Temp

Angus Donald is the author of the bestselling Outlaw Chronicles, a series of ten novels set in the 12th/13th centuries and featuring a gangster-ish Robin Hood. Angus has also published the Holcroft Blood trilogy about a mildly autistic 17th-century English artillery officer, son of notorious Crown Jewels thief Colonel Thomas Blood. Before becoming an author, Angus worked as a fruit-picker in Greece, a waiter in New York City and as an anthropologist studying magic and witchcraft in Indonesia. For fifteen years he was a journalist working in Hong Kong, India, Afghanistan and London. He now writes full time from a medieval farmhouse in Kent.

www.angusdonaldbooks.com

Also by Angus Donald

Fire Born

The Last Berserker
The Saxon Wolf
The Loki Sword
King of the North
Blood of the Bear

The Mongol Knight

Templar Traitor

ANGUS DONALD

TEMPLAR TRAITOR

CANELO

Penguin
Random
House

First published in the United Kingdom in 2025 by

Canelo, an imprint of
Canelo Digital Publishing Limited,
20 Vauxhall Bridge Road,
London SW1V 2SA
United Kingdom

A Penguin Random House Company
The authorised representative in the EEA is Dorling Kindersley Verlag GmbH. Arnulfstr. 124,
80636 Munich, Germany

A CIP catalogue record for this book is available from the British Library.

Print ISBN 978 1 83598 090 3
Ebook ISBN 978 1 83598 091 0

Map by Dave Slaney

Cover design by Blacksheep Design

Cover images © Adobestock; Shutterstock; Depositphotos

Printed and bound in Great Britain by Clays Ltd, Elcograf S.p.A.

Look for more great books at
www.canelo.co | www.dk.com

With thanks to Matthew Parris of The Times

and Matthew Paris of St Albans.

This novel is based on a true story.

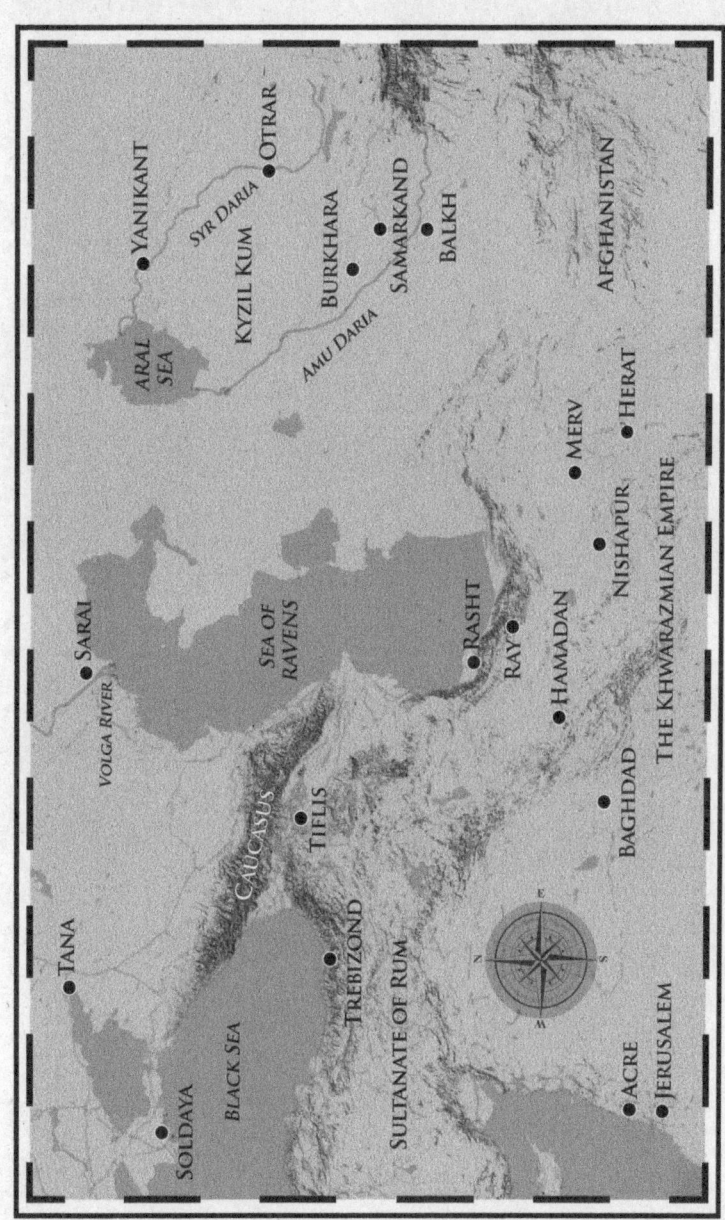

Prologue

July 1241

Frederick, Duke of Austria, flicked irritably with a mail-covered mitten at the fly dancing around his horse's neck. It was suffocatingly hot that noontide, even in the dappled shade under the elm trees. His lower back ached like the Devil, his padded linen undershirt was soggy with sweat, and he was regretting his decision to have his squire dress him in his full battle-gear that morning: a suit of iron-link mail that covered him from the crown of his head to the soles of his feet. He had been sitting astride his destrier under these tall elms for the past hour and more, waiting, waiting, and his famously short stock of patience was nearly at an end.

'Heinrich,' he snapped at the nearest rider, one of fifty knights and sergeants in a loose, murmuring pack all about him, 'is there any fresh word from the scouts?'

The knight, an older man with lines of worry carved into his lean cheeks, shook his head. The duke grunted with frustration and peered out through the leaves, craning his neck to get a better view of the valley below.

There, a little over a mile to the south, the slow, brown Danube spooled through the landscape. The great river turned south from its eastward route at the hamlet of Korneuburg, to the duke's left. The dust-hazed main road followed the river's course, cutting through broken terrain on the north bank, expanses of boulders and gorse mixed with small fields of golden barley. The duke's castle at Vienna was a mere hour's ride in that direction, only a dozen miles as the eagle flies.

I

'And you are certain of this information, Heinrich?' the duke said.

Heinrich von Leitzdorf straightened his back, looked his liege in the eye.

'The son of one of my oldest tenants, a steady, pious boy, said he saw a company of Tartars at Zwettl last night, just before dusk. More than two score, he said, a scouting or foraging party. He watched them advance east, then make their camp in a sheep pasture near his father's cottage. Unless they have managed to cross the Danube, which seems unlikely, or have turned back towards the rest of their Satanic horde, which is north of here, up in the woods of Bohemia, these scouts will pass us on this road today. Unless they do not. I cannot see the future. It is in the hands of God.'

The young duke nodded sagely. He looked round at the mass of brightly clad, murmuring Germanic horsemen gathered under the trees, then gestured for his squire to bring the wine flask.

He drank deeply and wiped his sweating face with his leather-covered palm. If his company departed now, he calculated, they could be back inside the walls of Vienna Castle by late afternoon – and he might even be able to take a cool dip in the Danube-fed castle moat before supper. That would be delightful, by Christ. Heinrich von Leitzdorf was right: only God knew where these swift-riding fiends were this hellish day. Perhaps they had disappeared back into the Realm of Tartarus.

A vast swarm of these creatures had recently erupted out of the East; everyone knew that. They had crushed the Russian dukedoms one after another. They had cowed the kingdom of Hungary with their ferocity, and destroyed the knights of Poland in one great battle at Leignitz just three months before. All eastern Europe now lay supine under the Tartar boot, with only little Austria still standing against them. The princes of France, Germany and England whined and quarrelled – and did nothing. The Pope issued decrees but dispatched no soldiers. Only Frederick of Austria and his handful of knights defied the heathen army. They would strike a telling blow for Christ this day against

2

this demonic foe. But where were they? Not on the Korneuburg road, that was certain. The duke made his decision; it was simply too hot. He opened his mouth to give the order, and stopped.

'Sire,' said Heinrich, pointing, 'look yonder, by that little copse of ash trees.'

Duke Frederick looked westwards at a small cloud of dust moving along the road towards them. As the dust drew nearer – and, by God, they were moving at a blistering pace – he began to make out the hunched shapes of individual riders and their dull iron armour, round shields and pointed helms topped with flowing plumes.

'About four dozen of the Hell-spawn, would you say, Heinz?' The duke grinned excitedly at his most loyal knight, the ageing constable of his castle. 'Few enough for us to challenge, eh?'

But Heinrich von Leitzdorf merely grunted a non-committal response to his liege. The lord of Austria was now bouncing in his saddle with glee, all discomfort gone.

'Yes, by God. We shall take them on. Heinrich – you take my lord Stephen of Dalmatia and his Hungarians and ride west to cut off their retreat back up the road. We'll wait for them to see you down there – then the rest of us will go straight in and fall on them. We'll catch these heathens like a walnut between two rocks.'

The duke made a pinching movement with his left hand, like a crab closing its claw. 'You understand me, Heinrich?'

'Indeed, sire.'

'Then, go. May God and all the saints ride with you!'

A little while later, the duke led his men out of the cover of the trees into the open, and onto the crest of the hill. With loud cries of 'For God and the Virgin!' and 'Austria for ever!', the thirty-five noble Germanic knights couched their lances under their right elbows, put back their spurs, and clattered down the rock-strewn slope towards the road, in one long, raggedy battle line.

The Tartars were quick to respond. They had seen the Hungarians burst out onto the road behind them, and now they saw the onslaught of the duke's knights coming straight down the hill. Despite being pinned against the riverbank to the south, they scattered in almost all directions. Those furthest east – the half a dozen Tartars nearest the hamlet of Korneuburg – galloped on and escaped into the jumble of thatched huts and barns and kitchen gardens, whipping their ponies into an undignified scramble to escape the eagerly pursuing Christian knights.

Those furthest west turned to face Stephen of Dalmatia's men, drawing short bows from scabbards on the horses' withers and loosing shafts at the gallop as they urged their mounts against their oncoming foes. Those in the middle of the Tartar pack split apart like a glass bowl dropped on a flagstone floor, the dagger-like shards splintering out as the line of knights swept into them.

Duke Frederick found himself face to face with a scowling devil under a black-plumed iron helm – a flat, pale face with twin spots of scarlet on the cheek, gleaming, deep-sunken black eyes and a feather of moustache above a snarling, gap-toothed mouth. The warrior effortlessly drew his short bow and loosed – and the wicked shaft thwacked into the painted leather surface of the duke's red-and-white shield, the iron point punching through and catching in the links of his mailed sleeve inside.

An instant later, the duke's lance took the enemy rider high in the left shoulder and ripped him out of the saddle. The long spear snapped mid-strike and Frederick immediately lost his grip on the shaft. Fumbling at his left-hand side for his arming sword, he saw with horror one of his knights arch his back in pain as a passing Tartar smacked a shaft into his upper spine from three yards away.

Screaming 'For God and the Virgin!' the duke drew his sword and kneed his destrier towards the nearest living opponent.

A clash of steel, the sparks visible, a glimpse of a dirty, hate-twisted face under a shapeless fur hat, and the duke was past his ferocious opponent, and reining in on the banks of the Danube. He immediately turned his horse, dug in the spurs once more and rode back into the fray. Another hideous foe: an elegant curve of silver catching the sunshine; his own straight blade, up fast, parrying, catching the weight of the blow. Then the riposte, completely by instinct, the long arming sword battering past the smaller man's defence and hacking into the side of his neck. Bubbling scarlet blood from his mouth; the Tartar slumping down in the saddle. Yet the warrior still had the strength to turn in the saddle and spit bloody defiance at the duke. Frederick closed in again, yelling, and finished him with a sweep of his sword that severed his ugly head from his body.

Gulping down air, his own blood fizzing from the heat of the action, Frederick looked about him, turning his head this way and that. His eye was drawn to one of the Tartars, a man taller than the rest, who was exchanging blows with three of the duke's sergeants at the same time. The Tartar controlled the horse only with his knees, and deftly fended off his three attackers with a small steel-plated shield and a slim curved sabre.

The man's head was covered with a domed helmet, adorned with a jaunty red plume, marking him out from the rest of these Hell-spawn riders with their black horsehair topknots. He seemed a superior kind of warrior – an officer, perhaps. More skilled than the rest. As Frederick watched, catching his breath, the Tartar slid under a sword blow from one of the sergeants, riposted with a lightning-fast slice that ripped open the Austrian's throat to the spine. The poor sergeant slid from the saddle, gargling blood. Yet this Tartar was still beset by two Christian enemies. He blocked a cut from one of them and forced the other back with a lunge, then chopped his iron shield down on the first sergeant's thigh, the rim striking hard and snapping bone. The sergeant screamed, and the Tartar tried to force his horse past him and into open space. But now the last sergeant was clubbing at his back, a crunching mace blow that clanged dully against the Tartar's lamellar iron-strip armour, making the man arch his spine in pain. The Tartar rounded on him, effortlessly turning his smaller horse and striking the last sergeant in a flurry of sword blows, almost too swift for the eye to see.

The Tartar was magnificent. Hell-spawn or not, Frederick thought, he fought like a lion, with a chilly ferocity, a merciless precision that was simply astonishing.

The Duke of Austria collected himself. He put back his spurs and his destrier leapt forward. 'For God and Saint Mary!' he yelled, as he closed on the Tartar and the outmatched sergeant, who was battling for his life. The duke swung his sword hard at the Tartar's lamellar neck armour and was aware that, even as he made his cut, the Tartar officer was hacking across the space between him and the sergeant and into the Austrian man's unguarded side. The Tartar's lateral blow landed an instant before Frederick's own powerful strike – which clanged against the back of the tall man's scarlet-plumed helmet just above the neck rim, at the level of his right ear.

Frederick saw the Tartar's head jerk back from the impact of the sword blow but, remarkably, he did not fall. In an extraordinary feat of horsemanship, he turned his nimble pony on a nail-head and came barrelling back directly at the duke. As he came on, one of the dismounted, wounded sergeants hacked wildly at the Tartar's passing leg; he missed, and the sword thwacked into the man's saddle flap, severing various straps.

The Tartar stood tall in the saddle to hammer a sword blow at the duke's head, and as he stood, his right stirrup strap snapped with a loud crack, and the man was dumped back against his high cantle. As the duke struck his own blow, desperately blocked by the off-balance man's small round iron shield, the Tartar was hurled from the saddle by the impact of the young Austrian's strike and his awkward stirrup-less seat. The duke's enemy spilled untidily from his saddle and thumped down hard into the dust of the road – and lay there in a crumpled heap, stunned and still.

Frederick left the man to his dismounted sergeants, to kill or capture. He turned his own destrier and looked for more mounted enemies to slay. Yet by now the fight was clearly over. The Christians were victorious – that was clear from their noisy exultations. His Germans were scattered all over the road, most of them with bloody swords in their hands. The Tartars had been

6

vanquished – the enemy saddles were all empty, the riders now lying prone in the dust, or fleeing for their lives on their swift little ponies. One of the fiends was gamely trying to swim his frightened horse across half a mile of swift brown river.

Frederick's breathing became calmer; he felt the hot glow of victory in his belly, and a slight feeling of nausea at the necessary carnage. The duke saw his constable Heinrich, trotting along the road towards him. He seemed to be unharmed, but he had a short black arrow tangled in his cloak-hem, which he seemed not to have noticed.

'We did it, old friend,' Frederick said. 'We did it. We struck a telling blow for Christ today.'

'Yes, sire. We did indeed.' But Heinrich seemed to be a little distracted; he was looking beyond his liege. A knot of bloody captives were kneeling in the dirt, hands held up high in surrender, with dismounted German knights and sergeants herding them into a line, with swords lofted, ready to strike down any who refused to obey.

'I regret to say, sire, that Otto von Lichtenberg has fallen,' the constable said. 'He is with God and the angels. Count Siegfried, too, is wounded – an arrow shaft in the ribs.'

'Still, it was a noble victory, eh, Heinz?'

'Indeed, sire. We must have dispatched two dozen of the devils between us.'

'Austria has stemmed the tide of evil, Heinz. We can be proud of our arms today.'

'Hmm… If you say so, my lord. If you say so. But what, may I ask, sire, do you intend to do with them?' He pointed over at the forlorn line of kneeling prisoners.

The duke turned to look. 'Them? No idea. Hang them all without delay, I suppose. As a fitting punishment and warning to the rest of their Hell-born breed.'

'Perhaps it may be wise to put them to the question first, sire. To gain a little intelligence. If we can find a good Christian who can speak their accursed tongue.'

'You take charge, Heinz, will you? There's a good fellow. They are all yours. Do what you will. Hang them, question them, chop out their black hearts and roast them. I care not.'

But Heinrich was already stepping down from his horse, oblivious of his lord.

He walked towards the nearest Tartar prisoner, and stopped before him, standing over the kneeling man and looking intently into his upturned face.

'Take off your helmet,' he said, in his native German.

The Tartar prisoner looked up at the knight out of eyes the blue of cornflowers. He was a man of about fifty years of age, square-jawed, lean, strong-looking. He looked slightly dazed. His head swayed on his neck and he blinked several times. Then he reached up and began to untie the leather straps that secured his helm. The steel helmet, with a short brim and cheek and neck flaps, was adorned with a scarlet plume, the only badge of its kind in that line of Tartar wretches.

'You understand me? My tongue?' Heinrich could barely hide his astonishment.

The man pulled the pointed iron helmet off his head to release a mass of long, grey-streaked, sweat-matted hair, which had clearly once been bright blond.

The kneeling prisoner replied slowly, 'I do... my lord,' in that same language. 'Also French, Italian, Latin, Turkish, Arabic, Persian and several other tongues beside...'

'Sire!' called Heinrich. 'Come here, I beg you – come and look at this one. Sire!'

The constable felt the presence of his young liege lord looming at his shoulder.

'God's blood,' spluttered the duke. 'I saw this one fight. He took on three of our sergeants – a veritable Trojan with a blade. Three men defeated before I felled him myself. But he is no Tartar. Surely not. Look at his eyes, Heinz – at his hair. Who are you? Tell me this instant, man. Be you heathen dog or good honest Christian? Speak up!'

8

'Jesus Christ is my Lord and Saviour,' said the man, making the sign of the cross with his hand, forehead to heart, left shoulder to right. 'God chose me as his servant. I have never denied my faith – and I never shall, even unto death itself.'

'Why then do you ride with these fiends from Satan's realm?' asked Heinrich.

The prisoner shook his head very slightly, winced, and said no more.

'Why do you keep company with the Devil's horsemen?' said the duke, shoving the kneeling man's shoulder hard. 'Tell me, man!'

One of the other prisoners spoke then, the words harsh, as alien as the barking of a hound to the duke's ears. To his surprise, the once-blond man answered him in that same hideous tongue. He appeared to be commanding the other prisoner to remain silent.

'Speak like a proper Christian – and answer me. Why are you with *them*?' The duke was growing impatient. The prisoner simply shook his grey-blond head again.

'Heinrich, seize that fellow!' The duke pointed at the kneeling Tartar who had just spoken with the strange captive. The older knight moved smartly to obey.

'Tell me,' the duke said, 'or I shall order your comrade's throat to be opened.'

'We are your prisoners – we have yielded to you. If you kill us, it runs contrary to all the laws of God and man. It would be nothing less than murder.'

The duke stared at the prisoner. He felt the stirrings of anger. He was not used to being gainsaid. 'Answer my question, then,' he growled. 'Why do you – who claim to be a Christian – ride with these Devil-spawn fiends from the bowels of Tartarus?'

The strange blue-eyed Tartar merely closed his eyes and began to mumble something – the familiar Latin words, '*Ave Maria, gratia plena, Dominus tecum…*'

'Talk to me – or I shall end your friend's existence this instant!' The duke could feel the hot fury rising in him, like a cook-pot coming up to the boil on the campfire.

'Kill him, Heinrich.' The duke nodded at the old knight, who immediately ripped his dagger across the Tartar's throat.

The blond man ignored the sputtering blood and continued with his prayer.

'Speak up – or you are next,' said the duke through his gritted teeth.

The kneeling man shook his head again. The familiar Latin prayer droned on.

'Heinrich!'

'Wait, sire! Look again at his face. I know this man. I have seen him before.'

The duke stared at the prisoner. He frowned. 'What? What do you mean?'

'In Pest, in the court of King Béla. In the spring. With the Tartar ambassador.'

'God's blood, you're right, Heinz. He was with their ambassador. He was the English translator with the Tartars when they demanded the submission of Hungary.'

Frederick seized the prisoner by the chin and forced his face upwards.

'You are the Englishman,' he said. 'You are the traitor to Christendom!'

Part I

Chapter One

Father Ivo of Narbonne strode through the gates of Vienna Castle, nodding at the men-at-arms on guard duty, who knew him, making for the stone tower on the western side. His robe swished around his ankles, revealing his hairy, sandalled feet. He was in a fine mood this morning and whistled a jaunty tune as he walked. Even the sight of the scaffold to his left in the castle courtyard, and its seven dangling, half-rotted bodies, could not sour his buoyant mood this balmy summer's day.

In his hands he clutched a fat sheaf of parchments, a vellum scroll and a little portable writing set – several snowy goose quills, a penknife, ink pot and a silver sander – all encased in a wallet of kidskin, and secured with a thong. A bulging leather satchel hung from his shoulder.

'Has he said anything yet to his interrogators?' Father Ivo said to Gutto, the gaoler, at the door of the castle keep that led down to the cells, where miscreants were imprisoned until meeting their fate. Gutto, a hunched, creeping man, small but powerful, shook his scabby shaven head.

'Not a peep?' said Father Ivo. 'Not even after Leitzdorf's men put the hot irons to him? Not after a month of rotting here? That tells us something, Gutto, does it not? That he is a man with an uncommon strength of will.'

The gaoler cleared his throat. 'He has not *said* anything, master, to the men-at-arms. Nothing to the men who beat and burned him.'

'But?'

'He talks in his sleep, master. He calls out in the dark of night when he is passed out from the pain. A name. He sometimes calls out a name.'

'That is most interesting, Gutto. What name does he call out when he is asleep?'

'A woman's name, master, I believe. Or it could be the name of a demon.'

'What name?'

'Saran – he calls out for someone named Saran.'

'Sarah?'

'No, master – Saran. And sometimes Sarantuya. He calls her "my love".'

'You have done well, Gutto. God will surely reward you for your efforts.'

The gaoler looked disappointed. So Ivo reached into his purse and pulled out a copper coin. 'Keep your ear pressed to his door at night, there's a good fellow,' he said.

'Yes, master,' said Gutto, smiling as he tucked the coin away deep into his rags.

'Now, to work. Has a suitable chamber been set aside for my labours?'

Ivo was shown into a small disused room on the ground floor of the tower, not much bigger than some monastic cells he had inhabited in his much-travelled life, but with a window that let in enough daylight for him to read and write on the table, and a stool on which to perch.

He gave it a cursory glance, dumped his writing materials on the table and said, 'Now, my good Gutto, you'd better lead me to this infamous Englishman.'

Keeping the satchel on his shoulder, he followed the gaoler down a slimy set of stone stairs into the darkness beneath, the chill rising with every step he took. It felt, to Ivo's lively mind, as if he were descending from the sunlit uplands into the open jaws of a great beast, down and down into the pitch-black belly of a monster. A sleeping dragon, perhaps. But was there a hoard of glittering treasure to be found at the bottom of these dark steps? Perhaps yes, there just might be. Not gold nor silver, not precious jewels, but something far more important. The truth.

Once inside the foul-smelling cell, when the light from the candle he carried had reached the rear of the space, Ivo saw the Englishman crouched like a beast at bay on the stones. The man was shackled by one ankle to a ring of iron set deep in the prison's floor. By the candle's mellow light, the priest examined the prisoner, who was naked apart from a soiled loincloth, and as lean as any living man he had ever seen. Ribs and spine jutted through the pale skin, cheekbones horribly prominent, the staring blue eyes, bright and feverish. Father Ivo could see the marks of the hot irons on his sides and thighs, angry burns, as well as cuts and bruises from the guards' cudgels.

Gutto made a soft enquiry about his safety, but Ivo waved him away. The gaoler shambled out and closed the door. The two men were enclosed together.

'A cup of wine before we begin?' said Ivo genially, producing a flask and cup from the leather satchel. 'Or a bite to eat? I have some bread and a pretty decent cheese. Ewe's milk, but it's not too tart. At least, I do hope it's not. Which would you prefer?'

The prisoner said nothing. He stared at the priest from his crouched position at the rear of the cell, his blue eyes in the skin-stretched face seeming to grow larger. There was something about his stillness, thought Ivo. Something impressive about his immobility. The long, matted hair about his shoulders gave him a leonine quality. He reminded Ivo of a Barbary lion that he had seen in the court of the Count of Toulouse, years before. Caged but vastly dignified, and definitely still dangerous.

'I do take your point, of course,' said Ivo. 'I must appear absurdly crass to you, to be making this obvious and clumsy approach. Trying to buy your soul with nothing more than wine and cheese. How impertinent you must think me! But my friend Gutto has told me that you have had nothing more than oat slop and river water for a month – so I thought we might have a cup of good red wine and a morsel of decent food while we sit together. No conditions are attached, I assure you. Please do not feel the need to make conversation – you may remain as silent as the grave while we enjoy our meal, if you wish. Oh... and is French all right? I can give you my German, if you prefer, or Latin, of course. But that, I am afraid, is the limit of my skill. Here, take hold of this while I cut you a slice of this bread.'

Ivo handed the man a clay cup filled to the brim with dark wine. He glanced at the iron chain restraining the prisoner. It was coiled a little, and he knew he was within striking distance of the captive. The caged lion. With part of his mind, Ivo knew that if this prisoner – a trained warrior – attacked him, he would be unlikely to emerge from the cell alive. But he was not afraid and, praise God, after only a moment's hesitation, the emaciated soldier reached out a long arm and accepted the wine, then took a sip from the cup. The prisoner nodded his thanks, but uttered no words.

Bread and a crumbling slice of cheese followed, passed as casually as Ivo could manage across to the captive, who was now seated cross-legged on the cold stone. He took the proffered items with a tiny incline of his matted – and, no doubt, louse-infested – head.

'I should introduce myself,' said the priest. 'I am Father Ivo of Narbonne, a humble clerk, but also a devout soul who has, from time to time, been charged with undertaking certain discreet duties outside the diocese by my lord bishop – missions, you might say, on behalf of the Catholic Church and, ultimately, on behalf of His Holiness Pope Gregory. I have been asked to come here by my lord bishop and question you, as an *enquêteur* – if you understand the term, an inquisitor – although I have no remit at all to compel you to speak or to use force against you in any way.

'If you chose to be compliant, I would speak to you about your actions over these past few years and the course of your life so far. I am tasked with persuading you to give an account of yourself, specifically to answer the question of why you should be riding with the Tartar host against fellow Christians. I am also here to hear your confession, if you will make it, and to offer you absolution for your sins. But, before we begin, I must apologise for the treatment you have received at the hands of these brutes here. And beg forgiveness for the hurts you have suffered. More wine?'

The prisoner now looked more surprised than anything else. But he held out his cup to be refilled, while he very slowly chewed a mouthful of bread and cheese.

'I also come today with distressing news, I'm afraid,' Ivo continued. 'The Duke of Austria, whose castle this is, is resolved to bring you to trial in his own court as soon as possible, on charges of high treason and crimes against Christianity. Austria, as I'm sure you are well aware, is now on the frontier of Christendom – the border march, if you prefer. Beyond this castle, the Tartar enemy rides unchecked across the whole of eastern Europe. And the duke, like any marcher lord, takes a robust approach to justice. In short, the date for your trial has been set for four weeks from today. All the local notables have been summoned to attend. And the duke also intends, if you cannot satisfactorily demonstrate your innocence, to hang you in his courtyard, as he has already done with the other seven Tartar companions captured with you. It is his crude notion of justice, I am very sorry to tell you.'

The prisoner's head slumped, his chin touching his chest, as he digested this information. He seemed to be praying. Then he raised his head, fixed his eyes on Ivo again, and a cold light of hatred seemed to gleam from under his brows.

'I am distraught to bring these tidings,' Ivo said. 'Four weeks is not a long time. His Grace the duke is somewhat... um, impetuous by nature.

'However,' he continued, with a bright new note in his voice, 'there is a chance that, if you were to explain your actions with regard to the Tartars, and make a full and frank admission of all your crimes, I may be able to persuade my lord bishop to intercede with the Duke of Austria on your behalf, and perhaps

His Holiness the Pope himself might even plead your cause, too. It is not impossible that, when all the true facts are known, after a suitable penalty, you may even be freed.

'I would, however, have to insist on a full, and – I must stress this – completely candid account of your actions, with nothing omitted, nothing distorted nor falsified. The truth and nothing less. I do hope you understand me. The alternative… Well, the alternative is that the duke will surely hang you inside a month. And no one will know of your travels, no one will remember your deeds and adventures, and nothing will be left of you on Earth. And, worse than that, you face an eternity in the fiery pit, for without my absolution you will die unshriven. I'm sorry to have to put it to you quite so bleakly, but this is the truth. I believe you understand how matters stand. Now, why not have another cup of this half-decent wine and tell me your name?'

The prisoner said nothing. But he *did* hold out his clay cup for more.

Ivo poured the wine. 'If you need a day or two to think on this, I understand that,' he said. 'I will leave you the bread and cheese, and the flask, of course. But time presses.'

Ivo got to his feet, brushing dust and dirt from his gown. He turned towards the door, took a step, then heard a voice – a voice weak from disuse, speaking in French.

'Who is your lord?'

Ivo turned around to stare at the prisoner, who repeated his question.

'I serve the Bishop of Bordeaux, a great man named Géraud de Malemort.'

There was a long, long silence.

'I know that name,' said the Englishman finally.

–

Some hours later, upstairs in the ground-floor chamber that had been given to him, an exhausted but exhilarated Father Ivo unrolled the kidskin wallet that contained his precious writing materials. He set out the ink pot and silver sander, selected a fresh goose feather, and began to sharpen it with his neat little folding knife. After a moment's reflection, he dipped the nib in the ink, shook off a few excess drops, and began to write on a large piece of parchment on the sloping table before him.

To Géraud, by the Grace of God, Bishop of Bordeaux, from Ivo of Narbonne, special enquêteur and humblest of his clerks, a rendering of his first encounter with the English prisoner presently held at Vienna Castle, in the Duchy of Austria.

My lord, it is with great joy and profound thanks to almighty God that I report to you that the prisoner has consented to speak about his life, and will attempt to explain how he came to be among the Tartar heathen horde at the gates of Vienna. He will continue to speak to me tomorrow of the course of his life that led him to this point. His name, he informs me, is Robert, and he is a knight of the manor of Hadlow in the county of Kent, in England. I intend to dispatch reports of our conversations to you regularly, in the prisoner's words, until the start of his trial in four weeks' time.

Robert of Hadlow says that his tale begins in the Holy Land, in the early spring of the Year of the Incarnation 1218, when he was abiding in that place as a brother-knight in the city of Acre, a stronghold of the Poor Fellow-Soldiers of Christ and of the Temple of Solomon, the military order better known as the Knights Templar...

Acre

March 1218 – 23 years earlier

A bead of sweat trickled down Robert's temple as he shook the dice in his cupped hands. The small pile of silver coins on the blanket in front of him was all wagered on this one throw, the remains of a far larger pile he had begun with some hours earlier – he knew not how many.

He was the dice-caster and his 'main' was six, the sum on the two dice from his first throw; he needed to throw another total of six – or a total of twelve – with the two dice to win his wager on this round. If he won, he would recoup all his losses and more. If he lost the throw, if he threw 'crabs' – two ones showing on the dice, or a one and a two – he would lose everything.

Hassan, a Christian from Tyre, who arranged this game of Hazard each night in the cramped, muggy space behind his wine shop in the Montmusart suburb of Acre, began to mutter angrily. The other three players, all local merchants, echoed his impatience.

'Throw those accursed bones, Templar,' said Hassan, 'and let us discover if God truly watches over your kind – as I've often heard you claim – or not!'

Robert could faintly hear the bells of the Tower of St Nicholas clanging away, signalling that the huge gates to Acre were ready to shut tight for the night. A good omen, he thought, the sound of holy ringing at the moment when his fate would be decided. The Almighty was with him.

He hurled the two ivory dice down the length of the grey blanket... but his attention was immediately wrenched away by a most *unholy* racket – the breaking of wood, a massive clattering as a table of brass jugs was upended – all before the dice stopped rolling. The door to the little storeroom behind Hassan's emporium burst open.

'Seize him!' thundered a knight, a tall man dressed in the white robes of Robert's Order. Two sergeants in black darted forward and gripped Robert's arms. He was hauled upright and pinioned.

'Caught in the act,' said the knight with grim satisfaction. Robert saw that it was none other than Jean de Malemort, the Seneschal of the Order, and second in rank among his Brethren only to the Grand Master William of Chartres himself.

As Robert was dragged from the stuffy room, he instinctively looked back at the grey blanket and saw that his dice had ended showing two ones – 'crabs', as that Hell-cursed configuration was called. He had thrown the dice… and lost.

Robert spent the night in a locked cell in the extensive sand-stone catacombs below the Templar castle at Acre, mostly on his knees in prayer. A little before dawn, the door opened and the brother-sergeant on guard outside ushered in a Templar knight, and muttered, 'Sir Gilbert of Hadlow.'

'Gilly,' said Robert, embracing his younger brother, hugging him hard to his chest, 'you should not have come to see me in my sad disgrace. It will taint you in the Grand Master's eyes.'

'I came to say goodbye, Rob,' said Gilbert. 'We received our orders last night. It's a good-sized expedition, fifty chosen knights and a hundred sergeants, and I am part of it. We set sail this morning – to Damietta! We are taking the fight for Christ right into the lair of the Sultan of Egypt.'

Robert looked into his brother's face and saw the high excitement and glowing pride of the youngster. He tried to smile, but all he felt was a cold sense of trepidation.

'So it's true,' Robert said. 'We heard the rumours, of course. That the Order means to attack Egypt directly. But I did not know that *you* would be chosen for the expedition.'

It would have been strange if Robert had *not* heard the rumours. For months, reinforcements had been arriving from across the seas, brother-knights coming from England, France, Burgundy, Italy and Spain, swelling the Templar ranks with their numbers. Gilbert himself, only recently enrolled in the Order in England, and determinedly following in his brother's footsteps, had arrived here in Acre only a month before, carried across the blue Mediterranean by the grand Venetian fleet.

'I volunteered,' said Gilly. 'The Pope's message spoke to my soul. God was calling me to the defence of his Holy Land. So I begged the Grand Master to accept me as part of the expedition.'

Pope Innocent III had long been calling for all the knights and princes of Europe to join in a great pilgrimage to restore the Holy Land to the true faith. Now, at last, John of Brienne, titular King of Jerusalem, was leading an assault on the heartland of their enemy, aided by the Knights Templar and Hospitaller, and an army of noblemen including Andrew, King of Hungary, Leopold, Duke of Styria, William, Count of Holland, Simon, Count of Saarbrücken, and many more besides.

This effort was sorely needed. The Latin kingdoms of the Holy Land, those few estates still ruled by Christian lords, had suffered defeat after defeat and clung on tenuously to a strip of land only a few miles wide along the coast. The Sultan of Egypt – conqueror of lands that stretched from Arabia to Anatolia – had outfought and outmanoeuvred the Christian armies time and again.

Jerusalem was in his hands and, despite the best efforts of the Christian knights, it remained under the green crescent banner, where it had been these past thirty years. So the decision had finally been taken to attack Damietta, the port of Egypt in the Nile Delta, to force Saphadin, as the Sultan was known, to bring his armies back from the Holy Land to defend his wealthiest city.

It seemed to Robert a desperate last throw of the dice for the Latin kingdoms. If this attempt on Damietta failed, the Christians would likely be swept into the Mediterranean.

Yet, despite the importance of this expedition, Robert was concerned for his brother, who, he knew, would soon be hurled into the fury of battle. Gilly was not a weakling, but there was an air of fragility about him that inspired protectiveness in Robert. It had been like this since childhood.

'I have just written to Father,' continued Gilbert, 'and told him about your predicament. And that I am to be dispatched to Egypt with the first of our knights. I only pray that the old man lives long enough to receive the letter. You knew that Henry had taken to his bed before I left England? I do not think he will ever walk or ride again.'

'You told me, Gilly. Our earthly father will soon be with our Heavenly one.'

'What will they do with you, Rob?' said Gilbert. 'Will they show mercy?'

'God chose me as his servant, Gilly – He will not abandon me. And I have served the Order faithfully these past ten years. That must count for something.'

'I shall pray for you,' said Gilbert. 'I shall pray for you every night, Rob.'

'And I you. I want you to promise me something, Gilly. You are not to court danger unnecessarily in Damietta. They will call for volunteers, they will ask you to risk your life for the cause. Do *not* do this again. If you love me, brother, remain silent when the call goes out for brave knights to undertake some fresh perilous mission.'

'Would *you* do that, brother?' asked Gilbert. 'The Robert of Hadlow I know prizes risk and danger more highly than anything else. Would he duck a challenge? No. The knight who won the First Lance badge for skill at arms three years in a row? A feat no other Templar has ever achieved. Would he shirk his duty? I think not.'

'It is *not* shirking. You already serve God by serving the Order. And to serve God is to serve mankind. There is no need to risk your life further. Others also seek glory. Let them step forward.'

'There is a whiff of hypocrisy on your words, brother. I know that you would *never* dodge a chance to strike a blow for Christ. How can you ask that of me?'

'This is not about me. This is about you, your life. Father will soon be gone to his reward and I... Well, look at me, in this cell, awaiting trial for my foolishness. Learn from my example. Do not seek out unnecessary risk in Egypt – that is all I ask.'

'I shall do as I think fit. As you would do. But I shall pray for God's guidance.'

At dawn, Robert was brought up to the Chapter House by the south sea-bastion to face the Grand Master. This great man was flanked by his Seneschal, Jean de Malemort, and the Commander of the Vault of Acre – the senior brother-sergeant of Acre – an elderly baseborn Parisian named Armand.

Only these three men were present – the guards were all dismissed – and they had gathered to sit in judgment over Brother Robert of Hadlow, and to determine his fate.

'Obedience,' said William of Chartres, seeming to taste the word. 'Obedience, poverty and chastity... these are the foundations of our Order, the bedrock on which our community rests. The statement of our purpose. Of all the strictures of our Rule, these are the most important by far.'

Robert, who was kneeling before the three most powerful men among the Poor Fellow-Soldiers of Christ in the Holy Land, found he could not lift his head to meet the Grand Master's stern gaze. He stared at the flagstone floor, and sent up a silent prayer to St Christopher, his favourite holy guardian, who had ever warded poor travellers and soldiers, to aid him in this time of trial.

'This is why we must resolutely set our faces against the vice of gambling in all its forms,' said Jean de Malemort. He and his two companions were seated on three large chairs. Armand, the Commander of the Vault, had shut his ancient eyes, perhaps to rest them.

'Gambling is a sin that has its roots in greed – in the unholy desire to gain material wealth,' Jean de Malemort went on. 'It is a cardinal sin, as well as running contrary to our Rule, which decrees that all Brethren must embrace poverty. Greed and avarice carry the sinner away from God, away from all spiritual matters, and towards the sordid pleasures of the Earth. Moreover, gambling leads to greater sins, excessive consumption of wine, and the temptations of lust and fornication.'

'My lord,' said Robert, finding his courage, 'since I joined the Order ten years ago, I have never once broken my vow of chastity. I swear this on my immortal soul.'

'I believe you, Robert,' said the Grand Master. 'I truly do. You are a fine knight, winner of the First Lance competition three times, if I recall correctly. In many respects, a paragon. No one has accused you of a breach of chastity... but there is the grave matter of your obedience. You were enjoined by the Seneschal, your superior in our Order, a man placed in authority over you by God, to cease attending these sinful games of chance, were you not? You cannot deny it. Yet you ignored the Seneschal's command and went again to the shop of the merchant Hassan in Montmusart anyway, to play at dice. You cannot say, therefore, that you have been perfectly *obedient*, can you?'

'I cannot claim that, in all truth, Grand Master, no, and yet I still hope...'

Armand let out a snore. Robert stopped, and looked at the elderly man with his eyes closed on the leftmost chair. Armand snorted. He opened one rheumy eye.

'This is the fornicator, eh?' he muttered. 'Don't do it, young man. Try to control your lustful urges. We all understand the temptation, by Christ. When I was a lively young sergeant, there was an Arab girl who worked in the bathhouse, pretty as a—'

'Commander, we are not investigating fornication today,' said Malemort.

'Why not? It is a terrible sin, leads to all sorts of trouble. They are all at it—'

'Commander!' The Grand Master's voice cracked like a horse-whip. 'Brother Robert has been caught in the act of gambling, playing at dice with the Arab merchants. If you have nothing useful to add to our deliberations, I beg you to hold your tongue.'

Armand took in a breath, as if he meant to argue, then slowly subsided.

'If I may plead my cause, Grand Master,' said Robert, 'I was merely trying to recoup my previous losses...'

'It matters not *why* you were disobedient,' said the Seneschal, 'only that you were. You disobeyed *my* explicit order, given not three days ago.' Robert saw the Grand Master nodding along in agreement. Armand had once more closed his tired eyes and was already gently snoring.

They found him guilty.

An hour later, stripped of his prized black-and-red Templar riding cloak, disowned by the Order to which he had dedicated ten years of his life, with an echoing belly, no money but a small silver St Christopher's medal on a thong round his neck, and dressed in a monk's habit of scratchy wool, carrying a six-foot pilgrim's staff and a water bottle, Robert of Hadlow walked out of the double gates of the citadel of Acre and took the main road to the east, heading towards the green-and-purple heights of Golan, and the vast emptiness of the great Syrian desert beyond.

Chapter Two

'Wait,' said Ivo of Narbonne. 'Are you telling me the Templars of Acre, those famed holy warriors, on the eve of the Damietta campaign, when they needed every trained knight for the grand assault on the Sultan of Egypt's homeland, expelled you from their ranks simply for *playing at dice?*'

'They did, Father,' said Robert. 'And were right to do so. Gambling is a grave sin – but it was more than that. I had been disobedient, which the Order cannot forgive in any brother-knight.'

Ivo made a note on his wood-covered tablet; he would write up the Englishman's account later in his chamber on the ground floor and send it to his bishop. For now, he scratched brief *aides-mémoires* with a stylus in the wax of the tablet. The chilly cell in the base of the tower of Vienna Castle had been made brighter that second day of their meeting by the addition of three wax candles in a brass holder; warmer, too, by the inclusion of an iron brazier filled with burning coals. However, while Heinrich von Leitzdorf, the castle's constable, had allowed these small comforts for the note-taking priest, he had insisted the English prisoner remain chained by the ankle to the stone floor and Ivo, seated on a stool, remain safely beyond his grasp.

'Have another slice of ham,' said Ivo, shoving the platter towards Robert across the stone floor with his sandalled foot. He bent to his tablet once more and scratched a word.

'And this fellow Armand, the...' He squinted at his notes. 'The Commander of the Vault. Did he truly fall asleep *twice* during your questioning?'

'He was a very ancient brother,' said Robert. 'More than eighty years.'

'And he has since been gathered unto God?' said Ivo.

'I would assume so. My trial in Acre took place twenty-three years ago.'

'Did you also know William of Chartres lived no longer than another year?'

The Englishman dropped his chin and closed his eyes.

'You had not heard that the Templar Grand Master was wounded in the battle for the Tower of Damietta and died afterwards?'

'I heard,' said Robert. 'And I grieve for him still. He is ever in my prayers.'

'So the only living man who was a witness to your trial in Acre and your subsequent expulsion from the Order was Jean de Malemort, the Seneschal.'

'And I.'

'What?'

'I, too, was there,' said Robert. 'I, too, was witness to the events that day.'

'Indeed,' said Ivo. 'You and Jean de Malemort. But only you two.'

The Englishman said nothing.

'I have one more question for you, before you resume your tale, if I may.'

There was a small, hard silence.

'Why east?' said Ivo. 'Why did you go *east* into the trackless deserts?'

'I do not comprehend you.'

'You had been expelled from the Order, rejected by your friends and comrades, you were sent away in disgrace from the place you called home. Why did you go east? Why not south to the port of Jaffa, where you might find a ship to take you back to England? Or, if you could not afford that, why not go north, to begin the long journey on foot? My question is… why *east*? Why go into the desert? Why go into the Syrian wilderness, where the Saracen armies of Saphadin held sway?'

The Englishman shrugged and looked away. 'God guided my footsteps.'

'Indeed,' said Ivo, and made another tiny note. 'I'm sure He did.'

The priest stared at his tablet, allowing the silence to grow, to balloon around them both in that dark, fetid space. The Englishman shifted a little, but said no more.

'Who is this woman Saran?' asked Ivo, puncturing the silence.

'What?'

'Who is Saran – or Sarantuya? Do not pretend you do not know the name.'

The Englishman looked at him, his eyes gleaming with hatred in the candlelight. 'I will *not* be interrogated,' he said. 'I will not have you snapping questions, yapping like a lapdog at every turn of the road. I shall relate my tale and you may listen, or we shall have no further commerce.'

Ivo sat back on his stool, cocked his head on one side, considering the half-naked prisoner. 'As you command, Sir Robert,' he said. 'I beg you, pray continue.'

–

The Englishman wandered eastwards, on stony paths, heading towards the distant purple and green of the mountains. He walked through a landscape torn by war: torched and looted by the victorious Saracen armies, with burnt-out buildings and ruined churches now marking the places where good Christians had once farmed crops and raised families. At the side of the road were scores of burial mounds, with simple wooden crosses hammered into the freshly turned earth.

These had once been peaceful Latin lands; now they belonged to no man.

Robert had no food and only a little water – and he suffered from the midday heat. At first there were many fellow travellers on the rocky road – some refugees like him, families fleeing the horrors of war – and he might have sought their kinship, and even their aid, but seeing his grim mien and shabby, beggarly clothes, they sensed his status as an outcast and instinctively shunned him.

Faint with hunger at the end of the first day's march, he *did* beg for a little bread by the roadside and received a crust or two, and more than a few curses and insults from many of the impoverished travellers, who despised his need. But Robert cared nothing for hard words; his raw shame surrounded him as an invisible grey wall, a shield from the contempt of his fellow men.

He walked into the hills the next day, climbing higher and higher, and found a refuge in a cave on the second night. He killed a nesting rock dove with a well-thrown rock and ate her flesh raw, along with two of her small, pearl-white eggs.

In the morning he arose, hungry again, to continue his march, ever eastwards. He passed through the drab grey hills and came down to the dusty yellow plain, walked through stunted groves of ancient silvery olive trees and fields of bright green unripe barley, before once more climbing to the heights and descending again to a vast inland lake. He drank sweet water until his belly protested, and swam, and slept deeply upon the rocky shore. Then, after filling his small leather water bottle and taking up his staff, he walked on into the desert, into the glory of the rising sun.

They waited for him in a narrow defile that afternoon, in a range of low hills beyond the river Jordan: three men – bandits, or perhaps deserters from the Saracen ranks, for they had the look of desperate men. Robert was unaware of them until almost too late. A flash of movement in the corner of his eye. Robert dropped to one knee and whipped his head round, just as a scimitar hissed over it.

He reacted by instinct. The long hours of practice at the padded pell with sword and shield; the many hard years spent training under several veteran sergeants in Templar precincts across Christendom. He had been well schooled in all forms of combat, with spear and shield, dagger and sword, on horseback and on foot, with arms and without. Before his disgrace, he had been accounted the finest man-at-arms, the most able of all, in the Templar citadel in Acre – three times named the First Lance, the man all the other brother-knights, each themselves skilled warriors, tried to emulate. All this knowledge and training, the scrapes and bruises, the hard knocks and early dawns in the practice yards... All this came to his aid now, and took possession of his limbs.

He swept the cedar-wood staff round, low, striking behind the scimitar-man's forward knee, and tumbling him sideways against a rocky outcrop. Then Robert sprang up and whirled to face the second man, a bald fellow – and a lunge from a wicked spear, aimed directly at his belly. The spear-point ripped through his monk's robe, just a whisker from his skin, as he turned again, and struck again, this time with the butt of the staff, jabbing up and cracking it into the bald fellow's cheekbone.

The attacker was knocked back, reeling, bloody. The third man came on with a nail-studded wooden mace, a bludgeoning tool, and Robert sidestepped, very fast, moved in and blocked its downward swing with the staff held between two fists. Then he whipped the right end of the staff around and thwacked it across the man's fat neck. A loud and satisfying contact, like a hard slap.

Mace-man howled and staggered away. But the first bandit, the shining scimitar still tight in his grip, was rising, cursing in Arabic and spitting in his rage. Robert made a hard downward chop of his staff on the top of the attacker's red turban, a blow that should have cracked his skull, and which felled him like a poleaxed heifer. Then the Englishman did the correct thing – the one thing his teachers had drummed into him from the beginning of his training. When you are overmatched, when you find yourself impossibly outnumbered, if it is perfectly safe to do so, you must quit the field.

It was not heroic, far from noble. But it was eminently sensible. Robert wasted no more time on the three bandits. He turned his back on them and took to his heels, sprinting straight down the path ahead of him as fast as his legs would churn. Which was when the fourth man – a great black-bearded Goliath – emerged from behind a huge round boulder on the path ahead of him, a long rusty sword in his massive hand. Robert skidded to a halt. The black-bearded giant grinned at him.

Robert glanced behind. Twenty yards away, the three bandits that he had already bested were gathering themselves for a second bout; the scimitar-man, blood trickling down his face, was astonishingly back on his feet. He must have a skull of iron, Robert thought – or, more likely, a steel helm hidden under the wrappings of that red turban.

Robert flicked a look back at Goliath, who was standing like a tree, swishing the sword back and forth. Robert smiled back at him and took two paces nearer, hefting his cedar staff.

'Come on, then, ugly one,' he said in gutter Arabic. 'Let us do this.'

Goliath let out a roar; he lifted the sword above his head and charged at Robert. The rusty blade was poised above the giant's head, ready to make a single downward killing strike. But, instead of shrinking away from the huge blow, the Englishman suddenly bounded forward to meet Goliath's charge, the staff leaping out in front of him like a spear, aimed at the big man's face.

Goliath snatched his sword blade down and across to block the blow from the staff, which it would have done very well had the spear-like jab not been a feint. Robert allowed the staff to slide over Goliath's shoulder and he hit the giant hard with his own shoulder, his six-foot form crashing into the centre of his opponent's chest with all the Englishman's weight behind it. The unexpected charge knocked the huge man sprawling on his back in the dust, with Robert landing on top of him.

The big bandit struggled to rise but the Templar was up faster, bouncing to his feet, still in possession of his cedar staff – which he stabbed down into the prone giant's open mouth. A snap of front teeth, a spurt of bright blood. A gargled shout of rage. For good measure, Robert jabbed down once again with the butt of the staff, crushing the right eye of the big man on the ground to pulp. He could hear the thud of footsteps behind him. He plucked the sword – a cumbersome thing – from Goliath's unresisting grasp, turned, and hurled himself at the other three attackers.

'Into thy hands, O Lord,' shouted Robert, as he flung himself at the enemy.

Sword and staff whirling, the Englishman charged the knot of bandits on the road. A sparking clash of steel and clack of wood, a shove of bodies, a spray of blood, and the scimitar man died with the rusty sword punched through his lower belly, above his groin. Yet Robert was not untouched in this wild melee. He mistimed a block with the staff and felt the nail-studded club crunch into his shoulder and rip up the side of his face as far as his left ear. He left the sword buried in the turbaned man's guts, swiped across with his staff, and shattered the mace-man's arm.

But he could feel his own blood streaming down his neck. And the glow of pain.

Goliath was roaring, stumbling to his feet, one hand cradling a ruined eye.

The bald spearman, who had hung back from the melee, his face bleeding, found his courage, bellowed that God was great, and hurled his spear straight at the Englishman. Robert twisted away, a swift but unnecessary move, as it happened, for the spear passed a good foot from his rapidly turning body. Instead, it sank into Goliath's ribs; the big man was now only one long pace behind him.

Robert regained his balance and shoved the slumping giant from him, hurling him aside from the path with the long spear wobbling from his bloody chest. He attacked the last two bandits standing. He jabbed the man with the broken arm in the belly with his staff and dropped him, gasping, to the ground, then he turned on the bandit who had hurled his spear and killed his own comrade.

This fellow, a skinny brute with a shaven head, was now waving a long knife. Robert fell instinctively into the second position – left foot advanced, right foot at a right angle, staff held diagonally across his body, ready to defend or strike – but the knife man clearly held the same views as the Templar instructors. He stared at Robert for a moment, then turned and ran back up the path as fast as his legs would carry him.

Robert looked about him. Goliath was not quite dead, but he was moaning and bleeding profusely by the side of the path. The turbaned man was gone, staring open-eyed at the sky. The man with the broken arm was gasping for breath on the ground. And the fourth had disappeared up the path. Robert wondered if he had gone for help. There might be a whole nest of them up there.

So he turned and began to jog down the path, ignoring his own wounds. He ran steadily, down into the valley and then up the other side. He ran for mile after mile, until he could run no more. Neck throbbing, sight blurring from exhaustion. He paused at a crest, sucking air, looking behind – no one there, and no dust over the path – before limping on into the thickening dusk.

He walked till moonrise, pushing himself, then left the path, and in the silvery light he clambered a hundred yards up a mountainside. Robert climbed up into a crevice, a place of cool shadows with one entrance, and there, where stone warded his flanks, he allowed himself to relax.

He prayed, grasping the silver medal on the thong around his neck, and giving up his heartfelt thanks to St Christopher for preserving him in the battle on the path. He prayed for his Brethren, and for his sick father, who might already be in Heaven. Then he took another moment to pray for his brother Gilbert, who would now be somewhere on the high seas, and at the mercy of the waves.

'Hold him in your keeping, holy Christopher,' he muttered. 'Ward him well and bring my brother safe to dry land – I ask in the name of Jesus Christ our Saviour.'

Next, he cleaned the mace-scrape on his neck as best he could without a mirror. His left ear had been partially ripped away from his skull. He decided to let it be, to let it clot, dry and, with the grace of God, begin to heal.

His left shoulder was badly swollen, and also excruciating, with a single nail-puncture, which he knew might well go bad and poison his whole body. And the spear tip that he thought had missed him had, he found, in fact scored a shallow bloody groove across his greyhound-lean belly. Yet it could have been far worse. Four enemies, all armed, and he only with a wooden staff. And he had survived, even triumphed. His old Templar instructors would have been pleased. He drank a frugal sip of his remaining water. And then, swaddled by cold, hard stone, he slept for a few hours.

The next morning he walked on into the Syrian desert. The water bottle was empty by midday, and there was nothing in sight but bare rock and shimmering earth. Occasionally, he heard the distant tonk of bells and the bark of dogs. But the shepherds avoided him, bloody and staggering as he was. He walked for many days, alone, parched, wounds throbbing, eyes seared by the glare.

At the fall of night he lay down where he was and slept, shivering in the icy desert air; by day he stumbled onwards, aimless, flayed by the brutal sun. Mad visions taunted him: he saw Grand Master William of Chartres ahead of him, beckoning, offering him a flask of cool wine; Brother Armand, Commander of the Vault, walked beside him, patting his swollen shoulder and urging him earnestly to 'Kill them all. Slaughter every last one. God will surely know his own!'

One day, at the very limit of his strength, Robert spied a patch of faded green in the distance, and an oily shimmer that might possibly have been water. He had seen so many charming visions in his parched wandering – lakes, oceans, crystal mountain streams – that he initially doubted this one, too; yet, as he approached closer, he saw that there was indeed a stand of scrubby palm trees providing a patch of shade and a pool of muddy water, with the tracks of animals in the black ooze at its edge.

He fell on his face, thrust his head in the brackish water and drank until his belly ached. Then he lay down in the shade of one of the stunted palms, wrapped in his rags, and determined that he would move no more. *This is as good a place as any to die*, he thought, and closed his red-raw eyes.

He slept. He dreamed a little: terrible dreams of war, blood and damnation.

He dreamed there was a man, a Bedouin by his dark face, headdress and robes, leaning over him and looking into his face. He dreamed the man and his friends bathed him and gave him water to drink and fed him broth and sops of bread and tended his wounds. Another man looked at his ear and, muttering, produced needle and thread and began to pierce his torn flesh with iron's icy touch.

Robert slept deeply again.

When he awoke, he was on the back of a swaying camel, with a sun-browned boy of eleven or so sitting behind him and holding him upright in the saddle with his skinny arms, talking quietly to the jolting beast beneath them, urging it onwards. All around him were men in black robes, perhaps thirty folk, armed with long spears and wide swords, with great curved, jewelled daggers stuck in their leather belts. Yet they offered him no insult, nor violence. There were two dozen camels roped together, and several horses, too, laden with boxes and huge jars, barrels and sacks of goods.

A camel train of merchants, he surmised.

That night they fed him again and when he had eaten, the leader of the train came to him in his place by the camel-dung fire. 'I am Aaron,' he said, setting himself down cross-legged beside Robert, 'a Jew of Sana'a, in the far south of Arabia. These are my people, my brothers, my sons and my cousins – we are the Habbani.'

Aaron was a man of forty years, Robert guessed, his skin tanned a deep, leathery brown by sun and wind, deeply wrinkled. His dark eyes were kind, with a gleam of wisdom, too.

Robert told the man his name, and admitted that he was a Christian of the far West, an Englishman, who until lately had resided at the Templar fortress at Acre.

'You are a great warrior, then?' asked Aaron. 'A noble knight, perhaps?'

'I am nothing now,' Robert replied. 'A penniless wanderer, a mere vagabond.'

'And that is your purpose in this life – to wander the earth until your death?'

They were speaking in slow, courtly Arabic. Robert had a fairly decent grasp of the tongue, garnered from the dice-men of Acre, enough for a little fireside conversation.

'I confess I have no purpose at all in this life,' he said.

The older man nodded wisely, silently considering the matter.

'We Habbani, too, are wanderers,' Aaron said. 'It seems God has placed you in our path for a reason. If you wish it, we will wander together for a time.'

'Where are you going?'

'North,' he said. 'Our journey together will take us into the cold north.'

Chapter Three

The next morning, after breakfast of camel milk and grilled flat-breads, the Habbani of Sana'a gave Robert a voluminous hooded robe to shield his head from the sun, and he mounted on the same camel. The boy, Ibrahim, climbed up behind and, once the train had embarked on its ambling way, began asking Robert questions about his life.

Had he ever fought in a great battle? Robert said he had not. Had he met the King of England? Robert had seen him, once, in a tall, golden pavilion beside a wide river at a marshy place called Runnymede, when all the high nobility of England had gathered to show the King their strength and resolve. Why did Robert not have a wife, being a man as well-seasoned as he was?

Robert, who was not yet thirty years of age, tried to explain his vow of chastity to the boy. 'I have promised my body and my soul to God,' he said. 'For the whole of my life.'

'Oh, indeed,' said his new friend, 'then you must be a very holy man.'

Robert's laughter prevented him from answering. Instead, he asked the boy about the people he was travelling with, and the valuable cargo they carried north.

'*Al-luban*,' the boy replied, breathing the word as if it were magic. But it was an Arabic word that Robert did not understand. They conversed gently, sporadically, all that day and the next, and at their nightly camps; Robert found he was increasingly able to understand and even join in with some of the conversation around the central camel-dung fire. After he had eaten and was lying back on his blanket, looking up at the myriad stars scattered like tiny, brilliant jewels across the velvet sky, he felt for the first time a lifting of the veil of misery that had fogged his mind for so many days. He got, then, on his knees and prayed, thanking God for his deliverance.

–

His command of the Arabic tongue increased over the next few weeks, as did his knowledge of his travelling companions. Jews from the deep south of Arabia, they were the sons and grandsons of merchants, the roots of their extensive family sinking deep into the soil of their arid homeland. These folk, he came to understand, had always made their living buying goods – the mysterious *al-luban* and semi-precious stones, such as onyx and cornelian, unearthed by delving in the hills around their home in Sana'a – and transporting them on the age-old camel routes that ran north from Arabia all the way up to distant Constantinople, seat of the emperors. Yet Aaron and his Habbani folk were going much farther on this journey than that great Greek city, Robert discovered.

'We are going to see fair Trebizond,' Aaron told him over their mutton and rice that night, 'then into the ancient kingdom of Georgia, and over the high Caucasus Mountains and beyond the Black Sea, to the lands of the wild Kipchaks and the barbarous Slavs.'

'Why so far, when you could sell your goods in Damascus and go home?'

'The further we travel, the more valuable our cargo becomes,' said Aaron.

–

One day, after Robert had been with the Habbani for more than a week, they saw a cloud of dust to the west. The men of the train looked to their swords, daggers and spears, and kicked their riding camels out in front of all the rest. Ibrahim and Robert followed – the boy chattering excitedly, Robert slipping out his cedar walking staff from the pack behind him, and wishing it was a spear.

It was another train from the Sultanate of Rum, to the west, with a string of mules and pack horses, and since it was late afternoon, and the Habbani sensed no danger from these newcomers, both groups decided to make their camp together that night. When the best carpets were laid out and the black camel-wool tents all erected, and hot, spiced wine was served, Aaron beckoned Robert to him. The Jewish headman was seated next to the leader of the new train from the land of Rum, a short, pug-nosed, luxuriantly moustached fellow with a green silk turban.

Robert bowed politely to the merchant of Rum and sat on the carpet between the two older men. 'This stupid fellow seems to have no Arabic at all,' said Aaron, 'and only a few words of Persian. Perhaps he may understand your Frankish tongue. Will you speak to him on my behalf?'

Robert spoke to the man in French, to no avail, then in Latin, and again received an uncomprehending shake of the head. They found a common tongue, and a happy gush of dialogue, in Turkish – a language that Robert had studied on the journey by ship to Outremer, out of boredom and aided by two Turkish crewmen, who had taught him their language and the little Persian that they had.

It had always been Robert's practice to listen to the tongues of the men he came across in his travels, to imitate them, and remember as much of their speech as he could. He had done this since childhood, even learning the harsh English that the servants in his father's hall used with one another.

Robert relayed his conversations with the Rum merchant to Aaron. 'This man is Suleiman Oktay. He is a trader and a follower of the Prophet. He says his road will take him west into the lands of the mighty Khwarazmian Emperor, Muhammad Shah.'

'Indeed?' said Aaron, perking up. 'And what does this Suleiman trade?'

'Grain, mostly,' said Robert, after conferring with the man. 'And dried fish.'

After an amicable few hours, filled with extravagant pleasantries and a good deal of friendly swapping of knowledge about the roads they had travelled, a small deal was struck between the two groups. The next morning, in the daylight, Robert presided over the exchange of a tiny pouch filled with cornelians – small blood-red beads that reminded the Englishman of a handful of redcurrants – for two sacks of barley, one large bag of salted red mullet and two fine camel-hair blankets.

The merchant, Suleiman, was pleased with his acquisition of the semi-precious stones, and sought out Robert to thank him and present him with a gift for his labours. It was an old sword: a Frankish arming sword, straight-bladed, a little rust-stained, and with the wooden hilt rattling loose on the tang. And with it came a battered leather sheath and a mildewed belt with an iron buckle.

'My father took this from the corpse of a Genoese man-at-arms during the sack of Constantinople,' said Suleiman. 'But he had no use for it – and neither do I. May you bear this weapon to better fortune than its previous owner. And, if you ever seek employment as an interpreter, the House of Oktay will always have a welcoming place for you. Go with God.'

Robert thanked him. The sword was no Excalibur, but it was exactly the kind of weapon he was familiar with, the preferred side-arm of the Templar knight, and he felt braver and stronger simply holding the old blade in its scuffed scabbard in his own two hands.

–

After rendering assistance to the Habbani in this manner, Robert found his relationship with the tribe had subtly altered. He was no longer the pitied recipient of their generosity but a valuable member of the train. He sat by their fires at night as an equal; he shared the food in their communal pots and slept in their tents without feeling like a beggar. The younger men asked his opinion on matters of the world, about the Frankish kingdoms of the West, of France and Spain. About his faith. And when Aaron suggested that he ride one of the few horses in the train, a sweet-tempered grey mare, he accepted the offer with alacrity.

He was assigned the task of scouting out the road ahead, looking for danger, but also – most crucially – finding rivers, ponds and oases in the parched desert, where they might water all their beasts at night and refill their leather water-sacks. Aaron himself often rode with Robert as they ranged far ahead of the train, the older man teaching Robert what lore he had about the finding of water in dry places, how to read the lines of the land, the hollows and hidden courses of old river beds. How to recognise the colours of the landscape: the vivid greens and barren browns, the yellows of tinder-dry pasture and lush purples of mountainside heather. Why one stand of palm trees might mean a sweet-water well, or a waterhole, and another stand a heartbreaking dust bowl.

They crossed rivers and forests and journeyed through the Sultanate of Rum, and into the high mountains where the Euphrates was born, and all the while Robert was learning to read landscapes like an unfamiliar book and find life-giving water for the train when there seemed to be none at all.

They encountered the folk of these lands, making trades wherever they might, with Robert, more often than not, acting as the intermediary. They met rascally Kurds and lean, bow-legged Seljuk horsemen, tight-fisted Greek Orthodox Christians and flowery-talking Persians. And even when his knowledge of tongues was not required, Aaron often chose to have Robert beside him.

One warm night, lying on his blankets by the fire and looking up again at the endless speckled sky, listening to the musical night-groaning of the resting camels, Robert felt at long last that he was at peace with himself. He was among friends, he had purpose of a kind, now, which was to travel wherever God guided his footsteps, and he surrendered himself fully into the hands of the Almighty.

'Lord,' he prayed, 'I know not what path you have set for me, but wherever it leads I will follow. I am your instrument. Your will be done, on Earth as in Heaven.'

He recalled the conversation he had had with Aaron over their supper. 'Our destination is Tana, a Venetian town by the Sea of Azov, at the mouth of the great river Don, in the land of the Slavs,' Aaron had said. 'We will trade our remaining goods there with the Italian merchants, then buy furs and amber, gold and grain and begin the journey south, all the way back home to Arabia.'

Robert decided that he would go with these good Habbani folk to Tana, by the Sea of Azov, beyond the very furthest limit of the Black Sea, and once there he would see where God should guide his feet thereafter. Perhaps he would remain with the Habbani and return south to Arabia – a land he had never seen, but of which he had heard so much about around the campfire. Perhaps he would continue on alone, travelling north into the wild lands of the Rus' princes as far as the frozen northern seas. He was wonderfully free of all his past obligations, except those he owed to God.

He sat up, and flexed his left shoulder. The swelling had long gone, although the joint was still a little stiff. His torn ear was mended, too. He got to his feet and threw another stick on the fire. He opened his pouch, found a rag and began to clean his sword with a little sweet oil. It was a small military practice that he had performed every night since he had been given the old blade. His calling had always been war; he had trained for it all his adult life. Now, as he looked at this old instrument of death in his hands, it seemed that the life of a merchant might be equally agreeable.

–

They came to Trebizond at the beginning of summer and, when Robert first laid eyes on the fabled city-state on the coast, he was astonished. After weeks of hard travelling through a largely barren wilderness, he found himself gazing in wonder upon a man-made jewel girded by the shimmering blue sea. Trebizond was a magnificent muddle of high, slender towers, wide avenues, filthy alleys, gold-roofed churches, colourful, jostling bazaars, and dense and festering slums on the fringes of the city, where the dregs of Black Sea humanity existed in cramped, violent, filthy squalor.

Trebizond was a kingdom whose exquisite noblemen called themselves Romans but spoke a very pure Greek. The nobles ate only the finest foods – fresh fish from the Black Sea, fine-milled white bread made from costly wheat, and venison hunted in the cool hills above the city. They drank the strong, dark local wines, mixed with spring water and sweetened with honey. The poor ate fishy porridge and gritty rye flatbread – but they, too, were proud of their city. And everywhere you looked in Trebizond were women, haughty, bare-faced and beautiful, imbued with natural grace.

'Oh, Trebizond is famous for them,' said Aaron, one hot and humid night in their cheap inn on the city's long waterfront. 'But the men are known to be vengeful. Have a care whom you bed!'

Robert vowed he would have no truck with the women of the city, bewitching as they might be. He might think himself a merchant now – or, in truth, a merchant's apprentice – but he was determined to keep his vow of chastity. He spent his days improving his knowledge of Persian with a shopkeeper friend of Aaron's, a man who had fled west from the Khwarazmian Empire fearing the wrath of Muhammad Shah, and helping his Habbani friends in the purchase of their trade goods. He finally discovered, too, the elusive meaning of the Arabic word *al-luban* – it meant frankincense, and Trebizond was avid for it. The lemony scent of burning incense filled the streets night and day, wafting in fragrant clouds from the doors of the many churches – Roman Catholic and Greek Orthodox, and even some of the Nestorian heresy – which filled this great shining city by the sea.

It was in this beguiling place that Robert fell into sin once more. He had received small gifts of money from the Habbani and their clients for his labours as a translator, and now he had a little leather purse that jingled with silver. Walking back to the inn one early evening, he heard a voice calling to him from a doorway. He turned to look and saw a woman, backlit by candlelight inside her tiny room, standing in the door frame. He could not see her face, which was in shadow, only her shape: a long, lean body, swelling to fruitful curves in the usual places. His reaction to her shocked him. A draw so powerful that he could not refuse it. He found himself approaching her, his feet moving in her direction without his volition, and responding warmly to her greeting in accented Greek.

'Come inside, handsome stranger, and spend an hour with me,' she said.

He was so close that he could smell her scent, hyacinth blossom and spikenard, and a musky, animal odour that was all her own. He could see her face now, painted artfully to make her dark eyes seem even larger, her mouth wide, red, inviting. He was drunk on her presence, so filled with desire that he felt he might burst. He gazed at her longingly and found that he could barely speak.

'Come inside, soldier,' she whispered. 'Come and have a cup of wine with me.'

Robert knew what she was. Yet he still found her intoxicating. His mind was filled with images of her naked flesh, of their two pale bodies entwined together on a bed. The warmth of her soft frame under his; the feeling of her eager tongue in his...

He opened his mouth, the impossible words seeming to stick in his throat.

'May God keep you, sister,' he said, and he physically shoved himself away from the door frame and stumbled off down the street. She called after him hatefully – calling him a coward and a weakling, accusing him of preferring the sin of sodomy. But Robert marched on. His face burning, his heart thumping wildly. His loins in turmoil.

A few streets later and he found himself pausing at an alley mouth, a dark, fetid channel between two large houses, where a group of five men were crouched over a large wooden tray, into which they were taking turns to throw a pair of ivory dice.

Without pausing for thought, Robert joined them. The company comprised three Armenian merchants, a Kurdish blacksmith and a tall, much-scarred Circassian warrior from beyond the high Caucasus. Robert untied the pouch of coins from his belt and found his new companions were suddenly eager for him to make a wager.

He won a little money, then lost a good deal more, and finally he gambled all of his hard-earned trading silver on one last, glorious fling of the clattering dice...

He stared with disbelief at the two white cubes. A four and a three. He had won. He had gained himself a handsome purse, which was stuffed with shiny silver coins.

He thanked his new friends for an hour of amusement and began to walk away, all thoughts of lust forgotten. Then he heard the growls of dissatisfaction from the three Armenians and loudest from the tall Circassian warrior, who had lost most of the silver he had gained. The big warrior glared at him, and he even looked as if he was ready to fight Robert for his winnings.

The former Templar merely turned to face the Circassian and stared coolly at the scarred highlander, with his right hand resting on the hilt of his old Genoese sword, his left holding the scabbard. He was ready to draw, ready to fight and kill – indeed, he felt eager for the exhilarating surge through his head, heart and limbs that came from engaging in combat. He raised his eyebrows in the unspoken question to his would-be opponent. *Do you truly want to do this?*

There was a long, prickling silence, then Robert half-bowed, bade the warrior a good evening, and walked away. The Circassian mumbled something rude and turned, too, going back to the tray and snatching up the dice. Back in the inn, Robert counted his fortune on the blanket on his cot. Then he knelt to pray, to ask forgiveness for his weakness and thank St Christopher for his strength.

–

Two days later the Habbani were back on the road, their camels freshly loaded, and the train headed west along the Trebizond shore of the Black Sea, heading into the lush, green lands of the neighbouring kingdom of Georgia. And ahead of them, scouting the way, rode Robert and Aaron.

They made some trades almost every day, in large villages and small towns, and it was then Robert began to understand the secret to these merchants' way of living. The Habbani always bought what was local and cheap, and transported it to places where it was neither. Sometimes this was on a risibly small scale: four baskets of dewy peaches purchased in one valley village and transported a few miles higher into the emerald hills, where the sweet fruit would not grow so easily. Or three sacks of sun-dried grapes, offered in exchange for a decoratively stitched Bedouin riding robe. Or a dozen amphorae of Trebizond wine sold to a thirsty headman in exchange for a fine woollen carpet embroidered with scarlet and blue silk.

Sometimes the trading they did was on a much bigger scale: they had transported their valuable frankincense – the yellowish dried beads of resin harvested from a scrubby tree found in the hills around Sana'a – a thousand miles north and sold nearly all of it to the churches of Georgia, which burned pounds of it daily. In return, they received bezants – fat coins of pure and shining gold.

They travelled further east, over the next few weeks, dropping down into Armenia and even venturing as far east as Azerbaijan, following the ancient paths of the trading world known so well to the Habbani, and obeying the dictates of the local goods they purchased and the markets in which they sold them. On the balmy shores of the Caspian Sea, near a little place called Rasht, Aaron sold the last of his wine and bought mountains of salted fish and sacks of beautiful seashells. Then he turned his train around and they headed north-west. Autumn was coming on fast, and Aaron said the train had to be on the other side of the high Caucasus before the weather turned. The traditional routes over the mountains, he told Robert, were all impassable from November through till March.

They reached Tiflis, the Georgian capital, after many weeks of travelling and a circuitous route, and there Aaron unloaded the remainder of the precious *al-luban* in exchange for a hillock of bright, finger-sized gold bars, which Robert and half a dozen men of the Habbani stood guard over with drawn swords until it had been safely transported to their fortified camping site. They had divested themselves, by then, of most of the bulky goods, and their cargo was mostly precious metal.

Aaron explained to Robert that, when they reached Tana, they would be able to exchange this accumulated treasure for huge bundles of thick furs – the lush, warm coats of bears, wolves and wild cats, as well as the dense pelts of sable, fox and pine marten – which were worth much more than their weight in silver when they had been carried south and sold to the men of the Latin kingdoms.

In the very last week of autumn, when the passes in the Caucasus were still viable, they headed north from the town of Tiflis on a narrow rocky road that wound through the foothills, and climbed through the verdant lower slopes to the great, grey, snow-capped wall of the mountains.

The crossing was a four-day ordeal of sleet and icy rocks and sheer exhaustion. And they lost one of the horses, an animal mercifully only burdened with dried goods, which slipped and fell from the narrow path to smash to its death on the wooded scree far below.

Robert had prepared himself in Tiflis for the arduous journey by buying a fine suit of warm clothes, leather gauntlets, sheepskin-lined boots, two fine woollen cloaks. And he was very glad of it when his breath steamed like dragon smoke in the mornings and he found his beard crusted with ice. He had also bought armour from a blacksmith – a good shirt of mail that fell to his knees, an iron helm with nasal guard, and a wooden shield with the red cross of St George on its white leather face – spending most of his saved trading money and his winnings at the dice tray.

When they had successfully traversed the high passes, the men and beasts of the train made their long way down the northern slopes and on to the plains beyond the Caucasus. They found themselves in icy, torrential rain, and were forced to take shelter for two days in a small bedraggled village called Magas, on the banks of a raging river. There they made roaring fires, dried their gear, rested, and listened to the endless hammering deluge on the red clay tiles above their heads. They bought and slaughtered three fat-tailed sheep and feasted – the whole train gorging, roasting the mutton over a hearth inside an abandoned cowshed they had secured for a few coins as a refuge.

The Habbani told stories of their ancestors, of heroic feats of the merchants' life, of fortunes won and lost, and old tales from their holy book, which, of course, Robert was often familiar with – David and Goliath, Samson and Delilah, stories of war and love – and the talk lasted deep into the night.

When the rain eased, they drove the camels north and west, travelling for two weeks through the lands of the wild Kipchaks, horse-warriors and herdsmen, natural fighters who eyed the wealth of the train like hungry wolves observing a limping newborn lamb. The Habbani kept their eyes open and their weapons to hand and, when they made their camp at night, they surrounded their tents and their animals with thick walls of cut brush and thorn. Each night four men stood guard.

It was during this time Robert first heard of the Mongols, a fierce people from the East who had challenged the Emperor of Cathay and conquered many of the peoples of the steppe, including the Kipchaks and their cousins the Cumans, who ruled the lands for a thousand miles east from the Caucasus. And every time Robert heard the name 'Mongol', the speaker's voice was fearful.

Chapter Four

'I beg your pardon, Sir Robert,' said Ivo of Narbonne. 'Did you say *Mongols*?'

'The people whom you call Tartars are, in truth, Mongols,' said Robert. 'The great Eastern king, Genghis Khan, united all the nomadic tribes of the eastern steppe under the shadow of his horse-tail banners – one tribe of which was called Tartars – but he renamed them all. He called all the steppe tribes Mongols, after his own clan. Most Mongols would be offended to be called Tartars.'

'Is that so?' Ivo made a little note in his tablet. 'And you truly had no prior knowledge of these savage peoples before you crossed the high Caucasus?'

'I have said so, Father. I have also told you that I will not be cross-examined, close queried and tripped up by your serpentine questions at every turn.'

'And I heard you, Sir Robert. But I must make a full account of your travels to my masters, not to mention the fact that, if I'm to intercede with the duke, I will need to know everything to be able to answer *his* queries. The trial will commence in just three weeks' time, mark you, and I must have *all* the facts before then if I am to have any hope at all of preserving your life. Surely you can understand this, Sir Robert?'

Robert said nothing.

'However, I do not wish to anger you,' said Ivo. 'You will notice I do not pester you about this Sarantuya person, about whom you seem so reluctant to speak. Nor do I wish to stem the flow of your tale. So, if you are agreed, I will reserve my questions until the end of the session and put them to you then. Will this satisfy you?'

Robert gave a curt nod.

'Very well, then,' said Ivo, 'please continue. You were in the flat lands of the wild Kipchaks, hearing tales of an even more terrible enemy – the Mongols.'

Robert said nothing for a while. He took a long pull from his cup of wine.

'I shall say much more about the Mongols – the people of the Eternal Blue Sky – in due course,' he said. 'But it was months before I even saw the *tumet* of the Great Khan marching in tens of thousands below their dancing horse-tail banners.'

Ivo opened his mouth to ask a question… then wisely closed it.

Robert gave him an appreciative grin. 'However, there is little of consequence to say about the journey north from the Caucasus, through the lands of the Kipchaks. We were attacked, once, during the night, by a dozen horsemen. But we fought them off with little difficulty – although the boy Ibrahim was killed by a spear-thrust. I grieved for him. After two weeks, we arrived at our destination, at the town of Tana, on the shore of the Sea of Azov, with our cargo intact, thank God…'

–

To Robert, the town of Tana seemed like an outpost at the edge of the world. A settlement built by Venetian merchants some years earlier to cater for the fur trade, it was a huddle of wattle-and-daub buildings surrounded by a palisade, crouched on the shore, near the reed-fringed estuary of the Don.

There were several wooden jetties spearing out into the grey river, with a dozen bulbous trading ships moored against them, and dozens of shabby wooden warehouses, forges and various workshops, and a scatter of brightly lit taverns and eating-houses. But the first thing Robert noticed was the big wooden-sided church in its own stone-paved square at the very centre of the town, with a huge gilded cross affixed to its roof. The cross reflected the afternoon sunlight like a blaze of the Lord's glory. It felt, to Robert, like a message from the Saviour, welcoming him to this wilderness.

Robert helped unload and settle the camels and the horses in a stable-compound attached to the biggest inn; then he washed his face and hands and changed his soiled linen for fresh and told his Habbani friends he was going to the church. Once inside, he fell to his knees and prayed for a time, alone, below the altar. He lit a candle before the statue of the Virgin beside the font, and offered another prayer to St Christopher, thanking him for warding him on the six-month journey.

He sent up another prayer, too, for his younger brother, Gilbert, asking the saint to ward him in Egypt, in the fiery furnace of battle. The stronghold of Acre and his Brethren of the Order; the war in the Holy Land, with all its myriad disasters and tragedies: all that seemed to belong to another life, he thought, as he sat back on his heels, and gazed up at the gold-painted crucifix that hung on the east wall behind the altar. Did the Latin kingdoms that his Brethren defended still exist? He could not know for sure. They had been clinging by their fingernails when he left Acre. One good Saracen push and they'd be gone. But surely he would have heard if they had fallen, even in the far north.

'You are a newcomer to Tana, my son?' said a voice in Italian. Robert turned to see a lean-faced, handsome young man in the robes of a priest, with a ring of glossy black tonsured hair. He rose and cordially greeted the holy man in that language, and discovered he was Father Pietro, a resident of Tana and the rector of this church of St Mary. The priest said he hailed from a little place near the great city of Pisa.

'You are an Englishman?' said Father Pietro incredulously, after they had exchanged their names and homelands. 'How come you to be so far from your home?'

Robert told the priest he had left England some years before to fight with the Christian armies in the Holy Land, but he had forsworn all bloodshed. He was a merchant now, he said, in a company of Arabian Jews who had come to Tana to buy furs from hunters in deep forests of the Rus' lands.

'Ah yes, the war in the Holy Land,' said Father Pietro. 'I am sorry to say that I understand it goes badly there for our Christian brothers. Some even say they cannot hold out against the foe.'

He smiled at Robert. 'But we are little troubled here by events in the Latin kingdoms. I shall introduce you to my Tana congregation. Italians like me, mostly Venetians, but all good Christians. More to the point, they are merchants to their marrow, experienced in all kinds of trade. I'm sure they can provide any help and information you and your companions may require.'

Robert was pleased to have made a new friend. And when Father Pietro offered, he agreed to make his confession and be shriven. He felt much refreshed in spirit afterwards and returned to the inn, and to his friends, lighter of heart and with a burning desire to drink a large quantity of wine.

The first soft flakes of winter began to fall the next day, and Robert, looking out of the door of the inn, knew he and the Habbani would now be obliged to remain in Tana for the next few months.

'All the routes through the Caucasus Mountains will be impassable to a train of our size until at least the middle of March,' said Aaron, over a convivial dinner a few hours later. 'So I have secured accommodation for all of us here, and storage for our goods. Take your ease, my friend, drink some wine, rest your body and spirit. We have travelled a very hard road together these past months. Sleep, eat, visit your fine church and pray for our souls. I will call if I have any need of you.'

It took Robert several days to get used to the static life. Every morning at dawn, when he rolled out of his narrow cot in the attic of the inn, he began to ponder where he and his friends would be riding to that day, what route they should take, and had to remind himself that they were going nowhere. He spent many a tedious hour staring out of the half-open shutters of the inn at the white landscape beyond, at the muffled, icy streets, watching the gentle fall of more snow and the bowed pedestrians, swathed in furs, shuffling past his watch-post.

He attended Mass almost every morning at St Mary's in the town square, wrapped in a leather-lined woollen cloak and hood, sometimes struggling through a full blizzard to get there, or slipping and sliding on the treacherous ice of the frozen-mud streets, but since this was often his only excursion from the stuffy inn during the day, he did not mind at all. The Habbani kept to themselves in a corner of the inn's common room, near the fire, eating, drinking wine, and singing their old Arabian folk songs; then sleeping for long periods like hibernating bears. However, Robert was often restless, fidgety, and, gradually, through his visits to the church and the offices of his new friend Father Pietro, he began to make the acquaintance of the residents of Tana.

The leader of the Venetian merchants was a man called Niccolò Ziani, an extremely tall man, balding, and with a narrow wedge-like face and a long aquiline nose. He was the richest man in Tana by some considerable margin, and the settlement's unofficial lord and master.

Ziani was involved, to a greater or lesser extent, in almost all the trading activity that took place in the town, either as the man who advanced the initial money for a particular purchase, or as the one who purchased the goods on behalf of others. He was even part-owner, Robert discovered, of the inn that housed his Habbani friends, as well as a dozen other prominent establishments in town.

Father Pietro introduced him to Ziani one Sunday morning after Mass, when a group of his congregation were milling around after the service, stamping their heavy boots and clapping their leather-gloved hands in the snow-filled courtyard of St Mary's.

'Signor Ziani, may I present Robert of Hadlow, a former brother of the Poor Fellow-Soldiers of Christ and of the Temple of Solomon, overwintering here in Tana.'

Niccolò Ziani, who was short-sighted, bent forward and peered down his long nose at Robert. 'A Templar, eh? What is a brother-knight doing up here in this God-forsaken wilderness? Taking the fight to the heathen Kipchaks, eh? Or have you set your sights on converting the pagan Rus'?'

'I have left the Brethren, signor,' said Robert, feeling a slight flush of embarrassment. 'I am a Templar Knight no more. These six months past I have been trading in the lands between Acre and Tana. I am no more than a merchant now.'

'I laud your wise choice, Robert,' said Father Pietro. 'Those Templars are suspected of a number of heresies. Some even claim they are *unchristian*. You risked being ensnared by their sins.'

Robert frowned.

'Nothing wrong with being a merchant, Signor Roberto,' said Ziani. 'Nothing at all. Who do you think donated the silver to fund the Army of Christ in the Holy Land, eh? Oh, I know Templars are cunning when it comes to matters of business – they say the kings of France and England are heavily in their debt – but it is we merchants who keep the world turning. Folk like me – and you!'

Robert found himself swept along with a dozen or so cronies of Niccolò Ziani to his huge house for the midday meal – a lavish affair that would have been a feast in any lesser household.

They sat at a long oak table and ate boiled duck hunted on the marshes of the Don, served with a piquant sorrel sauce, and roasted boar stuffed with plums and onions – the beasts taken in the dense forests far north of the river – as well as dripping platters of fresh roast beef and roast capons, fine white wheaten bread, boiled green vegetables, many types of cheese, fruits, nuts and sweetmeats. They drank wines made from grapes grown by the Euphrates and brought by ship in oak barrels from Trebizond across the Black Sea to this far corner of the Venetian Empire.

Ziani was a generous host, urging all his guests to eat a great deal and drink most heartily. He held court like a great nobleman of France or England, Robert thought, with no concern for the vast expense – a generous, open-handed lord, lavishing his great wealth upon his gathered vassals.

But this was a far more equitable table than that of a rich baron or count. Every man there – for no ladies were present – could speak his mind freely, and the talk ranged far and wide: the doings of the great kings and kingdoms of Europe; the progress of the wars in Italy; the success of harvests in many diverse lands and territories, from Scotland to Spain, and from Brittany to Bavaria.

And trade. Always trade. Discussion of the high quality of the black bear furs bought in the previous season – and other pelts of wild animals hunted in the frozen north and transported in massive bales down to Tana by shaggy Rus' hunters who, these refined, well-fed Italian merchants all agreed, were barely more civilised than the wild beasts they hunted.

'Father Pietro has a dozen of these hairy creatures staying in his rectory all this winter,' said Giuseppe, a short, hugely fat merchant who, it seemed, had taken too much wine with his dinner. 'What exactly are these Rus' brutes to you, Father?' he went on, already guffawing at his own enormous wit. 'Your slaves – or your house pets?'

Father Pietro smiled coldly. 'They are neither,' he said. 'They are my bodyguards.' He turned to Robert. 'Inside Tana is safe enough, but if you venture beyond the town on to the steppe, you are vulnerable to the local Kipchaks. They are treacherous thieves who'd slit your throat and steal the clothes off your back as soon as blink. I am a man of peace, but I find it prudent to be protected.'

'Trust a Pisan to know about treachery,' said Giuseppe, laughing heartily again.

Father Pietro said, 'Oh, I think the grand merchants of Venice know a good deal more about deceit and treachery than a humble priest from a village outside Pisa.'

Robert reflected that if there was anyone round the table who was humble, it was not Father Pietro. His pectoral cross was of solid gold and decorated with precious gemstones, and the buttons on his black silk cassock were made from tiny translucent seed pearls. Neither did he abstain from all the fine food and drink at this lavish gathering. He was a lover of luxury, that was certain, with very little sign of humility. But who was Robert to criticise? Father Pietro had been kind to him, offering much advice, and he had introduced him to Niccolò Ziani and all the present company.

The talk remained on treachery and deceit, and particularly on the iniquities of the merchants of Genoa, bitter rivals to Venice and never to be trusted, never to be admitted to Tana. Robert was struck by the vehemence of the hatred for the Genoese that Ziani and the other merchants displayed.

'Devil take all those Janus-faced whores,' said Giuseppe. 'Did you know the turd-eaters are expanding Soldaya, their Crimean port? Two of my ships have been attacked in the Black Sea in the past month. Those Genoese sailors are all thieves – and to my mind, no better than Barbary pirates!'

'Those Soldaya scoundrels are trying to steal the fur trade from under our noses,' chimed in the man sitting next to Robert, a merchant called Tommaso, 'offering prices far above those we offer the Rus' – cutting their own throats to ruin us.'

'And their spies are everywhere,' said Ziani. 'Everywhere, I say, perhaps even here in Tana. Listening in dark corners, reporting our movements, meddling. We must all strive to be vigilant.'

The conversation passed to commerce in general: to the alarming rise in the price of a bushel of oranges in Jaffa, caused by a blight in the groves that had reduced the harvest and created a scarcity; the falling cost of wool cloth from Flanders, and raw wool from the north of England – a glut on the market was responsible for that; and of the sudden availability of freshwater pearls in Damascus, transported west along the thousands of miles of roads by Persian merchants from Khwarazmia.

Silk Routes, they called them – a network of age-old tracks and pathways that led from the Mediterranean Sea through the Syrian deserts, through forests, over mountains, beyond great lakes and inland seas, across the desolate places of Asia, even from as far as the kingdom of Cathay.

Once talk on the Silk Routes began, Robert found himself entranced – engaged more viscerally than by stories of fortunes in gold and silver won by shrewd manoeuvres. He listened, absorbed, picking at a cluster of glossy hazelnuts baked in honey and slowly sipping his excellent wine, while the merchant Giuseppe told tales of the unimaginable wealth of the Emperor of Cathay: of his many castles built of solid gold bricks, with towers of creamy elephant ivory studded with huge pearls and surrounded by rivers of wine, endlessly replenished, and free for all to drink from.

Even the meanest peasant in Cathay was clad from head to toe in the finest silks, Giuseppe claimed, and rare and costly spices grew on trees by the side of the highway, free for any man to pick. Peppercorns, he said, were as common in that distant realm as barleycorns. Yet Cathay was no perfect paradise, he ruefully admitted to the table: parts of the countryside were ravaged by armies of cruel horse-warriors, Satan-spawned, with the heads of savage dogs, and who ate the flesh of their enemies. These soldiers were beasts in human guise who killed all men, women and children in their path, sparing none, and cut the tender breasts from virgin girls to roast and eat as dainties.

'Have you ever *yourself* encountered these terrible dog-headed warriors?' asked Robert, frowning at Giuseppe, who was crammed in a large armchair directly opposite him.

'He has never been further east than Tana,' said Tommaso. 'Old 'Seppe has never had any truck with hard roads, freezing nights and burning deserts – isn't that right, my fat little friend?'

'Giuseppe Bracco has pure salt water in his veins,' said Ziani, smiling down the table at his plumpest guest. 'He's a master mariner with nine trading cogs under his flag, and he knows the seas better than any other living soul. But he's never been to far Cathay. No Christian has yet done so.'

'I have this intelligence on the very best authority,' said Giuseppe, flushing, and not only from his intake of wine. 'My captain, Marco Stromboli, knew an old Greek spicer who had once ventured deep into the Chaldees' territory between the

Euphrates and Tigris and bought his precious wares in the bazaars of old Baghdad – and *he* knew a Persian fellow who bought silk in Samarkand, a glittering city where such tales are commonplace. I do not care to have my word questioned—'

'That is not completely true, Niccolò, you know.' Father Pietro absently touched the fine sleeve of Ziani's brocaded coat as he spoke, admiring its silky sheen and vivid pattern. 'It's not true that no Christian has ever seen far Cathay.'

'Indeed, Father?' said Ziani.

'Have you never heard of the legend of King John the Presbyter?'

'I have heard it, Father,' said Robert. 'The story of Prester John has been the subject of much discussion among my former Brethren – and for a good many years now.'

'Would you be willing to share your knowledge, Signor Roberto?' said Ziani.

'I think "knowledge" is too potent a word,' the Englishman said. 'But I have heard rumours, mere fragments of information, whispers on the winds. You may recall that there was a letter circulating in Europe some years ago that purported to have come from a King John of India, a mighty Christian monarch, who was said to rule a fabulously wealthy kingdom beyond the deserts of the East. The letter spoke of this king's desire to conquer the Persians, and all the Arabs of the Chaldees and even the Ayyubid Sultan of Egypt and all his Saracen armies and, in so doing, in defeating the enemies of Christendom, unite the world in the true faith of our Lord Jesus Christ.'

'And you believe this Prester John letter to be genuine?' said Tommaso.

'There are certainly *some* Christians in the East,' said Ziani, pouring Robert more wine. 'My Kipchak servants have occasionally mentioned them to me. Perhaps there is a great and noble Christian king who rules over them in splendour.'

'I could not claim that with any great certainty,' said Robert. 'And, indeed, many of my fellow knights were not persuaded by this letter – many of them believed it to be a clever forgery.'

'Tell us anyway,' said Ziani. 'A false rumour often conceals a genuine pearl of truth.'

'Very well, signor – I will tell you what I have heard. Prester John, or King John, as he is sometimes called, is said to be a descendant of one of the Three Magi who worshipped the infant Christ in the manger at Bethlehem. Other stories tell that he is descended from a long line of kings who were initially converted by Saint Thomas – Doubting Thomas – during his long wanderings among the heathens of the East. He is also said to be of the Eastern Church, which some call the Nestorian faith, and others claim is a heresy – for the Nestorians believe Jesus Christ had two natures, a divine nature and a human one, each one distinct but both present in the same body...' He trailed off, seeing Father Pietro's dark expression. 'I am no theologian, of course—'

'The Church is perfectly clear on this matter,' snapped Father Pietro. 'Jesus Christ is *both* God and man – indivisible – and to suggest otherwise is to propagate a vile falsehood. It is heresy. Pure and simple. And the only cure for heresy is burning. We have to root them out, these damned heretics, all of them. Burn each and every one!'

Robert studied a small wine stain on the beautifully embroidered tablecloth.

Niccolò Ziani said, 'Perhaps we should move on to another less troublesome topic. What news is there from Damietta? Has anyone fresh tidings from Egypt?'

It was the merchant Tommaso who answered him. 'I have tidings – all of them bad. Yet I hesitate to mention them in this august company before I have verified them.'

Ziani said, 'Tell us what you have heard. I, too, have heard distressing tales.'

'One of my captains reported that the Saracens attacked the Christian camp outside Damietta in October, and caused much damage. They slaughtered hundreds of knights and took several dozen prisoners – including a number of your Brethren, signor.' Tommaso looked at Robert.

'And there is worse news,' he continued. 'A great storm struck the Nile Delta earlier this month, on or around the ninth day of November. The Christians had built a great floating fortress to allow them to come close to the fortifications of Damietta, which guards the harbour and the gateway to Egypt. When this great storm struck, many of our people were on this floating fortress, which immediately sank beneath the waves. Thousands were drowned. This is what I've heard. Some say the attempt to conquer Egypt is over. They can't go on. Some say the Latin kingdoms are done.'

'I do not believe it,' said Ziani. 'I'm sure God would never allow such a thing.'

No one spoke. A pall of sadness hung over the gathering. Soon it broke up, each man heading home through the snow. As he was about to leave, Robert saw Ziani making a beckoning gesture.

'I saw your face when Tommaso was telling us of the disasters in Damietta,' Ziani said, when they were alone. 'I saw you flinch when he told us your Brethren had been killed or drowned.'

'I am a Templar no longer,' said Robert, staring at the rushes on the floor.

'Nevertheless, there will doubtless be people for whom you still care in their ranks. I shall be making my own enquiries as to who among the knights has been killed. Is there a name you should like me to enquire about? Or more than one?'

'Gilbert of Hadlow, my younger brother. He was at Damietta, as far as I know.'

'I shall find out what I can.'

Robert uttered his thanks and took his leave.

He walked back to the inn thinking of Gilly. And the drowned knights of Damietta. He knew he must face the fact that his brother was a knight and would encounter danger. But he still had that tight feeling in his chest when he contemplated his brother's death. Gilly had been a shy boy, kind, sensitive and swift to show his feelings – no milksop, but easily bruised by life at Hadlow Manor.

Robert remembered him clearly as a child of ten or so, who had been knocked off his horse when riding at the quintain, and was crying from the shock. His father, on witnessing this unmanly behaviour, had had him whipped by the steward, a brutal oaf called Aelle, with forearms like hams. And, of course, that beating had made young Gilly weep all the more. Robert, five years older than him and already growing his first moustache, had brought Gilly sweetmeats and hot buttermilk and comforted him, and thereafter had taken the time to train with him alone, in their leisure hours, encouraging him to ignore the pain and push on when things became difficult or when he was tired. They had trained together for months, every morning before breakfast. Robert had seen skill in his brother, which only needed encouragement to emerge. Gilbert would become a fine warrior one day.

Robert told himself he was simply helping make Gilly a more proficient knight, but he also knew that this kindness had a profound effect. He knew the younger boy looked up to him with something akin to worship. And when Robert, at eighteen, left the manor for London to become a novice in the Order of the Temple, Gilly had wept again at their parting, making his father seethe.

—

That feast was the first of several lavish meals that Robert took in the house of Niccolò Ziani, most often on Sundays during the dull winter months of inactivity. Yet he was not entirely idle in that long season. He set up a padded, man-high wooden post – a pell – in one of Ziani's empty barns, and trained alone with the sword, dagger and shield every few days to keep his muscles supple and his wind sound. Occasionally, he took his grey mare out of her warm stables, out of the gates of Tana and down onto the icy shores of the Sea of Azov to stretch her legs. They galloped along the freezing strand, wind in their hair, with the grey sea shimmering into the distance to merge with the horizon, and afterwards both man and horse returned to Tana much invigorated.

One day in early December he returned from his ride to find a servant waiting for him at the inn, summoning him to Niccolò Ziani's house.

The tall merchant was in his parlour, and greeted Robert briskly.

'I have news,' he said, 'which may make your mind a little easier, Roberto. The Christians are still outside the walls of Damietta. They have weathered their disasters and the siege continues. Furthermore, Gilbert of Hadlow is not dead – at least, your brother was not dead one week ago. But he is a captive of the Saracens. He was taken prisoner during the Sultan's raid on Damietta with eleven other men, two Templar Knights, Lanfranco Adorno and Guillaume de Toulouse, and the rest brother-sergeants of the Order. They are all twelve being held in a notorious gaol in Jerusalem.'

Robert smiled with relief and accepted the proffered cup of wine from his host.

'Thank you, Niccolò,' he said. 'I am in your debt for passing on that news.'

'Do not thank me yet. There is more. The Sultan of Egypt – who has long harboured a deep and abiding hatred of all your Brethren – has set the ransom at one hundred thousand marks in silver. That is for all twelve of them, by the way. And the full amount must be paid before a single Christian will be released from his captivity.'

'But that is preposterous – a king's ransom for a handful of poor knights?'

'It *is* preposterous. The Sultan means it as an insult. He knows the Templars will not pay – they rarely do – and even if they did, who even among the greatest princes of Christendom would lay out such a sum for members of a religious order? For three knights and some men-at-arms?'

'Has the Order replied to the Sultan's outrageous demand?'

'Not yet. But I have asked to be kept informed of the situation by my people.'

—

The holy season of Christ's birth came and went, marked by Masses and feasting, games, jests and contests of prowess. Robert easily won several bouts of sword-fighting with blunted weapons on St Stephen's Day in the snow in St Mary's courtyard, earning himself a crown of pine cones and a small purse of silver from Niccolò Ziani. What surprised him was that Father Pietro also took part in the sword bouts. Indeed, even more astonishing, the priest was a competent swordsman. When Robert congratulated Father Pietro, he said, 'I was brought up in the knightly way – my father insisted on it. He died a poor man, but he had trained as a knight before his family was ruined by his unwise commercial activities. So I studied horsemanship and swordplay. Only when I was older did I heed my true vocation to the Church.'

While Robert outwardly made merry with his friends in honour of the season, his belly was often clenched with worry at the thought of Gilly languishing in Jerusalem. He found he could not sleep at night for thinking about his plight. Yet there was nothing to do but pray and wait for news.

—

In the bitter days of January and February the Habbani began trading again, buying up the huge bundles of stiff furs – bear and wolf, pine marten and fox – which the Rus' hunters brought in.

'We will depart when the snows begin to recede and the trees are unlocked from their ice mantles,' Aaron told Robert, late one evening over several games of chess, a contest at which the Jewish merchant was by far Robert's superior.

'If it is God's will,' he continued, 'we shall have crossed the Caucasus by April and will be back in Sana'a by early summer and counting our profits. The question, my friend, is – do you wish to accompany us? We could use your skills with languages and you would be due a significant share of the train's profits at journey's end. Enough, perhaps, to begin trading on your own behalf.'

For some reason, Robert was hesitant. He was indeed tempted by a share of Habbani profits. But he also had half a notion of venturing further north and trying his hand as a fur-hunter. He could see that there was a good deal of money in this trade, and it appealed to his taste for adventure. A voyage into the unknown, into dangerous exotic lands. What could be more exciting and glorious?

Yet Robert was also afflicted with guilt. It was his fault Gilly had joined the Order. The youngster had wanted to emulate his elder brother. His hero. If Robert had chosen another path in life – perhaps if he had sworn fealty to a great English nobleman – then perhaps Gilly would also have chosen a less perilous calling. Instead, Robert had decided to become a Templar, and so Gilly had chosen to do the same. So Robert knew he was duty-bound to help his brother. Perhaps he should return to the Holy Land, so as to be near Gilly in Jerusalem. But what earthly good would that do?

'Must I decide today?' he asked, recklessly advancing a pawn.

'No, you may think it over for a time.' Aaron lanced across the board with his bishop, slaying one of Robert's knights. 'Check. And also checkmate, my friend.'

Aaron looked up. 'But you must make your choice before the equinox in ten days' time.'

Robert mentioned Aaron's invitation to Niccolò Ziani a few days later. They were alone and sitting by the fire in his hall, sipping their wine after another magnificent Lord's Day feast. 'So go south with the Jews, Roberto, become a frankincense trader, become rich. What could be more splendid?'

'It would feel like a giant step backwards,' Robert said. 'A retreat. I would be returning to the Latin kingdoms, or at least passing through them—'

'And you fear you would be shamed for your expulsion from the Order?'

Robert stared at the Venetian for a while, his expression one of cold fury. He had always been deliberately vague about his reasons for leaving the Poor Fellow-Soldiers of Christ; indeed, he had implied he himself had chosen to quit his Brethren.

'What? Did you think I would *not* make enquiries about you?' said Ziani. 'I invited you into my house, into my circle of friends. I would not do that without knowing something about you. The word is you were expelled for gambling at dice.'

Robert flushed with anger. He rose abruptly from his chair to leave.

'Do not be angry with me, Roberto,' said Niccolò, tugging on his long, thin nose. 'I care not if you have a fondness for gambling – nor do I care that you go to that tavern behind St Mary's Church every Tuesday evening and throw dice with all those drunken wastrels. I do not condemn games of chance, as your Order does. As a merchant, I take risks – I throw the dice. Indeed, it is your propensity to take risks that endears you to me. Listen to me for a moment, my friend. Sit down, I beg you. Listen… I have something important to say to you – and more tidings to impart.'

Reluctantly, Robert sat down. But he angrily waved away the proffered wine jug.

'The tidings are bad, Roberto,' said Ziani, pouring wine into a goblet anyway. 'You may need a drink. So, I must tell you, the Templars have let it be known that they will not pay over the ransom the Sultan demands. They say a hundred thousand marks is too great a sum to part with.'

'If the ransom is not paid, the Sultan will slaughter the prisoners,' said Robert.

'Not necessarily, no, and not necessarily all of them. The Sultan will probably assume that the Templars are simply negotiating for a lower price.'

'The Order often refuses to pay ransoms. They say a brother-knight should fight to the death rather than allow himself to be captured. It is part of their war doctrine.' Robert spoke these words with a leaden voice. Inside his head screamed the words, *My brother Gilly is dead!*

'Now listen closely, Signor Roberto. There is a way we can save your brother. Between us – you and I – we can preserve his life, and restore him to you and, at the same time, we can make ourselves wealthy. Are you listening to me?'

Robert stared. 'I'm listening,' he said. 'How could I not, if you speak of saving my brother?'

'Good,' said Ziani. 'Now attend closely. I have a proposition for you.'

Chapter Five

Robert felt the mare tiring under him and knew they must make camp soon. For a week they had been following the right bank of the river Don, heading north-eastwards, riding beside the water through a land of knee-high grass and bent, scrubby trees stripped bare by the long ravage of winter.

Here and there were patches of dirty snow. Indeed, on their third night out of Tana, camping tentless in a copse of alders, Robert and his Cuman guide Altan had been forced to huddle together as a storm hit, their blankets hooded over their heads as the snow howled about and ice shards lashed their faces. One of their horses had gone mad, snapping its tether and bolting, kicking and neighing wildly, thudding off into the whirling white, never to be seen again. How it had managed this feat, Robert did not know, since the beast had been – so far as he knew – securely tied to a tree.

But this afternoon the spring sun was shining merrily again, and the sky was an irreproachable periwinkle blue. If it had not been for his grey mare's leaden step and drooping neck, Robert felt he might have ridden on for hours into the fine golden evening.

Yet he knew he must halt for the beast's sake. He regretted the loss of the mad-driven horse, for he and the Cuman now had only four horses between them and thousands of miles to travel. Beside the exhausted mare, and Altan's mount – an ugly, brutal-looking broad-headed steppe pony, which seemed to be indomitable – they had one pack horse and one remaining spare riding horse.

'*Ezen*,' said his guide, jerking his white-bristled chin towards a bowl of lank grass beneath a rowan tree a hundred paces from the riverbank. 'We should make our camp over there. The horses need to rest or they are in danger of...' The rest of the sentence, Robert did not understand. Altan was speaking to him in simple Mongolian – something that Robert had insisted upon since their departure from Tana.

Robert looked over his shoulder at the sun, which was still a handspan above the empty western horizon. He turned back to his guide. '*Tiimee, amrakh ni mori...*' he said, which he firmly believed meant, 'Yes, we should rest the horses now.'

Altan smiled condescendingly at him and corrected his pronunciation. 'You learn a new language fast, *ezen*,' he said loudly and, swinging down from his pony's saddle, he added just under his breath, 'for a know-nothing *khuukhed*!'

Robert half-heard and understood he had been called a child by the old man. He did not bother to respond. At least the Cuman called him *ezen* – lord – to his face.

Altan was a slave – or he had been until a week earlier. He had been produced by Niccolò Ziani on the day before their departure with the words, 'This old Cuman fool claims he has travelled all the way from the Sea of Azov to the Altai Mountains and back again. He says he knows all the roads from here to the distant lands where the morning sun rises. He is probably lying, but he might be useful to you, Roberto. I bought him last year from Giuseppe Bracco as a groom for my horses. He cares for the animals beautifully, but he keeps stealing my finest stock and trying to escape on them. That was his trade before he was captured – a horse thief and bandit. Giuseppe used to chain him up in the stables at night, to stop him stealing. If he doesn't run off with your horses, he may be of some help. And if he gives you any trouble, slit the villain's throat. I'm happy to be rid of him.'

'What languages has he?'

'He has a word or two of Italian – simple commands. And his own tongue is Cuman, which is similar to Kipchak. But he says he also speaks fluent Mongolian.'

'Oh, indeed?' said Robert. 'Is that so?'

In truth, Altan's talents extended much further than fluency in Mongolian. He could ride like a centaur, tirelessly, effortlessly, as if his wiry body were an outgrowth of his muscular little pony. Robert, who was no mean horseman himself, had been impressed. The old horse thief could also shoot a small, powerful, recurved bow with miraculous speed and accuracy – on their second day of riding together, Robert had seen him chase down a jinking hare and skewer it from the saddle with one well-placed arrow. He could track a wild goat over the rockiest terrain, and had casually proved that talent as well. He was a Cuman horse-warrior, he proclaimed, a proud son of the steppe.

'Will you swear on whatever you believe to be holy to serve me faithfully until I release you from my service?' Robert had asked him in simple Italian.

'If you go east, I'll go with you, and be your faithful man for a year and a day.'

'Do you swear it? If you will do so willingly, I shall grant you your freedom.'

'I swear by Tenggri – by the Eternal Blue Sky above us – that I shall be your true and faithful guide and willing servant for one year and one day. But no longer.'

'Agreed. But if you play me false, if you desert me, betray me, or try to steal my property from me, I shall kill you, Altan. You understand that, yes?'

'I understand you will *try* to kill me,' Altan had said with an insolent leer. 'But the steppe is wide.'

His Cuman guide was, Robert thought, possibly the ugliest man he had ever seen. Only a little taller than a boy of ten years or so, but thick-chested, with short muscular limbs, and a round head with a fringe of light brown hair, a wide, flat face, squashed features, and leathery skin which was a mass of folds and wrinkles in which bright, swift-moving eyes as merry as a blackbird's were sunk. He reminded Robert of some of the hideous imps he had seen carved in stone, which guarded the roof of the Cathedral of Notre-Dame in Paris. Indeed, Altan was perhaps even uglier than those stone monsters.

Robert prayed that Altan was not, in his soul, as villainous as he looked. And, indeed, after a week of hard riding with the old man, he had no complaints except for his continued insolence, which he was gradually learning to tolerate. Save for this air of contempt for Robert, which he exuded with his every breath, Altan was not a bad travelling companion. He seldom spoke during the day's march and did not need to be shown how to make and break camp. They fell into their natural rhythms every night and morning without discussion – Robert tending to the fire and the food, and Altan looking after their horses, grooming, feeding and securely hobbling them.

This warm spring night, as they sat under the rowan tree sipping a meaty soup made from chunks of fresh wild goat, boiled over the fire and thickened with a little oatmeal, Robert asked Altan to tell him all he knew about the road that lay ahead.

'We stay with the water,' the Cuman said in Mongolian, waving away a loud, persistent mosquito, 'for as long as we can. Later there will be deserts, dry, very hard places to travel, and you will miss these wetlands like you miss your mother's sweet milk, *khuukhed*. But, first, we follow the rivers – this one, the placid Don, to begin with.' He made a sweeping gesture towards the bank, where a long-legged heron was stalking in a stately fashion through the reeds in search of prey.

'We stay with the Don up to where it turns north-east in a great sweep, in about another two or three days' ride,' Altan continued. 'Then we leave that waterway behind and cross the marshes to the east for a day or two, until we find the west bank of the Volga, a far mightier river, which flows all the way down to the greatest inland lake of all, to the peaceful shores of the shining Sea of Ravens.'

'The Caspian Sea?' asked Robert.

'It is the same, I think. There is a camel market there on the east bank near the mouth of the Volga, at a place called Sarai, where we would be wise to rest for a while. I know good people there. They will welcome us.' Altan took a slurp from his bowl. 'Then we follow the coast of the Sea of Ravens north and east, and we travel east for about twenty days across the cruel desert to another great inland body of water. This is the Aral, the Sea of Islands, they call it, and from there... Well, it depends on where your quarry is at this time. Perhaps the Great Khan will be close in that hot and dry season, perhaps he will be distant. But all men say he is coming west with his mighty army.'

My quarry. The Great Khan. As Altan rambled on about eastern lands beyond the Amu Daria and the Syr Daria, the two mighty rivers that fed the Aral Sea, and spoke of the cities of Otrar and Burkhara and Samarkand – of their great riches and beautiful women, their sweet fruit and plentiful grain – Robert's mind drifted back to the long conversation he had had with Niccolò Ziani by the fireplace in Tana, and the extraordinary proposition the Venetian had put to him...

–

'You must bear with me, Roberto,' said Ziani, pressing a wine goblet into his hand. 'There are a lot of miles to ride before we come finally to your brother's plight.'

The merchant settled himself in his chair and said, 'We spoke some weeks ago about a great Christian king in the East. You expressed some scepticism, if I recall.'

'Prester John, yes. I still cannot say if he is a living man or a mere phantom.'

The fire crackled and spat a spark onto Robert's knee; he batted it out.

'I believe Prester John to be as real as you or me,' said Ziani, 'and I have recently received reports confirming this from one of my spiderwebs of informants in the East. My agents speak of the rise of a very powerful king – Genghis Khan, they call him, or the Great Khan – who has humbled the Emperor of Cathay and conquered half of his territories. This most puissant Eastern monarch has united all the diverse horse-warrior tribes of the steppe under one banner. They say he has an army that numbers in the hundreds of thousands, and that he governs enormous fiefdoms and rules wide lands, possessing more territories and more wealth than all the princes of Christendom combined.'

'Do you actually believe these preposterous claims?' asked Robert.

'Maybe. I've had more than one report, and from people I have found reliable in the past. They speak of a great monarch, more influential than His Holiness the Pope, rich as old Croesus of Lydia, but who lives a modest life, in a plain felt tent like some penniless vagabond, in no more splendour than that upstart young monk from Assisi, Francis. You must have heard of him – the grubby fellow who goes about bleating that Christ intended us all to live in poverty. The fool.'

'You think this Genghis Khan is the true Prester John?'

'I believe he may be. I know from my informants that Genghis Khan is said to have Christians among his family and in his retinue – oh, they are heretics, and no doubt Father Pietro would damn them all to Hell and beyond. But they have accepted Jesus Christ in their hearts – I have had this from several excellent sources.'

'I'm not interested in heretics,' said Robert. 'I never have been – neither in associating with these misguided souls, nor in hounding them to their deaths.'

'Neither am I – but do not tell our good Father Pietro. These younger clerics are always so *zealous*, so intransigent, don't you find? He and Francis of Assisi make a pretty pair. Twin souls, twin zealots. But that is not important. Listen to the tale that I will tell you, which I heard last week. Tell me what you think when the story's done.'

Niccolò Ziani poured them more wine from the silver jug.

'The Great Khan has conquered all the territories through which the Silk Routes pass on the way to Cathay. You remember we spoke of these trade routes before?'

Robert nodded. He took a sip of his wine, struggling to curb his impatience. *What has this to do with Gilly?*

'Being wise, Genghis Khan saw the benefits of unfettered trade, and instructed some of his subjects who were followers of the Prophet to open negotiations with Muhammad Shah of Khwarazmia – you know of the existence of *this* great eastern king?'

'I've heard of him, yes, and his empire. He was mentioned often when I was with the Habbani. He rules beyond the Euphrates. The great king of the Persians.'

'Just so. Well, Muhammad Shah, or one of his servants, has made what I believe to be a grave error. It may even prove fatal – for the shah and for his empire. So, listen to this, Roberto... After an exchange of the usual diplomatic letters between the Great Khan and Muhammad Shah, the khan sent an enormous camel train loaded with goods south and west to the northern edge of the Khwarazmian Empire, to a rich city called Otrar, on the Syr Daria river, just beyond the Aral Sea.

'The camel train was accompanied by five hundred Muslim merchants and contained many valuable goods – rich silk cloth and fine glazed pottery from Cathay, large quantities of grain and jewels, and even a vast nugget of pure gold that was said to be the size and shape of a camel's neck. Can you imagine! And when the Great Khan's merchants arrived in Otrar, exhausted from their long journey, the local governor welcomed them, offering food and wine. And when their guard was down and they were at their leisure, he had them arrested as spies and put to death.'

Niccolò Ziani paused to let that egregious act sink in.

Robert watched Ziani, and sipped his wine. He was, in truth, thinking about a block of gold as big as a camel's neck. How much would that be worth? Would it be enough to pay the enormous ransom on his brother Gilly and the rest of the Templar captives?

'There was a great slaughter, and only one man of the five hundred strong mission – a lowly camel driver – escaped to report back to Genghis Khan,' said Ziani. 'He was alone and taking a bath when the Otrar guards began to massacre his companions, and he managed to hide in the fireplace of the bathhouse. Apart from that lucky cameleer, not one of the five hundred survived this disgraceful attack. The governor of Otrar, a nobleman named

Inalchuq, took all their goods into his own possession. He sent a decent portion of the spoils to Muhammad Shah in Samarkand, the Khwarazmian capital, a fitting tribute from a faithful servant to his king. But he retained the rest.'

Despite his worries, Robert found himself caught up in the merchant's tale.

'Surely the shah was angry that the Great Khan's servants had been murdered,' he said. 'It was a terrible crime. To murder ambassadors... Even the barbarous Rus' would not stoop to that.'

'You may very well think so. But when the Great Khan sent three more ambassadors to Samarkand, two of whom were Mongols of high birth, close relatives of the khan, and a third who was a respected cleric of the Muslim faith, and they demanded that the governor be handed over to the Mongols for suitable punishment... guess what foolish Muhammad Shah did next?'

Robert shrugged. 'This is many leagues beyond my understanding. Tell me.'

'He executed the Muslim cleric, and shaved the heads and beards of the Mongol princes, so as to shame them. Then he sent them back in abject humiliation to the court of the Great Khan.'

Robert was shocked. He sat back in his chair, and stared at the Venetian. Even among the heathens of the East, this must surely count as a gross insult to the Great Khan. An intolerable insult.

'It must mean war,' he said slowly. 'War between the Great Khan and the proud Shah of Khwarazmia. No monarch on Earth could endure such a gross and public humiliation.'

'Indeed, and the Mongols have a special reverence for ambassadors. To harm an ambassador, or any envoy of the Great Khan, is to harm the actual person of the monarch.'

'So what did Genghis Khan do to avenge this terrible affront?'

'Nothing – not yet. But he is gathering his strength in preparation for a great campaign. I have heard that the Great Khan dispatched only one final missive to Muhammad Shah. It read thus: "You have murdered my men and my merchants; you have stolen my property. Therefore, prepare yourself for war, for I am coming against you soon with such a host that you cannot hope to withstand."'

Robert took a draught of his wine.

Niccolò Ziani tugged his long nose again and smiled slyly at the Englishman. 'We Venetians have an old saying – "When blood flows, money flows alongside it."'

'You seek to profit from the coming bloodshed?' said Robert.

'I wish for *both of us* to profit from a catastrophe that will occur whether we desire it or not. The Great Khan is descending on Khwarazmia with righteous wrath burning in his heart. Cities will fall, men will be slaughtered, slaves taken, and a vast mass of plunder will be gathered by the victor.

'And I am convinced that the victor will be the Great Khan and his Mongol horde. He has hundreds of thousands of men at his command, remember. He will come down on the shah like a wolf on the fold. Khwarazmia will fall – and all its riches will be lost by the shah, by the foolish, greedy Muhammad Shah. Gold and silver, priceless fabrics and precious jewels will all cascade freely from his trembling hands. And I hope to gather up just a few of them for the House of Ziani.'

'Your words paint a pretty picture, signor. But those spoils would stink of blood.'

'Money has no smell, Roberto. As you progress in our profession, you will come to understand this. But let me ask you this question: To whom should those Khwarazmian riches belong? To Muhammad Shah? His own raggedy bandit clan came riding down from the barren steppe only two generations ago and conquered the Persians, the Arabs and the Kurds to found their own not-so-glorious empire on the piled-up corpses of their slaughtered foes. They stole their wealth from the Persians – and now, perhaps, the Mongols will take their riches from them. And, if we are clever and patient, and a little bit cunning, a small part of this vast treasure will come to us Christians – to me and you, Roberto. And to the Republic of Venice. Would you not like to be a very rich man?'

'St Matthew says, "It is easier for a camel to go through the eye of a needle than for a rich man to enter the kingdom of God,"' said Robert. 'I would earn my heavenly reward. But I would not besmirch my honour, nor would I wade through the blood of slaughtered innocents to win a few shiny baubles. If you believe that of my character, signor, you are much mistaken.'

Ziani looked away from the Templar, a look of irritation flashing across his vulpine features. Then he looked back at Robert and said, 'We are alone here. No one can hear us – there are no spies of the Church here, and none of your erstwhile Brethren. There is no one to judge you. So I ask you again, merchant to merchant – do you desire riches?'

'Not at the price of my soul,' said Robert.

The Venetian smiled coldly. 'Then do you desire to set your brother Gilbert free?'

Robert frowned at him.

Niccolò Ziani sighed. 'A hundred thousand marks,' he said. 'That is the price of your brother's freedom. An impossible sum – no? – but what if I tell you that it is a fraction of the amount that we will gain if we engage in commerce with the khan and his victorious horde. A hundred thousand is but one hundredth of the wealth we may gain from this war. I speak of the riches of an *empire*.'

'What do you wish me to do?' asked Robert.

'I wish you to help me forge a compact with the Great Khan – to make a treaty, a solemn and binding treaty, between the Doge and the Great Council of the Republic of Venice and his vast Mongol realm. This treaty would grant us – the Venetians – the exclusive rights to trade in all manner of goods with Genghis Khan's people in all the lands between the Sea of Azov and Cathay, under the personal protection of the Great Khan and with his full sanction. If you can secure this treaty, I shall advance to you from my own coffers the amount required to set your brother free.'

'You are able to pay out a hundred thousand marks in silver coin?' Robert was astonished.

Niccolò Ziani made a self-deprecating gesture with his hand. 'God has been good to me. And I shall have the help of my fellow Venetian merchants – but only if we achieve our treaty. Moreover, I shall negotiate with the Sultan of Egypt to reduce the amount considerably. But yes, since you ask me, I could readily advance you that sum. And we must also consider this: every week, every month, we delay in paying the ransom to the Sultan, the weaker your brother and the other knights will surely become. Have you seen a Saracen prison? A stinking plague pit would be a healthier place to lie. If you wish him to live, we must pay the ransom – and speedily. Help me and we will free him.'

Robert struggled for words. He had never imagined that a man – a commoner, not even a nobleman, let alone a king – might have this vast amount of wealth at his disposal. 'So... ah... you would exclude all other nations from trading with the Great Khan?' he said, mostly for something – indeed, anything – to say to Niccolò Ziani.

'So we may hope. But, in truth, we cannot prevent some local merchant of India or an itinerant peddler from Persia from trading on the other side of the world. But we Venetians *must* have exclusive right of trade on behalf of all Christendom.'

'You spoke before of plunder taken in war – not of peaceful trade treaties.'

'All the huge wealth of the shah and his nobles will soon be possessed, I calculate, by their enemies – the Mongol princes and generals and captains, and by the Great Khan himself, of course. And what will they do with these sudden riches? Why, they will seek out luxuries, novelties and pleasures. Choice wines grown on the banks of the Euphrates, thyme-infused honey from the slopes of Mount Olympus, gold-engraved armour from Germany, the soft cotton robes of Egypt to clothe themselves in the terrible heat of Asia... Warm woollen gowns, too, for the frozen winters on the steppe. Perhaps garments cut and dyed by the best Flemish masters. They will desire pure-blood Andalusian horses, high-bred camels from the Arabian Peninsula... And we Venetians will supply all this and more to the newly rich Mongol princes, who will have gold, silver and jewels to toss about like trudging peasants broadcasting their barley.'

'Silk, too,' said Robert, swept up in his friend's excitement. 'Do not forget the trade in silk, if we were contracted to be the sole importers for all Christendom, for thousands of bales of Cathay silk every year – for year after year. Why, the fortunes to be made could dwarf the treasuries of all the Templar preceptories combined.'

'I see you have the soul of a merchant,' said Ziani, approvingly. 'Now tell me, Roberto… will you undertake this task for me – for us. And for your brother Gilbert?'

–

'*Ezen*, rouse yourself!' Robert woke, slowly rising out of his dream like a man surfacing from a dive in a pitch-black pool. He found himself staring into the squashed face of Altan, the old man's bristled chin only inches from his own cheek.

'What? What is it?'

'The horses are restless. They can smell something – out there in the darkness.'

'Other horses? Other men?'

'Perhaps. We must be ready.'

Robert slipped out of his blankets, scooping up his scabbard belt and strapping it on over his thin calf-length linen chemise, which was all he wore to sleep. When the wide leather belt was snug around his hips, with the comforting weight of his sword on one side and a foot-long dagger on the other, he joined Altan's crouched shadow in the trees, where the Cuman thief was soothing the four horses, whispering to them in his own steppe language.

Then Altan tugged his sleeve and pointed out into the darkness, indicating north-west, and then flashed both his open hands twice at Robert. *Twenty men!*

'We must flee,' whispered Robert. He saw Altan's shadowy head nodding agreement. It was a cloudy night, no sign of a moon, with only the faint scatter of starlight to leaven the gloom. Then an ear-splitting scream filled the night air, and all around was movement, half-seen bodies of men rushing forward, the gleam of steel.

Chapter Six

Robert did not hesitate. He drew the sword and hurled himself out from the inky shadow of the tree. A knot of figures – not twenty men, more like seven or eight – were running down the slope towards the embers of the campfire and the two rumpled blankets where he and Altan had been sleeping.

He attacked them from the flank and took them by surprise, his first blow, delivered two-handed, hacking into the side of the neck of the nearest attacker and half-severing his head from his body. Robert ignored the falling man and barrelled straight into the next, shoulder-charging a big, full-bearded rogue and knocking him off his stride. A sword blade flashed in the starlight. Robert parried and counter-attacked, steel clashing, sparks flying, and the former Templar's arming-sword skidding along the enemy's blade and thumping into the meat of his arm. By now the night was filled with screams, curses and shouts of rage. The language used, Robert believed, was that of the Rus' – he had heard it spoken by the fur traders who had dealt with the Habbani – but it was too dark to make out the features of the shouting combatants. Robert had an impression of foul breath, bulk and beards. And blades. Too many blades. Someone shouted a question at him and, without waiting for an answer, hacked viciously at him with a long-handled Dane axe.

Robert was forced to duck the blow from the five-foot axe, close in a pace to his opponent, inside his killing range, and cut down hard at the fellow's shin with his sword. The cut landed, the bone snapped, the man fell sideways, yelling out in pain.

Another attacker was running at him, a big, fair-haired man, but before he could come close, this new assailant was suddenly jerked backwards, like a puppet on a string. As he fell back he clawed at his own eye, where a black arrow had sprouted.

Robert exchanged ringing cuts with another dark form, and sparks spewed red and gold from their blades in the night air. This man was very strong – Robert took a massive blow directly on the raised sword blade and felt the force reverberate the length of his right arm. He shoved the man away with his left hand, then scrabbled to draw his dagger. He heard another arrow hiss past his ear, but knew not where it struck.

His opponent was gone now. Then there was a volley of orders, harsh Rus' words he did not understand, and all the figures round him melted into the night.

Altan was beside him then, fresh arrow nocked to his string. 'They will be back – with burning *bambar*... with, uh, lights!' he said. Then some Mongolian Robert didn't catch – curses, anyway. 'Hurry! We must be off before they return.'

Robert wiped his bloody blade and dagger and sheathed them, then, fumbling like a hopeless drunk, his fingers catching on every buckle and strap, he saddled his horse and their spare mount, and helped Altan collect and roughly stow all their camping and cooking gear into the twin panniers carried by their packhorse.

In short order they were mounted and heading cautiously eastwards along the riverbank, Altan, unencumbered, on the lead horse, his bow in his hands, and Robert following with the pack-horse attached by a rope to the pommel of his saddle, and leading the other spare mount along with his left hand. His ears were alert, all his senses supremely heightened. Every snap of a dead branch, every click of iron-shod hoof on rock seemed deafening, and Altan kept turning in the saddle, gesturing to Robert to be quiet, making barely perceptible but extremely irritating shushing noises.

They got clear of the riverbank and the trees along its fringes and into a stretch of open countryside – scrubby heathland, spongy under hoof – and Altan urged his horse into a canter, so Robert was obliged to keep up. This was reckless beyond belief, Robert thought. The ground was puddled with large black shadows, and even when the pale sickle moon emerged from its blanket of clouds, he could scarcely make out the terrain beneath his horse's hooves. One misstep, one misplaced hoof down an unseen rabbit hole, and they would have a screaming horse with a snapped leg on their hands. Robert tried to listen out for their attackers over the thudding of their own hoof beats; and when he glanced over his shoulder, he could see nothing more than twenty paces away. He began to hope that they had lost whoever it was that had attacked them. Finally, Altan scrambled his horse down a slope into a narrow defile and reined in. Robert, breathless, and beyond fear now, halted his string of horses, too.

Altan slipped off his mount and silently handed his reins up to Robert.

The Cuman clambered up the steep slope using both hands and, lying on his belly, peered over the lip into the black and barren heath behind them, watching the path they had just taken. He was up there for a long, long time and Robert had just begun to dismount when the little man slid down the banks and came to his crupper.

'I saw them,' he said. 'A line of torches – still a large band, I think. Maybe fifteen men. Heading south-east. If we follow this ravine north, we can lose them.'

Robert saw no point in arguing, but he pushed the reins of the spare horse, along with those of the Cuman's own scrubby steppe pony, into Altan's hands. He kept hold of the rope attached to the packhorse. They set off, each mounted and drawing a second horse behind them. Northwards they travelled, all the rest of the long night until the sky began to turn grey in the east, growing lighter and pinker like a drop of blood spilled in a pail of fresh milk, until the sun poked its bloody head above the horizon. They rested the horses then for an hour and ate a few dried curls of last night's oatmeal, scraped from the unwashed pan. They drank and looked to the horses.

'You think we've lost them?'

'For now. Maybe. Maybe not. The steppe is wide.'

83

'Who were they?'

Altan said nothing. He looked away, refusing to meet Robert's enquiring gaze.

'You know them?'

The Cuman lifted his bristly chin then, and his blackbird eyes bored into Robert's.

'Saw them three days ago, on the skyline,' he muttered. 'I thought they might be following us. But I saw no sign for two days. I believed they were gone.'

'They were Rus',' said Robert. 'Why did you not tell me you saw them?'

'I should tell everything I see? Look, there is a pretty flower… up there, a hawk.'

'Why would they follow us?' Robert slapped the bundles in the panniers on the packhorse, and the animal stirred its legs skittishly. 'This is not worth three days' pursuit, and a bloody fight – and some of your comrades killed.'

The panniers contained spare clothes, Robert's iron mail, helm and shield, a few weapons, Altan's spare bow and a store of arrows, some extra camping equipment and bundles of dried food… and a few choice gifts for the Great Khan: a copy of the Holy Bible, made by the monks of a monastery in Ravenna, bound in finest kidskin and blessed by the touch of the Pope himself; a small relic, a fingernail of St Peter, encased in crystal and gold; a bundle of glossy black ostrich feathers from Egypt; and a pound of frankincense – the last of the *al-luban* of the Habbani, a parting gift from Aaron. They also contained a little coin and some trinkets for easing Robert's passage with officials.

Robert and Ziani had decided that gold and jewels would not impress the Great Khan – he must already possess wagonloads of treasures – but if he truly were the fabled Prester John, then a Holy Bible blessed by the Pope himself might well win Robert the great monarch's favour.

'More important than these gifts,' Ziani had said, 'is that you prove yourself to Genghis Khan as a man who is trustworthy.

Make him like you. Make yourself useful to him. Better than that, make yourself *invaluable* to him.'

The possessions and gifts bundled up on the packhorse might be worth a little something in terms of money, but they were not, as Robert had pointed out, worth killing and dying for. If these Rus' attackers had just been bandits after loot, there must be more lucrative targets on these lonely roads.

'No, not our possessions,' said Altan. 'They want *us*. To stop us, or kill us.'

Robert recalled the final conversation with Ziani just before his departure.

'Remember: the Genoese also have their spies,' the merchant had said quietly, although they were alone. 'We would be wise to assume they already know some, if not all our plans. Trust no one. Those Soldaya maggots would stop at nothing to wreck our efforts. The Genoese would deem murder a cheap way to thwart our plans. So beware! Be wary of every man and woman you meet.'

'The Rus' will not cease from following us,' Robert told Altan gravely. 'If they have tracked us for three days and a hundred miles, they will not give up now.'

'Do you know who they are?' asked the Cuman. 'Do you know who sent them?'

It was Robert's turn to look away. 'They are the servants of enemies of my friends in Tana,' he said. 'And they will surely kill us – or worse – if they catch us.'

They rode north as fast as they could push the horses, and with every stride away from the river, Robert began to feel a little more confident. At midday they paused, ate, drank a little, and changed horses. They took the time to distribute the baggage load carried by the packhorse between Robert's sweet-tempered grey mare and Altan's steppe beast. Then they saddled the other two horses and rode on in brilliant sunshine. Around mid-afternoon, Atlan stopped by a tall larch and, boosted by Robert, he climbed to the highest branch and looked at their back-trail. His face was grim as he clambered down.

'Dust on our trail,' he said. 'They have our scent.'

Robert was about to disagree with him, but thought better of it. 'How many?'

'At least a dozen, and they have spare horses, three or four for each rider.'

'Can we outpace them?'

Altan shrugged. 'The steppe is wide,' he said, swinging up into the saddle.

They rode on through the baking afternoon, pushing their animals as fast as they dared. By dusk, Robert could see the dust cloud behind them. They came to a wide stretch of river, infested with mosquitoes. Slipping from the saddle, they plunged straight in, swimming beside the horses to the far bank, a quarter of a mile away. When they emerged, dripping and exhausted, Robert asked, 'Is this the Volga?' He slapped at his neck, then examined his palm for the blood spot.

Altan laughed at him. 'This is the same river we've been following ever since Tana – the Don,' he said. 'It arches back on itself. You will know Mother Volga when you see her. You will see her in her full and shining glory in another day or two.'

They swapped the packs and saddles again and rode on into the night.

All four horses were exhausted now, and the men were too tired to speak. The ground was boggy here; insects still buzzed around their heads. The horses kept shying, disliking the soft suck of the earth, but Altan seemed to know the firm parts of the ground. It occurred to Robert that if Altan dropped the rope that led to the packhorse and simply rode away, there was not much he could do; he would be stuck in this insect-ridden marsh, splashing on hopelessly till the Rus' caught him.

'You shot straight, this morning. I believe you saved me,' he said, awkwardly.

Altan threw him a sour look. 'You fought almost adequately, too, *ezen*,' he said, then turned away. Robert heard him muttering, 'For a know-nothing *khuukhed*.'

But the Englishman smiled to himself, despite the insult.

Eventually, their combined exhaustion forced them to make a halt. They found higher ground, stripped the saddles and packs from their drooping horses and sat back to back, cross-legged, staring out into the dark with their weapons across their knees.

'You sleep, Altan,' said Robert. 'I will keep watch till the moon is high. But his companion said nothing. Robert, surprised, turned to look at the Cuman. His chin was already on his breast, his eyes closed. A moment later he let out a gentle snore.

'I might be a know-nothing *khuukhed*,' Robert said, 'but you are a tired old man.'

There was no sign of the Rus' come the dawn. Nor all that day, as they pushed on eastwards across the grasslands of the steppe, as endless as an ocean and equally beautiful. Two men and four horses passed the morning in a land that was endless on all sides, with Robert acutely aware of his smallness in the context of God's creation.

A little after noon they came across a lone shepherd and his small flock, and Altan galloped over to speak to the man, who brandished a knife at him and looked as if he were prepared to fight. Robert looked away and kept all three ponies trotting steadily eastwards, and a while later, Altan rejoined him. He was wiping blood from his own knife – a vicious-looking curved instrument, nine inches long, with a heavy bone handle – that he always wore in his belt.

'Did you kill him?' Robert said, shocked. 'There was no need to do *that*!'

Altan grinned and jerked a thumb over his shoulder, where a freshly slaughtered young sheep was slumped over the haunches of his horse. 'No, *ezen*, I only brought our supper,' he said.

They roasted the hogget that night at camp with wild garlic – and happily gorged.

The shepherd had seen dust – the passage of many horses – the old Cuman told Robert, but it had been well to the north of the track they were now following. When Robert asked him to assess the danger of their pursuers catching up with them, Altan just shrugged at him.

'The steppe,' he mumbled, through a mouthful of bloody meat, 'is wide.'

Robert found that he was beginning to resent that vague expression.

The next day they came to the Volga. And Robert was astounded that he had mistaken the quarter-mile-wide Don, which now seemed an insignificant trickle, for this vast expanse of water. He could barely make out the trees on the far side. The metallic colour of the river – a magnificent silvery azure – filled him with a deep sense of awe.

'She is the mother of all the lands around here and all the way north to the mountains,' Altan said. 'She is the rich, flowing heart's-blood of the Cuman steppe.'

'We cannot swim across that,' Robert said. 'Not with the horses and baggage.'

'There is a ferry. Downstream,' said Altan, grinning. 'Where Mother Volga spreads her legs.'

They camped far from the water's edge. And though it seemed they had lost the Rus', they still took turns on watch. Four hours awake, four asleep. Robert went first. Altan woke him when the moon was high and Robert sat with his back to the fire and looked out at the darkness, sword across his knees.

He thought about the Rus', and the Genoese merchants who had presumably hired them to kill him. Then he prayed for a while, eyes open, the words silent, spooling out inside his heart.

'Hear me, Lord Jesus. Comfort me, O Saviour, and protect me in my hour of peril. In the darkest part of the night, be thou ever my guiding light. And watch over my brother Gilbert, too, in his chains. Bring your sweet, holy comfort to his sorrowful heart and strength to his weary limbs.'

The next day, as they were approaching the place where Altan had crudely indicated that the Volga ferry operated, Robert spotted horsemen in the far distance – a dozen riders to the south.

They cantered off the riverside road, back into the shelter of a copse of birch, into a small hollow that shielded them from sight from the river.

Altan took charge of the four horses and Robert crawled forward out of the trees, painfully on his knees and elbows over rocky ground. At the top of a small rise he lay flat on his belly and peered out through the tough spiny marsh grass towards the landing site of the ferry, about four hundred yards away from his position.

He could see a small hut and a narrow wooden jetty lancing out into the shining water, with a wide, flat vessel tied up alongside it. Just south of the landing, he could see that the river divided into two streams around a thickly wooded island in the middle of the flow. The terrain was open grassland as far as the jetty, with a belt of woodland beyond, to the south of the crossing place.

There was a group of armed men at the landing, mostly fair-haired and bearded, in rough grey tunics and cross-gartered leggings, sprawled around on the ground by the jetty, some sitting and passing a skin of drink, some lying prone, asleep. There was a small fire smouldering, and a lean fellow in black, kneeling and stirring a pot suspended over the smoking fire. A pyramid of stacked spears, their steel points glinting, and a dozen tethered ponies, convinced Robert that these were indeed the Rus' warriors who had attacked them in the night. And when Altan crawled up the slope and took his place beside him, he was about to say so, when he was distracted by a small movement. There was an X-shaped frame set up by the water's edge, with something hanging from it. Robert had first assumed that it was a carcass — a deer or large sheep — hung up there to gralloch and carve for meat, and left up to keep vermin at bay.

Then the carcass moved — a twitch — and Robert could now see it was a man. A naked man, covered in blood, hanging limply from the X-arms of the structure. Even at this distance, Robert could tell he was very badly injured, perhaps close to death.

'They questioned the ferryman,' said Altan, 'to determine if we had crossed.'

Robert was suddenly filled with icy rage as he grasped the brutality of the Rus' pursuers. This poor fellow on the X-frame was no enemy. He was just a ferryman trying to make a humble living.

'How do we get across?' he said tightly.

Altan glanced sideways at him. 'We cannot cross here without the ferry boat.'

'Then we shall take that ferry boat away from these filthy animals,' Robert said.

Chapter Seven

Thirty paces from the Rus' camp by the jetty, but now south of it, in the wooded part of the bank, Robert paused, leaning his chest against the bole of a pine, craning his head round the trunk to see.

It had been a hard day's ride, south-west, then east, until they had found a suitable spot and secured the horses and baggage near a small beach on the western bank of the Volga. Then they had waited till nightfall and trekked north more than two miles on foot, coming up during the middle watches of the night on the Rus's encampment unobserved – at least, so Robert devoutly hoped.

Little seemed to have changed over the course of the last day, except that a large hide tent had been set up a dozen paces from the jetty, from which Robert could faintly hear the sound of snores. The embers of the fire provided a glow over the camp. And the Rus' seemed to have posted sentries.

One of them, a small fellow wearing a hood, was standing a stone's throw away, half-facing the woods, with his head thrown back staring up at the night sky. A crescent moon grudgingly offered its lemon light from a position just above the wooded island in the middle of the stream, to Robert's right. But drifting flocks of raggedy cloud regularly obscured even that feeble illumination.

God is with us, he thought, his hand going to his belt where the long, scabbarded dagger nudged his ribs. In the small of his back, he could feel the hard lump of his mace – a brutal weapon made of six flat flanges, blunt triangular iron blades affixed outwards in a ring around the wooden head, which meant anyone struck with the weapon felt the full force of the blow through one of the iron blades. It was a bone-breaker, a skull-smasher. Perfect for this night's work.

He touched his stubbled face then, where the smeared river mud had dried and cracked, itching his skin like the very Devil. He stopped himself from scratching and dislodging the cracked mask. He had shaved his beard off in Tana, echoing the fashion of the Italians, but on the road he had allowed it to grow back. He did not want any part of his body to reflect the moonlight, so he had dressed in dark clothes, slathered his face, and kept his weapons sheathed until the last moment.

It was time to act. He cupped his mud-smeared hands together and blew, making a hooting sound like an owl. The signal given, a black shape to his left – a smaller lump behind its own tree – moved. Robert thought he saw a flash of grinning teeth in the dark. There was a noise like a plucked string, and the hooded sentry was clutching his throat, coughing, blood gleaming in the moonlight.

Robert drew the mace from its place in the back of his belt, shoved away from the tree and sprinted out from the cover of the woods, running full pelt straight towards the enemy encampment. He ignored the arrow-struck sentry and hared towards the large tent, to the right of the campfire between the cooking space and the ferry. Only one man saw him coming – a fellow who was sitting by the fire and re-lacing a shoe. He squawked with alarm, dropped the shoe and rose, reaching for a sword on his belt – then Altan's arrow took him in the middle of his belly. He doubled over and Robert hammered the mace down into his skull as he ran past, dropping the man like a stone.

He was now ten paces from the jetty; a lean shape rose up from a dark fold in the ground where he had been lying, presumably asleep. He had a naked sword in his hand, and Robert skidded to a halt, just out of reach of his initial lunge. Robert drew the dagger with his left hand, keeping the mace in his right, and circled the man warily. He could not see the man clearly in the darkness, yet there was something familiar about his tall, slender shape and his long, midnight-hued robe.

Their plan had gone awry. They were supposed to reach the ferry, which was tied up to the jetty, with minimal interference. But even as he kept his eyes on the swordsman, Robert could hear the sounds of shouting behind him. A bowstring twang, a yell of pain and curses in the Rus' tongue.

The swordsman came straight at Robert, his blade arcing down from high on his left side, a blow that would have cleaved his shoulder had it landed. But Robert blocked with the dagger, the fine Damascus steel holding under the hard contact, and swung laterally with the mace. The man dodged away, the heavy flanged club grazing his ribs on the right side, and let out a gasp of pain. Then he was back, the blade darting towards Robert, flickering towards his face. He blocked with the dagger again, swung the mace again – and missed. The swordsman was wary now, circling, and as he moved the clouds opened a window of sky and the moonlight shone full on the swordsman's lean, dark face. He was quite unmistakable. He was Father Pietro.

The priest attacked and Robert, shocked by the revelation of his opponent's identity, was slow to react. He managed to swerve the downward cut, came in close and punched with the dagger. At the very last moment, he switched from a stab to the neck to a blow with his fist, still gripping the dagger handle, to the point of the chin. Father Pietro flew backwards, landed on his backside and, stunned, he struggled to rise. Robert stepped in, the mace lofted above the sprawling priest. In one blow, he could end this man's life. In one blow, he could bury the mace's flanges into his skull.

The blow never landed. Robert stopped. This was a man of God. This was one of the souls consecrated by the Church. A holy man who interceded with the divine. He could not slay him.

Robert stepped back.

'Next time,' he said, 'I will show no mercy. Leave us be, Father, and you shall live.' He turned to run. As he was sprinting for the ferry, he heard the priest shout out, 'Piss on your mercy. I piss on all of you, and all the Hell-bound duplicitous dogs of that thrice-damned whore Venice.'

Robert had no leisure to ponder the priest's words. He charged towards the water, feet pounding. He might have turned back to help his friend – for he could hear the sounds of battle behind him – but he and Altan had both sworn that they would stop for nothing to reach the ferry.

So Robert ignored the fight behind him and thundered down the slippery wooden planks of the jetty, leaping aboard the long, flat craft, which rode barely a foot above the surface of the water. He skidded to a halt on the slippery wood, turned, and immediately began hacking with his dagger at the thick hemp rope that secured the ferry to a post in the landing. He looked up once, quickly, and saw Altan, bloody and limping, but coming down the wooden jetty towards him. God be praised. Altan had his bow in one hand and a slim, curved sword – a scimitar – in the other. Behind him loomed Father Pietro, who was urging on a huge fellow, a man wielding a long Dane axe. Scattered along the bank now were a dozen others, pointing and shouting, and a handful of fallen bodies, too.

Robert cut through the last strand of rope, looped his left arm around the post to hold the ferry, flipped the long dagger in the air and caught it by the point, then he drew back his right arm and hurled the dagger hard, end over end. The spinning knife smacked into the axeman's face, ripping away a flap of cheek flesh. It stopped the Rus' dead in his tracks.

Altan threw himself onto the boards of the ferry, thumping down in a bloody heap, just as Robert unlinked his arm and shoved hard against the mooring post, using his whole strength. The lightly built ferry – by God's grace – slipped easily and smoothly away from the land and coasted out a dozen yards or more into the moonlit waters of the Volga.

The Rus' with the torn face was kneeling on the jetty, clutching his wound, and beside him stood Father Pietro, tall, dark and furious, sword in his right hand, as the gap of water between the priest and the ferry increased from a dozen paces to twenty and the current took them.

'You will burn in the fires of Hell, you foul Templar heretic – you and all your filthy kind!' shouted the priest, his hate-filled words travelling to them clearly across the silvery-black water.

Robert stared back, puzzled. *Why would the priest be hunting us? Why does he hate us so?*

He could not think on that now. Robert bent and picked up a punting pole, and dug it into the river bed, pushing the ferry even further out into the fast-running Volga. Altan was on his feet by then, too, and scrabbling to pick up another long pole. The Rus' on the bank were a hundred paces away from them now. But one of them had found a bow, and a moment later a shaft slammed into the wooden decking. A fine shot at this distance and in darkness. Robert and Altan were both now at the blunt stern of the vessel, poling the craft hard away from the land and, with every heave, they put another good twenty paces between them and their bank-bound enemies.

Another arrow hissed through the night, and flew between the two men before disappearing into the shimmering waters. But a third one flew true and sliced the lower part of Robert's right calf, just above his boot top. The Rus' with the wounded face shouted out something – an insult or threat. But its power was lost in the growing space between them. Soon there were no more arrows either.

In a few moments, the enemy were no more than a grey blur on the fast-receding coast, with only the orange-red pinprick of their campfire to mark their position.

There was no way to tell how fast they were moving, for they could see nothing of the banks in the darkness, but Robert and Altan knew they were on the western branch of the Volga, as it bifurcated at the island. It was an unwieldy craft to steer for men unused to this kind of labour – and Altan's left leg was badly injured, which drained his strength considerably.

Robert examined his own wound: he had taken a shallow but painful cut, no more; the arrow had been at the extent of its reach when it hit him. So he did most of the poling, trying to angle the ferry across the river to hit the coast of the long island. He judged that if they made landfall on that tree-filled haven, they would be safe till morning, and with daylight they could reckon their position.

The land came as a shock to Robert, the ferry grinding on rocks and bumping into the half-submerged roots of trees, and he was thrown off his feet, and landed on top of Altan's wounded leg while the older man was sleeping. The scream the Cuman let out, followed by a volley of curses in his own tongue, would have alerted anyone in the vicinity – had there been anyone near them at all.

Mercifully, the island seemed to be uninhabited. They tied the craft up and, in the light of a shielded candle-stub, looked to their wounds. Altan, they discovered, had a long slice along the outside length of his right thigh – a sword cut, still bleeding. Robert doused it thoroughly with boiled water from his drinking flask while Altan cursed him in Cuman and called him a clumsy child in Mongolian – and Robert ignored his invective and bound the gash tightly with a strip of linen torn from his chemise.

'What is the name of this island?' he asked Altan as he worked on his leg.

'Pig,' said the old Cuman.

'I am being as gentle as I can,' Robert retorted angrily.

'That is what it is called – Pig Island.' Altan began laughing weakly. 'It used to have wild pigs living here. But they all died or were eaten by Volga boatmen.'

Robert, too, began to laugh at his misunderstanding, the danger and excitement of combat making him giddy with mirth. Eventually, sobriety returned to them both.

Robert's own wound had dried and scabbed over within the hour. Neither of them was in too perilous a state, he reckoned, although his great fear was that the wounds would go bad, as many did. He turned away from Altan and knelt on the decking of the ferry craft in the dark, and prayed to St Christopher to keep all corruption – which came from the Devil – away from their injuries. Then they wrapped themselves in their cloaks, lay down and slept fitfully on the boards.

–

The sun rising over the heavily wooded island cast long shadows over the mist-covered river, and they could only just make out the western bank they had left in such a hurry the night before. Altan pointed a gnarled finger north and west, to indicate where the ferryman had been tortured, but it was too far away to see anything of the Rus' camp. After a quick wash in the river, Robert knelt to say his morning prayers, and beseeched almighty God to welcome the poor ferryman into Heaven.

They had no food, and neither man was in the mood to linger on the island, so they shoved off before the sun was fully above the horizon. Both straining at the poles as best they could with their injuries, they directed the ferry back towards the western bank.

It took them an hour of hard effort with the poles, and a pair of long oars they found lashed to the rail. And the current kept tugging them further and further south. But once they were safely landed on the western bank, several miles south of the island, Robert disembarked and tried to find the beach where they had left their four horses and all their baggage.

This occasioned a brief argument with Altan. The Englishman insisted they had been swept too far south down the river. The Cuman, who seemed unusually irritable that day, swore they had not come far *enough* downstream. The sound of distant neighing ended their dispute. It was coming from beyond a spit of land a little further south and, with Altan smirking triumphantly, they pushed the ferry craft out into the river once more and glided just a few hundred paces downstream.

Reunited with their possessions, they ate a few slices of cold mutton and munched double-baked barley bread and drank some river water, and Robert looked at Altan's wound once more. It was angry red and swollen, and trickling watery blood, so he washed it thoroughly again, this time using a flask of tart wine-vinegar from their stores.

The Cuman bore the treatment without a word. And returned the favour to Robert's shallow wound. The vinegar stung like a thousand wasps and Robert was hard-pressed not to cry out. But he saw Altan watching him as he worked, looking for a sign of weakness, so he remained impassive.

With the baggage loaded on the ferry there was more discussion – what next? Both agreed that, rather than cross the river – which their Rus' pursuers might expect them to do – they should continue downstream on the ferry craft until they came to a town called Sarai near the mouth of the river, where it emptied into the Sea of Ravens. There was, however, disagreement about one matter.

'We cannot take our horses on the water,' said Altan. 'But Sarai has a camel market. We will stay with my friends. They will help us buy camels for our journey.'

'Those horses cost a great deal of money. You wish me to simply abandon them?'

'You hoard coin like a merchant,' Altan sneered. 'If you wish to keep your precious horses, we must leave the ferry craft and ride them south on this bank for ten days. And then how to cross?'

'There is plenty of room on the craft for our beasts and us. We take them with us.'

'Horses don't like boats. They might stand still a few hours, to get to the other side of the river. But not several days' travel on the water. They would get sick or go mad. They could easily injure themselves kicking out in their panic, or hurt each other – or us!'

'So we take them across the river and ride them south on the far bank.'

'We have already spoken of this. The Rus' will look for us on the other side when they find the means to cross. It is far better if we go now by water. Much faster. And the Rus' cannot follow us. It is best if we set our horses loose here, and best if we buy camels down in Sarai for the desert.'

'Best if we buy camels? And whose coin do you propose that we spend on that?'

'Lord Ziani's coin. He has plenty. Now, decide! The ferry craft or the horses?'

Robert said his farewell to the mare by rubbing her nose and giving her the last of the feed corn by hand. Then he released her, and the three other horses, with brisk, affectionate swipes on their haunches to set them on their way as free creatures of the steppe. Robert and Altan then sorted through their gear, and piled all of the now-unnecessary horse tack on the beach. As they worked, Robert saw that Altan was moving stiffly and favouring his wounded leg. His face was pale and drawn with pain. Robert realised that he had been correct to choose the waterborne method of travel. Riding would have been excruciating for his companion, with his wounded leg protesting at every jolt of his horse. The water route was a far better option.

Yet Altan made no complaint as they worked. Indeed, he barely spoke. At mid-morning, with their gear neatly repacked and loaded on to the ferry craft, they shoved off, briskly poling out into the middle of the stream. The craft was immediately drawn downstream by the strong current and needed only the lightest touch of the steering oar to keep it firmly in the centre of the river.

There had been no sign of the Rus' all morning. Indeed, they saw no one for the rest of that hot day. Robert took the steering oar at a little after noon and allowed Altan to rest his leg and sleep in the shade of an awning he had rigged between the side rails. The Englishman kept the craft moving steadily ever southwards. And, at dusk, he directed the ferry towards a stretch of grey sand on the eastern bank. As the craft ground up noisily on the strand, Altan awoke and sat up, yawning and looking about him. They tied up the craft and made camp above the beach, Robert making barley flatbreads, cooked on hot rocks, to eat with dried goat's meat and a handful of sweet raisins.

'How is your leg?' Robert asked as they prepared for sleep. 'Do you desire me to clean it again and change the bandage?' Altan merely grunted something unintelligible but clearly rude, closed his eyes and pulled his cloak tight around him.

Over the next few days, Robert saw no trace of the Rus' as they slid swiftly down the river towards Sarai. Robert privately believed they must have given up the chase. Whatever the Genoese were paying them, or whatever reward they were offering, it must now seem to them a bad bargain. Between Altan and himself, he reckoned they had accounted for at least half of their number either dead or wounded. And with half their strength gone and their prey growing ever more distant, even the most determined Rus' mercenary-bandit must feel discouraged.

What disturbed Robert's mind was the presence of Father Pietro among his pursuers. He thought about the priest often, as he and Altan glided easily down the mighty Volga. There was little else for him to do. What did it mean that Father Pietro was leading these brutal hired men? He had claimed that he was a Pisan – but was he, in fact, Genoese? No, no – the Genoese dialect would have swiftly given him away. Those Venetians would have spotted the lie immediately. So he was truly from Pisa. So why was he, then, in the pay of Genoa? Robert puzzled over this for some time.

Had the Genoese offered him irresistible riches – or perhaps even a share in the wealth of the trade with the Mongols? It was possible. Father Pietro also seemed to harbour a burning hatred for Robert personally – and for Venice. But why, if he were *not* Genoese? Robert pondered the riddle every day as they wafted south towards Sarai, but try as he might, he could find no satisfactory answers.

What Robert did conclude was that it must be assumed that Father Pietro knew everything about his intent to make a treaty with the Mongol khan. So how did that affect his mission? Not at all. He would continue. He had no choice. He could not give up while Gilly's fate hung in the balance. Ziani would be willing to pay to free his brother *only* if Robert secured a treaty for Venice.

They saw few people as they travelled down the river. Some of the low, bedraggled villages on the riverbanks yielded raggedy gawkers who came out of their mud huts and watched them slide by, sometimes with a wave or some shouted jest or invitation. Their grubby children pointed and laughed at them. From time to time, they saw fishing craft, which ranged in style from sleek canoes to single-masted fishing smacks. They tried fishing themselves on the fifth day, and hauled a huge dragon-snouted fish from the water, as big as a goat, which they grilled on the campfire that night.

By day, when Robert was not poling the craft or fishing, he overhauled his kit, cleaning and sharpening his weapons and armour, scrubbing at patches of red rust on his iron-link hauberk, fixing a loose flap on his helmet. But there was plenty of time for staring at the lush banks as they slid by, too, and thinking about ordeals to come.

'Drink your fill, *ezen*,' said Altan one dawn, as he watched Robert scoop a helmet full of water from the river. 'And remember that sweet taste in the desert.'

The river traffic increased the closer to the delta they came. They began to see true ocean-going vessels, with several masts, capacious bellies for cargo and ranks of oars. Sometimes they caught a glimpse of chains and a waft of stench from the slaves below deck. Robert examined each vessel carefully, but there was no sign of the Rus'.

The town of Sarai, when they finally reached it on the seventh day of river travel, came as something of a disappointment to Robert. He was used to the timber-framed, barley-straw thatched houses of Kent, or the airy brick-and-marble colonnaded mansions of the Mediterranean. After so many days of hard travel by road and river and two bloody fights, he had been secretly imagining a luxurious fleshpot of the Orient – if not quite a city with golden castles, and ivory towers studded with pearls and perpetual rivers of cool red wine, then at least something more glorious than this.

Sarai was a town of mud – baked yellow-red mud – with squat, ugly houses pocked with tiny square black windows, like dead eyes, and dry poles sticking out from the walls of the buildings like short, skeletal limbs. There were towers, domes and thick walls for defence, and all of it was made from the same sun-dried earth. Even the local mosque – a squat, castle-like building with four crenelated turrets and a stubby minaret beside it for calling the faithful to prayer – was made of the same drab earth, except that this place of worship had a few simple designs swirled into the baked mud on either side of the closed wooden door, which was painted a dusty black.

As Robert poled the craft towards a mud-brick jetty in a harbour lined with beige houses, an odd notion struck him: that Sarai might well have been built by a giant's children making mud pies.

The people of Sarai were drab, too, in muddy-coloured robes and hats made of dusty felt cloth. The women were all veiled – not that he was especially interested in them that bright morning – and there seemed to be an inordinate number of muscular, spear-carrying men with daggers in their belts, black turbans and fierce expressions.

With the vessel tied up at the jetty, Robert set to unloading the baggage, dumping it on the harbour front, while Altan, still limping from his leg wound, went into the town to seek out the people he claimed were his friends. Robert found himself surrounded by a crowd of dirty, sallow-featured boys, staring at his square-jawed, sweaty, brick-red, extremely English face and his long bedraggled blond locks.

He tried the boys in Arabic, but that tongue elicited no response except nervous giggles. He gave them a little rudimentary Mongolian speech, but they had evidently never heard of that language either. He tried a few simple phrases in Persian, to no avail. Then, as a private joke, he tried them in Ancient Greek – he had heard that Alexander the Great had visited these very regions in antiquity.

However, before he could discover if the ragged youth of Sarai had received any education in the Classics, the crowd was driven away by the arrival of a moustachioed man, with a grey turban and brown gown, swinging a black staff with a silver knob, who addressed Robert in fluent Turkish.

'You must be the Englishman,' the fellow said, flicking his staff at the heels of the departing urchins. 'I am Tolon Kopti. I welcome you to Sarai. My good friend Altan tells me you have a large bag of silver coins that you are very keen to give to me.'

Chapter Eight

'I come to you with some grave tidings this morning, my friend,' said Father Ivo.

Robert regarded the man in silence. He cocked his head on one side to indicate polite interest, but he was less concerned with his news than with the satchel under the inquisitor's arm, which had a pleasingly food-like bulge. On his last visit to the cell, the priest had brought him a length of spicy Vienna sausage. Robert's mouth was suddenly filled with saliva at the memory.

'I have told you before that the Duke of Austria is a man of very little patience.'

'You did, Father.' If there was no more of that sausage, Robert thought, a little of the ewe's cheese would also be very fine. He had not eaten since Ivo's last visit, which had been more than two days earlier. A little bread would be enough. The gaolers, knowing he was being fed by Ivo, had even stopped serving him the oat slop.

Robert forced himself to ignore his hunger like a soldier. Was he a beast, a mere animal? No. He was a man. He was a disciplined knight – a proud Christian warrior.

He straightened his spine and said, 'What tidings, Father? Please, share them with me.'

'I am sorry to say the duke has advanced the date of your trial. It is now to be held in the great ducal hall above us in just one week from today. So, if we are to have any chance of mitigating your sentence, or persuading the court that your actions are excusable, you need to complete your story before then. Which means you will have to relate your adventures more swiftly. More succinctly.'

'More succinctly?' said Robert.

'Indeed. Simply cut out the people who have no great bearing on your actions. Your slave Altan, for example… Do we need to hear quite so much about this fellow?'

'Altan was no slave. He was my *guide*. I freed him on our first acquaintance, after he had made his solemn oath to me. He served me loyally until—'

'Well, if you must make continual references to your sla— your Cuman guide, then do we need to hear about this new fellow… uh… this Tolon Kopti? In this mud-coloured camel market…' Ivo reached into his wide sleeve and pulled out his little wood-covered tablet. He consulted it for a moment and said, 'In the town called Sarai, near the shores of the Caspian Sea. Is this Tolon Kopti vital to your narrative? Could we not move ahead to the time where you first met the Great Khan?'

Robert's stomach growled. He was no beast, but his empty belly made him seem like one.

'I can tell you are hungry,' said Ivo. 'I have a little more of that Vienna sausage and some rye bread in my satchel, and a flask of good wine that I could share… Ah, wait! No, I have a better idea. Your keen appetite may help focus your mind on the story. No irrelevant details. You shall eat, and heartily so, when we finish our session today, and I go above to write up my notes.'

Robert looked at the priest with contempt. His stomach squeezed itself once again, more loudly this time. If he had not been chained to the ring in the floor, and if he had been in his full strength, he would probably have murdered the man before him – *this* man of God before him; he would not make the same mistake he had made with Father Pietro. There was little mercy left in Robert now. It had all been burned from his soul. Unaware of the Englishman's dark thoughts, Ivo was setting up a candle-holder and lighting half a dozen wicks to see his tablet clearly.

Instead of murdering the priest, Robert said shortly, 'Tolon Kopti was a rich Sarai camel merchant. A good man. We stayed at his house for a full month while Altan – my *friend* – rested his leg, received physic for the sword wound from local doctors and wise men, and while God healed him. Tolon Kopti was openhanded to us with both his hospitality and his time and, when the day came to buy camels from him, he gave us a fair price. I have not seen him since the day Altan and I rode out of Sarai, heading east on our camels, with two other beasts in a small camel train behind.'

'Very good, Sir Robert,' said Ivo, infuriatingly. 'Very... um... succinct.'

'Shall I not describe, then, Father, our sufferings on the journey east, across more than five hundred miles of parched steppe in high summer? Shall I neglect to mention that magnificent, awe-inspiring landscape, with nothing to see but dust and withered grass from one horizon to the other? Shall I not describe our pains, indeed, our agonies, when our tongues dried to leather in our mouths for lack of water? And how the skin of my face blistered and peeled off to reveal the raw flesh beneath? Shall I say nothing of how we crossed the great Ural river and both of us nearly drowned in its mad, swirling currents? Shall I not tell you about how we eventually found the Aral Sea after weeks of wandering lost in the oven-like heat, and came down at last into the lands called Turkestan – nor about our entrance into the Khwarazmian Empire – the realm of Muhammad Shah – and how we eventually found the northernmost town of the empire on the Syr Daria river? Shall I tell nothing to you of any of that long, hideous journey?'

'I believe you *have* just told me of it. And while stories of hardships endured are sometimes most edifying, since they remind us of our Saviour's Passion, and benefit us that way, I would still prefer – indeed, I must *insist* – that you stick to the bare bones of your story. Time is short. We must waste none of it. As I have said, your trial is in one week's time. Did anything of great moment happen on the steppe road? Did you meet any of the wild Tartars whose ranks you later joined?'

'No,' snapped Robert. 'We were attacked once by a pack of Kipchak bandits on horseback, but we outran them. We both survived.' He fell into furious silence.

'And…?' said Ivo. Robert shook his head, determined to say no more.

'Perhaps I have misjudged the urgency of your appetite. Your hunger makes you ill-natured, I believe. Please, my friend, have a little wine. Let me get out the bread and sausage from my satchel. We will have a morsel and then you may resume your tale. But, do not forget, the duke will bring you up to his court in seven days, so, if you could, I earnestly beg you to try your hardest to—'

'To be *succinct*?' snarled Robert. Yet when Ivo passed him a slice of bread and a chunk of spiced sausage, he readily accepted them. And the brimming cup of wine, too.

–

After weeks of dust and flies, of the seasick jolting pace of the camels – after each day had blurred into another under the endless blue, with nothing but miles of drab emptiness in all directions – Altan let out a croak of joy and pointed into the distance, at a low object on the southern horizon and the brilliant sparkle of moving waters.

He wielded his camel stick and urged his tired beast, and the spare animal tied behind him, into a jogging-trot, cawing, 'Yanikant… Yanikant,' like a dying crow.

Robert, who had been sunk in an exhausted daze, was confused by his cry. He encouraged his two beasts into a stiff-legged run, and when he had caught up with the Cuman, he yelled, 'What? What, man? What in God's name does "Yanikant" mean?'

'Yanikant means food, Yanikant means wine, Yanikant means a hot bath and a willing whore. Yanikant means *tansag baidal*! Ride, *ezen*. Stir your lazy foreign bones!'

They dismounted by the wide gates and led their camels inside the town of Yanikant, and Robert knew he was gawping like a half-witted Kentish yokel come up to London with his flock for the first time, but he truly could not help it. *Tansag baidal*, he would later learn, meant 'luxury' in the Mongolian tongue – a condition both despised and hungered for in equal measure by the iron-hard horse-warriors of the Great Khan.

And luxury was on display everywhere he looked in the town of Yanikant.

The central square was lined with stalls and booths displaying goods and chattels of a richness that Robert had never seen before in all his travels. To the left of a glorious mosque – a white marble edifice inlaid with ceramic tiles of gold and sea-green, amid repeating patterns with Arabic lettering declaring the greatness of God – were a dozen market stalls for soft, thick carpets, which hung from the sides of the stalls like trophies, marvellously patterned rich fabrics in red and purple yarn that glowed like the pelts of mythical beasts in the slanting sunlight. Beyond the carpet-sellers, the gold and silver workers had laid out their wealth of glittering wares on shining bolts of aquamarine and scarlet silk – cloak pins, buckles, oil lamps and gleaming candlesticks. And the Yanikant armourers were next, with racks of scimitars, spiked helms polished to a shine, small iron shields with holy words imprinted on them in gold letters for extra protection in battle.

To the right of the mosque was the sprawling food market, with grilled meats cooking over braziers, wafting their stomach-wrenching scents abroad, and stalls displaying fresh breads, sweet cakes, plump vegetables and mounds of fruit: green striped watermelons, red grapes, purple-black plums and pyramids of cheerful pomegranates, and so many varieties of apples in so many different hues, from glossy crimson to buttery yellow, that they made Robert's desert-dulled senses whirl…

–

In the black and stinking Vienna dungeon, Father Ivo cleared his throat noisily.

'Succinct... Yes, Father,' said Robert. 'I will be brief. Now, pass me that wine!'

–

The colourful, exuberant town of Yanikant was a wonder to Robert after such a long time in the wilderness. He and Altan swiftly found a place to stay in a clean guest house. They washed, ate, drank some well-watered wine, and slept for a day and a night. Then they ate, drank and slept some more. When he felt recovered sufficiently from his desert ordeal, Robert wandered out of the guest house one peaceful morning and began leisurely to explore the noisy, bustling streets.

He soon found himself in an area lined with shopfronts and warehouses, and felt his merchant's instincts beginning to emerge again. He walked along the shops and eyed the goods on show. He ate a skewer of delicious spiced lamb, sitting on a carpet opposite a warehouse-cum-shop full of implements, and watched men haggling to purchase rakes, pitchforks and iron-edged spades.

He wandered on, not knowing what he was looking for until he found it. In a large warehouse at the edge of the town, he introduced himself to a middle-aged fruit merchant who spoke some Turkish and, after a few pleasantries, they sat down together and began to discuss business. Eventually, after hours of wrangling, Robert purchased several sacks of dried apricots as well as a bushel of green walnuts from the man. And, after a little more talk, Robert was persuaded to buy a quantity of barley. The merchant threw in two nets of watermelons for good measure.

When the deal was concluded, over a cup of iced sherbet, Robert sought the latest news from his new acquaintance. It was good and bad. War was coming; every trader along the Syr Daria knew this, which meant that the price of goods would surely rise.

Muhammad Shah – may his glorious rule last a thousand years – was preparing his armies for battle, the merchant told him, and dispatching his regiments to the most important cities of his realm to keep them safe. The barbarians were coming west. Their savage khan was angry about the humiliations he had received in Otrar. But the Emperor of Khwarazmia was well beloved of Allah, and he would swiftly see off these unruly steppe bandits if they dared show their ugly faces here.

A few days later, Robert and Altan guided their heavily laden camels out of the gates of Yanikant and on to the wide, well-worn road running south-east from the town, a route which ran along the banks of the Syr Daria. This valley was the golden thread that linked all the trading towns along its length, a ribbon of humanity slanting down along the river and drawing sustenance from it.

To the east was endless steppe, stretching all the way to Cathay, if Altan's stories were true. To the west, beyond the river, was the Kyzyl Kum, an uncrossable expanse of sand and rock.

Over the next few weeks, in blazing summer sunshine, the two travellers, their four camels, their goods and belongings, sweated their way south-east along the line of the Syr Daria valley, trading as they went – and gathering any information they could about the Mongol approach. The towns they entered were each different from the last, but each had a similar feverish air. A palpable sense of fear. Almost panic. Everyone they met knew the Great Khan was coming, and while a few believed the shah would protect them, many more were in great fear for their lives and livelihoods.

Robert sold his walnuts and apricots in Jand, the next town along the river, and picked up a dozen baskets of pomegranates; then, at the market in Signak, four days' ride south-east of Jand, he traded his barley for wooden casks of wine and his pomegranates for a dozen bundles of sheepskins. In the full roasting heat of the summer season, some time around St Bartholomew's Day, towards the end of August, Robert and Altan found themselves outside the walls of the fortified city of Otrar.

Otrar was situated at the confluence of two rivers, the mighty Syr Daria and a smaller tributary called the Arys. The city, which was home to as many as fifty thousand souls, stood on a high plateau some sixty feet above the surrounding farmlands and was fortified with high stone walls. There were two strong gates. The first guarded the entrance from the main road heading north-east towards the empty steppe and the Silk Routes that led towards the formidable Tien Shan mountain range. The second gate was in the south-west of the roughly circular city, and that led down to the green waters of the Syr Daria. Robert and Altan entered by the more northerly gate, on foot, leading their camels, and were immediately swallowed by the crowds of Kipchaks, Tajiks, Uzbeks, Persians and other folk who made up this city's diverse population at the edge of the Khwarazmian Empire.

A trumpet squealed, and a shouting soldier on a beautiful black horse – clearly an officer, by his cracking whip and all the gleaming bullion on his elegant silk coat – forced all the foot traffic on the crowded street to crush to one side and clear a narrow path. Important personages were coming.

Robert and his lead camel found themselves hemmed in by the crush and stink of humanity as a full squadron of Muhammad Shah's Persian lancers jingled past. As these long-nosed horsemen trotted by, Robert marvelled at their exotic uniforms: dazzling corselets of polished steel scales, worn over sky-blue robes with baggy yellow pantaloons spotted with blue, their pointed steel helmets adorned with peacock feathers. Robert even caught a glimpse, in passing, of the governor of Otrar himself, the infamous Inalchuq – the man, he recalled, who had murdered five hundred Mongol merchants and stolen all their goods. The man who had humiliated the Great Khan's three ambassadors was revealed to be a jolly-looking little fellow, running to fat, in a bejewelled scarlet turban, being carried along in a golden palanquin by four burly slaves. The cavalry and their master were on their way to the citadel, it seemed, the brick-built fortress at the heart of the city of Otrar.

Yet peacock-plumed Persian cavalrymen were not the only Khwarazmian troops garrisoned in Otrar that summer. Muhammad Shah had reinforced this city, his northernmost stronghold, with more than ten thousand troops from regions right across his empire. There were sun-dark Armenian hillmen – stocky, grinning fellows armed with war axes and spiked shields, who had marched fifteen hundred miles to roost here in their barracks inside the citadel. There were wiry Afghan tribesmen from Balkh lodged in the citadel, too, their beards gleaming with perfumed oil, wielding needle-sharp javelins, and with the handles of their long, wide-bladed fighting knives sticking out of their belts. There were five hundred archers from Isfahan, in the heartland of Khwarazmia, lodged in their own comfortable barracks in the south of the city, and infantry from Zaranj – a thousand silk-clad spearmen, who marched, stamped and wheeled every day at dawn on the flats outside the city.

In the days that followed, Robert made an effort to make a mental note of every type of Khwarazmian warrior he encountered in Otrar: every regiment, every company, every commander's name he could discover. He tried to make assessments of how effective each band of warriors might be in battle. The words of Ziani sounded in his ears: 'Make yourself invaluable to the Great Khan.' But he also strove to be unobtrusive while gathering this information, and he was careful to present himself as nothing more than a simple merchant, interested only in commerce and in profit and loss.

He and Altan put up at an inn near the northern wall that first day and, when they had seen their camels unloaded, fed, watered and housed, they immediately ventured out to see the city sights. There were no restrictions to their wanderings over the next few weeks, save from entering the citadel, where Zaranji guardsmen barred all who did not possess the governor's token.

Robert and Altan soon made it their practice to take a cup of peach juice each afternoon at a stall in the square outside the citadel. They made the acquaintance of the stallholder, a rascally one-eyed Tajik, and sought his opinion on a variety of Otrar matters, which he was never reluctant to share.

It became a calming, pleasant ritual – the sweet juice, the relaxed conversations, a general watching of the world over the rim of a cup. But one day was a little unusual. They watched for most of the afternoon as a succession of couriers and soldiers of various types went in and came out of the massive double gates of the citadel. There was a feverish urgency about their movements, a military briskness hitherto unseen, and which seemed most incongruous in the heat of the day.

Altan casually asked the juice-stallholder what all the bustle was about, and the Tajik told him that tidings had been received that a strong Mongol force had broken through the high passes of the Tien Shan mountains, surprising everyone in Khwarazmia with their extraordinary feat, and these Mongols were now infesting the Fergana Valley – the fruit and grain basket of the northern empire. The enemy were in great numbers, looting and burning farms and orchards in the valley.

'This Fergana Valley. How far is that from Otrar?' Robert asked Altan later.

'At least three hundred miles, I believe. Although I have never seen it myself, *ezen*. I confess that I cannot guide you to the Fergana. I only know the better-used northern steppe routes.'

Robert grunted in disappointment. 'Then I must find a man who *does* know.'

They remained in Otrar for a month, waiting to hear fresh news of the movements of the Mongol army, and Robert spent much of his spare time making a crude map of the city, its walls and fortifications. He chafed at the delay – and fretted a good deal over Gilbert's well-being, too. The thought of his brother languishing in gaol tormented him at night, when he tried to sleep. The sooner he made the treaty, the better. But for now there was nothing to be done but watch and wait.

He did not even know for sure if this Mongol force was still in the Fergana Valley. Nor did he know if Genghis Khan was with them – although that seemed likely. He was occasionally tempted just to get on his camel and trust that God would lead him to the Great Khan. But he knew there was little point riding into the harsh wilderness with no reasonable plan of action.

Rather than kick his heels in the city, Robert spent several mornings watching various Persian cavalry regiments perform exercises on the flat ground outside the northern gates, and he returned to the city each afternoon increasingly impressed. These lancers were highly skilled and disciplined.

He also continued to enlarge his circle of acquaintance among the local merchants.

'You bought three bales of sheepskins in the heat of the summer?' said Karacha, a merchant who owned a row of warehouses along the northern wall of Otrar. He was a handsome young man with a long Persian nose and a black chin-beard and long moustaches, oiled, curled and perfumed with sweet oil of attar. He and Robert were drinking iced watermelon juice together while sitting cross-legged on a purple carpet in the rear of Karacha's guest hall, just off his largest storeroom. It was the third or fourth time they had met, and both men seemed to be enjoying their new friendship.

Despite the cold drink, Robert's thin linen shirt was soaked through with sweat.

'I did indeed. The Signak merchant was selling them too cheaply,' said Robert in his rapidly improving Persian. 'And I strongly suspect that it will not *always* be summer.'

'It will not always be summer, eh? Hmm. I am awed by your wisdom,' said Karacha, a twinkle in his eye. The two men had taken to each other from the first. Robert liked the way the merchant infused much of what he said with humour. He seemed trustworthy, too, although he was very skilled in bargaining. 'You fair-skinned Rus' are rarely so far-seeing or shrewd!' Karacha added.

When anyone in Otrar had questioned him about his homeland – which, admittedly, had not been very often – Robert had always claimed to be a Rus' trader from Novgorod in the far north.

'I heard more and more of you Rus' were coming east these days,' said Karacha.

Robert leaned in. 'I believe you are a man I can trust, Karacha,' he said. 'So I will tell you, in strict confidence, that I am not a Rus'. I am from a country called England, far to the west of here.'

'I am utterly astonished,' said Karacha, smiling to show that he was speaking in jest. 'But, now that I think on it, I can clearly see that you are no Rus'. You are entirely sober, in the first place. You have not the foul stink of beer or wine – of *al-kuhul*, as the Arabs call it – on your breath. I have never met a Rus' – not one – who was not at least slightly intoxicated from dawn to dusk, and I have met dozens on my travels north of the Sea of Ravens. But you may trust my discretion, my friend. I give you my sacred word as a merchant. I shall never tell a soul. However, if I may be so bold, what is your purpose here? It cannot be to sell old sheepskins for a few handfuls of silver.'

'I shall reward you with my full confidence,' said Robert, 'since you have sworn to keep my secrets.' He liked this fellow. Karacha had bought a large portion of his goods and had paid a fair price in silver dirhams. Robert knew he was taking a risk, but he felt in his gut that the danger was worth the prize. It felt almost exactly like the assessment he made before a risky throw of the dice.

'I am, in truth, an envoy,' he said. 'An ambassador from my own people in the West to the Great Khan. We wish to do a great deal of trade with the Mongols in the coming years.'

Then he sat back and watched Karacha's expression change. The young man's smile slowly drained away. His usually tanned skin now looked very slightly green.

'You know, my friend, that what you are saying is the blackest treason?'

'I know that Governor Inalchuq has forbidden any resident of Otrar to have any commerce with the Mongols on pain of death. I heard the announcement proclaimed from the citadel's walls.'

'Then you must also know, Robert, that it is my duty to report your words to the governor's officials and his Zaranji guards, and when I do this you will be taken up and executed as a spy.'

He stared at Robert, appalled. 'Why did you tell me, Robert? Why, in the name of God?'

'Because I do not think you will betray me. Because I believe that I can trust you. Because I know that *I* would never betray *you*. I consider you a dear friend, Karacha. I would never tell the governor or his officials, for example, that *you* are still trading with the Mongols yourself. Never. Nor that in the back room yonder, you have a number of bales of silk and several boxes of Cathay spices, which arrived yesterday. My Cuman guide Altan sniffed them out. He has a very keen nose.'

Karacha no longer looked pale. Now twin spots of anger coloured his cheeks.

'This is how you repay my kindness?' he said, hissing the words. 'You seek to bend me to your will by the threat of exposure. You, who have eaten my salt—'

'Calm yourself,' Robert said. 'As I said, I shall never betray you – as long as you do not betray me. We are bound together by our secrets. All I ask from you is information.'

'What information? What terrible secrets must I now confide to you simply to preserve my life from the governor's executioners?'

'Do you truly fear them so very much?'

'Of course I do. They strangled my poor father.'

'Why?'

'Over a pure-bred Asil mare – a horse the governor desired and which my father refused to sell. Inalchuq had my father arrested on false charges and put him to death. They strangled him with bowstrings in the traditional manner – and claimed it was a courtesy. They demanded I deliver the mare to the governor's stable. But I slit that sweet horse's throat rather than give her to that man. Inalchuq has never forgiven me. He is my enemy. Were I to be arrested, I'd not see another dawn.'

'I am sorry to hear that, my friend. Forgive me for pressing you. But also know this – Inalchuq shall never learn any of your secrets from me. You have my oath on that.'

'Hmmf. So tell me, *friend*, what is this information you seek from me?'

'I seek to know about the Mongols,' said Robert. 'Their whereabouts, the names of their high commanders, and how... and how I might contact them.'

'You ask a great deal.'

'But you possess this information. I know that you communicate with them.'

'Perhaps.'

'My friend, we must help each other. If you help me find the Mongol army, I swear you shall not suffer for it. Indeed, I am minded to reward you handsomely.'

Chapter Nine

Robert and Altan rode out of the gates of Otrar at dawn the next day, astride two geldings, with a mule bearing their possessions. They trotted east towards the brown foothills of the Tien Shan, which they meant to cross before the autumn rains set in.

They had presented their four camels to Karacha as a gift, in grateful thanks for his help in providing the information about the whereabouts of the Mongol army.

Robert had also invited him, in the future, to act as the trade agent in the East of the Doge and Great Council of Venice, under his authority, when he had secured his precious treaty with the Great Khan. Karacha had been unimpressed by this offer – he seemed to believe it a hollow promise – but he was pleased by the camels. Mostly, however, he seemed glad that Robert was leaving Otrar.

The latest reports from the citadel held that the Mongol horde was still in the Fergana Valley, Karacha told him, which was to be found about three hundred miles as the eagle flies south and east from Otrar. He also furnished Robert with a set of landmarks and directions to follow.

The Mongol commanders who occupied the Fergana Valley were a pair of generals called Jochi and Jebe, and they were said to be close to the Great Khan. General Jochi was the khan's eldest son – though there were rumours that he was illegitimate. General Jebe was a daring cavalry commander who had once been the Great Khan's mortal enemy, but was now somehow his most trusted adviser.

Once clear of Otrar and the surrounding villages, the land quickly became a parched and barren desert, a place of choking dust and shimmering heat and a few miserable scrubby bushes, with never a blade of grass to be seen. The nights were freezing and fireless, for they were riding into the unknown and did not want to draw attention to themselves, and they followed faint tracks or paths in the sandy rock that often petered to nothing unexpectedly. They passed a few herdsmen from time to time, minding their sheep and goats, but they strove to avoid all contact with humanity.

Robert suspected he had lingered too long in Otrar, and that his clandestine activities had been noted by city officials or had been reported to them. Karacha had told him that an Uzbek mendicant – a notorious informant of Inalchuq's – had come to his house and asked questions about the blond 'Rus' trader. Naturally, Karacha had told the beggar nothing, but all the signs had been ominous.

So Robert had decided to leave the city as quickly as possible, and he spent a large part of the first day's ride twisting in the saddle to look at the trail behind them. He could easily imagine a squadron of Persian lancers galloping after them and hauling them both back to the citadel in chains for trial and execution. And while he did not particularly fear death – his faith had always made him strong in that way – he knew that if he were to be killed, there was no hope for Gilly. So they rode hard, pushing their geldings to the limit each day and camping at night without a fire to warm their bones.

After three days of travel, Robert began to be a little easier in his mind. He believed they were now beyond the reach of Inalchuq and his Persian lancers, and before him the land was beginning to rise, with the white peaks of the Tien Shan growing closer, it seemed, with every passing hour. They halted at midday on the fourth day in the shade of a stunted thorn tree to drink well-watered wine from leather sacks and give the tired horses and mule a mouthful of oats and a drink of water, too.

Altan was looking at his gelding's off hind hoof, and levering out a small lodged stone, when he stopped, dropped the hoof and looked round, listening hard. He lifted a warning finger to Robert and put it to his own lips in the universal sign for silence.

Robert strained his ears, but could hear nothing beyond the moan of the wind as it whipped dust devils across the empty grey sands.

'Persian lancers?' Robert whispered in Mongolian.

Altan shook his head. 'No, not those puffed-up goat-molesters…'

There was a rattle of hooves on stony ground and ten riders appeared, seeming to spring up directly from the earth itself. They surrounded the two men and their beasts, in a loose circle, with their compact bows out, arrows nocked, strings drawn. They were short, wide-bodied men with weather-beaten faces, eyes sunk deep into folds of leathery skin. They wore brown robes of wool, belted, with swords hanging from straps, and leather boots with the toes curling up at the front.

Some had floppy, wide-brimmed leather hats, others felt-and-fur hoods. The most striking ones were bare-headed, and had shaven a wide strip over the top of their heads to leave a fringe of jet-black hair at the front and long hair clumped over both their ears and at the back, which had been tied and braided into three glossy plaits.

'If you touch a weapon, you die,' growled an older man in the centre. He was a broad-faced, strong-looking brute on a stocky steppe pony with a wide and ugly head, its nostrils flaring as it took in the scent of the two geldings and the mule.

'Make a sudden movement, you die,' the man said.

Then, 'Who are you?'

Robert smiled at him. A genuine smile of happiness. For the man had spoken to him in the Mongolian tongue – in swiftly delivered but still perfectly comprehensible Mongolian.

'I am an ambassador from the court of the Doge and the Great Council of Venice,' he said. 'And I seek an audience with the Great Khan of the Mongol nation.'

The new arrivals bound their hands in front of them, but did not abuse Robert and Altan much more than that – a buffet or two to make them move – nor did they pillage and rummage through their personal belongings, as Robert had feared they might. The Mongol scouts – for it soon became clear that this is what they were – lifted them back up onto their horses and, leading the pack mule, made them ride for the remainder of that day and all through the night, too. They stopped only twice to eat and drink from their water flasks, and the prisoners were also allowed a little refreshment, and by the break of dawn they came into sight of a sprawling camp of felt tents, horses and vast herds of sheep and goats.

Robert had believed he was as fit and strong as any man in the world, but the relentless pace the Mongols set was a trial even for him. He realised that the month of idleness in Otrar had taken its toll. With his back as tight as a drum, his thighs aching and the inner part rubbed raw, he had to be lifted bodily down from the gelding outside a large tent in the centre of the Mongol encampment.

'I demand to see the Great Khan immediately,' said Robert loudly. 'I am an ambassador – do you understand? A high envoy from Christendom to your people. You will inform the Great Khan I'm here to see him on behalf of my exalted Venetian lords. I do not expect to be kept waiting.'

The captain of scouts with the elaborately shaven head came to stand in front of him. He stared contemptuously into the Englishman's face from a few inches away. Then he punched Robert full strength in the mouth, a stunningly hard blow that nearly dropped him to his knees.

'You? An ambassador?' the captain said. 'My shit-crusted hole you are. With only one servant and one mule carrying a few trinkets? I don't think so. You are a spy. A dirty Khwarazmian spy. Or perhaps even a cunning foreign assassin. My *noyan* will know exactly what to do with you.'

He punched Robert again, harder this time, rocking his head back.

Robert and Altan were forced to sit on the ground outside the low circular tent made of felted wool – a *ger*, it was called in Mongolian – with a red lacquered door set into the tent's southern side. Their hands were still bound, and Robert's head was ringing from the blows he had received.

He faded in and out of wakefulness as the hours passed. He was weak and hungry and very tired, and he dozed a little with his chin on his chest. They were each fed a bowl of fresh, warm mare's milk at about midday, and drank it down gratefully. As the hours dragged by, and the sun began to sink, Robert began to revive, and asked Altan if he understood what was happening, and why they were being made to wait here, down in the dust, trussed up like a pair of sacrificial lambs.

The older man grinned at him. 'They don't believe you are an envoy, *ezen*,' he whispered. 'That one who hit you, Chuluun, the leader of the *arban*, the squad that captured us, he wants to kill you. But dare not to do it, in case you are what you say you are. They wait for their commander, their *noyan*, to come back from hunting wild goats up in the foothills. He will decide our fate.'

'What about the Great Khan?' said Robert. 'Where is he?'

'Far away. To the north. But he is coming. I listen to their chatter. Genghis Khan is coming here in a terrible rage and he will drown all the Khwarazmians in their own blood.'

'What is this army, then?'

'This is no army. This is one *mingghan*, a thousand men, under a leader named Khuyag. Noyan Khuyag. They are a guide *mingghan*, a force of scouts and information-gatherers, pathfinders. They smooth the army's road, clear away any obstacles, look for any dangers, before the rest of the *tumen* comes to a new place.'

'So we wait?'

'We wait, *ezen*. Maybe we can try to run when it gets dark. But if they catch us, we will be deemed to be guilty and…' Altan made a squelching noise.

'So we wait. Now, tell me again, Altan, since we seem to have plenty of time on our hands, tell me how they order their troops, their companies and their armies. A *mingghan* is a force of a thousand horsemen, you say, and commanded by someone called a *noyan*...'

'The patrol that captured us is called an *arban*, just ten riders. This is the smallest group of Mongol troops. They will all share one tent while on campaign, all cook their meals together in a single kettle, like a family. Ten *arbat* – that is how you say *arban* when there is more than one of them – make up a *jagghun*, a hundred warriors under a captain, an *akhmad*, who is responsible for their discipline. Ten *jagghut* make up a *mingghan*, a regiment with its own identifying name, which is commanded by a *noyan*. This scouting *mingghan* all around us is called the Golden Eagles. Look, see that big, ugly banner-man standing over yonder by that big black *ger* with the red door?'

Robert looked in the direction Altan was indicating with his chin. He saw a huge warrior beside the entrance to a squat round tent, holding a long pole with a large square piece of yellow silk at the top on which he could just make out the crude images of three brown birds, stacked one on top of the other. The top of the pole ended in what looked like a rope made of knotted horsehair.

'...and ten *mingghat* make up a *tumen*,' said Altan, 'which you might call a battle, or division, of about ten thousand men. A general will command a single *tumen*, or several *tumet*. Then you have the bodyguard of the Great Khan, the *kheshig*, whose lowliest members outrank all other Mongol soldiers, even the highest-born general. There's the Day Guard, the *turghaut*, and the Night Guard, the *kabtaut*, and...'

Robert found his attention was drifting away from Altan's words. The Mongol system of units of ten, and multiples thereof, had been explained to him by the Cuman before on the road east. But, as he repeated the alien terms again in his head – *arban*, *jagghun*, *mingghan*, *tumen* – and tried to fix them in his memory, his eye was involuntarily drawn to an enclosure about thirty paces away.

Inside the circle of latticed fencing, a young horse was running free – a stocky, large-headed steppe stallion, muscular and squat. The animal seemed to be wild, untamed, and very resentful of being enclosed by the light willow fences that surrounded him.

The steppe stallion ran around and around the perimeter of the fence, lashing its hooves out behind it from time to time. A spirited animal. A dangerous one, as well. As Robert watched, a slim figure slipped through a gap in the lattice fences and began to move towards the wild horse. The figure wore the voluminous brown Mongol robe – a *deel*, Altan had called it – and a floppy felt-and-fur hat, and also the heavy curled-toe riding boots he had seen on his captors in the *arban*.

The young Mongol had a rope bridle in his right hand and was making odd cooing noises as he slowly approached the horse. The Mongol was moving in a gentle circular path, never heading directly for the frightened animal. The horse stopped running, looked at the Mongol and snorted threateningly. Robert could see the warrior's face for the first time: pale skin, large dark eyes and high cheekbones. He looked not that much older than a boy. The horse whinnied, showing big yellow teeth, then thundered away around the perimeter, kicking up spurts of dust with each stride.

The Mongol horse-breaker patiently followed the animal, still making soothing noises, creeping ever closer. This time the breaker managed to get a hand on the horse's neck before the beast took off again. The stallion thundered away, kicking out wildly at the Mongol boy, who dodged out of the way as the lethal hooves whipped out only inches from the front of his *deel*.

Robert was entranced by this contest of boy versus beast: human patience against atavistic fear. He forgot all his discomforts, his fears. He simply watched the Mongol and the stallion in their strange enclosed dance. The youngster was undeterred by the skittering horse, and moved forward, slowly, carefully, once again, singing a low, throaty tune as he approached the frightened stallion.

Robert looked back at Altan, who had his eyes tightly closed. He was still droning on about the structure of the Mongol army. '…and it is arranged into three wings – the left wing, which is also called the east wing. The right is the west wing, and the centre – as well as the reserves, of course, and each commanded by kinsmen of the Great Khan or a tried and trusted general…'

When Robert looked back at the boy and the horse, he saw that the Mongol had managed to slip the rope bridle over the stallion's head, and was stroking the creature and muttering to it, his right hand holding the bridle, his left caressing the animal's neck.

Then, with one lithe movement, the boy swung his right leg over the flank of the horse and leapt smoothly up onto its back. The young animal took off like a frightened fallow deer, thudding around and around the fenced-in willow circle, with the Mongol sitting upright on his back.

A group of Mongol onlookers had gathered at the lattice fence to shout and cheer on the rider, who gripped the galloping beast tightly with his knees, had the rope bridle in one hand, and a clump of thick black mane in the other. Robert was filled with a strong desire to cheer the boy on, too.

The horse thundered round and round, eventually coming to a quivering stop, quite close to Robert's position. His eye caught the rider's and he smiled at him in encouragement. The boy – a handsome youth, almost pretty – stared back at him blankly.

The comments were coming in thick and fast from the other onlookers. Some of them ribald or mocking, Robert could tell, even if he could not quite hear the words. The boy was grinning cheerfully at his friends gathered at the willow fence line, and was saying something to them, a retort, when the stallion, which was clearly a cunning creature, gave a great wriggle and heave, a flick of its back legs, and bucked the boy clean off its back, immediately taking off again in its wild, circular, willow-hemmed flight.

The boy thumped down hard on his back on the sand; his fur hat was knocked from his head to reveal long, glossy black tresses.

The belt that held the robe closed was loosened, the garment opening to reveal a small but definitely feminine breast embossed with a cherry-pink nipple. The onlookers hooted and jeered as the girl, grinning ruefully at them, hastily wrapped herself up again.

Robert's mouth fell open in surprise. He could now see clearly that this rider was a female, even dressed again in the heavy enveloping robe and with the floppy hat retrieved and pulled down over her ears. She walked like a woman, her singing was that of a woman, yet her courage, as she once more approached the shivering horse on the far side of the ring, was as high as any man's.

The wild stallion allowed her to approach. Then, when she was within an arm's length, the beast bolted and cantered around to the other side of the enclosure. The girl turned and plodded towards the animal's new position. This time the horse allowed her to come right up close. She was still singing softly as she reached for the bridle and began once again, stroking the animal's sweat-streaked neck. They stayed together for a long time, her head pressed against the horse's damp flank, and Robert could see the creature slowly becoming calmer. He was aware that Altan had stopped speaking and he, too, was watching the drama of the young woman and the wild stallion.

Then she mounted again, smoothly swinging her legs over its back, and after an initial flinch and shy and breaking into a swift trot, the stallion consented and walked with the girl on its back all the way around the ring, a full circuit of the perimeter. The girl's friends all cheered, and made catcalls. She modestly looked down and stroked the beast's neck, as if to give all credit to the animal.

'Here they are, Noyan Khuyag! These are filthy spies who claim to be high envoys!'

Robert looked up and saw a tall Mongol with a plain, square face looking down at him. His thick woollen robe was embroidered at the lapels with complicated red and blue stitching, fancy work, which was also lightly spattered with fresh blood from the chase. His large round head was bare, displaying the shaven skull strip, brow fringe and ear plaits of a warrior. A magnificent silver-hilted curved sword hung from his belt at his left side.

'Who are you?' said the *noyan*. 'Speak the truth to me – or you shall die.'

'I am an ambassador from the court of the Doge and the Great Council of Venice,' said Robert. 'I seek an audience with the Great Khan of the Mongols. I demand you take me to him.'

'He lies. There are only two of them,' said Chuluun, the *arban* leader. 'We scouted their trail and there are only these two men. They are surely spies from Otrar.'

'You may be right, Chuluun. But they also present a large problem for me.'

'Shall I cut their throats, *Noyan*?'

The tall *noyan* said nothing for a time. Then he said, 'Gag them. Put them in my *ger*. Put two guards on the door. I'll send an arrow rider to report back to General Subutai and the main column. Maybe he will tell us to dispatch them both immediately. And maybe not. We shall see very soon.'

Robert and Altan were lifted to their feet. Stinking rags were shoved in their mouths and bound in place. Then they were marched through the red lacquered door of the *ger* with the banner-man outside and thrown onto a pile of furs and blankets to the left of the doorway. Once they had righted themselves, Robert began to look around. Even under a possible sentence of death, his curiosity was piqued by the living quarters of these folk. The exterior of the *ger* had been a uniform mud-coloured brownish grey, apart from the bold splash of red made by the lacquered front door.

Inside the *ger*, it was a different world. There were soft crimson and blue woollen carpets covering the floor, and plump leaf-patterned silk pillows around the curving walls. At the north side of the man-high tent stood a low, padded platform covered in scarlet silk, supported by a polished wooden frame – a piece of furniture that was a cross between a bed and a wide, cushioned throne.

The walls were hung with heavy blue cloths, like tapestries in a Christian castle, some of them made of plain shiny silk, but many of them patterned with dots and stripes and squares. Weapons and tools hung from hooks on the walls; there were bags of gear stored beneath in large felt boxes.

In the centre of the *ger* was a square hearth marked out with oiled black stones, and an age-blackened cauldron was hanging over a mound of just-glowing embers, emitting a trickle of steam. An old woman dressed in black, gnarled and bent, crouched over the smouldering hearth, stirring the cooking pot. She paid no attention at all to the two prisoners' entrance. She simply ignored them.

Robert was suddenly very hungry. He could smell the food the old woman was cooking. Mutton. Some kind of stew. He wondered if they would feed him before they cut his throat – he could not see why they would. He closed his eyes and began to pray silently to St Christopher, clutching the medal round his neck with his bound hands. He prayed to the Virgin, too. '*Holy Mother, guard my brother and deliver him from captivity. If I must pay for this with my life, so be it.*'

The lacquered door opened suddenly, a blast of cold air came in, and Robert opened his eyes. Someone had barged into the *ger* – a woman. The horsewoman who had so tamed the wild stallion.

She stared hard at the two prisoners, seemingly in disgust, and then said something to the old woman, which Robert did not catch – something about the food she was cooking. And something else about a problem. The old woman answered grumpily in the affirmative. The horsewoman threw one more look at the two bound prisoners, and muttered in revulsion. Then she went over to the far wall and took down a dagger from its peg. She pulled the curved steel from its scabbard, tested its keenness on the ball of her thumb and, satisfied, she fixed her eyes on the two prisoners once more.

Robert could see a spot of blood on the woman's thumb. The blade was sharp. High-quality steel. That should, at least, make their ends swift. *Into your hands, O Lord, I commend my spirit*, he prayed silently, trying hard to master his sudden fear and calm his swift-beating heart.

The woman glared at him and said angrily in Mongolian, 'Let us solve this problem now! Yes?' Holding the sharp blade low in her right hand, she advanced towards Robert.

Part II

Chapter Ten

In his writing room on the ground floor of the tower, Father Ivo opened his leather satchel and removed a vellum letter. He opened its folds and held it up to the light from the window, and once again read the opening words with a voluptuous shiver of joy.

> To Father Ivo of Narbonne, special enquêteur, at the Castle of Vienna, Austria, from Géraud, by the Grace of God, Bishop of Bordeaux, greetings.
>
> I read with interest your letter of the fifteenth of August, Year of Our Lord Twelve Hundred and Forty-one, concerning the interrogation of the Englishman now confined within the lower parts of the castle and, while I commend your industry and thoroughness in this matter, I have several questions to which I require answers…

An hour later the special *enquêteur* was forty feet below his writing room, in the company of the subject of the letter himself.

'Sir Robert,' he said cheerfully to the blinking prisoner, eyes dazzled by the candle held in the priest's large, hairy hand. 'I have some wonderful news this morning. I have received praise from my master Bishop Géraud and, furthermore, he has vouchsafed in his latest missive that, should you continue to co-operate with me, fully and honestly, he will shortly be writing to the Pope to beg His Holiness to intercede with Frederick of Austria and ask him to show mercy on you.'

'Your bishop is very good, Father,' said Robert. 'I am grateful. Yet I cannot help but notice that you did not bring your food satchel with you. May I ask why?'

Ivo was busy lighting the other candles in the chandelier.

'What? Satchel? Ah, that satchel… What can I have done with that thing?'

Ivo cocked his head. He could hear a tiny squeaking noise. Was that rats? The upper castle was overrun with them. What must this dank and stinking dungeon be like? No, he realised with quiet satisfaction, it was the sound of the prisoner grinding his teeth.

'Let us begin,' he said. 'My master wishes me to ask you this concerning the Jews of Sana'a with whom you travelled from the deserts of Syria to the shores of the Sea of Azov. You were employed by their leader Aaron as translator. Is that correct?'

Robert said nothing.

'The bishop asks this… Why did this company of Jewish merchants, much practised in trading in the region, not *already* have a translator – someone, much like your good self, versed in all the tongues of the peoples they were likely to meet and trade with. It seems a little strange, does it not?'

Robert remained silent.

'This troubles my master, you see, Sir Robert. He feels that, perhaps, if you cannot explain this curious fact – and several other small matters – to his satisfaction, then perhaps your whole narrative must be cast into doubt. And, if that occurs, and Bishop Géraud comes to the conclusion that you have, in fact, been lying to us, then he feels he will not be able to intercede with the Pope on your behalf, and he must allow the justice of Duke Frederick to take its dreadful course. The trial will take place in six days from now. So perhaps you might like to explain this inconsistency to me, Sir Robert. Why did these travelling Jews not already have a translator in the company?'

'I told you before, priest, that I would not be cross-examined and badgered on every twist and turn of my story. I told you—'

'Ah, there it is,' said Ivo, reaching into his sleeve and pulling forth a package wrapped in cloth. The scent of meat and onions came at Robert like a waft from Heaven. He stopped talking and his mouth was immediately flooded. 'How can I have forgotten this delicious little morsel? And I believe… ah, yes… that I have a small flask of good ale, too, tucked away here.'

Ivo smiled at the starving prisoner, crouched in the near-darkness, tethered by an iron chain. 'Would you care for a piece of this fine beef pastry? Hot from the duke's ovens?'

'You are transparent, priest,' said Robert. 'And cruel. Indeed, I think you are *unchristian*. Do you believe your crude attempts at manipulation go unnoticed?'

'Does that mean, Sir Robert, you would *not* care for a slice of hot beef pie?'

Ivo tore the loaf-shaped pasty in two, releasing another cloud of intoxicating steam, and offered one half to Robert. 'You were going to tell me all about these kindly wandering Jews and their mysterious lack of a translator…'

'God will surely punish you for this, Father,' said Robert. But he accepted the food and, through a mouthful of beef and flaky pastry, he mumbled, 'They had one before me – the Jews. A translator. A very learned man, they said. They set out from Sana'a with a scholar called Joseph, but he died in Gaza, bitten by a poisonous adder. That is what they told me, anyway. That was why they needed my knowledge of languages.'

'Indeed.' Ivo produced his tablet and stylus and made a small note on the wax surface. 'That would certainly explain the mystery of the missing translator. So… shall we move on? My master also had a small enquiry about the Venetians residing at Tana. Why did this man – this wealthy merchant-prince Niccolò Ziani – commission *you*, a penniless and, not to put too fine a point on it, *disgraced* foreigner, to seek this important trade concession with the Great Khan, who is also perhaps the legendary Prester John. And why was he willing to spend his own hard-won money ransoming your brother Gilbert? Why not send one of his own people, a member of his own family, or a colleague – or go eastwards himself and save the price of that enormous ransom?'

Robert shrugged, and swallowed with some difficulty. The priest passed him the ale flask, and the prisoner drank deeply, half-emptying the small vessel.

'Can you explain his extraordinary generosity? It seems that many people have been unduly kind to you in your travels. First the wandering Jews, and now this Venetian magnate.'

'God chose me as his servant,' said Robert. 'And I knew He would not abandon me. Perhaps He moved all these folk that I met to kindness.'

'Do you claim that God directed Niccolò Ziani to send you east on his behalf?'

'I do not know,' said Robert, wiping his lips with a filthy, manacled hand. 'Perhaps. I cannot claim to understand God's mysterious purposes. Nor can I know what is in the mind of another man. Niccolò Ziani liked me, I think. He trusted me. Also, the road east was – is – perilous. He would likely not be robust enough for the rigours of the journey. He was a merchant, a soft man. He wanted a man who would not fear the danger. A highly skilled knight – a First Lance – who had no attachments in Christendom.'

Ivo bent to his tablet again. 'No attachments in Christendom,' he repeated as he scribbled his note. He looked up. 'And you were such a man – with no attachments? Apart from your poor brother, of course. No lingering attachments, say, to any of your Templar Brethren?'

'I told you,' Robert said. 'The knights expelled me from their Order at Acre.'

'Yes,' said Ivo. 'You did indeed *tell* me that.'

'You do not believe me?' Robert sounded tired.

'Let us say only that there might be other explanations for your departure.'

Robert stared at him but said no more.

'Now then,' said Ivo, 'if you are sufficiently refreshed in body, let us continue with your *fascinating* narrative, Sir Robert. And remember, haste is of the essence. In six days you will go before the duke and his court. This wild young Mongol horsewoman, this steppe hoyden, was about to cut your throat, if I recall…'

Robert, his hands bound and mouth gagged with a stinking cloth, looked up at the lithe young woman standing over him with a dagger in her hands. Her oval face was oddly alluring for a heathen, the mouth wide and generous, her cheekbones high, the nose narrow and well sculpted; her large eyes were the deepest, darkest colour he had ever seen. She still wore the same knee-length *deel* she had worn while taming the horse, woollen leggings and leather boots with curled-up toes, but her head was bare and her glossy raven locks tumbled about her shoulders.

He had never expected the person who killed him to be quite so beautiful.

'I am told you understand a little of our tongue,' she said, her voice soft but firm. 'So I shall tell you this: there are two armed men outside the door who will cut you down without hesitation if you try to escape. And, if you rise quickly from this carpet without permission, or make any sudden moves at all, I shall kill you myself. Is that clear? Now give me your hands, *gadaad khun*, and I shall loose your bonds for a little while. You cannot eat my mother's food with your hands bound.'

And, as Robert offered up his wrists, she slipped the dagger between them and cut the rope. Then she did the same with Altan. By the hearth, the old woman was spooning out some kind of thin stew from the blackened pot on the coals into two big clay bowls.

A few moments later, Robert had ripped out his gag and was sipping a hot, oily mutton broth with chunks of stringy meat, fat and gristle, and finding it as sweet as ambrosia.

'Thank you,' he muttered, his head lowered to the steaming bowl.

'You are a guest in my *ger*. No guest of my home goes hungry – even a *gadaad khun*.'

'What will happen now?' he asked her a little later, when the portion of *shulen*, as this traditional Mongol mutton stew was called, was finished, and his empty bowl was set aside on the carpet. He found he greatly disliked her calling him *gadaad khun*, or an 'outside person' – which meant, in other words, a foreigner.

'It depends on my husband, Noyan Khuyag. He says you claim to be an envoy from beyond the Sea of Ravens, but you may instead be spies of Shah Muhammad.'

'We are no spies. I am Robert, my servant here is Altan. We simply desire an audience with the Great Khan. We have gifts for him and an important message from my masters. If it pleases you, I should like to speak to the Great Khan. A good man's life will be put at hazard by any delay.'

The young woman laughed. It was a charming sound to Robert's ears, like a mountain stream bubbling over rocks. Her words, though, were far less charming.

'You think you can simply ride up the Great Khan and shout out a greeting to him?' she said. 'Invite him to share your water flask? As if he were no more than some half-asleep shepherd boy minding his flock? No! He is the Khan of Khans, the Lord of the Steppe. He does not converse with any passing vagabond *gadaad khun*!'

'We are not vagabonds. I am a warrior of great renown among my people. Altan, too, is a skilled fighter of the steppe. We can both provide valuable assistance to the Great Khan.'

'What kind of assistance? What aid can you offer to mighty Genghis Khan, who commands countless multitudes, who cradles entire nations in the palm of his hand?'

'I shall tell him that when I see him,' said Robert.

The young woman laughed again. '*If* you see him. You should worry about seeing another dawn, *gadaad khun*. My husband may well cut off your yellow-haired head.'

'Maybe. I do not think so. Maybe I can help him, too. What is your name?'

'My name is not your concern. But, since you are a guest, I will tell you. I am Sarantuya. This is my mother, Temulun. But hush now, I hear my husband outside.'

—

'Ah, indeed,' said Father Ivo, in the black Vienna dungeon. 'This person was Sarantuya. This is the woman you call out to in the night-time.'

'You told me, priest, that you would reserve all your questions until the end of our interview,' said the prisoner angrily.

'Yes, that is quite so… Forgive me, Sir Robert. Here, you finish the rest of this beef pasty, I am not so hungry today. And do, please, continue with your narrative.'

—

The door of the *ger* was wrenched open and Noyan Khuyag strode inside. Robert caught a glimpse of another man a dozen yards behind him – an older warrior in knee-length lamellar armour, a protection made from overlapping iron scales sewn on a leather coat, and a curved sabre hanging by his side. There were other warriors, too, outside – half a dozen gathered round the armoured older man.

Khuyag came into the *ger*, leaving the door half-open and the others beyond the threshold. He took one look at Robert, who was scratching his ear, and let out a yell of rage. In a stream of rapid Mongolian, too fast for Robert to comprehend, Khuyag berated his wife for loosing the captives' bonds. Then he gave her a hard slap across the face that knocked her back, and then another that smashed her to the floor. Robert was on his feet in an instant, ready to intervene, when the tall *noyan*, faster than thought, whipped the sword from the sheath at his waist, even as he was turning towards Robert. He put the point to the base of Robert's throat just below the Adam's apple, and pressed.

Robert stopped, and slowly lifted his hands in the air. Khuyag was glaring into his face.

'Sit down, *ezen*,' said Altan. 'Sit down and be calm – you may live a little longer.'

Robert backed away slowly and sat back down in his former spot on the carpet at the curved cloth wall of the *ger*. The *noyan* turned back to his sprawled wife and resumed barking at her, and at his mother-in-law, occasionally waving the curved sword wildly, and pointing it in the direction of Robert and Altan. His lovely wife Sarantuya got to her feet and, keeping her head submissively low, she went over to the far side of the *ger* to busy herself with some small domestic matter.

There was a shouted question from outside the open door, or perhaps an order. Something angry, whose meaning Robert did not catch. Noyan Khuyag went back to the red lacquered portal and pushed it fully open. Then he bowed and uttered some formal words of greeting, and the older man and two of his younger lieutenants stepped briskly over the threshold and entered the tent.

'That him?' said the older man, staring hard at Robert, examining him minutely.

Khuyag assured the older, clearly senior man, that this was the spy they had captured. Robert was taken aback by the servility in the *noyan*'s manner. As if he was in the august presence of the Great Khan himself. And there *was* authority here. And great power, too. A presence. Could this older man perhaps even be Genghis Khan? The Great Khan? The legendary monarch Prester John?

The newcomer was in his mid-forties, but clearly as fit as a younger man; above average height, broad-shouldered, barrel-chested, and with his legs bowed from a lifetime of riding. He had a bald head with a large forehead, a few faint scars, a straggly beard and a wispy moustache. His eyes were large and very light brown – indeed, almost yellow. They seemed to shine like lit candles with intelligence.

'This one is not a spy. Look at him, Khuyag. Spies operate in the deep shadows – they hide themselves among others. This fellow blazes like a fiery torch in the night!'

He then did something that surprised Robert. He sat down in front of him, crossing his legs, only a foot or two away from the Englishman and at the same level with him. Leaning forward, he stared intently into his face.

Nothing was said for several moments. Then, 'You claim to be an ambassador?'

Robert nodded.

'Do you know that, under our strict Mongol law, it is forbidden to claim falsely that one is an envoy? And the penalty for a false claim is death?'

Robert shrugged. 'I have nothing to fear,' he said. 'I speak only the truth.'

The older man smiled coldly at him. 'That is very rare,' he said. 'So tell me, stranger, which mighty king sent you to us? What is your purpose in this land?'

'I am called Robert of Hadlow, an English knight from a distant land, many months' ride towards the setting sun, but I come as an ambassador of the Doge and the Great Council of the Republic of Venice, with a message for you, Great Khan…'

The older man snorted. Then he began laughing, his body rocking back and forth in mirth. Eventually, he calmed himself. 'I have been impolite,' he said, wiping tears away. 'I have not introduced myself to you. I am not the Great Khan, I am merely Subutai *Baghatur*, Lord of the Mountain Wolves, General of the Left Wing. The Great Khan is still in the north with his armies.'

Sarantuya came forward, eyes lowered. Robert could see her cheek was red and swollen where Khuyag had struck her. She offered the general a big clay bowl of some whitish liquid.

'Give this bold fellow a bowl of *airaq*, too, woman,' said Subutai. 'I cannot believe he is a skulking spy. And, if he is… Well, he will have a decent drink before he dies.'

'I have journeyed for many weeks, General, seeking the Great Khan, to offer him my services while I am a guest in his lands. I have rare skills as a warrior, and much battle lore. I am also here to invite him to join my masters in making a trade treaty. I have valuable gifts, too, for Genghis—'

'Oh-ho! Gifts!' interrupted the general. 'The *elchin said* has gifts for us! He is generous!' He turned his head to look up at Noyan Khuyag, who was standing over them, scowling down at the pair sitting together on the carpeted floor of his *ger*.

'Have you seen these fine gifts, *Noyan*?' said Subutai.

Khuyag merely shrugged.

'Did you see them – and desire to keep them for yourself?' said Subutai.

'He had a single pack mule with him, loaded with a few trinkets…'

'They shall all be returned safely to you, *elchin said*,' Subutai reassured Robert, patting his knee, 'along with all your possessions, or I shall take a few heads from this Golden Eagle *mingghan* by way of punishment. Perhaps even your head, *Noyan!*'

Robert felt his belly muscles unclench at the general's use of the term *elchin said*, which he knew meant 'great envoy' or 'ambassador'. He took a sip of the mildly alcoholic drink in his hand – fermented mare's milk, he believed – about the same strength as good Kentish ale. It was creamy and sweet, though he could feel the alcohol burning the cut on his lip from the blows he had taken.

'My gifts for your master are very precious,' Robert said. 'They are holy treasures from the West, although as the *noyan* says, they are few in number.' He wiped a trickle of the *airaq* away from his cut lip. 'We have travelled a long road to meet your Great Khan. And it was, sadly, not possible to bring a profusion of bulky and burdensome gifts with us. However, I possess something that may be of even greater value to you, General – and to the Great Khan as well, of course.'

'What might that be?' Subutai was smiling most genially, as if they were old friends, sitting together enjoying a drink. Yet his diamond-hard, nearly yellow eyes gave the lie to this conviviality:

Robert could feel them boring deep into his skull like a red-hot carpenter's awl.

'Information. My servant and I have spent the past month in the city of Otrar. While we were there, I made certain observations as to the dispositions of the shah's troops, of the numbers of his soldiers in the garrison, of the state of the fortifications. Indeed, I have made a map of it all—'

'Now you *are* sounding like a spy, *elchin said*!' said Subutai, with a hearty – and wholly false – chuckle. 'Can I have been mistaken about you?'

'I only seek to aid the Great Khan in punishing the city of Otrar for its shameful treatment of his envoys. I acted in Otrar only in the interest of Genghis Khan—'

'And perhaps also in your own interest?'

Robert smiled back at Subutai, holding his gaze. 'I believe that my interests and those of the Great Khan align in this matter. And in many other matters, too.'

'We shall discover that in time, *elchin said*. All things are made clear with time. You speak Mongolian badly, like a child, or like a wild Cuman dog –' Robert sensed Altan stirring beside him at the insult – 'but I shall find someone who can teach you our language and our ways. You have travelled across the world, I see. You must rest with us for a while. Do you possess other tongues?'

Robert admitted that he had a little Arabic, Persian and Turkish, as well as his own tongue, which was called Norman French. He also confessed that he had Italian, Latin and Greek... And Subutai listened to these unfamiliar names, nodding wisely as if he, too, was a student of these tongues.

Then, when Robert had finished listing his linguistic accomplishments, Subutai said, 'Now, tell me something else, *elchin said*, and answer me honestly. I can see that your face is a little bruised, your lower lip is split open. You have clearly been beaten, injured by some rough person or by some persons, I would think. You were attacked by bandits on your long journey, perhaps?'

'It is nothing,' said Robert. 'I fell over on rocky ground when I was arrested by your men.'

Subutai put his head on one side and frowned at him. 'Now I think you *are* lying to me, *elchin* said. Why would you do that? Tell me the truth — for your life depends on it. Have you been hurt by someone? By this fellow here? By Noyan Khuyag?'

'One of the troopers struck me. It is a small thing, of very little consequence.'

'On your feet. We will go and seek out the fellow who dared to strike you.'

Feeling oddly ashamed, Robert got to his feet, with Altan doing the same, and they followed Subutai out of the *ger* and into the warm early evening sunshine.

A squad of half a dozen Mongol soldiers closed in around them, with Khuyag running on ahead. It took no time at all for the *noyan* to locate the leader of the *arban* that had captured them, and two of Subutai's men seized the miscreant and forced him down onto his knees in front of Robert.

'Is this the man?' snapped Khuyag. 'Is this the soldier who struck you?'

Robert simply nodded.

'You, wretch, will beg forgiveness from the *elchin said*,' Khuyag roared.

The man on his knees looked up at Robert with terrified eyes. Chuluun was his name, Robert recalled. He babbled something, much too fast for Robert to catch.

'In the name of Jesus Christ, I forgive you for the blow,' said Robert.

Then one soldier seized both the man's arms and held them behind his back. A second Mongol drew his curved sword and, without a single word, hacked Chuluun's head clean off with two swift, powerful blows of his blade.

Robert was appalled. As the severed stump of the man's neck spurted and trickled gore into the dust by his feet, he rounded on General Subutai, who had watched the episode calmly, with his arms folded and without uttering one syllable.

'Why did you allow that? I had forgiven him. There was no need for it!'

'You are the *elchin said*, are you not? An ambassador from the West to the Great Khan? To Mongols, the person of an envoy is sacred – he must not be harmed, never, not for any reason at all. This foul maggot insulted you, and he struck you. How can the Great Khan punish Otrar for slaying *his* envoys, and not punish this wretch?'

Chapter Eleven

They remained, at all times, a good half-mile from the walls of Otrar, well beyond the longest bowshot, and rode through the many small abandoned villages that surrounded the city, through their neat kitchen gardens and elegant orchards, the lands here made fertile by the joining of the Syr Daria and the river Arys. It was a placid, homely landscape: mud houses, painted red or blue or simply whitewashed with lime, and thatched with millet straw; small fields of stubble and bright green weeds, the crops gathered in; the land irrigated by deep ditches, which also marked the boundaries of the village fields. But everywhere was eerily quiet. There were no human voices to be heard, and no clucking poultry, no lowing of beasts of burden, no cows requiring to be milked.

With the arrival of the first contingents of the Mongol horde, the people in Otrar's outlying villages had immediately fled for shelter inside the city, with all their goods and animals. Robert could well imagine the crowded streets now, filled to bursting with new refugees and their herds of sheep and cages of chickens, their shelters clogging the tiny squares and narrow alleys.

Subutai commanded three *tumet*, three divisions of ten thousand men each. But this advance part of the Mongol army was still about forty miles behind their general and following the trail of the Golden Eagles, the scouting *mingghan*, but apparently coming up fast. The bulk of the main Mongol army – perhaps another ten *tumet* under the Great Khan – had still not arrived in Khwarazmian territory from the north. Furthermore, Robert knew that a third Mongol army, almost as powerful as Subutai's thirty-thousand-strong force, lay somewhere to the south of them under the two warlords General Jebe and General Jochi – the army now camped in the Fergana Valley that Robert had attempted unsuccessfully to locate. He had known that Genghis Khan commanded a mighty host and many generals – but he had never realised quite how powerful the Lord of the Steppe truly was.

There was no sign yet of the Mongols' opponent, Muhammad Shah, but rumour had it that the Khwarazmian emperor was to the south of Otrar, near his fabulously wealthy capital Samarkand.

Robert, astride his gelding, which had been returned to him along with all his belongings, clattered over a narrow wooden bridge across a deep irrigation ditch and up the slope of a small hillock that had been planted with apple trees, some heavy with autumn fruit. He reined in the gelding at the summit of the rise, with Altan halting beside him, and gazed south-west at the city.

If anything, the fortress of Otrar looked even more formidable from this vantage point. It was built on an oval of land half a mile across that rose sixty feet above the flood plain, and atop this outcrop of land were walls twice the height of a man. It was well defended, too, Robert knew, having been garrisoned by ten thousand men of the shah's finest regiments. Robert and Subutai had discussed the military composition of this much reinforced garrison at length over the past week.

This was Muhammad Shah's strategy for winning the war. The emperor of Khwarazmia had a score of large fortified cities similar to Otrar scattered across the northern part of his domain, and he had filled them with his best-trained and bravest soldiers – five thousand here, ten thousand there – confident that behind their strong walls, they could hold out for months against steppe horsemen, who, while superior at speed and manoeuvre, were unversed in the patient tactics of siege warfare.

'They have plenty of food, deep wells and high walls,' he said to Altan.

'And thousands of brave men who will defend those walls to the death,' replied the Cuman, shaking his head. 'And they are adequate fighters. It will be no easy task.'

There was a rattle of hooves behind them, and Subutai and half a dozen of his Mongol attendants came clattering up the slope and halted their mounts beside them.

'Ho, *elchin said*!' Subutai called out jovially. 'Tell me what *you* see that I do not!'

Robert scratched at his beard. 'I see months of hard labour ahead of us, General. Months of trench-digging, fortification-building and slow, grinding bombardment. And many hard, bloody assaults against those high walls. Even then, victory is not assured.'

Subutai laughed. 'I asked you to tell me what I *do not* see,' he said.

Robert shrugged. 'As you wish. There, by the mosque, the tall blue tower, west of the main gate – you see it? – the wall is a little weaker there, I think. I have seen this place with my own eyes. The old stones of the wall have crumbled a little and the locals have carried many of the larger ones away and used them to build new homes.'

'Good,' said Subutai. 'And that blue tower makes an easy mark to aim at.'

'You need another two points of attack,' said Robert. 'At least two more.'

'Yes, and you shall find them for me, *elchin said*,' said Subutai.

'There is something else I must tell you,' said Robert. 'You see that glint of gold, high on the left? That is the roof of the citadel. A second bastion inside the already formidable fortress of Otrar. Even if you do manage to overrun the outer walls, General, you will still have to storm the walls of Governor Inalchuq's stronger inner fortification.'

'Yes, first the outer walls, then the citadel. It will not be swift, I know. Nor easy. But before we begin our labours, I shall go and offer them the Great Khan's Choice.'

'What is that?' Robert asked.

The general smiled crookedly at him. 'You will see, *elchin said*, you will see.'

–

The next morning, an hour after dawn, Robert and Altan, accompanied by Subutai and Khuyag and six Mongol troopers, all carrying large round shields made of woven rattan and faced with very tough ox-leather, rode slowly towards the northern gates of Otrar.

They paused often, scanning the double portal intently, looking for any signs of hostile activity, before riding another few dozen paces forward and halting again.

Robert hoped that the defenders – a crowd of dark heads above the gates, and the hundreds on either side of the walls – would understand they came to parley. If they decided to shoot arrows, or hurl lethal missiles, despite the protection of the shield-men, all their lives were in God's hands.

It had been nine days since the beheading of Chuluun in the Mongol encampment on the road to Otrar. Since then Robert had been almost constantly in the company of either Subutai or Khuyag.

They had helped – in Robert's case, rather clumsily – to pack up the *noyan's ger* and his entire household at the command of the booming Mongol drums, and transport the whole *mingghan* fifty miles down the road towards Otrar. For the past five days they had been freshly encamped, with all their herds, women and children, five miles north and east of the walls of the city. The first *tumen* of Subutai's command had also reached them – ten thousand men – and they had thrown a cordon round the whole city, with strong Mongol encampments set up on all sides. Otrar was surrounded.

When General Subutai's party was a hundred paces from the double gate – well within reach of a lethal arrow – the great portal partly opened and a dozen horsemen came boiling out of the gate in a cloud of dust and cantered down the road towards them.

Robert watched them approach impassively. He now understood the terrible meaning of the Great Khan's Choice, and he had agreed to translate the general's words when the Choice was given to the men of Otrar. He wondered what effect it might have on these proud Khwarazmians.

In part of his mind, he recalled the story Niccolò Ziani had told him in his cosy firelit hall in Tana about the actions of the ruler of this city: '...when the Great Khan's merchants arrived in Otrar, exhausted from their long journey, the local governor welcomed them, offering food and wine. And, when their guard was down and they were at their leisure, he had them arrested as spies and put to death.'

Robert could now make out the faces of some of the Otrar contingent that was approaching them. In the centre was the governor of the city, Inalchuq himself. This morning the little despot's turban was a fine sky blue and bedecked with rubies the size of pigeons' eggs. And beside him was the austere captain of the Citadel Guard, a haughty Persian aristocrat called Koorush, with several kings in his lineage. On the other side of the governor was Inalchuq's chancellor, Haq Bey, rumoured to be the richest – and also the most corrupt – man in the whole of Otrar, which was a feat all in itself. He knew these powerful men only by reputation, never having met any of them himself.

The Otrar delegation clattered to a halt a dozen yards away, and the eight Persian lancers fanned out on either side, which made Khuyag growl under his breath like an angry dog. But Subutai hushed him, and they sat and waited for the enemy riders to settle.

The general caught Robert's eye, and nodded to him. A signal. Then he said loudly, 'I am Subutai *Baghatur*, Lord of the Mountain Wolves, General of the Left Wing. I am the true and faithful servant of mighty Genghis Khan, Lord of the Steppe, and I speak today with his voice.'

Robert translated this as best he could into the courtly Turkish tongue, which he knew was the language of all these higher-ranking servants of Muhammad Shah.

'I am Inalchuq, son of Kamalchuq, Governor of Otrar, beloved cousin of His Imperial Majesty Muhammad Shah, King of Kings, Blessed of Heaven, the Lion of Samarkand, may his glorious rule last a thousand years! Why do you invade his lands and come to my gates garbed for war? I order you to withdraw, to depart this land immediately and return to your own home, lest the fury of my lord destroy you!'

'You will say only this to him, *elchin said*,' Subutai muttered to Robert. 'Only these words, yes? You understand me? Say these words and then we will depart from here. You shall give him the Great Khan's Choice – no more and no less than that!'

Robert glanced at Subutai and nodded. Then the general said, very slowly and clearly, 'Surrender to me now and receive my mercy, O people of Otrar, or I shall annihilate you all and leave not one stone of your city standing on another. Throw open your gates this day and kneel in the dust before me, and all who are innocent shall be spared. Dare to resist me, and I shall slay all living things inside your walls. It is time for you to make the Great Khan's Choice!'

Governor Inalchuq gaped at Robert as he made the translation. He looked as if he could not believe his ears. 'There is no need to be so hasty, young man. Ask your master if he would care to drink an iced—' Inalchuq began saying, but Subutai spoke right over him.

He said to Robert, 'Tell this gaudy little monkey-man that he has till sunset to make the Choice. Call him a monkey – use that word. Tell this ridiculous little monkey-man he must give me an answer by dusk.'

Robert said the words he was told and watched Inalchuq's jaw fall open.

'Do you realise to whom you are speaking…?' the governor began.

But Subutai was already turning his horse's head and, moments later, he was spurring his mount and galloping away up the road, with the rest of the escort scrambling to keep up with him.

Robert took a moment to look over at Inalchuq and meet the fat little man's astonished gaze one last time, before he, too, turned his gelding's head, dug in his spurs and galloped off up the road after his new master.

The engineers arrived the next day with the second and third *tumet* of Subutai's command. The city of Otrar was now surrounded by a force of thirty thousand Mongol warriors. And Robert and Altan found themselves living in a city – albeit, a city made entirely of low, round, grey-brown felt tents.

Subutai had ordered Khuyag to offer Robert his hospitality, and the question of whether or not he was an envoy seemed to have been settled. Whether or not Subutai trusted Robert was unclear, but he acted as if he did. Robert, in turn, tried to behave like a loyal servant of the Mongol lord.

There was no news of the arrival of Genghis Khan, and Robert knew he had to bide his time outside Otrar and simply wait. There was nothing else he could do. He tried not to think about what life must be like for poor Gilly, rotting away in gaol in Jerusalem – if, indeed, he was still alive.

To ease the imposition on the *noyan* and his family, Robert had presented Khuyag with half a dozen flasks of the sweet wine of Samarkand, which he had purchased in Otrar. The *noyan* had been delighted, and seemed keen to be friendly with such a high, important personage as the *elchin said*.

'My *ger* is yours,' the *noyan* had said. 'You are my honoured guest for as long as you choose to stay.' And then he'd slapped Robert very hard on the back.

Khuyag insisted on opening the Samarkand flasks that evening and drinking the liquor from a huge pewter bowl, quaffing the expensive wine in great slurping gulps as if it were no more than small beer – or the Mongol fermented milk drink, *airaq*. They ate tender roasted kid that evening, with millet porridge, and drank many toasts to the good health of the King of England, the Republic of Venice and, of course, to their mighty lord Genghis Khan.

Khuyag soon became drunk, red in the face and boisterous – asking Robert about the lands through which he had travelled, about the battles he had fought, the men he had killed and the women he had ravished. How many horses did he own in his homeland? How many sheep and camels? It must be a great number for such an important man. Robert drank as sparingly as he could, with all due courtesy, but soon he felt the heat of the wine in his blood, and allowed himself to speak imaginatively of the upland pastures of northern England and their numberless flocks of sheep; of the magnificence and splendour of the court of the child king Henry – none of which, in truth, he had ever seen with his own eyes.

Deep into the night Khuyag grew morose, and complained bitterly to Robert that he lacked strong sons to say the proper rites over him when he was dead.

'I have no children to mourn me,' he said, leaning on Robert's shoulder. 'No son. Not one child. My wife has a dry womb. There's no life force in her belly.'

Robert could not help but glance at Sarantuya as he said this. The woman, eyes lowered, was pouring out the last dregs of the wine into her husband's pewter cup.

'Perhaps I should find myself a second wife,' the *noyan* slurred. 'A better wife.'

The Englishman saw that Sarantuya portrayed no emotion as she heard these words. She had heard them before. She simply cleared away the dirty plates and the bones of the kid and departed to the woman's side of the *ger*. Much later, lying in his blankets in the darkness of the tent, Robert heard Khuyag unsuccessfully trying to couple with his wife, harsh words of recrimination, a slap, then snoring. He turned over in his blankets and tried very hard to sleep.

–

The engineers soon began constructing their big trebuchets and smaller mangonels on sites selected with advice from Robert

– and with Khuyag looking on sourly. But while the Englishman had received a lengthy training in fortress bombardment from the expert brothers at Acre, he soon realised that the knowledge of these people – squat, black-haired folk in blue jackets and leggings with wide-brimmed straw hats on their heads – surpassed his own. What puzzled him further was that they barely seemed to understand his Mongolian, and had no Turkish or Persian either.

'These people are not real Mongols,' said Khuyag. 'They are Jin artisans who surrendered to Genghis Khan rather than have their cities destroyed.'

'They are truly Jin from the land of Cathay?' Robert was fascinated.

'They are burrowers in the dirt. Marmot-men. They kill good men from afar with their machines and without ever seeing their enemies' faces up close. They are not proper horse-warriors like you or me, *elchin said*. They are not *real* men of war.'

The marmot-men were, however, industrious. They quickly levelled places in the ground for the massive trebuchets, selecting three sites all around the city, digging out the yellow earth and smoothing it down to a perfectly even surface. On each of the three sites, four trebuchets would be set up. They immediately began constructing their huge artillery machines from baulks of cut timber they had brought with them on enormous ox-carts, pulled by a dozen of these great beasts.

Their leader was a tall, immensely fat man in a blue silk robe who received streams of officers all day and night in his command tent and, while he might not look much like a man of action, he certainly stirred his scores of blue-jacketed Chinese workers to labour their hardest. And, even as these twelve artillery machines were being constructed, other marmot-men were occupied in building a packed-earth wall ten feet high, three feet thick all the way around the besieged city.

The wall was meant to protect the Mongol troops from any rescue attempt by the shah – should the emperor venture north and fight. But it also reinforced a not-very-subtle message to the city: *You are surrounded. We shall remain here until your city has fallen.*

The trebuchets were assembled in a matter of only four days, and one crisp autumn morning Robert, Altan, Khuyag, and a score of his men, watched as the long arm on the first machine was hauled down by a dozen sweating Jin engineers using a dozen ox-hide ropes, gradually raising the counterweight – a massive rope net filled with boulders – high in the air. The first missile, a stone the size of a human head, which had been carefully chipped into a perfect sphere, was rolled into the leather sling at the end of the throwing arm – a twenty-foot-long stripped pine trunk. The restraining ropes were released at a brisk shout of command from the Chinese battery commander, the counterweight dropped, and the throwing arm was flipped high in the air to thud against the padded horizontal bar at the top of the massive machine.

The round missile exploded from its sling and arced high in the air before smashing itself to powder against the walls of Otrar, slightly to the left of the Blue Mosque that was its target. And while it must have sounded truly alarming for the besieged troops inside Otrar, it seemed to have no impact at all on the city's defences.

Altan said dismissively, 'All that sweat – and nothing to show for it!'

Khuyag made a frustrated hissing noise and said something rude, but his words were drowned out by the shouts of the engineers and the creak of ropes and beams as the machine was prepared for another shot. Just then the second trebuchet in the battery freed its ropes, and a second ball flew through the sky and struck the city wall, thirty feet to the left and a little lower than the first strike. The moment after that, the third and fourth trebuchets of the battery both dispatched their missiles.

'Watch the marmot-men at work for a week – or better yet, a month – and you will see something,' said Robert. 'Each strike weakens the wall. And the trebuchets will try to concentrate their power in one spot. After a thousand strikes…'

'We have not the leisure to watch for a week,' said Khuyag, 'and certainly not for a month.' He was in a foul mood. Once again, he had drunk to excess in the *ger* the night before. 'We have orders to make a sweep to the south. The general wants to know where the shah's army is, and to determine its strength. He invites you to join us, *elchin said*. Will you ride to seek the enemy?'

'It is my duty, *Noyan*, to greet the Great Khan here and to present my gifts to him.'

'The Great Khan is still in the north. Did they not tell you? He will not come here for at least another month. Would you prefer to sit for all that time in the *ger*, spinning yarn, with only women for company – like a timid little marmot-man?'

Robert smiled thinly at his host. 'I would not. I will ride out with you to find the enemy. It is my pleasure to serve the Great Khan in any way, no matter the danger.'

'Have no fear, *elchin said*, you will not be killed by the enemy. My men will keep you safe. Subutai would have my head if I let one of the shah's lancers skewer you.'

Chapter Twelve

Robert was astonished once again by the speed and endurance of the Mongol horsemen. He and Altan had nearly ridden themselves to exhaustion on the first day, simply trying to keep up with the hundred-man-strong *jagghun*, which was led on this scouting mission by his host Khuyag. The *noyan* had command of the whole Golden Eagle *mingghan*, and this company – called simply No.4 *jagghun* – was considered the best of the ten that made up the *noyan*'s reconnaissance regiment.

They had set off well before dawn, leaving their encampment, which was to the north of the main army, and circling the sprawling camp, with its vast herds of horses and flocks of sheep and goats, before crossing the Arys over an ancient wooden bridge and thundering down the east bank of the Syr Daria, galloping roughly south. Khuyag had given them each two spare horses to ride and, when they paused briefly a little after noon, to switch their saddles to fresh beasts, Robert was forced to admit that these hard-riding Mongols were his superiors in matters of horse-craft.

He chewed a strip of raw mutton, which he had been given as his rations, and drank some fresh mare's milk, too. He tried to ignore the rank taste of the mutton. He had seen Khuyag lodge a dozen slices of the dried meat beneath his saddle that morning before they set off, and by the time the meat was given to him at noon, it had been thoroughly tenderised by a mixture of the horse's sweat and the weight of Khuyag's posterior. He ate the limp, leathery meat nonetheless – there was no other food. But when he heard the order to remount, his limbs almost failed him. He had to use every ounce of his strength simply to haul his tired body back up into the saddle.

'Not too tired by our little ride, *elchin said*?' asked Khuyag, who was smirking at him.

'Not at all,' Robert replied, forcing up a grimace in return. 'In truth, I find it quite refreshing to travel at such a calm, leisurely pace for a change.'

Altan brought his pony next to Robert's. 'He is testing us, *ezen*, do you know that?' he muttered. 'Mongols do not ride at this reckless speed without due cause.'

'That much is obvious,' replied Robert.

They rode all afternoon, again at a blistering pace, through the cultivated lands that ran in a strip along the banks of the Syr Daria, then further east into higher ground. At dusk they came down into a valley and camped that night on the shore of a lake a few miles east of the river, in a recently abandoned fishing village. So recently abandoned, in fact, that the embers were still glowing in the hearths inside the reed huts there, and Robert found a clay pot of fish stew still steaming beside one such fireplace. At the approach of the Mongols, the villagers had fled – he knew not where. And he was too exhausted to care for the fate of a few fisherfolk in the back of beyond.

After he and Altan, Khuyag and Taghachat, the *jagghan* officer, had each wolfed down a bowl of *shulen* – boiled up at camp that evening from the same revolting horse-tenderised mutton – Robert asked Altan if he knew anything of what lay west beyond the Syr Daria. Khuyag, whose elaborately shaven head had been nodding on his chest, perked up at this talk.

'I never yet ventured over that side of the Syr Daria, *ezen*,' said Altan, picking a shred of mutton from his front teeth. 'But I have heard stories about that place. Men call it the Kyzyl Kum – the Red Desert. A bleak landscape of dry earth and rocks occupied only by wild foxes and evil spirits. To enter the Kyzyl Kum is to seek your death, they say. It is an evil place. There is no water at all till you reach the Amu Daria on the far side of the red sands. It is a hard ride of twelve days to that mighty river – a four-hundred-mile journey across an expanse of empty, haunted wasteland.'

'What of the towns, oases and strongholds there?' asked Khuyag. 'General Subutai said there might be some rich settlements to be found in this Red Desert.'

Altan looked over at the *noyan* and shook his head. 'I cannot tell you, *ezen*.'

'I heard that in the south are the cities of Burkhara and Samarkand,' said Taghachat, surprising everyone. 'Places where the wealth of the empire is all piled up in mountains of gold.'

'Mountains of gold?' said Khuyag. 'You idiot! Who told you this nonsense?'

'We caught a man trying to escape Otrar a few days ago,' said Taghachat, sounding hurt. 'When we put him to the question – asking where all the treasure was – that is what *he* told us. In Burkhara and Samarkand, he said. Mountains of glittering gold and treasure. He said something else. The cities had no walls. The red desert was their only defence – all the protection they needed.'

–

They found the forward elements of the shah's army in the broken lands fifty miles to the south, in the scrubby Tien Shan foothills, with the high peaks stretching away to the east like a jagged, snow-capped wall. The scouts, who ranged far out in front of the rest of the *jagghun*, spied a detachment of the shah's Persian light cavalry, and came galloping back to report to Khuyag.

An ambush was swiftly prepared.

The twenty enemy riders were gorgeously dressed in scarlet silk tunics, blue spotted pantaloons and purple turbans encompassing spiked helms, the troopers trotting in pairs down a narrow defile, flamboyant helmet plumes nodding, backs as straight as their gleaming steel-tipped lances, as if they were on some parade ground.

They might have looked magnificent, and the courage they displayed in the short, bloody engagement that followed was beyond question, but the shah's cavalry never stood a chance. The Mongols, easily outnumbering the Khwarazmians by more than four to one, came clattering out from their places of concealment in the canyons that branched off the road and swamped the shah's men with the stunning force of a rockfall, the No.4 *jagghun* men piling into the foe with a wild and savage joy.

Robert drew his arming sword but never needed to use it, since he was warded throughout by four Mongol riders and Altan. These five bodyguards never let a Persian lance come within ten feet of him.

The black Mongol arrows, loosed from the saddle with incredible speed by the ambushers, slashed into the shah's lightly armoured men, sometimes punching men clear out of their saddles with the force of the strike. Their bright, silk-clad bodies were swiftly riddled with lethal shafts. Some of the Persians tried to flee but were cut down by arrows, or hacked from the saddle by Mongol sabres. Khuyag soon had to call out for the slaughter to cease, so at least one of the foe should be left alive for questioning.

Only one Mongol was killed in the short fight – a deep lance thrust delivered during the initial thundering attack – and two others were lightly wounded by Persian blades.

The horses were rounded up, the saddlebags ransacked for loot, and the lone Persian survivor was soon screaming under the knives of the *noyan's* men.

Robert muttered a prayer for the poor man's soul. Then he was handed a pair of ripe, dusty-black figs, a big cube of soft, sweet ewe's cheese, a hunk torn from a loaf of fine-milled bread and a flagon of wine – all of which had once been intended as a Khwarazmian trooper's evening meal – and he sat down on a convenient rock with Altan and they feasted like kings.

It was a joy to eat something – anything – that was not mutton, and to take a drink that was not made from mare's milk. To Robert, that simple meal tasted like a man's heavenly reward.

'The main Khwarazmian force is about seventy miles south, according to the prisoner,' said Khuyag a while later, when he joined Robert for the last of the wine. 'He said it was on the northern shore of a lake, and their army was a hundred thousand strong... I think he lied to me.'

'Is he still alive?' asked Robert.

Khuyag laughed at that.

'He must have been lying,' said Robert. 'A hundred thousand? Three times the size of Subutai's force? No. If they were truly that powerful, they would already have relieved the siege of Otrar – and utterly destroyed or scattered Subutai's men to the winds.'

'Maybe he lied. Maybe not. It doesn't matter. We shall see with our own eyes.'

–

Sharp chips of stone cut into Robert's elbows and knees, and he shifted his weight a little – but very, very slowly – to ease the pressure. He was lying flat on his stomach on a spur of mountainside that speared out from the foothills of the Tien Shan mountains above a long blue lake that ran roughly east to west. It was four days since they had left Otrar and all of Robert's muscles were protesting, for he had spent most of those four days in the saddle keeping up with the blistering pace of the *jagghun*, yet he felt satisfied to be using some of the military skills he had trained in for so long to good purpose. Below him on the north shore of the lake, basking under the late autumn sunshine, was a vast settlement of tents – several thousand of them. They ranged from plain, humble pyramids of white canvas, arranged in straight lines and blocks, each shelter no taller than a man, to tents that were larger, gorgeous structures of coloured silks, set in their own spaces, surrounded by smaller shelters, and often topped with floating green banners covered in script. The nobles' abodes.

In the centre of the encampment was an oblong golden pavilion with the largest banner of all – a long red flag depicting a huge golden lion. The tent was ringed by scores of men – impressively bearded fellows in green-and-gold uniforms, with shining steel helms, and holding pikes twice as tall as they. They seemed to be posted there to keep the rest of the camp at a safe distance.

'Is that big golden one the shah's *ger*?' Robert whispered to Khuyag, who was lying beside him, peering under a shading hand at the extraordinary sights below.

They had been there an hour, having made their way up to this vantage point – crawling the last two hundred yards painfully over rocks on their knees and elbows – from a grassy bowl of land where two arms of the mountains met: the place where Altan and the rest of the *jagghun* were now taking their ease and tending their horses. Khuyag had said he would go alone to spy on the enemy, and Robert, who was fairly sure Khuyag was still evaluating him, had volunteered to go too. The Englishman had no idea if he was passing the tests Khuyag set him. Neither did he care very much.

'If it is not, then these Khwarazmian lords are even richer than we imagined.'

Robert made an attempt to count the numbers of the tents, to get an idea of the strength gathered here, but he soon lost his tally. Many horsemen were moving about, large formations of riders, thousands of them raising dust that clouded his view. At the far end of the mass of tents he could see squares of infantry at their drill, performing manoeuvres, wheeling and changing shape, now charging and coming to a sudden stop. He could even dimly hear their high, warlike cries.

There were pickets posted on the roads that led from the encampment – cavalry and infantry – and Robert could see a squadron of fifty horse setting out east, on the road that led to their position.

'I have seen enough,' said Khuyag, punching Robert's arm. 'Let us go home.'

–

'What, in your opinion, is the true size of their army, *elchin said*?' asked Subutai.

It was five days later and Robert, Altan and Khuyag and the No.4 *jagghun* had just arrived back in the Mongol camp to the north-west of Otrar. They had been immediately summoned to the command *ger* of their general, to make their report.

Subutai's tent was thirty feet across the middle, and twice the height of a man. It was not as grand as the shah's golden pavilion on the lake, but infinitely more practical. The whole edifice of felt sheets, wooden poles and willow latticework was mounted on a massive wheeled platform, which could be pulled by oxen – fourteen of these beasts – for many leagues across the steppe.

'The enemy is *not* a hundred thousand strong, General, as was first reported. I do not believe so. But it *is* a large host and Shah Muhammad is with them, which will make the soldiers fight all the harder. I would say sixty thousand, or maybe even as few as fifty thousand troops. But they overmatch your strength, General. They are perhaps twice as many as you. They looked ready to move out. Certainly, we observed much activity in the camp. If they marched swiftly north to us – and combined their attack with a sortie from the besieged city – we would have a cause for some concern. My advice, if they came north, would be to retreat swiftly. It was a favoured doctrine of the wise Christian warriors who schooled me from a young age.'

To Robert's surprise, Subutai chuckled at his comment, and slapped his thigh.

'Retreat!' he said, laughing again and sitting back on his cushion. 'Retreat if they come north? That is what we *want* them to do, *elchin said*. One great battle to defeat the shah – that's what we seek – and then the whole of Khwarazmia is ours! If the shah comes up here with his fifty – or even sixty – thousand men, I shall send messengers to Jebe and Joshi in the Fergana Valley, yes, and to the Great Khan in the north as well, if necessary, and we shall unite and crush this upstart Persian popinjay between us. If *only* they were so reckless as to come north towards us! What say you, *Noyan*? Will the shah come here with only a paltry sixty thousand at his command?'

'I do not know, *Baghatur*. I cannot say what is in the shah's mind. We came as close to them as we dared, the *elchin said* and I. But even then we could not easily reckon their numbers. I would say *more* than sixty thousand. But I believe what the *elchin said* is correct — the shah was with them. But whether he will come north… Yes, perhaps he will. I would feel compelled to by honour.'

'Let us hope that he does. All this news is good — very good. You have served me well, Khuyag. And you, too, *elchin said*. I congratulate you on your successful mission.'

Subutai beckoned to one of his servants, who brought over a leather bag full of *airaq* and refilled all their cups. He was beaming at them both as he drank the cloudy liquor down in one draught. 'Your Mongolian is improving, *elchin said*,' he said after a while. 'But you still make mistakes. You sound like a stupid Cuman. I have picked out a teacher for you to study with. A wise person, and patient with dull-witted men, who can help you become proficient in our tongue.'

He winked at Khuyag, a mischievous little twitch of his bright yellow eye.

Robert did not understand what was happening. Some small jest was being played. Khuyag scowled at his lord, his sallow cheeks colouring red. 'You do my humble household far too much honour, *Baghatur*,' he said with an obvious tone of resentment.

'Who, then, is to be my teacher?' asked Robert.

–

Sarantuya used a riding switch made of stiffened leather held in an outstretched hand to point to the cook-pot that hung over the hearth in the centre of the *ger*.

'*Khoolny sav!*' she said.

Robert repeated her words.

'No, *elchin said*,' Sarantuya said. '*Khoolny saaav!*' Robert tried hard to copy her intonation.

She pointed the riding switch at a quiver full of Mongol arrows hanging on the wall beside his head and said, '*Chichrekh*. This thing here is called a *chichrekh*.'

Robert prided himself on his talent for languages, but he was finding Mongolian difficult to learn. Perhaps because he was being taught by a woman. A very beautiful woman.

He had two brothers growing up: Henry, named after his father, was the elder, and he stood to inherit the manor when his father died; and Gilbert... But he had no sisters. He had, of course, known a few village girls when he was a lusty stripling – he was no blushing virgin – but since he had joined the ranks of the Poor Fellow-Soldiers of Christ and of the Temple of Solomon as a young man, and taken his vows, he had had almost no commerce with living, breathing women at all.

There were none in the Templar precincts but carved stone statues of the Blessed Virgin Mary and other female saints – and even the local women who washed the vestments of the knights, and who cooked their meals, were excluded from the common rooms of the Brethren except during certain hours when the knights were elsewhere. He found Sarantuya a most distracting mentor.

She had a natural grace, a fluency, as she moved around the *ger*. She held herself like a warrior, always balanced, never awkward. Her movements were almost dance-like, elegant. He found himself staring at the curve of her high cheek while she was speaking to him, and sometimes a little shamefully trying to delineate the shape of her body through the thick *deel* she wore. When she looked into his eyes, he actually felt slightly drunk, as if he was drowning in those two black pools. And sometimes he believed he could see right through her eyes and into her pure and shining soul.

The shameful glimpse of her naked breast when she was taming the stallion rose, deliciously, in his mind from time to time, and he found he could not concentrate on the difficult Mongolian words.

He cursed himself for a lustful sinner. From time to time, he called on St Christopher to strengthen his spirit. She was a good, honest woman, the wife of his generous host, and he was a man sworn to a life of chastity. '*Banish all these impure thoughts from* my heart, holy Christopher,' he prayed, 'and keep me safe from all the Devil's snares and the corruption of my carnal lusts!'

'*Khuchtei*,' said Sarantuya, clutching her bicep with her left hand. 'This word means "strong".'

Robert half-heartedly repeated the word.

'*Khuuuchtei.*' Sarantuya stepped forward and grasped his own arm above the elbow, hard, her fingers digging in like claws. And he felt a jolt of lightning from her touch.

'*Iluu khuchtei*,' she said, smiling up at him in a friendly way. 'More strong.'

She touched her own right arm, then his arm with her left hand.

'Strong... more strong. Stronger. Do you understand now, *echin said*?'

—

After his daily lesson with Sarantuya, in the early morning, Robert usually saddled his gelding and rode towards Otrar to watch the progress of the siege. One chilly day, as he trotted towards the marmot-men of the Yellow Battery, he pondered something Sarantuya had said to him earlier.

She had been telling him some of the legends about the early life of Genghis Khan – who had been apparently born clutching a blood clot, which was a portent of the rivers of gore he was destined to shed – and she had used the word 'uncle' to refer to the great lord of all the Mongols. He was fairly sure that he had heard her correctly. But what did this mean? If the Great Khan was her uncle, surely she would not be married to a mere *noyan* – a commander of only a thousand men – and living in an ordinary *ger*? She would be a royal princess, would she not? A member of the Golden Kin, as he had heard the family of Genghis Khan were commonly called.

Perhaps he had simply misheard – or 'uncle' was just a term of respect used by non-relatives. After all, 'sire' did not literally mean that one's lord or king was one's 'father'.

He greeted the artillery captain of the Yellow Battery, and asked him how his beloved trebuchets were faring that morning. The marmot-man – never so-called to his face – was a soft, middle-aged fellow called Deng, who hailed from the Jin Empire in distant Cathay, and who had been captured by the Mongols at a large northern city called Zhongdu. He had struck up a friendship with Robert, and had told him once in his halting Mongolian – which, oddly, Robert found less easy to understand than the full-spate torrent he received from Khuyag and his troopers – that, at the siege of Zhongdu, when he had been defending the city with his battery against this very Mongol army, they had used lumps of precious silver and gold to hurl at their foes when they had run out of stone missiles. After he had been captured, during the sack of his Jin city, his foes had given him a stark choice: serve the Great Khan – or die.

'Since you ask, the arm on No.3 machine is cracked and needs to be repaired,' said Deng. 'We cannot use it. But my other children are full of zest and vigour!'

He smiled up at Robert on his gelding. 'See, *elchin said*… See what damage my powerful wooden children have already wrought on the shah's feeble walls!'

Robert looked at the walls of Otrar – at the section in front of the Blue Mosque, where the trebuchets had been pounding away for five weeks now – and saw that his friend Deng was correct. There was a deep V-shaped depression in the wall, a large notch perhaps forty feet down and fifty feet across at the top, and a tumbled mass of masonry before the breach, reaching right down to the plain. The broken masonry formed a kind of rough narrow stairway up to the gap in the walls, and even as he watched Robert heard the creak, whistle and thump as the furthest trebuchet loosed its ropes and a missile arced through the sky and landed on the edge of the V-shape in a puff of dust and disappeared inside the city. A trickle of rubble rolled down the stair, one big pale sandstone block bouncing all the way to the very bottom like a ball.

'They come out at night to try to repair the breach in the darkness,' said Deng. 'So we give them a ball every hour or so after dusk, just to keep them hopping.'

'How soon before it is ready to assault?' Robert asked.

'Another two days,' said Deng. 'We have started another breach further along – to the west. See there!' Robert followed his pointing finger and saw a smaller but still significant indentation about a hundred feet along from the original.

'When that one is bigger, we will join the two. Make one big breach they cannot repair – or easily defend. Then Subutai can send in his assault *mingghat* to capture it – those poor brave fools.'

'You have done well, Deng. Has the general praised you for your work?'

'Subutai *Baghatur* came to see us yesterday. He said he would give me a chest full of silver when the city falls, and a hundred slaves to tend my wooden children.'

'And the other batteries? Are they doing as well as you?'

Deng looked slightly put out. 'The Red Battery in the south has made a breach of sorts. A clumsy hole, no subtlety. Good for nothing but a diversionary attack. But the Blue Battery has hardly chipped the stones of Otrar. This is the breach, *elchin said*. This is where the assault will be.'

Robert gazed at the large V-shaped indent in the walls, and at the Blue Mosque behind it – and at how much more of its tall, turquoise-clad tower was visible now.

He could picture the narrow streets still hidden by the battered walls in that part of Otrar. There was an orange-seller who once had his stall there – a funny little man who would make up flattering bits of poetry in Persian about passers-by, hoping to entice them to buy his fruit. And, of course, the little green door that led to the long, low warehouse of the young merchant Karacha.

He had sat for many hours with the trader, almost directly under the place where the breach now was. What did Karacha's warehouse look like? he wondered. The last time he had seen it, it had been filled with bales of silk and sacks of grain and boxes of fruit, and the air had been pungent with spices – much of which had been gained from his illicit trading with the Mongols. Had his merchant friend managed to move his goods out in time? Well before the arrival of the Mongols? Of course, he would have. Karacha was a practical man. A born survivor. He would be long gone by now, with all his wealth and stock. And Robert was glad of this. Because when the Mongol assault got through that breach, there would be appalling slaughter.

And once the city of Otrar was taken, no one inside the walls would be safe.

When Robert returned to the *ger* that evening – having ridden slowly all around the walls to make his full assessment – he was struck by an air of expectation in the Mongol camp: a general, wide-reaching feeling of barely suppressed excitement.

The younger warriors engaging in rough horseplay in the chilly evening air outside their *ger* seemed even more exuberant than usual. They strutted and posed, many stripped to the waist to show off their white, wiry bodies and their archers' muscles. Some of them were engaged in mock-wrestling matches with their friends. Women, too, seemed to be full of a strange novel energy, several calling out friendly greetings to him as he rode through the well-trodden paths between the tents on the tired gelding, asking him to come and share a cup of *airaq* with them. He wondered if it was the knowledge that two breaches were practical – that is, that they were ready for an assault – which gave everyone such an air of jollity. He doubted it. Storming a breach was a grim, murderous affair, and no cause for any kind of celebration.

He discovered what was afoot back in the *ger*, when Khuyag's mother-in-law, Temulun, was handing him a steaming bowl of *shulen*, and a spoon with which to eat it. Khuyag was sprawled on his low couch-throne in the northern part of the tent, lolling like a sulky barbarian king. He had a leather sack of *airaq* by his knee and he was drinking with determination, refilling the bowl after every draining gulp, deliberately trying to make himself drunk.

His face was dark, reddish with the alcohol, and something else besides.

When Robert had finished his greasy mutton stew, Sarantuya brought him his own cup of *airaq*. He smiled up at her and asked what news there was in the camp that day, taking care to pronounce the Mongolian words as precisely as he was able.

'Have you not heard, *elchin said*?' she said. 'The Great Khan draws near. Our scouts have made contact with his outriders. Genghis Khan will be here in a week, if he hurries a little.'

Robert sat upright, spilling his *airaq*. A week? The Great Khan would be here in a week. Then he could begin the negotiations. If he were able to accomplish this quickly, and if he braved the winter weather on the return, he might be in Tana by Ash Wednesday. Gilly could be free by Easter!

'He can take his time, if he wants to,' slurred Khuyag. 'Why not dawdle a month longer up in the north? Or stay away for another year – or two… Hey, why not?'

Once more, Robert had no idea what was happening. 'You do not wish to greet the Great Khan?' he asked his host, puzzled. 'You do not revere him?'

'No, *elchin said*,' Sarantuya said. 'The *noyan* is delighted at the prospect of seeing the face of our beloved Khan of Khans. Oh, yes!'

She was speaking for her husband – something Robert had never seen before. 'But my husband is preoccupied by another matter. He has been granted a great honour by our general. A reward for his successful scouting trip in the south. Noyan Khuyag and the Golden Eagle *mingghan* will be the tip of the spear in the assault on the city of Otrar in two days. If he succeeds, he will be honoured with the title *baghatur*. You see, Subutai seeks to impress the Great Khan with his skill. Subutai has ordered that the city of Otrar is to be captured *before* the Lord of the Steppe arrives.'

Chapter Thirteen

'Haste is the enemy of siegecraft!' That was one of the Order's maxims that Robert had absorbed in his first year as a beardless novice in London. The Englishman pondered this bit of Templar wisdom as he lay in the darkness of the *ger* and listened to the snoring of Khuyag only a dozen feet away.

The Templars had other sayings, too: 'Failure breeds failure,' and 'Retreat saps morale,' and, more appropriately in the case of the siege of Otrar, 'God is watching – seize the moment!' That was a great favourite among the younger, more aggressive brother-knights.

But Subutai was *not* being too hasty in ordering his assault on Otrar – Robert had seen the breaches himself and determined attackers might force their way through them, if God willed it.

He knew, too, that it would be a brutal fight, accompanied by a terrible slaughter. So he understood the *noyan*'s reluctance to sacrifice the lives of his men, and perhaps his own life, in this most dangerous of assaults. Robert had a decision to make. And perhaps a dangerous action to take part in. There was the treaty to consider, of course – and Gilly. Always Gilly. He was no good to his younger brother dead. But he needed to impress the Great Khan. He needed to make the khan feel that Robert was – what was Ziani's word? – invaluable. And how better to speedily gain Genghis Khan's admiration and friendship, than to put his own life in peril in the Great Khan's cause?

It was an appalling prospect. And he was not immune to terror. Yet, if he lived, he must surely be rewarded. Perhaps with the treaty that would release Gilly from his torment. This would be by far the greatest gamble he had ever taken. So, as was always his practice, he looked to the Almighty.

He remained lying in his blankets, motionless; the Templars taught that God was everywhere – in the cloisters, on the battle-field, even in this stuffy felt tent in the eastern wilderness – and that he listened to all earnest supplications from the faithful.

Robert began by silently reciting the Lord's Prayer, as Christ himself had taught his disciples: '*Our Father, which are in Heaven, hallowed be thy name...*' When he had finished and was feeling calmer, he opened up his heart and asked the Almighty a simple question: '*Is it your will, O Lord, that I hazard my own life in the service of these heathens in order to save my brother?*'

He listened for a long, long time in the darkness of the tent, as the *noyan* snored, grunted, broke wind – and heard nothing beyond all those familiar, human sounds.

Then, just as Robert teetered on the lip of sleep, almighty God sent his holy messenger to him, in the shape of a shining vision of St Christopher.

The saint appeared in his mind in a white linen shirt and plain hose and sandals, and a billowing brown traveller's robe, with a cedar walking staff in his right hand.

On his shoulder sat a little boy, of about three or four years old, a boy of such blinding purity and glory that it could only be the Christ child. No, Robert could see now. It was *not* the Christ child – it was his brother Gilly, as a little boy, and he was sobbing. He looked up at Robert, his eyes wide as platters. 'They are hurting me, Rob, they beat me and starve me. Make them cease, I beg you!'

Then St Christopher spoke to Robert in a deep voice. 'Fear not the fires of battle, faithful pilgrim, your life is in God's hands! He loves you and holds you in his safekeeping. You shall *not* fall in this heathen struggle. Put your trust in the Lord. Take strength from his holy grace!'

The next morning, Robert unpacked his belongings from the large black case made of stiffened felt he had been given by Sarantuya. With Altan's help, he took out all his precious war gear and piled the necessary items outside the *ger* in the autumn sunshine. And then they began to inspect, clean and repair every item.

He scrubbed his mail coat with fine river sand and water, paying particular attention to the many spots of rust which had bloomed on the iron links during his long travels; and when the metal was shining and clean, he spread it out to dry on a bush before oiling it. Then he took out his flat-topped wood and leather shield, replaced a mildewed arm-strap, nailed down a corner that had come loose, and repainted the white leather-covered surface with a mixture of dried mare's milk powder and mutton grease. The red cross in the centre of the shield he made brighter by rubbing with a piece of madder root, which he then varnished over with egg white.

He set the renewed shield to dry against a large stone, admiring its bold symbol of the Christian faith, which now seemed to glow, very appropriately, like freshly shed blood.

He would fight in the breach under the protection of the Holy Cross, and that thought gave him comfort. Then he set about sharpening his arming sword and dagger, using a whetstone, while Altan, sitting beside him, took a soft rag and oil to his steel helm, to give it a proper warlike shine.

'You need not do this,' said Robert. It was the first time he had spoken to the Cuman that morning. 'You have no obligation to risk your own life alongside mine.'

'I swore an oath — did I not? To guard and protect you. You are foolishly going into danger. How could I *not* go with you? Would you have me break my word?'

'I could command you to stay here in the camp when the *noyan*'s attack goes in. Indeed, I believe I shall do so. Altan, you are hereby commanded to remain—'

'Foolish child,' Altan interrupted. 'You chatter too much. Finish your work!'

It was a far harder task to persuade General Subutai that Robert should be allowed to accompany the Golden Eagle *mingghan* in the first assault on the city of Otrar.

Robert and Altan were granted an audience with the *baghatur* in the great tent on wheels that afternoon. But Subutai was in a foul mood, busy with his plans for the attack, and in no humour to indulge the whim of a foreigner.

'You are the *elchin said*,' the general bellowed. 'You are an envoy – not a common warrior. If I allow you to be killed, the Great Khan will take my head, too!'

'I am both,' said Robert. 'And I shall not be slain. I had a vision last night, sent by God. He promised me that I shall not perish in this fight. But, if I am proved to be wrong and I fall to the shah's men, then it is clearly God's will that I perish!'

'The Eternal Blue Sky does not make such promises to mortal men,' Subutai sneered. 'Your Cuman will tell you. We are born under the vault of Heaven and we die under it, and Tenggri cares not how or when we fall. He is indifferent to our fate. All he decrees is that *one day* we must all perish.'

'God has promised that I shall live,' replied Robert. 'And my faith makes me strong!'

'I could have you bound and gagged and left behind with the women.'

'Yes, you could insult and humiliate me, this is true,' said Robert. 'But would that please your Great Khan? To know you laid hands on the envoy of a foreign land?'

'I will take no responsibility, *elchin said*. I will not sacrifice even one of my brave riders to protect you. If you choose to seek death, I wash my hands of you.'

'I absolve you of all responsibility, General. And now I must take my leave.'

–

Robert rode his gelding through the Mongol camp before dawn the next morning, looking about him as if with new eyes. He looked into the solemn faces of the people he passed, and sensed the same leashed excitement as in the days before, but today he found them all to be beautiful. The babies looked especially wonderful to his eyes in the cold morning light, each one a perfect little soul; the grown men all seemed sturdy, robust creatures built of sheer vitality – all human strength incarnate. Every young woman appeared to be as fresh and lovely as the dawning day itself.

The iron-link mail coat was slightly loose around his shoulders, and the links crunched together a little as he moved with the horse. He realised that he had lost a considerable amount of weight since embarking on this arduous journey. He wore a plain black surcoat over his mail and had slung the freshly painted shield over his back. At his waist on the left was the arming sword, at his right a dagger with a razor-sharp nine-inch blade hung in its sheath, a replacement purchased in Sarai for the weapon he had hurled at the Rus' at the ferry. And if these were not weaponry enough, he had tucked his flanged mace, that killing club, in his belt near the base of his spine. The slung shield tapped against it as he rode through the mud lane between the dozens of *gers* in this part of the camp.

He kept his face impassive, but in truth he was filled with a horrible icy fear – and he readily acknowledged this truth to himself. However, he was determined that he would not let that fear prevent him from doing his duty. He muttered another prayer to St Christopher as he rode along, beseeching the saint once more to ward him in the fray, and guide his sword arm in the name of Jesus Christ. His enemies this day were Saracens – followers of the Prophet Muhammad – the same foe his Brethren had faced in the Holy Land for a hundred years. Surely God must condone their deaths. They were infidels – the eternal enemy. Furthermore, he would be killing for Gilbert this day – killing Saracens here to free his brother from torment in a Saracen prison in Jerusalem.

'I put my trust in you, O Lord. Let your will be done,' he said out loud, terrifying a goat that skittered from under the path of his horse's hooves, bleating in distress.

The Golden Eagle *mingghan* was formed up just inside the encircling wall that the marmot-men had built, but still a good half-mile from the walls of the city. The Mongol riders already sat waiting in three thick, loose lines of men and horses.

To their right was another *mingghan*, whose name Robert did not know, and beyond that, yet another. Subutai had committed three thousand of his riders to capturing the breach – one third of his army. If these three *mingghat* won through, thousands more Mongols would surge in after them.

He lifted his eyes to the battered walls and saw that the breach was – as Deng had promised – considerably wider than before. The marmot-men had done their work well. A length of wall fifty yards long had been lowered, and before it lay a jumbled stairway of broken stone from the walls right down to the plain, a rough stairway up which an agile man might clamber to reach the summit.

The indentation in the wall was much deeper on the left, the eastern side, where the original breach had been made, but the wily engineers had managed to join up the first hole with the second, the smaller one. It would be treacherous underfoot, easy to slip and turn an ankle. And for the Mongols, trying to force a way through the gap at the top would be a terrifying foretaste of Hell.

Yet it could be done – yes, Robert believed it could be done. He could now see the tiny black figures of men scrambling over the upper parts of the rubble stairway, defenders attempting to shore up the gaps with bricks and baulks of wood. He heard the thump of a trebuchet, and watched a missile arc through the air and crash into a hunched group of the shah's men on the right-hand side of the breach. They vanished in a huge puff of dust, snatched away to the next world in an instant.

He halted his horse beside Noyan Khuyag, who ignored him. Taghachat, who was the *noyan*'s second in command, gave him an affable – even carefree – grin and a little wave. Robert grinned back, aiming for the same fine insouciance in the face of death – when in truth his guts were filled with iced water. He nodded to Altan, too, who was beyond Taghachat, but received only a scowl in return. The Cuman had ridden out before dawn to tell the *noyan* that Robert would be joining his assault.

The four men sat in silence for a while, their horses a length or two ahead of the three loose Mongol attack lines. The gelding stirred restlessly under Robert's thighs, snorting and violently nodding its head, seeming to protest its owner's current folly, and he quieted it with a soft stroke of his hand on its neck. He could clearly hear the gentle murmuring of the Mongol cavalry behind him – men exchanging words of comfort with comrades, old jokes, a few boasts, too – and the continual chink and click of the accoutrements. Then Khuyag turned his head to look at Robert for the first time. His bloodshot eyes were glassy, as if he were in a trance. He seemed not to be entirely present.

'I must be the first through the breach, *elchin said*,' he said. 'It must be me. Yes? I will not allow *you* to steal my glory, foreigner. I shall be first into Otrar and thereby earn my status as *baghadur* – hero! You will remain behind me at all times. This is an order. You understand?'

'I hear you, *Noyan*,' said Robert. 'That honour shall be yours alone.'

Then came a distant rumbling rattle and both men looked towards the city walls. Prompted by a trebuchet strike, a new section on the extreme right had collapsed: a small avalanche of grit, small rocks and larger stones, bouncing down like tumbling skittles, a yellow cloud of dust rising.

Taghachat said, '*Noyan*, look, our attack flags are flying!' and pointed behind them.

Robert turned and saw that two Mongols were standing on the flat top of the encircling wall, each with a big yellow flag in his hands, waving it back and forth.

'The Golden Eagles will advance!' bellowed Khuyag. 'For… ward march!'

And the *mingghan* began to walk slowly towards the battered walls of Otrar.

The gelding could sense Robert's fear and excitement; it badly wanted to run, and the Englishman had to restrain it so as not to canter wildly out in front of the advancing Mongol line. They were three hundred paces out from the wall when the *noyan* gave the order to go up to the canter and then swiftly up to the full gallop, and with great relief, Robert finally allowed the animal to stretch out its long legs.

They thudded over the hard ground, once a field of barley, the Englishman revelling in the thunder of thousands of hooves on the sun-baked earth, and the beginning of a mad, surging sense of reckless joy. Robert saw that the walls of the city, now racing towards him, were thick with the helmeted heads of the defenders.

He shouted out the name of Jesus Christ and found himself filled with a wonderful, calming sense of his holy power. A few moments later, the arrows began to fly from the battlements and fill the air around the galloping men with their lethal hiss.

Robert heard grunts of pain behind him as the shafts struck home in the Mongol ranks, but he did not turn to look. He spurred on and, in no time, he found himself beneath the breach, reining in beside a jumble of rock and stone, and leaping from his horse's back. The Mongols in the second and third ranks of the charging *mingghan* behind them were loosing their own arrows now, shooting from the saddle above the heads of the rapidly dismounting men, trying to weaken the double-rank of Khwarazmian defenders, hundreds of them clutching spears and shields, that had appeared high above them in a bristling line at the summit of the breach.

Robert drew his arming sword, and hooked his left arm through the loops of the shield. A wicked javelin, hurled from above like a thunderbolt, landed in the earth by his right foot, sinking in six inches. He shouted, 'For God and St Christopher!' and plunged forward, upwards, scrambling onto the nearest stone block and beginning his ascent to the breach. His heart was hammering, his breath sawing in his throat, but he was buoyed up by zeal. He was aware of the *noyan* a few yards ahead, forging upwards, scrambling up the slope, and there was Taghachat just a pace behind his commander. Robert stole a glance behind him and saw Altan coming up, stumbling on the rubble and shouting something about staying back, calling him a foolish child.

All round Robert were climbing Mongols, shouting, cursing, leaping up the rubble stair towards the top. The air all about him was thick with arrows and spears, slicing past like a lethal rain. Through the flickering missiles he could see above him the grim, bearded faces of the defenders – Armenian hillmen, he thought, armed with spears, axes and spiked shields, the men all linked together in a tight wall. Behind them stood a mass of archers from the heartlands, from cities like Isfahan and Zaranj; hundreds of Afghan javelin men were up there, too, hurling death down upon them.

Robert lofted his shield, sucked in a great, hot breath, and continued to climb.

A pair of arrows, one after the other, thwacked into the face of his shield and he hunched a little under the wooden protector, raising its edge to eye level before taking another step up the unstable stairway. Another arrow hissed past his ear; one snagged at his black surcoat. One hit his shield and bounced away. He sensed the men of the *mingghan* around him, just shapes and colours: Mongols shouting; flat, snarling faces, cursing and climbing. But he felt himself surrounded, too, by a blaze of bright colour and noise, a blaze of glory. But men were staggering and falling. Dying. The blizzard of missiles never slackened. Something clanged off his steel helm, jerking him back.

He recovered his stance, forced his legs to move, shoving his body up the shifting slope of small stones and dirt beneath his feet with his will alone. His belly now seemed filled with sour and bitter soup; he could taste it in his throat. He was possessed by a desperate urge to empty his bladder and bowels. A Mongol, his chest transfixed by a javelin, blundered into his path and collapsed, coughing blood.

Again Robert yelled, 'For God and St Christopher!' and felt his strength rise. He forged upwards, thighs burning, boots slipping in the rubble, eyes smarting from the swirling yellow dust, leaping from one boulder to another, up, up, ever upwards.

A hurled javelin skimmed his mailed shoulder, a glancing blow that ripped through surcoat and iron links without harming him, but which knocked him to his knees. Mongols were dropping all about him now, scores of men cut down by shafts and spears, bleeding on their knees, one man screaming with an arrow embedded in his eye. There were bodies, stacked, to both his left and right. He saw Taghachat cowering behind a huge boulder, his round shield studded with half a dozen shafts. Yet still the *mingghan* battled onwards, upwards. A rock the size of a pig, falling from above, bounced past his head and effortlessly swatted away a man just behind him.

Khuyag was just a dozen yards ahead. Alone. He had an arrow in the meat of his shoulder. But he was still staggering up the loose scree towards the thick line of foes now just a few yards away at the summit. Robert forced his body upright, and began to climb again, following the line that Khuyag had taken, trying to join him. There were three or four men on either side, Altan at his right shoulder, his shield hoisted high, cursing and spitting unintelligibly foul words of pointless rage.

Robert snatched a glance behind and saw that the second wave of Mongols had dismounted and was coming forward, the first men now on the very bottom of the slope. The Mongol arrows still flew as well, hissing like adders as they passed him on both sides. The attack was still going forward, grinding up that terrible blood-slick slope. He trod on the body of a wounded man and heard him scream, ignored him and pushed on, the summit now only three paces away. There was a sharp crack of stone on stone and he sensed rather than saw the trebuchet missile – a head-sized boulder – plough into the line of defenders, punching a ragged hole in the defence as it ripped their bodies away. For a brief instant, a wide gap was created in the enemy battle line. And Khuyag was in there, shoving his body into the space, hacking at

Armenians on either side with his sword. A Mongol joined him, lunging with his spear at a terrified archer.

Robert found a further surge of power – God-given, without a doubt – and his shaky legs carried him right up hard against the bristling wall of Khwarazmian axemen.

He shouted 'For Christ!' and hacked at a bearded face, the man shrinking away from the blow. A Mongol arrow flashed past his cheek and took one enemy – a man directly to his front – full in the face, knocking him back. Into the gap his falling body made, Robert shoved his shield, his body following that cross-blessed protector. His sword flickered out, slicing a man's throat, taking a life. An Armenian hacked at him with a shining blade. Robert blocked with his arrow-stuck shield, feeling the axe sink into the wood, and his counterstroke with the sword cracked into the man's skull.

He felt the full red rage of battle possess his limbs, and give them extra strength; he struck left and right, punching with his shield, hacking with the sword, trying to widen the gap that had been made in the enemy line. Khuyag was away to his left, still battling. Altan was now on his right. Both men were fighting like demons, slashing and cutting, killing Armenians with awful efficiency. Demon-like men – enemies? comrades? – were screaming, howling, spitting out their rage around him now. Robert cut down a slender archer with his sword and, with his backstroke, drove back a yelling Armenian axeman. But for every man he felled or forced a few paces backwards, another two Khwarazmians seemed to spring up into the space he had just created. He killed again, and again.

He caught a glimpse through the throng of the tower of the Blue Mosque, and saw how scarred and chipped its once beautiful tiles had become after weeks of the trebuchet onslaught. Then it was gone from view, filled by a knot of shouting, red-faced, bearded men. He parried a mighty axe blow with his arming sword and the old Genoese blade shattered under the force of the collision. As Robert ducked to avoid the second axe strike, hurling aside his stump of a sword and groping for the flanged mace at the small of his back, Altan stepped forward, stabbed, twisted his blade and eviscerated the axeman before his lethal blow could fall on his master.

The air hummed, reeking with blood and shit, with piss and mortal fear. The noise was deafening: shouts and screams; a weird low moaning from the wounded. Robert, gasping for breath, stepped back a pace from the line, brandishing his mace and battered shield.

The enemy line once more was full and whole – a barrier of snarling faces and polished helms, linked round shields and steel points – and his booted feet were mired in a slurry of entrails and dust.

There was no sign of Khuyag. Altan had disappeared among the crush of yelling *mingghan* men pressed up against the still-intact wall at the summit of the breach. A pair of howling Mongols appeared at his shoulder, charged forward, and were instantly cut down by the swinging blades of the axemen. A javelin, hurled over the heads of the Armenians, hammered into his shield. The point, splintering through just above his forearm, knocked him staggering backwards. He stumbled down the slope, lost his footing in the treacherous rubble, and crashed painfully to his knees.

A Persian arrow, loosed at close range, chopped the top-right corner off his shield and grazed his face, opening up a cut above his brow that immediately began bleeding a torrent. Robert, still on his knees, wiped the streaming blood from his eyes and looked back down the slope. The attack had faltered. The slope was now littered with hundreds of dead and dying Mongols. The arrows lay in drifts like black snow. And the troops of the third wave of Mongol attackers were milling around at the bottom of the slope. Hesitating. One of their officers was yelling at his men, grabbing and shaking them, urging them to climb the blood-soaked rubble stairway to Hell, but many Mongols were drifting away now, loosing shafts, then edging back towards their tethered horses.

Ten yards above Robert, at the face of the enemy wall, a maddened, blood-soaked figure was still hammering at the wall of enemies with his sword, the blade held in both hands. It was Khuyag, battle-deranged and badly wounded. As Robert watched, an officer behind the wall – a young man – gave an order and pointed directly at Khuyag.

Robert had a flash of recognition: the elegant oiled beard, the long Persian nose.

It was Karacha, the Otrar merchant, his amusing friend, no longer sipping sherbet in a colourful silk robe and loose trousers on a pile of cushions, but very brave and fierce in a shining coat of metal plate, sword in hand, a steel helmet with a nodding plume on his handsome head.

An Afghan spearman, responding to Karacha's order, stepped out of the ranks and hurled his javelin at Khuyag, who saw it coming and twisted his body away. The long missile caught him anyway, punching into his ribs on his left side. Khuyag wheeled away down the slope, the spear in his flesh, and fell down, convulsing, yet still trying to rise only half a dozen yards from Robert.

A trio of arrows pattered about his body. A spear landed in the earth beside Robert's skinned right knee. All around him, the Mongol wave was retreating; the warriors were stepping back down the slope, shields high, their bodies hunched behind them. Some Mongols were even running full pelt down the slope, skipping like goats from rock to rock. The attack was over. The assault had failed. Robert, too, had the urge to flee. His earlier rage was long gone; he longed to bound away like the others, as fast as he could down the dusty stair. To safety. No one could blame him for it.

The attack had failed. There was no point in dying uselessly here.

He looked up at the wall of enemies that still filled the bloody breach; it was thicker than ever. He saw the merchant Karacha again, still behind the line, directing the archers with a cold and ruthless efficiency. Their eyes met. A bearded Armenian right next to Karacha was in the act of loosing a shaft directly at Robert, and he saw the merchant quickly raise a hand and seize the Armenian's bow, pulling it, spoiling the man's shot.

Robert looked over at Khuyag, still trying valiantly to rise again, cursing and spitting blood, and he knew then he could not play the craven. He hauled his own body upright, threw aside his ruined shield, and staggered over the rocks towards Khuyag. He seized a double handful of the Mongol's *deel*, and with a massive heave he lifted the *noyan* onto his shoulders. An arrow slashed through his surcoat sleeve, the point snagging on his mail coat beneath. Then Altan was beside him, his shield lifted high in protection. Helping to guide Robert's shaky booted feet as he lurched unsteadily down the rubble stair with the limp *noyan* slumped like a corpse over his back.

Other men came running to his aid, too. He half-saw Taghachat on his left, face bloody, helping to support the *noyan*'s lolling head, as their tight group of survivors stumbled, slipped and half-fell down the last part of the rubble stairway, and staggered towards the remaining horses on the flat, arrow-strewn ground below the victorious walls.

Chapter Fourteen

'So he will live, *elchin said* – this is what you are telling me?' said Subutai. 'You believe that big, donkey-headed drunkard Noyan Khuyag will live to see another dawn?'

It was the morning after the disastrous attack on the breach, and Robert was sitting with the general in his huge wheeled *ger*, drinking fresh mare's milk and eating ripe peaches. He had just finished making his report to Subutai on the disastrous assault on the Otrar breach, but he knew the general had also received several full accounts from his own people.

'I have no gift of prophecy, General,' said Robert. 'Nor am I a Hospitaller. All is in the hands of God, but yes, I think it likely that the *noyan* will live for a while. If his wounds do not sicken and corrupt, and if he's allowed to recuperate for some months.'

'I suppose you think yourself a hero, *elchin said*. A true *baghatur*. A man to whom we must bow down and show gratitude? We should feel honoured that you bravely carried the *noyan* safely back down from the breach. Is that what you think?'

Subutai was furious. And Robert knew he had every right to be. More than seven hundred Mongol men had been killed in the assault on the breach, and twice that number had been wounded and injured, with a good many of those likely to die, and Subutai had nothing to show for it.

The dead and wounded had been left scattered all over the slope, and Robert had heard from Altan that the enemy had come down from the breach after the attack to slit the throats of the wounded.

Subutai had thrown three full *mingghat* at the walls and lost two thirds of their number for no gain. No wonder he was angry. Genghis Khan was coming, and his master would not be impressed.

'I did what I thought my duty, no more,' said Robert. 'I seek no gratitude.'

Subutai made a disgusted growling noise with a mouthful of juicy peach. He swallowed mightily. 'Tell me, then, O humble *elchin said*, since you insisted on being present during that stupid bloodbath below the walls of Otrar, why did our assault fail?'

The Englishman pondered his reply. 'In the event, the breach was not wide enough. The defenders were also too numerous – and they were clearly forewarned of our intentions. And your Mongol soldiers… Well… Your men are cavalry, very fine cavalrymen, but they are not infantry. They are used to swift movement and fast action, not the dull, trudging push of patient spearmen. The attack up the slope was not pressed with determination. At the top, only a handful of our warriors were actually testing the Khwarazmian defences. Many watched from below, loosing their arrows. Too few men actually climbed up into the fight. And there should have been a diversionary attack at the other breach. To thin their numbers and confuse them about our true intention—'

'Enough! That's enough for now. I will hear all your suggestions later. Tell me this… Khuyan commanded the assault. Did he, in your wise opinion, fail in his duty?'

Again, Robert thought long before answering. He was torn between honesty and protecting his host, the man whose *ger* sheltered his body at night.

'The *noyan* fought bravely. He was the first man to attack the breach—'

'That is not what I asked. Did he fail in his duty?'

'If his duty was to fight with all his courage and strength, then yes, most certainly Khuyan did his duty… to the best of his ability.'

'Khuyan's duty was to lead his three *mingghat* to victory.'

'If his duty was to capture the breach, the answer is obvious. Why ask?'

Subutai laughed. 'I believe that the Great Khan will relish conversing with you, *elchin said*. You are as hard to grasp as an oiled snake. The khan will like you.'

Then he called for a servant to bring a moist cloth to wipe his peach-sticky hands. Another servant brought out a warm, damp towel for Robert's hands, too.

Subutai finally leaned back on his silk cushions, and let out a long breath. 'We have endured a setback, *elchin said*,' he said. 'And the Great Khan will not be pleased. We need to consider our next move carefully. What is your counsel? How would you take the city?'

'I have the seed of an idea, General. But, first, may I ask you a question?'

Subutai inclined his balding head, his yellowish eyes glittering with interest.

'How soon will I be granted an audience with Genghis Khan?'

'If you continue to prove useful to me, *elchin said*, I shall recommend to the Great Khan that he speedily grants you an audience. If you are *not* helpful to me, if you are obstructive, or refuse to answer my questions, then who can say when – or even if – the Great Khan will have time for any such meeting, even with so great a personage as the ambassador of the Republic of Venice?'

An hour later, back in the *noyan's ger*, half a mile from Subutai's massive tent on wheels, the stink of blood was thick in the air. Khuyag had been wounded in the shoulder, a deep puncture wound, and in other places, too. Arrow cuts, mostly, some mitigated by his armour, but which had caused him to lose a great deal of gore. Sarantuya had cleaned his many wounds, washing them with rice wine, packing them with a herb salve, and bandaging them tightly with clean linen strips.

The javelin in the ribs – the last wound he had taken – might well have killed a lesser man, but the *noyan* had been extraordinarily lucky. The spear had broken a rib and ripped a long bloody trench in the flesh of his left side, but it had not penetrated his lungs, nor his viscera. Robert had examined the wound closely before it was bandaged, looking for the telltale red bubbles that would mean the lung had been pierced. But he saw nothing but the slow ooze of watery blood coming through the half-dozen big horsehair stitches that his wife had sewn in his mangled flesh.

'God clearly watched over him in the battle,' he said to Sarantuya, when they had finished their ministrations. The woman was washing her gory hands in a basin of water, and looked up at him from under a heavy curtain of her midnight hair.

'You think your God was in that terrible place of death and pain?' she asked.

'God is everywhere,' Robert replied. 'Mountain, valley, desert and sea.'

'Then he is nowhere,' she said. 'He is nothing. If your god is equally present in the hideous slaughter of battle, and also in the joy of lovemaking, in the nursing of a newborn baby, and in the daily shitting out of a good turd, then he is undiscriminating. He has no sense at all of which place is right and which place is wrong. He is no more than an empty space. A void. A nothingness.'

Robert could sense the anger coming from her like steam off a boiling pot.

'God preserved your husband, lady. Without God he would surely be dead.'

'No! *You* preserved him. *You* saved him and brought him home from the breach.'

Robert did not know what to say to that. It almost sounded as if she was berating him for bringing her wounded husband back alive from the battlefield.

'You do not believe, Sarantuya, in the power of almighty God, then?'

'Come with me, *gadaad khun*,' she said, rising to her feet and taking his hand in hers. Robert felt a rush of hot confusion. He intensely disliked her calling him 'foreigner', but the touch of her warm skin against his palm was intoxicating.

Sarantuya led him briskly out of the *ger*, and he followed unresistingly.

They stood together in the late autumn sunshine by the entrance to the tent. And Sarantuya pointed upwards with both arms towards the cloudless heavens.

'There is the true god, *gadaad khun*,' she said. 'That is Tenggri – the Eternal Blue Sky. When the Sky Father and the Earth Mother came into being, all the people of the world were created between them on the steppe. But Tenggri also creates death. Human beings were created to die. Accordingly, all men and woman pass away in death until Tenggri breathes life into them again.'

'What of the soul? What of the spirit that makes you, Sarantuya, you? You will die, and I will die, but if we put our faith in Christ, our souls shall live on for ever.'

'Where is your soul? Can you show it to me?' Sarantuya cocked her head on one side, and looked up at him.

'I cannot. The soul is invisible – it lives inside our hearts. But it is *eternal*.'

Sarantuya snorted with disbelief. She pointed over at an ornate spear that had been thrust into the ground just to the right of the *ger*'s entrance. The ten-inch steel blade gleamed; the wooden shaft had been carved with symbols of animals – deer, yak and hawk. Ribbons of red and yellow silk and dozens of black braids of horsehair were attached high up on the shaft, just below the blade.

'That object,' she said, using the special tone she used when she was teaching him, 'is a *sulde*. That is the Spirit Banner of Noyan Khuyag and his household.' She gestured at the upright weapon. 'No, do not touch it, *gadaad khun*. That spear contains the holy essence, the sacred honour and the fighting spirit of my husband. See there the many horsehair strands, affixed below the blade – they come from the very best stallions in our family herd. See them dance in the wind? When Tenggri moves the horsehairs with his wind, he infuses them with his power.

'When my husband dies, his spirit will go into that spear, into those horsehair braids, and there they will stay until Tenggri gives him life again as a newborn baby. That is Noyan Khuyag's soul. There. You can clearly see it, no? Where is yours?'

'Is this what all the Mongol people believe?' asked Robert.

Sarantuya laughed, which surprised Robert – faith was no cause for mirth.

'Some believe this, some do not. Some worship only the mountains or the rivers. Some of our warriors are devout followers of the Prophet Muhammad, and some adhere to the Yellow Religion of the Chinese, which insists you must not kill any living thing. Those bald fools! Some are even worshippers of the Christ child – like you, *elchin said* – and who believe in the wisdom of a long-dead prophet called Nestorius. Each may choose what they wish to believe. Tenggri or Buddha or nothing at all. Is this not the only way to have harmony among so many different peoples?'

'That is not something we would allow in my land,' said Robert. 'Nor in many others. Men die for their faith. But tell me... what does the Great Khan believe?'

'Genghis has a Spirit Banner – indeed, I have been told that he is so great a personage that he has *two*. A white one and a black, one for peace, one for war.'

'He worships Tenggri? I heard a whisper that he might be a follower of Jesus? Even that he might be a Christian? Have you ever heard the name of Prester John?'

Sarantuya shrugged. 'No. And what does it matter what he believes? That is his affair. Neither does the Great Khan tell his people which god they must bow before. All are equal in his eyes. Christian or Muslim or Tenggri, they are the same to him.'

Robert was so astonished by this, he found he had nothing to say to her.

–

The arrival of Genghis Khan whipped the whole encampment into a frenzy. All the men who were not on duty set about cleaning and mending their gear, sharpening swords, making arrows, combing their horses' coats, oiling hooves and plaiting tails.

If the Great Khan ordered a grand review of his army, they wanted to be prepared. No man wanted to seem unkempt before the Khan of Khans, and their officers berated and chivvied any who had so much as a loose thread on his *deel*.

The women were equally energised: sweeping out the *gers* with wiry gorse-bush brooms, sending clouds of dust flying in the air outside their doors; beating carpets with willow wands; washing all their cushion covers, clothes and bedding near the rivers and drying them on bushes.

They brewed *airaq* and dried venison strips in the sun, in case the Lord of the Steppe stopped by their *ger* and required feeding. The older women also cooked special rice flour dumplings, filled with shredded mutton and cabbage, or salted cheese and honey, and fried in best mutton grease.

The children were excited as well, stealing dumplings right out of the hot pan, despite the scolding of their elders, then running outside the *ger* to leap on their ponies and ride out recklessly fast to meet the first elements of the approaching Mongol host. These swift, shrieking ragamuffins, some no more than six or seven years old, but already riding like centaurs, accompanied the sedate columns of *mingghat* as they approached besieged Otrar, greeting the new arrivals with shrill cries of welcome, and pleas to be recruited into their ranks. Subutai, flanked by his bodyguards, rode out to meet the Great Khan in a more dignified manner, and personally escorted him into the camp.

Robert and Altan were also caught up in the whirl of preparations. Robert bathed himself thoroughly in the river Arys, and washed his whole body twice over with rough hearth-ash soap. Afterwards, Altan trimmed his long blond hair and his bushy beard. Then they carefully looked over the precious gifts that Niccolò Ziani had given them in what seemed like another age. Something had chewed the peacock feathers – a hungry rat, perhaps, or a tribe of marauding mice – and they now looked sadly tattered. Robert gave them to Sarantuya, saying they were a mark of thanks for the hospitality. She accepted them, frowned at the rat-gnawed edges, and gave him only muted thanks.

Robert then rooted out the Ravenna Bible, which had been blessed by Pope Honorius III, and examined it with awe. It had been bound in soft kidskin, which had been covered in a thick, protective double-wrapping of waterproof waxed linen, which had thankfully defied all the rats and, more importantly, more than one dunking in various rivers on the way east. They both looked at the decorated inside of the Bible, marvelling at the illustrations in metal leaf and paint. The huge initial letters of each book in the holy tome had been coloured with gold and silver, painted in sky blue or scarlet, or brilliant greens, and adorned with caricatures of weird beasts and trumpet-playing angels.

It was a glorious object, a triumph of craftsmanship – as was the tiny crystal box, bound in gold wire that contained the fingernail of the Apostle St Peter, the Rock on which Christ had built His Church. The mere touch of these two items gave Robert a sense of virtue, and even of holiness.

He allowed himself to imagine that these two simple but magnificent gifts might inspire Genghis Khan – who now seemed unlikely to have any link to the fabled Prester John – to embrace the faith and eschew his pagan sky worship. And Robert discovered within himself a fresh zeal to accomplish his mission. He would shortly meet the Great Khan, secure a fine treaty with the Lord of the Steppe, and, after returning west in triumph, arrange for his poor brother Gilbert to be speedily freed.

Robert pulled a clean white surcoat with a crimson cross painted upon his chest over his *deel*, and dispatched Altan hotfoot to Subutai's *ger* with word that he was ready to meet the Great Khan.

'Tell him to inform the Khan of Khans that the ambassador of the Doge and the Great Council of the Republic of Venice wishes to present him with precious gifts.'

Then Robert accepted a cup of *airaq* from Temulun, Sarantuya's ancient mother, and sat down to wait. He waited all that afternoon and, in the evening when Altan finally returned, the Cuman said he, too, had been made to wait outside Subutai's *ger*.

'But you *did* deliver my message to General Subutai, did you not?'

'I told him that you were ready,' said Altan. 'And he acknowledged my words.'

'Did he say *when* Genghis Khan would have time to see me?'

'He did no more than grunt at me, *ezen*, then waved me away.'

'It's too late now for an audience. Do you think he will see me tomorrow?'

Altan shrugged. He was eating a big bowl of *shulen* and eating it unnecessarily noisily, slurping a good deal. He kept his eyes doggedly on his food as Robert spoke.

'The Great Khan must know I have been waiting weeks to see him,' continued Robert. 'He cannot delay us much longer. This is an important treaty – I am sure Subutai will have told him. It will be as beneficial for Genghis Khan as it is for Venice. Why is he keeping us waiting?'

Altan mumbled something through a big, wet mouthful of mutton stew that might possibly have been, 'The steppe is wide!'

–

Robert waited three days, then a full week. Then he resigned himself to proper knightly patience. He rode out into the wilderness for a couple of days with Altan, to give their horses a good run before the cold season set in, and he also spent some time playing dice with Deng, the commander of the Yellow Battery, in his tent near the front lines, and losing a stack of silver pennies from Ziani's diminishing hoard. He did, however, gain information from the engineer to offset his loss.

'Did you hear, *elchin said*, about the assault on the southern breach?' Deng said, collecting up his winnings and pouring them into his leather belt-pouch.

Robert had not. 'Another game?' he said hopefully. 'Double the odds?'

'No, *elchin* said. If I take a little money from you, no one is hurt. If you win a great deal from me – or I from you – then one of us may become angry. And perhaps we will no longer be friends. We have amused ourselves for a time. Better stop now, eh?'

'This assault,' Robert said, chewing a fingernail. 'I heard nothing about it.'

'It was a small affair. One of the Great Khan's newly arrived *mingghat*, full of youthful fire, and looking to impress the khan, or perhaps shame Subutai, attacked the southern breach three days ago. General Odegei's men led the assault, I believe.'

Robert realised that it must have taken place while he and Altan were away.

'They went in at night, charging up the slope using ladders and ropes, hoping a sudden attack would work. But with just one *mingghan*. They were repulsed. Bloodily so. And now Genghis Khan is angry with General Odegei, or so I hear.'

The trebuchet batteries had orders from the Great Khan to continue their bombardment, despite the advent of winter, which caused serious problems for the hard-working marmot-men. Robert listened attentively to Deng's woes as he was served fragrant tea by the engineer's servant. The big machines had kept pecking away at the walls, day after day, but at a much slower pace, barely quicker than the enemy could repair the damage. It had turned cold at night, too, and the pine-wood throwing arms of the trebuchets became brittle if they froze, and were prone to snapping under the strain. One throwing arm of a machine in the battery had snapped only three days before and the flying splinters had killed one of Deng's best engineers.

Worse, the defenders of Otrar had become emboldened by the failure of the two assaults. Two days ago, a force of Afghan javelineers had crept out of the city and fallen on one of the batteries – not the Yellow Battery, thank God – but they had slaughtered some of the Jin crewmen of the Blue Battery and many of the local workers, too. They had managed to set two of the battery's trebuchets aflame before running back to the safety of the city. The two machines had since been repaired or replaced, but it was an unhappy omen. Deng shook his head and sucked his teeth in regret.

Yet not all the news was bad. While Robert kicked his heels around the camp, waiting for a summons from the Great Khan, agonising about the delay and what that might mean for Gilly, he was heartened by Khuyag's recovery. While the *noyan* was still very weak, he was getting stronger.

When Robert examined the injuries three weeks after the disastrous attack in the northern breach, he saw that they were all scabbing nicely and there was no smell of corruption. Khuyag was now able to hobble about the *ger*, and even went outside for the first time since he had been wounded to do his personal business. The *noyan*'s mood, however, remained morose. He seldom spoke, save to curse Sarantuya if she failed to bring him what he wanted quickly enough.

Robert did a calculation one day and realised it must be only a few days until the Feast of the Nativity, the day on which Christians celebrated the birth of the Saviour. He consulted Sarantuya, and received directions to a *ger* on the far side of the Mongol encampment in which a group of Nestorians were said to worship their God.

On the eve of Christmas Day itself, washed and dressed in his best clothes, Robert presented himself outside this *ger* and, after the usual introductions, he handed them a generous gift of a package of frankincense, in remembrance of one of the Magi who had given a similar gift to the Christ child in Bethlehem. Robert then asked if he might join their service of Mass this holy night.

The service was not a joyful experience for Robert. Instead of the familiar sound of struck bells, the Nestorians loudly beat flat metal shingles to mark the usual offices of Holy Mass. And these strange Mongols – men and woman who called themselves

Christians – seemed bemused by the gift of frankincense, as if they had never seen, or even heard of, this most holy incense before.

Their so-called Christian rituals were subtly different and spoken in the Mongolian tongue, which gave Robert a strange, uncomfortable feeling. Latin, surely, was the only proper language for the true faith of Jesus Christ. But most unsettling of all was the fact they had no crucifixes, no images of Christ suffering in his Passion. They venerated a plain unadorned wooden cross instead, a drab, dull object, which felt completely wrong. Almost like a blasphemy.

Yet he kept his mouth shut and joined in and took what comfort he could from the Mass. As he received Holy Communion, and recited the Lord's Prayer in bad Mongolian, he felt a longing, an almost overwhelming desire to be back home. Back in the little chapel in Hadlow, perhaps, with the priest droning on and his father grumbling to young Gilly about sitting in a draught. Or with his Brethren in Acre, attending the church of St Anna. How he missed the camaraderie of his knights and the sense that what they were all striving for was right and true. Here he felt miserably alone.

Robert even wondered then, in that stuffy, crowded Nestorian *ger*-church outside the walls of Otrar on Christmas Eve, whether the rest of his own world still existed. Were any of the Latin kingdoms still holding out against the Sultan of Egypt? Perhaps, in the twenty long months he had been gone, the Christian realms had been swept into the sea. Perhaps even the Order of Poor Fellow-Soldiers of Christ and of the Temple of Solomon was no more. How could he know out here?

'Almighty God,' he prayed, when that strange service was nearly concluded, 'grant me this from Your mercy. Watch over my people, and my Order, and the holy homeland of your son Jesus Christ. And move the heart of the Great Khan, stir his mind and cause him to offer me an audience. Bring us together in your name, and open his ears to me, so that we may swiftly agree upon a fine, honourable treaty, which will allow me to return home and rescue my brother from his suffering.'

Chapter Fifteen

Two days later, Robert's prayer was answered. Altan came running into the *ger* with snow on his boots, startling everyone, and almost bursting with his excellent news.

'The general says it will be today,' he panted. 'Subutai will come in one hour to collect you – and he will escort you into the Great Khan's presence. The Lady Sarantuya is to accompany us and act as translator, should you need her assistance.'

It was the largest *ger* Robert had ever seen. Much like Subutai's, it was built on a vast flat wooden platform and constructed of wooden lattices and ash poles and huge pieces of thick grey felt cloth, but despite its great size – it was a good fifty paces across – it was oddly plain. Where Subutai had silk wall hangings in marvellous patterns and colours, the Great Khan's walls were adorned with plain black cloth. While Subutai and his guests reclined on soft cushions as wide as a man is tall, and filled with airy goose down, the Great Khan sat on a plain blue square of dense matting, with his advisers and generals on similar mats on either side, conversing freely, some – shockingly – even interrupting the khan while he was speaking.

Robert, Altan and Sarantuya approached the Lord of the Steppe, and made their bows before him, and then Subutai *Baghatur* introduced the Englishman.

'I present to you, O Great Khan, Robert of Hadlow, *elchin said* of the Republic of Venice, a land far to the west, beyond the Sea of Ravens. He has gifts for you.'

The half a dozen men chatting on the mats all fell silent and Genghis Khan looked up at the Englishman. And, for the first time, Robert looked into the eyes of the most powerful lord on Earth.

-

'Finally,' said Father Ivo, making a note on his little wooden-backed tablet. 'You have finally brought us to your meeting with this Tartar potentate. It has taken you long enough. So, did you receive your treaty? Did you get the heathen king to agree?'

'All in good time, Father,' said Robert. 'There is a great deal of this tale left to tell.'

'There may be a great deal of story to tell, but there is not a great deal of time. You have five days before the duke will bring you up before his court. Five days before His Grace may well decide to hang you. May I suggest that you try a little harder to speed your story along?'

'I shall try, Father, to speed the story along, as you ask. But it is a long tale and there are parts that must be told in order, for the whole to be comprehensible. I cannot just leap ahead to the end.'

'Five days, Sir Robert. You have five days before an end may be made of *you*!'

-

The Great Khan looked unremarkable, at first. An older man of near sixty years, dressed in a plain blue woollen *deel*, baggy blue leggings and reindeer-skin boots, with slightly narrow but very shrewd eyes, and smooth, lightly tanned skin, with a few wrinkles from sun and wind around the eyes and mouth. Both his ears were pierced and twin gold earrings hung from the lobes. His forehead was high, lightly creased, and he wore a plain white linen cap, which covered any remaining hair on his round head, with a long white cloth tail that fell down his back, to protect his neck from the harsh steppe sun.

His eyebrows, moustaches and wispy beard were all long, grey and silky. But most striking of all was his serene expression. He gazed calmly up at Robert, observing him in great detail, from his Mongol boots, cloth belt and *deel*, to the flowing white surcoat he wore over the top and the blood-red cross emblazoned on his breast. His gaze lingered on his blond hair and beard and his blue eyes – and yet he took in this outlandish-looking foreign ambassador without betraying emotion at all.

'You are the warrior who fought in the first breach in the walls of Otrar with the Golden Eagle *mingghan*, are you not?' he said. His voice was deep and musical.

But there was something extraordinary about this ordinary-seeming man: he radiated power, like heat coming off a stove. Robert could feel it warming his face.

'I had that honour, Great Khan,' he said. 'I am sad we were not more successful.'

'I thank you for your great service to my people. Your courage has been noted.'

'Your Majesty is most gracious.' Robert turned slightly and beckoned Altan forward. 'I shall, if I may, present these marvellous gifts, a fitting tribute to you from the Doge and the Great Council of Venice. I have brought these items over half the world to give to you, as a gesture of our goodwill towards the whole Mongol nation.'

Robert took a square package from Altan's hands, took two steps towards Genghis Khan and knelt, keeping his eyes down, and held out the small square object towards the Great Khan. The Lord of the Steppe did not move, but one of the younger men sitting next to him got quickly to his feet and went forward to take the package from Robert's hands. He carried it back to the line of men sitting around the khan, promptly drew a knife from his belt and began to slice at the wrapping.

Robert had to bite his tongue to prevent himself begging the impatient fellow to stop hacking away so crudely at the waxed-linen coverings.

'Who's that clumsy man?' he whispered to Sarantuya, at his elbow.

'That is Odegei, Genghis's third son. His second son, Chagatai, is sitting on his right. His youngest son, Tolui, is the young man on his left. His eldest son, Jochi, is not at court at present. He is off with his *tumen* scouting the Syr Daria north of here.'

Once he knew, Robert could see the resemblance between the khan and his sons. Odegei, the one wielding the dagger on the package, looked most like him: he was in his middle thirties, with a wider and much coarser face than his father, but similar features and the same shrewd, narrow eyes.

'It's a book,' said Odegei, sounding disappointed. Then he casually tossed the gift over to his father, who caught it effortlessly in the air with his left hand.

'It is *the* Book,' said Robert, watching as Genghis Khan turned the Bible over and over in his hands, and finally opened it to look at the beautiful illustrated pages.

'It is the true word of God,' Robert continued, 'which has been blessed by the touch of Pope Honorius himself. There are, in truth, no more than three or four similar Bibles in the world. It's a holy treasure, and the wisdom contained within its covers is the foundation of the Church and the whole Christian faith. I sincerely hope, great lord, that you will treasure and revere this gift for all your long life.'

'You are most generous,' said Genghis Khan quietly, looking up again and smiling, before handing the Bible to one of his servants. 'I shall indeed treasure it.'

'I have one more very special gift for you, Your Majesty.' Robert found he was sweating heavily, although the huge, draughty tent was very far from warm.

Once more he beckoned Altan forward and, this time, he removed the crystal box from its silk bag before kneeling and presenting it to the Great Khan. Once more, Odegei came forward and snatched the gift from him. Genghis Khan's son peered at it, examining it inches from his face.

'Is that a little bit of... fingernail?' he said, incredulously. 'Yes, it's a tiny sliver of a dead man's nail! Eugh!'

'It is a holy relic,' said Robert stonily. 'It is the sacred fingernail of St Peter, one of the disciples of Christ, and later an apostle. St Peter founded our Church in Rome.'

Genghis Khan looked briefly at the gold and crystal box before passing it over his shoulder to a servant. 'It is very fine,' he said. 'I thank you for both your gifts.'

'That holy relic has been known to do miracles,' said Robert, feeling unnerved by the lack of enthusiasm displayed by the khan. 'A blind boy in Ancona who prayed before St Peter's fingernail was cured of his sickness overnight! A lame old woman was made able to walk just by its touch!'

'Oh,' said Odegei. 'It's a *magic* fingernail! That will be *very* useful.'

Robert wasn't quite certain – but he thought he heard the Mongol prince snigger.

Genghis Khan shot his third son a hard look. Then he turned back to Robert.

'We thank you for your most generous gifts, *elchin said*. Please convey our pleasure in due course to your masters in Venice. You now have our leave to depart.'

Subutai was at Robert's elbow and was tugging him away from the group of Mongol men sitting on their plain blue mats, now all conversing animatedly again.

Robert turned to the general and hissed, 'I have not had the chance to speak to him about the treaty yet. I have not even mentioned it. I must be granted more time.'

'Be patient, *elchin said*, the Great Khan has a great deal on his mind. He has a city to take, a war to win… an empire to conquer. You will have your chance soon!'

—

'Do not be downhearted, *elchin said*,' Sarantuya said the next day. She was making fletching for hunting arrows, gluing small feathers onto flint-tipped reed shafts and tying them in place with silk thread. It was fine work, requiring deftness. She didn't look at him while she worked but Robert, entranced, watched her slender fingers dancing over the reed with feather and thread – so nimble, so precise. So entirely beautiful.

'Be patient. Did you expect the Great Khan to begin a detailed discussion of gold and silver, swords and sheepskin, coloured beads and...' She seemed to flounder trying to think of other trade goods. '...peacock feathers at your very first meeting?'

Robert shrugged and scowled. He found he was filled, these days, with a restless impatience that he had not felt since the last long, dull, snow-bound winter in Tana.

It was snowing once again, thickly now, and the siege had ground to a halt with the trebuchets only loosing perhaps once or twice a day to show they were still present. The Mongol soldiers were all huddled round their hearths in their *arbat ger*, when not on duty around the encircling walls, and Robert was beginning to feel confined, bored – eager to agree a treaty and go home and begin negotiations for Gilbert's release. He realised that his brother had by now been confined for more than a year. What would a year in a dark, damp cell do to the young man's body? Or to his soul?

'Patience is a virtue, I am told,' said Robert, smiling at Sarantuya. Altan, who was playing a complicated Mongol game with Khuyag involving stones on a board, looked over and laughed at him. 'It is not one of *your* virtues, *ezen*,' he said. 'You are an adequate fighter, I will admit, but you have all the patience of a greedy child.'

Robert ignored him.

Khuyag said, 'The Great Khan must think about overcoming our enemy first, *elchin said*. The Khwarazmians laugh at him, safe and snug behind their high walls.'

'What if I were to *give* him Otrar?' said Robert. 'What if I held the key to opening up the city? What if I opened it and allowed him to surmount its walls?'

'Are you drunk?' scoffed Khuyag.

'He must reward you,' said Sarantuya. 'The khan could deny you nothing.'

'Be quiet, woman! The *elchin said* is either slobbering drunk or he has gone mad from sitting around in the *ger* all day long. If there were such a key to open the city of Otrar – and there is *not* – our friend does not possess it. Unless he has another one of those magic fingernails and intends to wield it ruthlessly. Ha ha!'

'There!' said Sarantuya, rubbing her hands to rid them of strands of dried glue. 'That is another batch of twenty shafts made up.'

She got to her feet. 'You may be right, husband. The *elchin said* has been kept inside the *ger* too long. I propose a hunting trip. There are deer in the eastern valleys, I am told, and we could use some meat for our pot. If the snow stops tonight, let us all ride out at dawn and look for the herd.'

Khuyag coughed wetly. 'I am not yet ready to chase after deer,' he said.

'But the *elchin said* should have some sport, breathe some fresh air,' she countered.

'You take him out, then,' said Khuyan. 'And bring me a fresh deer liver to roast. I need some good bloody nourishment to strengthen my own blood.'

–

It felt good to be alive that dazzling dawn. Robert and Sarantuya cantered away north-eastwards from the dirt and bustle of the Mongol encampment and soon entered a pristine snowscape, which seemed as if a human had never set foot there before. Altan had cried off the hunting trip, saying he had a runny nose and fever – the same illness that afflicted Khuyan and was delaying his recovery.

Therefore, Sarantuya and Robert rode out alone, the Englishman a little self-conscious of that fact, since he had rarely been alone with her before outside the walls of the *ger*.

He asked questions to fill the void – many questions, mostly about Mongol hunting practices – and Sarantuya patiently answered him, describing in detail the *Nerge*, the great hunt, which was not only a way of feeding the tribes of the Mongol nation but also an effective training for warfare.

'I hope you will see it, one day, *elchin said*,' said Sarantuya. 'It is a glorious spectacle! Magnificent – but sad, too! Khuyag took part in one last year with the khan in the high country of the Kara Khitai. And I was fortunate enough to accompany Genghis Khan in his kin party. We began with a line of warriors so long that it stretched out of all sight – someone told me the line was as long as a man could ride in two days. Dozens of *mingghat* were involved in the great hunt – some say all the riders of the Mongol army who were available to the Great Khan that year.'

'I would like to see that one day,' said Robert. She seemed to him to be more fully alive that morning, away from the confines of the *ger*, away from Khuyag. She seemed excited, even joyful, her dark eyes sparkling, her slim body upright in the saddle, full of grace and power. Her mount that day was the same stallion she had tamed in the willow enclosure on the day that he had first seen her, the young animal now thoroughly broken to the saddle. Her hair was unbound this day, as it had been then, and flowed free, black and glossy as jet against the blinding white of the snowfield.

Indeed, she looked astonishingly beautiful. When he looked at her he lost his breath.

'A visible landmark is agreed by all the commanders of |the units, an end point, the killing ground of the *Nerge* – are you paying attention, *elchin said*? – and then, when the killing ground is agreed, the long line of warriors begins slowly to advance, each warrior remaining within arm-touching distance of his comrades on both sides.

'As the hunting line advances, the extreme left and right wings begin to slowly converge upon the centre. Like two great arms reaching forward to grasp each other. Each *mingghan* obeying the commands of the drums and the flags, to co-ordinate their movements, until the wings join up many hours, or even days, later, and a huge circle – a noose – of mounted warriors has been formed over a vast area of land. It is an area the size of a tribal hunting ground, ten or twenty times as large as the land occupied by the city of Otrar and all its villages, and this noose contains thousands of animals – musk deer, wild sheep, saiga antelope, black-tailed gazelle, yaks, camels and wild ponies, but also tigers, leopards and wolves... Then the vast ring begins to tighten—'

'Look over there,' said Robert, pointing to their right. In the far distance, a good half-mile away, Robert could see a line of tiny shapes, running in single file across the snow. It was a small herd – half a dozen red deer, running across the pristine fields to the north, heading to the safety of a little white-capped copse on the horizon.

'Did we frighten them?' he asked. 'Have they seen us?'

'They don't run from *us*,' said Sarantuya. 'They only seek the wood's shelter.'

She reached behind her and took the small recurved bow from the wide leather holster on her stallion's flank; she had a quiver of arrows by her knee, but did not withdraw a shaft from it yet. Robert touched the Mongol spear he had borrowed from Khuyag, pulling it out of the little socket by his right stirrup before dropping it back in its place. It was not Khuyag's Spirit Banner, of course – merely an ordinary battle spear, of which the *noyan* had several – but still a formidable weapon: a twelve-foot wooden lance with a foot of steel at the end and a sickle-shaped hook behind the long blade for pulling an enemy off his horse. He looked at Sarantuya. She grinned and nodded once in confirmation, and they both began to advance silently on the distant copse.

'As the noose of men grows tighter and tighter, the animals inside the ring begin to panic,' Sarantuya said, speaking very softly now, even though they were still four hundred paces from the copse which hid the deer, 'and these creatures in their frenzy try to break out of the line of men.'

They were advancing at a walk; their hoof sounds were deadened by the thick snow. 'Some succeed,' said Sarantuya, 'but most of the animals are confined in a smaller and smaller area. I have seen wolves snapping at lions, and wild goats butting yaks in their fear and in a desperate effort to escape. No man may kill an animal, not even in self-defence, until the Great Khan gives the word.'

The copse was getting close. 'On that day,' she said, 'the Golden Kin – we members of the khan's family – gathered on a bluff overlooking the valley in which the noose of the *Nerge* had gathered all the animals. It was a disturbing sight, *elchin said* – thousands of animals, all mad with terror, fenced in by the wall of horse-warriors. Snarling, bleating, lashing out with claw and hoof—'

Robert held up a hand to silence her. He thought he could see something moving in the copse. A dark shape fifty paces away. He wiped his eyes with his gloved hand, trying to ease the ache from the snow glare. They slowly advanced another twenty paces.

There was an explosion of noise, a cracking of branches, and a huge stag, with antlers as wide as Robert's out-held arms, crashed out of the dark wood, heading across their line of advance.

And behind the stag came a line of leaping red deer.

Three, four, five animals came bounding out of the darkness and cover of the wood and galloped straight across their path. Robert immediately put back his spurs and urged his gelding forward, and the eager horse responded by surging from a walk to the full gallop in a matter of moments. He took both the reins in his left hand, plucked the Mongol spear from its socket and flipped the shaft under his right armpit, taking aim at a fat young animal two places behind the great horned stag that was streaking away, leading his deer tribe across the dazzling snow.

'Not the doe!' yelled Sarantuya. 'She is carrying. Spare her, *elchin said*.'

Robert glanced over his shoulder and saw Sarantuya was only a length behind. She had dropped the reins around the pommel of her saddle and was guiding her stallion with her knees. In her hands, the recurved bow was already drawn, a black shaft nocked. Even as he watched her, she loosed, and the speeding arrow smacked into the haunch of the last deer in line, a young buck.

The impact of the arrow strike threw the buck's back legs off their course; the animal faltered, twisted awkwardly, the shaft stuck deep in his flesh, then it recovered. And bounded onwards, now three full lengths behind the last galloping deer of the herd.

Robert slammed his heel into the gelding's flanks, urging the horse to even greater speed. And his mount responded, leaping forward like a greyhound. Robert saw another arrow flash past and appear in the wounded deer's neck, above the right shoulder, the steaming blood running thickly down the animal's tawny flank. Robert's horse was only yards away. The buck was failing fast, mired in its terror, its blood flowing freely, its movements becoming wild and uncoordinated.

Robert changed his grip and drew back his right arm. He hurled the lance with all his strength at the animal's right flank.

He knew the throw was good even before it left his hand. The heavy spear plunged into the young animal's running side, the blade entering deeply, crunching through the ribs, punching into the cavity inside, the sharp blade slicing through organs and arteries, lungs and ligaments, creating massive damage. The animal ran on for another three full bounding strides, and then quite suddenly collapsed, tumbling horn over hoof, then coming to a sliding halt in a bloody sprawl in the snow.

Robert reined in, panting, his breath making great clouds in the air. Sarantuya hauled up beside him an instant later. They grinned at each other like happy children.

—

'Yet not all the frightened animals captured in the *Nerge* are killed, *elchin said*,' Sarantuya informed him solemnly, after wiping a dab of deer-grease from her lips.

'Some are trained to be hunters for the Great Khan. There was an old man of the Merkit tribe who trained a leopard cub. The animal wore a gold collar and the khan would feed it raw meat.'

They were sitting on a fallen trunk in the gloom of the copse, next to a crackling fire on which they had roasted two chunks of meat cut from the deer's haunch. The heat of the fire had melted the snow round them, and the overhang of the trees above gave their eating spot a cosy, cave-like feel.

Robert could smell her scent, even above the notes of roasting meat and his own fresh body sweat. She smelled of grass, and a sweet flowery tang which was perhaps jasmine. Sarantuya had even thought to bring a leather sack of *airaq* with them to drink, and a few millet flatbreads, and the meal – just the two of them eating together – had an intimate, yet also an oddly festive feel. Robert could feel himself relaxing for the first time in a long while. He smiled at Sarantuya, enjoying the look of her, the planes of her face, the mere fact of her presence with him.

'But mostly the animals are killed,' she said. 'It is a great and terrible slaughter. Enough meat is harvested in just one day to feed the Mongol nation for half a year.'

'Is that why you said "sad"?' said Robert. 'The death of so many beasts is sad?'

'Yes, the death of any creature is a cause for sadness, do you not think so?'

'I believe God had a plan for all of us – and for all his birds and beasts, too. Some are alive only to provide sustenance for Man. To feed and clothe him, to serve him, too. Like that fine steppe stallion of yours. He was born to serve you, and only you.'

Sarantuya looked away. 'And women? Do they live only to serve men?'

There was a tone in her voice that made Robert frown. He saw that she now had a tight, fierce expression on her lovely face. He said, 'I know little about women. I had no sisters. And I have never had a wife or a sweetheart. I know even less of God. I cannot claim to understand His plan.'

'You had a mother, yes? Did she live only to serve your father?'

'She loved him. And he loved her. She died in childbirth. The baby girl, too.'

'I am sorry to hear it.'

They sat together quietly for a while. Robert poked at the fire with a stick.

'That must have been very hard for you, the death of your mother,' she said finally.

'I think my mother's death took the greatest toll on my brother Gilbert.'

'How so?' said Sarantuya.

'He became very quiet afterwards. He had been a happy little boy, always playing in the woods and fields around Hadlow, running down to the river Medway, always smiling, laughing. Then, when our mother died – he was about seven summers then – he suddenly became silent, and sly, slinking like a cat in the dark corners of the hall.

'He spent a lot of time with dear old Goody, our cook, helping her in her kitchen, allowing her to pet him and feed him her sweet pastries, and with Father Thomas, the Hadlow priest, who told him that his mother's death was God's will – as it was. But when Goody died, suddenly, of an apoplexy – she just dropped dead one day about a year after my mother died – my brother Gilbert had a fit. He seemed to be possessed by a demon and he went... Well, he went a little bit insane.'

Robert paused and took a sip from his bowl of *airaq*. 'Gilbert blamed Father Thomas for the deaths of Goody and our mother, and... and he tore down the crucifix in our chapel and hacked it apart with an axe. Then he pissed over the broken splinters. As I say, he went a bit mad. He got better after a few weeks. But it was a terrible thing. All Kent was shocked. He had to do penance for Father Thomas. And Gilly caught such a beating from our father that he was bedridden for days.'

'Did you not grieve for your mother also?'

'I did. I prayed for her. And I sometimes wept. But time heals all. And I know that God has a plan for all of us – the living and the dead. She is with the angels now.'

'Did your father never remarry?'

'No, Henry's health began to fail soon after. He is very ill now, near the end. If he is not already dead. I do not know. I suspect I shall not see him again in this life.'

'So sad. Tell me some happy thing – tell me something joyful to lift my heart.'

'Are you not happy? I am. I am filled with joy just to be here with you, Sarantuya. Alive. Healthy. In this snowy wood, in this very moment. Just us two alone.'

Sarantuya looked at him. Her dark eyes seemed to glint as if wet. 'You speak dangerous words, *elchin said*. I shall pretend I did not hear. Do you know the Mongol penalty for a married woman who makes love with a man who is not her husband?'

'From what I have seen of your folk, I assume the penalty for adultery is death.'

'It is death,' said Sarantuya. 'But adultery can only occur between two people of *different* households. It is only adultery when a married man of one *ger* lies with a married woman of another *ger*. The Great Khan has decreed that matters of the *ger* should be decided within the *ger*, and matters of the steppe decided on the steppe.'

There was a heavy silence between them, and each looked intently into the other's eyes, their faces inches apart. They were so close, Robert could smell her breath, a sweet milky scent from the *airaq*.

'Tell me, *elchin said*,' said Sarantuya, breaking the silence, 'why did you not marry? You are a fine-looking man. Strong. Brave. Slow to anger. Why did you never find yourself a good woman and set about raising sons with her? Are you not capable of begetting children? Or would you not like to have little ones? For myself, I would give anything to have a child – I would do *anything*. But I have never been blessed. My belly remains flat. Khuyag tells me my womb is unwelcoming.'

'I am fond of children. My older brother has a fine sturdy boy. But I made a vow to God, when I joined the Order, that I would preserve my chastity for His glory. I swore I'd never marry or lie with a woman. And I have never broken my promise.'

Sarantuya stared at him, astonished. 'Do you not find women or girls to your taste? You do not like us? I know that some men prefer to bed pretty young boys—'

'Christ, no, that is an abomination. I like women very well. But it is in the resisting of their charms that I make my commitment to the Lord, and thereby prove my worth. I serve God, not my own desires, and by serving God, and his only son Jesus Christ, I am in truth serving all mankind.'

'Your God is cruel to demand this. How does forsaking love benefit Him?'

'By resolutely turning my back on carnal sin, I honour the Almighty's commandments.'

'You are strange, *elchin said*. I have never met a man like you before. Do you not dream of lovely young women sometimes, when you are alone in your bed? Do not armies of pretty Christian girls come unbidden into your mind when you sleep?'

'Never!' said Robert stoutly.

'No?' she said. 'You have *never* dreamed of making love to a woman?'

The Englishman, reddening slightly in his confusion, declined to answer.

Chapter Sixteen

The shape of the burnt-out farm building was just another lump of darkness in the night. There was no moon, and a shifting blanket of cloud only occasionally allowed a glimpse of the speckle of stars. Robert pressed his body against the brick wall and looked south towards the loom of the fortress of Otrar. He could see the torches of the sentries high on the walls, tiny blazes of light, two hundred yards ahead of him. Only a few sentries were out this cold night, walking back and forth along the wall to keep warm, perhaps men who were being punished for some small military crime.

He was wearing a coat made from marten furs, given to him by Subutai, a thick wool tunic and tight leggings, and a turban of black cloth wrapped around his head, which meant that he was able both to withstand the cold and to blend in with the night. The snows had melted, but the air felt no warmer than when the earth had been covered by a frozen crust. Nonetheless, Robert was glad the snow had gone. He savoured the concealing darkness. He had blackened his blond beard with soot from the *ger* stove, too, before he set out on his mission, as well as his hands, face and neck.

He turned his turbaned head, very slowly, and looked behind him at the line of the Mongol-built wall that surrounded the whole of the Otrar area, and thought he could make out the boxy frames of the four mangonels of the Yellow Battery in front of it. The battery was silent that night, with only the occasional wink of a lantern to show that men were guarding it from an unexpected sally from the city. The trebuchets loosed their missiles now only during the day, and the intensity of their attack on the walls had lessened a good deal since the arrival of the Great Khan. Every commander knew that Genghis's sons Odegei and Chagatai had been given overall command of the capture of the city – and that Subutai had been demoted and humiliated in the eyes of all by having these two members of the Golden Kin set in authority over him.

Yet, if Subutai was bitter about his treatment, he did not show it to Robert when they were sitting in Subutai's *ger* discussing his plan to give Genghis Khan the 'key' to capturing Otrar. The general had decided not to discuss Robert's risky plan to take the city with his Golden Kin superiors – for his own private reasons – and he had brusquely ordered Robert to hold his tongue as well.

'Keep this only between us,' he had said. 'Yes? You want to talk about Venice and trade with the Great Khan, *elchin said*? Then this is the best way to command his attention. Execute your plan successfully. Hand him the city on a golden plate and the khan *cannot* refuse to grant whatever your heart desires. He would be seen as ungrateful, a miserly monarch who did not reward his servants.'

'But I have already risked my life for him – in the assault on the breach,' said Robert.

Subutai laughed. 'What you do not understand, *elchin said*, is that among the Mongols, success is *everything*. A Mongol does not expect to receive praise for trying his hardest. He either accomplishes what he sets out to do – or he fails. The assault on the breach failed. Khuyag failed. You failed. I failed. There is no reward for failure.'

'I shall do this,' said Robert slowly, 'and with a willing heart. But if I survive and I am successful in opening the city for the Mongol army, I must insist – indeed, I shall absolutely demand – that the Great Khan receives me *immediately* to discuss a treaty with Venice. I want this to be clearly understood between us, General Subutai.'

'It is understood. And, if you are successful, I shall make it my task to aid you in any way I possibly can to have a profitable meeting with the khan. Your success shall be my success. If you win through tonight – if your plan succeeds – we will both prosper.'

Robert waited until the two nearest sentry torches high up on the walls were moving away from him, then he scuttled forward away from the ruined building through the darkness – a hundred paces, then another fifty, being careful where he placed his boots on the uneven ground – before crouching in a frozen irrigation ditch, a mere fifty paces from the rubble of the stairway before the breach – the very place he had so disastrously attacked two months before. He could smell the decomposing bodies even in this bitter cold – a rotten, oily, stomach-turning stench.

The denizens of Otrar had half-successfully barricaded the breach at the top of the stony slope with baulks of wood, old furniture and new slabs of masonry, but when they had come out to try to dismantle the stairway, a few *jagghut* of Mongol cavalry had launched an attack and killed several of the Khwarazmian workers with arrow showers before they could all scramble back up to safety.

Now, the breach was half-blocked, enough to keep out a major attacking force, but the broken stone stair remained in place in front of it – along with the decomposing bodies of hundreds of men. Some were Mongol attackers killed in Khuyag's assault; some were corpses made more recently.

As he watched the moving torches of the sentries above him, which were approaching his position, Robert took his mind back, as he often did, to the long ride home with Sarantuya after their hunting expedition. They had both been quiet, walking their horses side by side, with the limp carcass of the young buck roped behind Robert's saddle. There had been a bitter-sweet intimacy between them in those hours – although nothing had occurred that might trouble a confessor.

Sarantuya had not committed the crime of adultery. Robert had not broken his vow of chastity. They had not even touched each other. They had merely talked for hours and shared their innermost thoughts. Nevertheless, while he might not have sinned in body, in his mind, he was as guilty as the worst felon. Robert experienced a whirling surge of emotion merely being in her presence, which he knew was deeply wrong. He felt a deep yearning, a kind of madness, which even he – a man who had shunned women – had been forced to recognise. It was love. Robert had fallen in love. And that knowledge was a weight in his heart. He felt his love for Sarantuya so strongly, it made him dizzy.

'This woman is the wife of another – a comrade of mine,' he had told himself. 'I can never possess her. I can never even tell her that I desire her – that I want her more than my next breath.'

He clenched his fists tight and tried to banish all these sinful thoughts from his heart.

'Khuyag is a brother in arms – a brother in all but name. And I am a brother-knight sworn to celibacy. I *must* remain staunch.'

But the Devil spoke to him often, teasing and taunting, in the long hours of the night, when he could sometimes hear Sarantuya's breathing. 'You are no longer a Templar, Robert of Hadlow – the Brethren rejected you in Acre. You're just a man, in a strange land, with the same wants as any mortal. Why wallow in suffering? The *noyan* is a brute, a drunkard, unworthy of your brotherhood.'

The torches were travelling away from his position again, as the sentries made their rounds, and Robert could hear the Devil's voice, even now. He had to move. He had to banish the seductive voice in his head with cold, hard action. He vaulted out of the frozen ditch, ran forward as silently as he was able, and began to climb the rocky stairway, finding it difficult in the darkness, slipping and stumbling. He climbed a dozen yards up the slope and felt something give under his right foot – and there was a terrible rumble and rattle of stones bouncing away.

The noise went on for a long time and seemed deafening to him – surely a giveaway. At any moment Robert expected to hear the shout of a sentry's challenge from above. And see lights. He froze in his position, his chest and limbs pressed tightly against the uncomfortable rocky slope, clutching at the gritty stones. His breath sounded too loud in his ears. His heart was thumping like a drum. He slowly twisted his neck to the right and peered up the slope, but he could see nothing above but the uneven, broken line of the half-repaired barricade.

He shifted his head again slightly and a sudden hideous waft of corruption filled his nostrils. The face of a dead man was only inches away. The soldier – a Mongol, he guessed, though he could barely tell – was lying upside down, perhaps fallen from above, and was facing him, his open mouth level with Robert's brow. The man had lost most of his teeth, either before death or after. Something was gently moving inside the dark cavity of his mouth. Robert caught a glimpse in the starlight.

Maggots.

Was this a foretaste of his fate? A warning? A message from God to reprove him for his arrogance in attempting this feat? Would his own body, too, soon lie unburied, discarded on some foreign field? God grant it should not be so. He turned his face away from the dead man's, closed his eyes and listened. All was quiet above. He waited a little longer, listening hard. Still he heard no sound. Robert pushed up from the rubble and, as quiet as a tiptoeing mouse, began to climb again.

Near the top of the slope, he paused once more, cramming his body into a large dark rocky crevice just below the line of the barricade. He could see flickering lights. He could hear a man's voice talking in Persian to his comrade above him. He listened hard: the fellow was saying something about a girl who was teasing him, accepting his lavish gifts but refusing to submit to his advances. His friend told him that many women he knew were difficult in this same way. But there was one dancing girl down in Samarkand whom he favoured above all the others… The two sentries were about three yards along the wall from Robert. And they had evidently stopped their patrol to converse with each other. Robert was almost overcome by a mad impulse to join in their conversation: to tell them that he, too, loved a woman he could never hope to possess.

Instead, he reached very slowly behind him, feeling around the back under the heavy marmot coat. He slowly drew the dagger with the nine-inch blade from its scabbard, and held it low in his right hand. A brutal tool of war. A killing steel. He silently urged the men above to shut up about their minxish women and move along. If one of them took it into his head to peer over the barricade – just a quick glance down at the long rubble slope – he was finished. He would kill them both, if necessary – he knew that he could do it – but he had no wish to end their stupid lives. Quite apart from the potential noise the two killings might generate, he felt a kind of kinship with them: they were all three tangled up in love's silky bonds.

Move, you stupid bastards. Move. The words were only spoken inside his head.

The two Persians exchanged a few more banalities about life and love, and then began to grumble enthusiastically about the scarcity of food in the long-besieged city.

The city grain stores had run dry, it seemed. Except for the governor's personal supply of barley in the citadel caverns, there was no bread to be had anywhere, not even for gold, nor for jewels – nor love. The people of Otrar were already eating their horses; soon it would be the turn of the cats and dogs. Even rats were being hunted down by the city's children. Robert set himself to remember all the details. Subutai would be pleased to know that his long siege was bearing fruit.

At last, the two sentries moved apart, one heading along the battlements to Robert's right, the other returning leftwards. When they were a dozen paces from him, Robert finally let out a long, huffing breath, and he realised that he had been holding it for what seemed like an age.

He waited a few moments more and then, as smoothly and quickly as he could, he slipped over the top of the barricade and onto the old stone walkway behind.

There was a set of stairs to his left – he remembered them well – and soon he was a shadow slipping down them towards ground level, and hugging the shadowed exterior wall like a ghost. He reached the street level, and drifted into the alley behind the Blue Mosque, stepping over chunks of broken masonry, the loose stone rubble crunching alarmingly under his boots. He turned right and found himself once again in a main thoroughfare, empty at this hour, and three doors along, he found himself knocking softly on a small green door set into the side of a long, low warehouse.

There was no reply to his knocking. He knocked louder.

Just as Robert was about to abandon the attempt to rouse the inhabitants of the warehouse and to seek somewhere to pass the night, the door jerked open and a sleep-fuddled, grey-bearded old man poked his head round the green-painted wooden jamb.

'Who knocks at this time of night?'

'I must speak with Lord Karacha – it is important,' said Robert in Turkish.

'He sleeps now – come back in the morning like a civilised person.'

The old servant began to shut the door, but Robert lunged forward. His shoulder hit the wood, with all his weight behind it. The door sprang back and struck the servant in the forehead, sending him tumbling backwards. Robert moved fast. He was inside in a trice, with the door shut and bolted behind him – and he had his dagger pressed under the chin of the dazed servant an instant later.

'Do not cry out, man. Take me to Karacha. I swear I do not mean to harm him.'

The servant goggled at him; he was a small fellow, shrivelled and trembling.

'Do not hurt me, lord,' he said. 'I beg you – I have a wife and little ones.'

–

'I had not expected to see you again, Englishman,' said Karacha, pouring out a cup of wine and offering it to the intruder, who was now sitting on a pile of silk cushions before him. 'Then I saw

218

you fighting like a fiend at the bloody breach and suspected one day this meeting would occur.'

'I apologise for the manner of my arrival.' Robert took a sip of the wine – thin, vinegary stuff, a far cry from the hospitality he had received here only a few short months before.

He made no comment on his host's reduced circumstances. Instead, he smiled at his companion. Despite the arduous – and, if he were honest, terrifying – journey he had undertaken to reach this man, this merchant, this friend, he did not feel fatigued. He was filled with a quickening sense of anticipation, brimming with a new-found energy.

Karacha had not screamed out or called for the city's soldiers when he had been roused in his bedchamber by the old servant. He had woken, seen Robert, grimaced, pulled on a robe, and invited Robert to come down into his hall at the far end of the warehouse for refreshment. But he looked wary – like a man inviting a wolf into his hall.

'I am heartily sorry for disturbing you at this hour, Karacha,' Robert continued, 'but I could think of no other way of contacting you.'

'You are here now. And so am I. To what do I owe the honour of this disturbingly clandestine visit? Have you come to sell me sheepskins? I would gladly take them from you this cold season.'

'Do you remember our conversations before I left Otrar?'

'As if they took place yesterday.'

'You remember that I said to you that I would reward you handsomely.'

'How could I forget?'

'Well, it is now time for your reward.'

'Oh, happy day!' said Karacha, smiling broadly again. But his smile never reached his eyes, which remained cold, hard and even more wary than before.

The two men stared at each other for a while in silence. Robert saw that his friend's face was thinner – drawn with hunger, perhaps, or by some terrible sorrow.

Finally, Karacha said, 'Perhaps you might like to tell me more about my handsome reward, since I'm forgoing a night's sleep while I wait to hear of it.'

'I shall. But firstly, I must ask you this question. Do you believe that Otrar can withstand the might of the Great Khan and all his Mongol armies?'

'Perhaps. It is possible the shah might come and drive the Mongols away.'

'I have seen your shah's army – I saw fifty thousand of his men waiting for marching orders in the south near Samarkand three months ago. But the shah hesitated. He could have come up to you then and, perhaps, relieved the siege. He chose not to. Now the Great Khan has three times that number of warriors. Indeed, he is *hoping* that the shah will come to him up here, so that he may crush him. I am sorry to say that the fall of Otrar is, my friend, inevitable. Your city will be taken, sooner or later. And every man, woman and child inside the walls will be put to the sword. If you look into your heart, my friend, you will recognise this to be the honest truth.'

'So my reward is knowledge of my doom? You are most generous, *my friend*.'

'I would preserve you and all your family from certain death. And make you very rich into the bargain – perhaps the richest man in all Khwarazmia.'

'I'm listening. And how would this miraculous transformation occur?'

'You would join forces with me, in a business sense, and act as my agent in buying or selling goods in Khwarazmia on behalf of the Republic of Venice. Do you not remember that I offered this position to you before I left the city in the autumn?'

'You talk of trade at this time of war? When there is nothing in Otrar to eat – let alone buy or sell. You talk of trade with Venice – a place I have never seen, never heard of before meeting you. With a Mongol horde at my gates? Are you mad?'

'You would rather wait till the Great Khan's horde are no longer at the gates, but inside your walls, and the utter destruction of every living thing in Otrar begins?'

'What do you want?'

'I want you to be my agent on behalf of the Republic of Venice.'

'I would like you to explain this, if you please. How can *I* trade with Venice?'

'I told you that I was the high envoy of the Doge and the Republic?'

Karacha nodded slowly. 'That was the truth, then?'

'I am here to make a treaty with Genghis Khan – a solemn, binding and exclusive treaty with the Mongol nation on behalf of my masters. The Lord of the Steppe will conquer Khwarazmia in due course, and once that happens every Mongol commander, from the meanest trooper to the Great Khan himself, will be swimming in the loot of a mighty empire. Gold, silver, jewels, silks and all manner of precious goods will fall into the possession of the victorious Mongols. If I can establish a treaty with the Great Khan, this abundance of wealth will flow like a great tide towards Venice, and you and I can grow rich on that tide, taking our fair portion of the profits of this westward flood of goods. You know the silk trade, if I recall. Imagine if all the silk in Khwarazmia came into the possession of a few Mongol lords… Think how cheaply they might sell that silk to us. Now consider how rare and expensive that silk would be in the West, where only the very richest can afford it.'

'I understand you, Robert. I have been trading silk for years, as did my father before me. But two things I must question. Will Genghis Khan truly win this great war against Khwarazmia? And can you really induce him to make a treaty with Venice?'

'The Mongols will surely triumph against the shah,' said Robert. 'They have conquered half of Cathay, as well as all the Kara Khitai realms north of here. Genghis Khan has united the warring tribes of his steppe lands – disparate folk who had been killing one another for centuries. I *know* he will triumph – I tell you that there are a hundred and fifty thousand Mongols on the Syr Daria right now. But even if you do not choose to believe it – consider the fate of Otrar, of your family, if you chose the wrong course. The shah has abandoned you to your fate – and, sooner or later, the Great Khan will knock down your walls and slaughter you all. Every single one of you. I can prevent that from happening. I can save you, if you will only help me. And, as for the treaty, I have the help of Genghis Khan's greatest general. Subutai *Baghatur* is my good friend. He will help me persuade his Mongol overlord to set his great seal to the treaty – but first I must gain favour with the Great Khan himself. Once that feat is achieved, the khan will agree to the treaty – I am sure of this.'

If he does not, Robert thought to himself, *Gilly is a dead man.*

Karacha stroked his little black chin-beard thoughtfully. 'And how do you plan to win favour with the Great Khan?'

'I will make a gift to him of the city of Otrar. In truth, *you* will give him Otrar!'

Karacha sat back on his cushions. It was clear he understood Robert's words. But he still looked shocked. 'What you are asking me to do is treason. A terrible crime. A sin. The blackest sin. You ask me to betray my city, my government, my shah… Do you know that I am commander of the Third Division of City Militia? You ask me to betray my comrades, my soldiers, my servants?'

'They are dead whether you help me or not,' said Robert cruelly. 'The Great Khan will kill them all. But you can save yourself – and your family. And what has the shah ever done for you? He has thrown your city to the wolves – he might have relieved Otrar months ago. But he did not. Instead, he left you to your doom. And Governor Inalchuq – you once told me he was your enemy. Do you truly care if he, or any of his greedy sycophants, survive the destruction of your city?'

Karacha stared at him, saying nothing. He swallowed hard; he swallowed again, his Adam's apple bouncing, but still the merchant had no words to share with Robert.

'When we sat down here tonight, my friend, you said to me that you suspected this day would come,' said Robert. 'What did you mean by that?'

'I thought you might come. I saw you in the breach and I know you saw me. I thought you might come offering something to trade, food or wine. Or possibly that, for our friendship, you might offer me a chance to escape. That is why I did not permit the Armenian to slay you.'

'I *am* offering you a chance to escape. You help me open the city of Otrar to the Great Khan – and your life, and the lives of all your family members, shall be saved. I swear this to you on my immortal soul. Then we shall both of us set about becoming richer than old Croesus of Lydia.'

'I no longer have a wife or a child,' said Karacha. 'My wife died a month ago of a fever – we have much sickness here. My only son died a few days later.'

'I am sorry to hear it. But you still live. Your wife would not want you to die needlessly. And you are young – you can remarry when this whole business is done with. You might have more children – a dozen offspring, two dozen, if you wish it.'

'This whole *business*,' said Karacha listlessly. He looked at the carpet.

'Dawn is coming,' said Robert, 'and I must go back to the Mongol lines. Make your choice, my friend. Will you live and be rich, and perhaps happy again one day? Or will you choose to die?'

'That is no choice at all,' said Karacha.

Chapter Seventeen

It was impossible to see with the naked eye at this distance: some five hundred paces. Robert realised that if he had not been told the precise area in which to look – just to the left of the scrubby bush, below the reddish stain on the rock – he could never have correctly identified the spot. But when he concentrated hard, squinting, he thought he could make out a faint vertical line of shadow as the large canvas sheet that tightly covered the wooden cargo door, painted the exact same grey-yellow hue of the sand-stone plateau, shifted in the wind. Then his eyes misplaced it again.

Karacha was a cunning man; Robert knew this. But this hidden exit from the tunnel leading out of the young merchant's warehouse seemed particularly inspired. This was how Karacha had managed to continue trading with the Mongols despite Inal-chuq's ban on that intercourse; this was how he had continued to trade right up to the arrival of Subutai's *mingghat* outside his city's walls.

Behind that yellowish canvas sheet was a wooden door, Robert had been told, which was barred with iron from the inside, and which led to a wide set of steps and a passage that rose in a gentle spiral through the massive sandstone outcrop on which the fortress of Otrar had been built. The tunnel then emerged in the darkest corner of Karacha's warehouse. The merchant's father had built this passage twenty years earlier using a team of imported – and highly rewarded – labourers from Yanikant, and swearing them to secrecy afterwards. Karacha had been able, via this route in times of peace, to smuggle illicit silk and spices into Otrar, and fruit, grain and sweet wines out of the city. But since Otrar had been encircled by Subutai, Karacha had reckoned the passage too dangerous to use – and neither had he dared to reveal its existence to the governor of Otrar's officials. So the passage had lain quiet and abandoned – indeed, almost forgotten – for the length of the siege so far.

Until Robert had come knocking at that green warehouse door a week before.

Robert had not *known* of the existence of this secret tunnel, but he had guessed it, or something similar, existed. How else could the merchant bring all his contraband into the city?

It had not taken long for Karacha to reveal its existence and location to his unexpected guest – once he had made up his mind to betray Otrar, he became a willing conspirator. And the two men had talked into the small hours; indeed, the sun had nearly risen before they completed their plans.

Then, after a meagre bowl of porridge, Robert had spent the day sleeping in Karacha's dark warehouse, before creeping over the breach again the next night, down the rubble slope, sprinting across no-man's-land in the darkness and returning safely to Khuyag's *ger* a little after midnight.

'He will signal when the door is unbarred,' said Robert to Khuyag, who was on his left, both men mounted on steppe ponies. Robert had judged his gelding too high in the shoulder for what he had in his mind.

Sarantuya's husband was nearly recovered from all the wounds he had taken at the breach and, on being told of the Englishman's secret mission, the *noyan* had insisted that he and the five hundred or so survivors of his Golden Eagle *mingghan* be included in this attempt. Khuyag and his men sought revenge for the hurts they had received and the good men they had lost in that breach. But General Subutai had given Robert another *mingghan*, as well, to help him carry out his plan.

A plan which was, in fact, simplicity itself.

The commander of the Black Lynx *mingghan*, a heavily armoured regiment, sat his muscular pony on Robert's right.

Noyan Tuguldur was a middle-aged Mongol, with a scar that bisected his face from right eyebrow to the left corner of his mouth. The Jin sword that had given him this mark had also sliced off the tip of his nose. Yet the *noyan* of the Lynxes remained a jolly fellow, who was clearly pleased to be going into action, and who treated Robert, whom he saw as Subutai's lieutenant and adviser, with great respect, almost as if the Englishman were also his senior officer.

'You are quite certain we can ride our horses inside this little marmot hole, *elchin said*,' Tuguldur asked, his hideously scarred face smiling up at Robert's.

'The merchant says it is as tall as two men and one and a half times as wide as his outstretched arms. He says he has transported bales of raw silk up those steps, big, heavy bales that must be carried by four men. So I would think we can ride inside the passageway.'

'If it is not big enough – no matter,' said Tuguldur. 'Black Lynxes can fight on foot just as ferociously as from the saddle. That is probably why Subutai *Baghatur* chose us for this task.'

From his other side, Robert heard a disbelieving snort from Khuyag.

'You are both clear on your ultimate objective?' Robert pointed at the city's northern gate, which was about six hundred paces along the city wall to their left. This cold morning, the walls and towers of that daunting barbican were thick with many extra men, who were watching this collection of fifteen hundred Mongol cavalry massed in front of the rubble slope of the original – and now fully blocked – breach. The summit of that fateful breach, too, had been massively reinforced with archers, axemen and javelineers.

Robert had considered making this attempt at night. He had balanced the danger of moving a mass of cavalry, in darkness, across rubble-strewn ground that might easily break a horse's leg, against the risk of being clearly observed by the enemy in daylight, and had decided that it would be much wiser to keep his plan as simple as possible.

'You and your officers have memorised the map – and the directions I gave you?'

'We know where we're going,' said Khuyag, and Robert glanced over at him. Once again, he wore that not-all-there, trance-like air, a glazed-over look in his bloodshot eyes.

'Fear not, the Black Lynxes will fulfil their great and glorious mission and—'

Robert cut Tuguldur off with a raised hand. On the battlements, a stone's throw along from the breach, a large flag had been raised. A green banner with three golden coins in the centre – the standard of the Third Division of the Otrar City Militia. It was Karacha's battle flag. No mistaking it as it rippled in the breeze. It was the signal.

'Do not delay too long, Noyan Tuguldur,' said Robert. 'Stay on our heels.'

He turned to Khuyag. 'Time to go, friend! Let us take this city for the Great Khan!'

–

The Golden Eagle *mingghan*, with Khuyag and Robert in the lead, Altan just behind the Englishman, and Taghachat supporting his *noyan*, galloped straight towards the rubble slope below the breach. They hoped to appear as if they were making another doomed attempt on that damaged section of the wall. To aid in this deception, the trebuchets had been hurling their missiles all morning at the defenders on the summit of the breach. The hooves of their ponies splashed and splattered in the mud, decreasing their momentum, and they had to ride around many chunks of masonry, the remains of ruined houses and tumbled stones fallen from the shattered walls.

The snows were long gone, but two days of chilly drizzle had made the ground before the fortress soft and spongy. As they approached the foot of the rubble slope, the arrows began to patter down upon them, and Robert found he was hunching his mailed shoulders against their fall. This was the price they must pay for attacking in daylight. *May God grant it worthwhile*, he thought.

The *noyan* bellowed a command and his five hundred riders turned their ponies' heads and began to gallop across the face of the sandstone plateau, heading east towards the concealed door.

They were there in a dozen moments, and Robert lifted his leg and slid from the saddle of his charging mount before the animal had come to a halt. He rushed towards the canvas sheet, seized it with both hands and, using all his strength, he hauled at the material, trying to drag it from the wall.

It was clamped in place, and even his full strength was not enough. Then Altan was beside him, and Taghachat, too, and together they ripped the canvas free. Khuyag and his men were milling around, shooting their bows from their saddles up at the battlements above, and their enemies responded by hurling rocks and javelins. From the side of his eye, he saw a Mongol trooper spitted, the man hunched in the saddle, the javelin rising out of his body like a sapling. But there were far fewer Khwarazmians on this part of the wall. No more than a handful, for most of the defenders were still massed at the breach, waiting for another foolhardy assault that would never come.

They stripped the canvas clean away to reveal a brown wooden door, hinged on the left side, and Robert found the handle, an iron ring set in the right side of the door at about waist height. He twisted the ring and pulled hard, straining at its weight, and slowly, slowly, squeaking, shrieking, shuddering, the door swung open to reveal a square, black interior and the beginnings of a dusty sandstone stairway.

'Torches,' yelled Robert, but the *noyan* was far ahead of him. Khuyag had a burning pine-brand, with a head of cloth soaked in oil, clutched in both his fists and, as Robert watched, he passed it to Taghachat, who set fire to a bundle of a dozen more torches. The Golden Eagles were still milling around outside, below the walls – and Robert could see they were taking horrific casualties from above. There was a sudden hammering of hooves and

Robert looked round to see the full-strength Black Lynx *mingghan* thundering directly towards them across the open ground.

He yelled, 'Inside – everyone inside,' and, grabbing a torch from Taghachat, he ran to his pony and swung up into the saddle. 'We will go in first, *Noyan*,' he shouted at Tuguldur, who, with the first *jagghun* of his thousand men, was now almost on him. 'The Golden Eagles will lead the way.'

But the Black Lynxes waited for no man. When they charged into battle they did not stop to listen to mere orders. Tuguldur, now looming over him, snatched the burning torch from Robert's hand and, without a moment's hesitation, he rode straight into the dark opening with a reckless and almost magnificent disregard for personal danger. And his thundering horsemen followed after him.

Robert could hear the dull clattering of their hooves on the sandstone steps and the heroic shouts of 'Give me victory... or give me death!' as hundreds of Mongol riders surged into the square entrance and swiftly disappeared up the sandy stairway, some men even riding two abreast alongside their *mingghan* comrades.

Robert shouted, 'Altan, to me. To me, now. We must get up there quickly!'

He forced his pony into the jostling stream of men, only vaguely aware of Altan and Khuyag on their mounts behind him as he kicked his animal up the broad winding stairway, one turn, and then another, other horses barging into his, squeezing him against the walls, the animals neighing madly, men shouting joyfully, their voices echoing, bouncing off the sandstone. A Mongol careered into him and he backhanded the man hard across the face, pushing his horse ahead of the furious man, upwards, round another turn until, in seemingly no time, he burst out of a large open trapdoor into the huge space of Karacha's long warehouse inside the Otrar city walls.

The first thing he saw was Karacha, cowering in the corner, a round metal shield above his head, his sword abandoned, as Tuguldur rained clanging blows down on him from horseback.

'Leave him!' bellowed Robert. 'He is a friend.' Tuguldur, in full fury, stopped his blow mid-strike, turned in the saddle and looked quizzically over at the Englishman, screwing up his hideous face in incomprehension. But he had stopped striking Karacha's shield.

The warehouse was filled with horses and riders, snorting, shouting, a hundred hooves clattering deafeningly on the wooden floor, but two Mongols were already dismounted and tugging at a long, sliding door in the front of that huge space. And more horsemen were erupting out of the black hole in the floor every moment, brandishing their weapons, yelling their savage war cries.

'This is this fellow's warehouse. He's on our side,' Robert shouted at Tuguldur, pointing at Karacha. 'Remember the city gates, *noyan* – you must get your men to the gates immediately!'

Tuguldur saluted with his sword. At that moment, the long door to the warehouse was slid back, letting in a wall of blinding light and a fine view of the dusty street outside.

'To the city gates,' yelled Tuguldur. And he turned his horse towards the wall of daylight.

'No, no, that way!' shouted Robert, pointing left. 'Follow the street round that way!'

'To me, brave Lynxes!' yelled Tuguldur, and he cantered out of the warehouse and into the streets of Otrar, his *mingghan* flooding out after him.

'That cut-faced goat-fucker shall not take the gates without me,' bellowed Khuyag. 'Golden Eagles, to me. Follow me – to the city gates! Forward, men! To the gates and glory!' Khuyag galloped out of the open sliding door and disappeared up the street. Yet there were still horsemen appearing out of the trapdoor. Dozens, scores of riders, most instinctively, made their way out into the street to join the stream of yelling Mongols heading east. Robert dismounted and threw his reins to Altan. Then he stood in the centre of the warehouse, arms wide, directing the riders into the street.

When the flow from the trapdoor had finally slowed to a trickle, he gathered a few of the Golden Eagles to him – only a dozen, but all Mongols from No.4 *jagghun*, men whose faces and names he knew – and he told them they had been chosen to be the *elchin said*'s personal escort in the city. And they were to wait in here with him.

Then, with Altan's help, he pulled the door closed. And, as he pulled the portal the final few inches to close it, he paused a moment and listened. He could already hear the sounds of battle – the clash of steel, the shouts and screams of injured men in Mongolian, Turkish and Persian. He could smell smoke on the air, too: the city already burning. Through the crack in the door, he saw a squad of thirty Persian spearmen in sky-blue silk tunics jogging past. Then a pack of Afghan cavalry. He hastily closed the door the last few inches and pulled the locking bolt across.

He went straight over to a dazed Karacha, and gripped his shoulder hard.

'You have done it, my friend,' he said, smiling at the merchant. 'Whatever happens now, you have played your part and played it admirably. I congratulate you.'

'I truly thought that Mongol brute was going to chop me in half,' said Karacha. But he managed a small, tight smile in return for Robert's.

'Stay close to me – and Altan, whom I think you will remember. You will be safe. But first we must sit tight here for a while. If the Black Lynxes and the Golden Eagles can capture the northern gate, then Subutai is ready to commit his whole force – three full *tumet* – to the attack. The whole of Otrar and its environs will be engulfed by his righteous fury. We will be better off staying in here.'

'I need a very large cup of wine,' said Karacha.

–

They waited until dark. Karacha packed his most valuable goods, his coin and treasure, into a large wagon, one pulled by four of the Golden Eagles' steppe ponies. He refused to leave without it.

'I have laboured ten years to amass this wealth, Robert,' he said. 'I will not abandon it to the looters. I care not that I lose my father's house, my flocks, my other warehouses and the goods in them. But this wagon and its contents I must have. *We* must have it, my friend, to create our future.'

Robert had planned to leave by the same route he had entered – back down the sandstone stairway to the base of the walls – but encumbered by the four-wheeled vehicle, that was impossible.

'We shall exit by the main gate, then,' he said. 'If you must keep your wagon.'

When they finally ventured out into the street, it was to plunge into a foretaste of the Devil's realm. All Otrar was aflame, or so it seemed, and the night-time city was lit by weirdly flickering reds and oranges, the air filled with the crackle and snap of burning wood and the screams of stricken folk. Black smoke rolled through the streets in great banks, choking and blinding them, which was a mercy of sorts, because it obscured the hideous scenes of destruction and carnage on every side. There were corpses *everywhere* – men, woman, even children had all been butchered; some of the bodies had been literally hacked apart. Many had been decapitated. Even Robert, who had been bracing himself for this horror, was shocked. Hot tears ran down Karacha's cheeks.

The party around the heavily laden wagon hurried on as best they could, but the corpse-clogged streets slowed their advance to little more than a crawl. The wheels of the wagon rolled through puddles of blood, garishly illuminated by torch-like buildings. One of the troopers attached a Golden Eagle flag to a spear and set it above the wagon, which acted as a protective talisman.

They came across an especially tall mound of bodies at a cross-roads – a place where Robert had once bought packets of honeyed nuts from a street urchin. The reeking pile of carcasses here was shoulder-high. The dead were old folk, mainly – although it was sometimes difficult to tell – with a sprinkling of young women and children. These corpses had been ordinary citizens who had apparently surrendered to the rampaging Mongol cavalry in the hope of receiving mercy.

Their hands had been tied behind their backs and their heads had been removed, probably with a couple of hacks of a sword. Then the headless bodies had been tossed on the pile with all the rest. The severed heads, perhaps two hundred of them in total, had been stacked neatly in three small pyramids by the wall of a house by some tidy-minded murderer. The men's bearded heads were all gathered in one gory pyramid, the women's in another, and the children's in a third.

Robert gazed at one head in particular – it had once belonged to a cheerful young nut-seller of his acquaintance, the Khwarazmian lad apparently still grinning at him, even in the grotesqueness of death.

The Mongol troopers kept their countenance throughout, but they were sometimes obliged to clear the torn bodies and parts of bodies aside, to allow the wagon to roll. Emaciated cats and dogs, mules and horses, were among the dead clogging the street. It took them near an hour to travel the six hundred yards to the gate. Robert spent most of that time fighting the urge to vomit.

He remembered the words Subutai had made him say to Inal-chuq when they met outside the gate to parley: 'Surrender to me now and receive my mercy, O people of Otrar, or I shall annihilate you all and leave not one stone of your city standing on another. Throw open your gates and kneel in the dust before me, and all who are innocent shall be spared. Dare to resist me and I shall slay all living things inside your walls.'

Subutai had been as good as his word.

They reached another cross-street and Robert looked west into the heart of the burning city. There was still fighting taking place in and around the citadel, the governor's redoubt, the archers on its battlements still loosing a lethal rain of arrows onto the mass of Mongol riders milling about below. But, as far as Robert could tell, the rest of the city had by now been completely overrun by Subutai's men, and the sack of Otrar was progressing almost exactly as the general had threatened.

He could see large crowds of victorious Mongol soldiers surging through the streets, some staggering drunk, barely able to walk, more sober ones pulling terrified Otrar citizens from their houses and putting them to the sword. Other Mongols were busy looting, breaking open doors and carrying out goods – high-quality cloths, silk hangings, mattresses, bedding, iron-bound coin chests, wooden furniture, copper cooking pots, baskets of fresh bread, skinned animal carcasses, barrels of sweet white wine... anything of any value that the exuberant soldiers could lift and carry away.

Then the smoke cloud ahead parted and more than two score mounted Mongols, perhaps half a *jagghun*, trotted out of the grey, greasy murk, heading straight towards them.

Their captain shouted something, pointing at Karacha's silk gown and turban – an order to attack, perhaps. Just in time, one of their Mongol escort shouted out that they were Golden Eagles, from the *tumet* of the West Wing, and their leader was a trusted lieutenant of Subutai *Baghatur*.

These Mongol riders reined in and gawped as the fully laden wagon rolled past them over the gore-stained cobbles. Robert was pleased to see some of Subutai's men were still under discipline.

As they passed by, their captain called out to the men of the escort, 'Good hunting, brothers!' and saluted crisply. Robert just nodded and smiled tiredly back at him.

When they finally reached the gate – sick at heart, in Robert's case – it was evident a fierce battle had recently been fought over that strong barbican. There were hundreds of bodies scattered round the base of the two towers, both Khwarazmian and Mongol, but the Mongol dead were being collected by slaves and stacked neatly to one side of the open space before the portal. The double gates of the barbican were wide open and all that stood in the way of their exit was a middle-aged *noyan*, and his young lieutenant, sitting on steppe ponies in the middle of the archway.

'What you got there, soldier?' asked the *noyan*, who sounded more than a little drunk. 'Some choice plunder, I have no doubt. The sharing-out place is by the apple orchard south of the West Wing encampment. You had best go straight there with all that lovely loot. Make sure you deliver it to the Chinese officials posted there – every trinket, every coin, every sweet drop of wine – or Subutai will have your heads before morning.'

'Not loot,' said Robert. 'It is this gentleman's property.' He indicated Karacha.

'He looks like one of *them* – a dirty cloth-head,' said the *noyan*.

'This high-born Persian is under my protection,' replied Robert, giving the *noyan* a glare. 'We're taking Lord Karacha to meet Subutai *Baghatur*. Where may he be found this hour?'

'Last I heard, *ezen*, he was up yonder at the citadel, where those mule-stubborn cloth-heads are still foolishly defying us. You are going the wrong way. Wait, wait... Aren't you the *elchin said*? I have heard of you – a big *gadaad khun* with yellow hair like a demon, who speaks bad Mongolian.'

'I am he. If Subutai is busy, I will attend the general when he is at leisure. Now let us pass!'

The *noyan* bowed to him in the saddle and guided his pony out of their way. He gave a crisp order to the guards and the heavily laden treasure wagon slowly rumbled out of the gates of Otrar.

Chapter Eighteen

The *ger* was empty when Robert returned to it. He guessed Sarantuya and her mother were watching the fall of the city from some convenient viewing place. And Khuyag, he supposed, was still fighting somewhere inside the walls, perhaps with Subutai. So he quickly arranged for Karacha to stay with the senior man of their escort, and enjoined him to watch over the merchant and his precious wagon with equal care. The fellow was called Minquat, and his *ger* was only a few hundred yards from Khuyag's, and it seemed as good a place as any to lodge the exhausted Karacha. Robert did not feel confident enough yet to introduce a new guest into his *ger* without the *noyan*'s say-so.

Despite his own tiredness, he took himself off to the Arys and washed his whole body and long hair thoroughly. He had a place that he often liked to make use of, a few hundred yards away from the nearest *gers* on the outskirts of the Mongol encampment. The river there had carved out a sheer sandy-earth bank into something resembling a small cliff, and Robert liked to bathe in the shallow pools below, his body mostly screened from view by the five-foot-high bank.

Now, as he squatted in the shallows, scrubbing his body with fine river sand, he watched the city of Otrar burn a mile away, a dull red glow on the horizon beneath a thick cloud of smoke. He watched the endless columns of red sparks rising into the black sky above the walls, as if each tiny ember were the soul of a dead man ascending into Heaven. But that could not be true – Otrar had been a city of heathens; as far as he knew, there had not been a single Christian living within its walls. The burning city *was* strangely beautiful, he thought, considering the horrors it contained.

As he emerged, and dried himself on his shirt, he felt the first pang of guilt: this terrible carnage was his doing; the countless dead littering the streets were killed by him, indirectly. The destruction of so much that was good – a city of tens of thousands of people – must be laid at his door. And for what? So that Niccolò Ziani and the people of Venice might become richer? *No*, he thought, *not only for that – it is so that Gilly might live. I did this terrible thing to save my brother.*

He told himself that Otrar was doomed anyway. It was always going to be destroyed. He told himself that the city and its inhabitants had been marked for death the moment that Governor Inalchuq slaughtered the five hundred merchants. What Robert had done in opening the city to the Mongols was part of a larger pattern – ordained by God – and what he had said to Karacha was true: the shah had abandoned Otrar to its fate. Sooner or later, the Great Khan would have torn down the walls and slaughtered them all. The argument was good. But it did not make him feel much better.

When he was dressed again, he knelt on the riverbank, closed his eyes and prayed to the Virgin, begging Mary, the holy mother of Jesus Christ, to intercede for him with the Almighty and grant him absolution for his sins. He prayed for the countless dead of Otrar – and for Gilbert, too.

Then he slowly made his way back to the *ger*, now feeling both very hungry and utterly spent.

Sarantuya and her mother were back in the tent when he arrived, and the two women both had an air of almost hectic gaiety. Over roasted kid and rice, and a flask of wine, Robert described how he and Khuyag had entered the city through the secret passage – and thereby caused its downfall.

Sarantuya was all praise. '*Elchin said* – you have behaved like a hero! The Great Khan will surely reward you. You have saved the lives of many, many Mongols.'

'How so?'

'Genghis Khan *had* to take Otrar – for the sake of his reputation. He had been grossly insulted – he could not let that pass. If you had not found a clever way inside the city, the Great Khan would have ordered another bloody assault on another new breach in their walls. And another, if that one failed. And another. I have no doubt that the Great Khan would have been successful – in the end – but thousands of our soldiers would have perished to give him his victory. Subutai will have lost only a few hundred today when he stormed the city. Did you hear Khuyag was right there at the gates to greet him? He and that ugly fellow from the Black Lynx fell on the defenders from behind, and overwhelmed them. Khuyag is a hero, too. I am so proud to have *two* heroes in our *ger*!'

Even Sarantuya's sour-faced mother seemed pleased with Robert that day, giving him an extra portion of the juicy roasted kid and urging him to drink up his wine, even often refilling his cup.

Robert yawned. 'Where is Noyan Khuyag now?' he asked Sarantuya.

'He sent Taghachat to us with a message. He says he is flushing out the last of the stubborn defenders in the southern quarter of Otrar. Which probably means he and his *mingghan* are stripping that part of the city of all its loot. I don't expect him before dawn.'

Altan was also missing; while Robert was bathing, he had gone to see a friendly young Mongol widow of his acquaintance. He, too, could not be expected to be back till the morning. Which meant it was only the three of them in the *ger* that night, celebrating their victory around the hearth. It was, nonetheless, a convivial gathering, with Sarantuya telling them stories of her carefree childhood growing up in the great northern forests on the fringes of the steppe. And, when invited to do so, Robert also spoke of his youth – of his long training as a knight, how he had been sent away at the age of seven to Rochester Castle to learn the arts of war at the household of a Kentish nobleman.

He spoke about the Templars and how he had later joined their ranks; about the training he had completed, the ordeals he had suffered. The wine flowed. And, with it, laughter. He described his adventures with the Habbani in the desert. And how he learned to find water for their caravan.

'You've led an interesting life, *elchin said*,' said Sarantuya, when Robert's stories were told.

'Please, Sarantuya, do not call me *envoy*. My name is Robert!'

'Robyert, Robyert. I like this name, *elchin sa*— I shall call you Robyert. Does the name have some deeper meaning, some allusion? Tell me – what does *Robyert* mean?'

'It has no meaning. It is just a name. It was my grandfather's name.'

'My name is Sarantuya. It means this!' She got up and walked unsteadily over to the red lacquered door of the *ger*. She pushed it wide open and stood in the space. Her lovely face was tilted upwards, and her features and midnight hair were illuminated by a shaft of silver from above.

'This is my name,' she said. 'This is me. *Sarantuya* means "moonlight".'

'A beautiful name,' said Robert, gazing at her with something near awe.

'People who are close to me call me Saran,' she said, coming back inside and sitting down next him, smiling shyly and putting a soft hand on his brawny arm.

Temulun muttered something that Robert did not catch, but her tone was clearly disapproving.

The meat and wine had their predictable effect on Robert and, after some happy hours spent conversing with the two women, he indicated that he wished to sleep and the party broke up.

Lying in his blankets in the warmth of the *ger*, he felt for the first time a genuine sense of contentment. He had triumphed that day. Despite the horrors of the ravaged city, and the guilt, he had won his battle. He was alive, whole, and very shortly he might expect to receive his reward.

Not long after that, he fell asleep.

–

He dreamed of Sarantuya – or Saran, as he now thought of her. He dreamed that his beautiful Mongol girl came to him in the darkest part of the night. He was lying on silken sheets, on his back, in a chamber in a high castle tower somewhere in England, and she came to his bedside, naked but for a silk gown open at the front to reveal her long, slim, white body. He could smell the warm scent of her skin, milky, musky and intoxicating. She put a finger to his lips, bidding him to be silent, and then guided his hand to cup her left breast, and caress its perfect cherry-tipped nipple.

He was immediately as hard as an oak branch – so eager, so ready for her loving – that the knowledge that this was the blackest of all carnal sins was nowhere in his dreaming mind. She straddled him, lowering the fork of her body onto his, allowing him to enter her without difficulty. Smoothly, joyously, they began to move together in a rocking rhythm as old as humanity itself.

Their movements became faster, more urgent, and soon they were bucking and thrusting, grinding their bodies into each other. The sweat began to flow; Saran's fingers were now digging hard into his shoulders. She was making tiny whimpering noises. He spanned her slim waist with his hands, fixing her on him, thrusting upwards, and thrusting again, moving in unison with her body.

In his dream, they seemed to be melting into each other, their flesh becoming one writhing, grinding body, one spirit, one mind, and Robert, his scalding desire spinning higher and higher, let out a long moan, which Saran immediately silenced with a cool hand over his mouth. He was at his apex, a soaring peak, and his long-clenched loins exploded in a fine, roaring surge of love. He felt her body clench, like a gripping fist around him, and she, too, let out a small noise, and sagged back.

Robert fell back on his blankets, spent, his whole body liquid, awash with love.

She lay on top of his sweat-damp body, holding him tight, her smooth face pressed to his beard, their breath mingling, their hearts beating together, and then gradually slowing at the same pace. Then with a single, hard kiss on his lips, she lifted herself off, wrapped the loosened silk gown about her body and walked across the chamber towards the arched window in the stone wall – through which she slipped like a elf-wraith or some other kind of spirit, soaring up and away, disappearing into the pure moonlight that meant her name and into the endless void of the night.

–

Robert awoke the next morning with a deep sense of happiness, which immediately began to fade when he realised that he was alone in his blankets in the fuggy, sleep-stinking *ger*, with Sarantuya's clattering mother – hungover – grumbling as she tried to light the hearth and set a pot to boil. There was no sign of Saran. Hot yellow sunlight was streaming through the door into his eyes.

Robert's fine mood collapsed. He, too, had a pounding head from the excess of wine. Yet worse than that was the knowledge his lovemaking with Saran had been no more than a dream.

–

'I present to you once again, O Great Khan, the *elchin said*, the ambassador of the Doge and the Republic of Venice, who most courageously and selflessly aided us in capturing the city of Otrar.'

Subutai spoke the words sonorously, his introduction booming across the crowded *ger* and, this time, instead of receiving him seated on a plain mat and surrounded by his close family, Genghis Khan strode towards him across the middle of the tent, arms outstretched in a welcome.

The Lord of the Steppe was dressed in impressively regal style that morning to celebrate his victory. He wore a surcoat of gold brocade over a tunic of sea-green silk embroidered with crescent moons, billowy clouds and serpent-like dragons. He had a

241

curved Chinese sword at his waist, and when he embraced the Englishman in a bear hug, Robert felt its jade handle dig hard into his ribs.

'I am mindful, *elchin said*, that I am in your debt,' said Genghis Khan. 'You have delivered Otrar to me by your cunning, if what General Subutai tells me is true. He says you persuaded a traitor to open a way into the city for my men. Your excellent service to me shall not be forgotten. And I mean to reward you handsomely.'

Robert, who was standing only a pace in front of Karacha, considered taking issue with the word 'traitor', but thought better of it and bowed very low instead.

Genghis Khan clapped his hand once and a servant appeared, the crowd parting before him; he bore a green velvet cushion on which was a long, slim, dark object.

'I am told that while assaulting the walls of Otrar some months ago, your sword was broken, and so, if you will permit me, I present to you this, which I hope will prove a worthy replacement.'

The khan took a scabbarded sword from the cushion and presented it with both hands to Robert, who received it with trembling fingers. He could hear the murmuring in the crowded *ger* as he examined it closely. It was a truly beautiful thing: three feet of gently curving elegance. The long handle was fashioned from dark, glossy wood, studded with three gold buttons, with a wrist-loop of plaited black yak hair adorned with a golden tuft at the end. The scabbard was a black lacquered sheath trimmed with gold, top and bottom, and the blade, he saw when he part-drew it from its glossy sheath, was a single-edged length of shining steel. He had never possessed such an item before, and he fell to his knees to offer up his humble, genuine gratitude to the Khan of Khans.

'That is not all,' said Genghis Khan. 'This sword is only a symbol, a token of my second precious gift to you.' He clapped his hands together once more, this time for silence.

'Hear me, all you of the Mongol nation, and be attentive to my words,' he began.

'This Englishman, this *gadaad khun*, now known to you as the *elchin said*, has proved himself the equal of any Mongol in courage – and in cunning, too – and I hereby grant him, now and for all time, the glorious title of *Baghatur* in honour of his heroic actions in our righteous war against the Shah of Khwarazmia. Henceforth, he shall be known to all as *Elchin Baghatur* – the Hero Envoy!'

Every person in that tent began cheering, clapping and shouting Robert's new name.

'Great Khan, this is too great an honour...' Robert began. He was almost overwhelmed by all the dense, swirling emotions inside his heart.

Genghis Khan lifted a single finger for silence – and was immediately granted it. 'I have not finished, *Elchin Baghatur.*' Robert immediately ducked his head in submission.

'I have been told,' the Great Khan continued, 'that you have but one old servant to help you in your daily needs – a miserable Cuman dog. I find this too modest a retinue for a man of your exalted standing in my army. Therefore, for my third gift, I hereby appoint you the role of *Akhmad* or Captain of the No.4 *jagghun* in the Golden Eagle *mingghan*, and second-in-command to our good and loyal soldier Noyan Khuyag, with whom, I believe, you are acquainted. You shall have a hundred Mongol warriors to lead into battle, to obey your every command. And to support the dignity of your new elevated position, I shall give you twenty ponies from my own herd, yours to pick out as you choose, as well as one hundred fat-tailed sheep and one hundred goats!'

The *ger* was filled again with cheering at the Great Khan's extraordinary largesse. Robert found he had a hot tear in his eye, too. 'Great lord,' he said, 'you do me too much honour!'

Genghis Khan embraced him again, this time crushing the beautiful new sword that Robert was clutching hard against his chest. Then he turned and walked away.

Robert found himself surrounded by a sea of smiling Mongol faces, with many folk, unknown to him, pounding him on the back and expressing their joy at his elevation. Some, of course, he did know well. Khuyag was there, already red-faced from too much wine, but beaming happily at him.

'We shall fight together, shoulder to shoulder, *elchin said*,' he slurred, then hurriedly corrected himself, 'I mean *Elchin Baghatur*! We shall slay the cowardly shah himself – for who can stand against two heroes such as we when we fight together? My courage and your cunning, together!' Then Robert was swept away by the crowds pressing in on him. He caught a glimpse of Sarantuya at the back of the throng and, when their eyes met, she gave him her most demure smile.

Taghachat was beside him now, and he put a horn-like claw on Robert's arm.

'They have given me to you, Captain, I'm to be your *jagghun* lieutenant, and with your permission, Altan and I will now ride out immediately to secure those twenty ponies. The khan's herd-master will have sniffed out the news by now, and he will be trying to conceal the best ones from our eyes. But we shall find them, worry not, *Akhmad*. I'll gather up the khan's sheep and goats, too. I know where they are. Altan and I will fetch them here and add them to the *jagghun* herds.'

Robert nodded. He realised he was still clutching the sword to his chest. 'Here, give me that,' said a deep voice, and a strong hand ripped the sword from his grasp.

It was General Subutai, standing in front of him. 'My gift to you is less lavish, but I think you will find it as useful. It is as important as the sword to Mongols.'

He was holding a wide leather belt in his left hand, with a golden buckle, several gold bosses and clasps, and a slender sling arcing down to hold Robert's new sword. Robert allowed the general to fix the belt around his waist, to adjust it properly, and to attach the fine sword so that its curving black scabbard hung comfortably at his left side.

The weight of the weapon felt good, natural, and Robert had the strangest sensation that he was now somehow... whole. Complete.

'You must always take this belt off before you pray,' said Subutai. 'It is a symbol of your submission before Tenggri – or any other god you favour. The Mongol belt holds all things in life in balance. It represents the natural order of the world, the balance of a human spirit. It holds the world together, just as it holds the *deel* together around your waist. If you do not take this belt off when you pray, you will have bad luck – and your prayers will not be answered. When you take it off, you are allowing yourself to be unmanned, unstrung – humbled before God. Furthermore, Mongol men give belts to show that we consider the receiver a trusted comrade and friend, almost like a blood brother – and, by this gift, I now consider you one of mine!' Subutai grinned at him and put a hand on his shoulder. 'And, as your friend, I have something to ask of you—'

'General,' Robert interrupted him, 'I am very grateful for this fine belt – and mindful of its great import – but before you ask anything of me, there is some more urgent business with the Great Khan, I believe. The treaty with Venice…'

'Ah, yes, I said I would help you with that matter. And I shall. But first, I must ask you if you would be willing, with your fine new scouting *jagghun*, to—'

'I beg your pardon, General,' said Robert. 'But I cannot agree to anything – nor will I discuss any matter with you – until I have been allowed to speak to the khan about the treaty with Venice. It is the sole reason I am here. Will you *not* help me to speak to him, as you promised you would?'

Subutai stared at him for a few moments, his odd yellow eyes boring into his face. Robert wondered if he had been too forthright – even rude to this powerful warlord.

The general said, 'Very well, let us seek out the Great Khan. I am nothing if not a man of my word. The Lord of the Steppe is occupied with other matters now but, since you insist, you shall have your chance to speak to him of this matter. Come along now!'

The general began to push his way through the crowded tent, shoving lesser men out of his path with impressive strength.

Robert followed in his wake, marshalling the arguments that he would make to the Great Khan. He must be persuasive. He must think like a merchant again – bring to mind his travels with the Habbani. He must make the treaty seem beneficial to the khan…

Robert found himself face to face with Genghis Khan once more. Subutai was whispering in his ear and the khan was staring directly at Robert, his face impassive.

Did he seem angry? Robert could not tell. There were about twenty people gathered around the Great Khan, mostly Mongols in *deel* or long silk robes; he recognised his sons Odegei and Chagatai and a general called Jebe. There were a few women, too, with powdered faces and tall, slender lacquered headdresses in the shape of square towers. Robert paid them no mind. He was rehearsing his speech in his head: he must be enticing, compelling but not too forceful, stressing that an exclusive treaty with Venice would be for the betterment of the whole Mongol nation.

'*Elchin Baghatur*,' said Genghis Khan, still unsmiling. 'I thought we had concluded our talk, but my servant General Subutai here informs me – to my delight, naturally – that you and I have yet more topics to discuss. You have my ear. A brave man, a *baghatur*, will always command my attention. Speak now! What is it that you wish to say to me? Speak up, brave captain of Mongols!'

'O Great Khan, I am grateful for all the gifts you have bestowed on me. So grateful, indeed, that I also wish to honour you – and the whole of the great Mongol nation – by making to you a gift of my own. I offer you, in all humility and sincerity, the opportunity to create a binding tie, a bond of silk and steel, with the greatest trading power of Christendom, the magnificent Republic of Venice.

'I am, as you know, the representative of the Doge, its ruler, with plenipotentiary powers granted by him to make a trade treaty with you – an exclusive treaty with the Mongol people and its Great Khan, to trade goods, and services, too. What I suggest is very simple… The Venetians would buy goods from you – items such as silk, wool and furs. We, for our part, would provide the Mongol nation with our luxuries, such as fine jewels fashioned by the greatest artists in Europe, Damascus steel swords and plate armour. We could send you artisans to build exquisite palaces in marble and brick, learned masters to teach philosophy—'

'*Elchin Baghatur,*' said Genghis Khan coldly. 'As intriguing as your offer sounds – your *gift*, as you call it – this is not an auspicious time to be discussing the trade in silk or swords, or jewels. I have a war to conduct in Khwarazmia. I have other far weightier concerns on my mind at present.'

'Great One, I have been waiting to speak to you about this for months, waiting patiently. Kindly tell me… when *would* be an auspicious day? I would be pleased to make an appointment with your servants, and we could then discuss—'

'*Elchin Baghatur,*' said the khan, 'You will listen to me now.' He did not raise his voice, but the words came out in a terrifying whisper, a tone that set all the hairs on Robert's neck on end. It was the rasping sound of steel being drawn, or the warning cough of a lion making ready to charge.

'I will speak plainly,' he said, 'since you are a foreigner, not used to our Mongol ways. I shall say this very clearly so that there can be no misunderstanding. *I do not wish to make a treaty with you or your Venetian masters at this time.* Do you think I do not know why you are here? Do you think my people have not reported your ambitions to me? I know what you seek, and I know all the benefits – or otherwise – that might come from making this arrangement. You do not need to cajole me as if I were some stupid goat-herder to whom you wish to sell rotten meat in a crowded bazaar. I know what it is that you want and, at this time, I have not decided whether or not I will grant it.

'So I ask you to be patient a little longer. Do you think you are the *only* one who has come to me offering fine jewels for a part of the trade in silk? The leader of those foreigners *over there* also wishes to make a treaty with me. He says he represents the Republic of Genoa, another great power in the West – greater, he says, than Venice. He has been here a full month, waiting patiently for my decision. He is less importunate than you, *Elchin Baghatur*. More courteous. You must wait. Just as he and his friends must wait. Patiently, peacefully, until I decide. I will have no quarrelling, no bloodshed. You will wait, as the men of Genoa wait. When it pleases *me*, I shall summon you!'

Robert looked over to where the Great Khan was pointing. A dozen paces away was a group of men: people that he had not yet noticed in the crush. They were taller than the average Mongol and wore rough woollen tunics in plain earthy colours, baggy trews, heavy boots. Their faces were big, red and lumpen, and a few of them had hair the colour of straw. In the centre of the group, standing apart from the rest, was a tall, thin man in the austere robes of a Catholic priest, his glossy black hair cut in the tonsure. And he was now staring directly at Robert.

It was Father Pietro. The sword-wielding priest Robert had last seen at the Volga ferry.

Part III

Chapter Nineteen

'This Father Pietro...' said Ivo of Narbonne, fumbling with a sheaf of documents, several sliding off the pile on his lap into a stinking puddle on the stone floor. He retrieved them and, shaking off the filthy water, he said, 'This priest was an agent of the Republic of Genoa, yes? Your enemy – the one who tried to kill you on the road east from Tana – and you discovered him unexpectedly at the court of the Great Khan in the eastern wilderness, in attendance on that puissant monarch, yes?'

'As I have described,' Robert replied. He was slowly chewing a large mouthful of bread and ham, trying to master his urgent desire to wolf it down whole.

'That must have been a little disconcerting,' said Ivo.

Robert did not bother to reply. He vividly recalled his internal explosion of fury and frustration. That thrice-damned priest had followed him all the way to the court of Genghis Khan, and was even now poised to snatch the glittering prize from his grasp.

But Robert had said not a word to the priest that day. The only contact came when Father Pietro brushed past him in the Great Khan's *ger* a little while later and the priest had hissed at him, in Italian, 'Ziani lied to you, Templar. Your brother Gilbert is a prisoner in Soldaya. The Venetians have been using you to secure their treaty, like the snakes they are!' Then the man of God was gone, swallowed by the crowd in the *ger*.

'I felt some disappointment, Father. I cannot deny it. Is there any wine?'

Ivo absent-mindedly passed him a sloshing leather flask. He was still leafing through his damp notes. He had accumulated quite a stack of them by now.

'There is also another small matter that my master the bishop wishes you to clarify, Sir Robert,' Ivo said. 'He enquires whether your conscience is clear about betraying the people of Otrar to their fate. You said before that you had triumphed. But, in your own words, there were fifty thousand souls in the city. And all perished – men, women and children – apart from the traitor Karacha.'

'He was no traitor,' said Robert. 'He was a man who did not wish to die in the cause of his enemy – Governor Inalchuq. Any man might feel the same.'

'Nevertheless, he consigned fifty thousand of his friends and neighbours to the flames. He opened the gates of his own home to his country's enemies!'

Robert took a swallow of wine. Then a long, deep breath. 'To answer your bishop's question, Father, my conscience is *not* unburdened. I was partly responsible for the death of that multitude. I often pray for the souls of the people of Otrar, and beg for forgiveness for my part in their fate. Yet I also know that had I not been there to persuade Karacha to open his secret door, the outcome would undoubtedly have been the same. Otrar was doomed. And war is war, Father. I pray that you may never stare into its terrible face, but when warlike men of conflicting allegiances are pitted against each other in anger... blood will necessarily be shed.'

Robert paused for a moment. 'God *allows* this to happen.'

'That's a fine argument, Sir Robert. Who are we to question God's will?'

Ivo looked at Robert for a while. 'But God is not the only one who makes complex and ineffable plans, is He? Mortal men are also wont to lie and scheme, are they not?'

Robert said nothing; he stared down at the stone floor of the cell.

'I must urge you again, Sir Robert, to be completely candid with me if you wish to be spared the full rigour of the Duke of Austria's justice. The trial is in four days' time, do not forget that. Be completely honest. It is not only that there are many inconsistencies in your narrative. Those may perhaps be explained away, and indeed you have done so – quite expertly, I may say. But your demeanour, your behaviour, your attitude, are at times odd. You seem to embrace the Tartar – or, as you say, Mongol – cause with all your heart, and you happily ape these heathens and their godless, bloodthirsty ways. You do not, to my mind, behave like a man who is only interested in making a treaty – in short, as an envoy. Can you imagine, say, the noble Spanish ambassador to the court of King Louis of France charging into a bloody breach during a siege of a town held by one of His Most Christian Majesty's enemies?'

'Things are different in eastern lands,' said Robert. 'And I am a trained knight.'

'Hmm… What you say is true, but you do not persuade me,' said Ivo. 'But, nevertheless, you placed yourself in mortal danger for the Mongol cause – and more than once.'

Robert said, 'God chose me as his servant. I knew He would not abandon me.'

'Your piety, at least, does you credit. Perhaps, if I may, I will share something with you of my own life. Of my own experiences. Will you permit me?'

Robert shrugged.

'I was not always a loyal son of the Church. For a time, in my youth, I fell into the blackest sin – and my sin was heresy. I became involved with a group of sinners, miserable heretics of the worst stamp, in my southern homeland of Provence. We called ourselves Christians, and each other Good Men and Good Women, yet we were not. The rest of Christendom called us Cathars and heretics and reviled us – rightly so. We were mired in sin. I shall not sully your ears with the shameful details but, by the power of Jesus Christ, I was saved. I was saved by a holy man called Géraud de Malemort, who later became the Bishop of Bordeaux, and who is still my master. He persuaded me to return to the sanctity of the Church and to confess my sins, and although initially reluctant, I eventually did so. I was shriven. I was received into the Church and my soul was saved.

'Years passed. I studied very hard and was duly ordained as a priest. But, as penance for my former sins, I was tasked with investigating and reporting on other Cathars, men and women I had known, some of whom were even former friends, exposing their heresy to the cleansing light of Jesus Christ's one true Church on Earth. I was forced to use subterfuge, at times, and pretend still to be one of their heretical brethren to expose them, and ultimately to save all their immortal souls.'

'You were an informer!' said Robert. 'A spy who befriends and then betrays.'

'I was what I still am – an *enquêteur*. I made investigations and enquiries, some clandestinely, but I only sought out the truth, I hunted it down, then I reported it back to my lord bishop.'

Robert's disgust at this revelation was plainly written on his face.

'You may not approve of my life's work,' said Ivo. 'My vocation. But *my* conscience is clear, Sir Robert. I know in my heart that I do God's holy work. I serve only Him. I serve the glory of God – and Géraud, my lord bishop, of course.'

'You berate me for Otrar, yet how many poor souls did you cast in the flames?'

'That is not the point, Sir Robert. I do not tell you this to be judged by you. I tell you this to make you understand that I, too, am used to telling untruths, and fabricating convincing stories. I am well used to concealing my true purposes from other men. I am familiar with working in the shadows, living a contradiction in dangerous, unfamiliar places where one must profess one thing in public while secretly believing another.'

'What has this to do with me?' said Robert. 'I have told you the truth.'

'I do not think you have. I recognise myself in you, Robert of Hadlow!'

Robert's lean features gave a little twitch of revulsion, but he held his tongue.

'Suspicions are all very well,' said Ivo. 'I am often suspicious of men who confess to me. And, often, I am right to believe that they lie through their teeth. But, in this case, I have evidence, and the word of a man that you know – and who is brother to my lord bishop. You said that Jean de Malemort was one of the men who sat in judgment on you in Acre. One of the three Templars who caused you to be expelled from the Order. So I ask you this… Did you have any private dealings with Jean de Malemort, either before or after your examination by him and the other two?'

Robert did not reply. Nor did he move. And his extreme stillness was, in itself, a kind of confession. He stared back at Ivo, unblinking, and saying nothing.

'Too long. You waited too long to answer, Sir Robert. Jean de Malemort was Seneschal of your own Order – I beg your pardon, your *former* Order.' Ivo's tone was caustic. 'Of course you had dealings with him before your trial. How could you *not* have interacted with him, perhaps even on a daily basis, before you were expelled? Yet you checked yourself, wondering, perhaps, if you might reveal something important by admitting that you had had private dealings with this man? And you *have* indeed revealed something. You clearly have something important, something crucial, to hide in your relationship with him. A secret of some kind.'

'I am tired. I was thinking. It has been a long time since I was in Acre. Yes, I may have seen him around the halls. I recall he gave the knights their daily orders.'

'Did you have any meetings with him? Just the two of you, alone, discreetly behind closed doors? With no witnesses or notes made on what you discussed?'

'No. I do not recall any. We never had any meetings at all of that nature.'

'Indeed? No secret conversations about an important mission to the East?'

'No. Nothing of that kind. I swear it.'

'This is most curious. My bishop has a letter, sent from Acre by his brother Jean. In the letter, the Seneschal implies that he dispatched one of his best Acre knights, a brave man, on a perilous mission into Syria. He says he prays daily this brave Christian's life may be preserved among the heathens.'

'What has that to do with me? I was expelled from the Order in disgrace.'

'So you have said. But it occurs to me that this might have been a ruse. It seems possible that Jean de Malemort dispatched *you* on the same mission that he mentions to his brother. In truth, it seems to me to be entirely possible – even likely.'

Robert's eyes sparked with anger. 'I have told you several times. I did not have any private or secret meetings with Jean de Malemort. He did not send me on any mission. I was expelled from the Order for gambling at dice. I have no more to say on this matter.'

The two men looked at each other in silence for what seemed like an age.

'It is possible that I am mistaken,' said Ivo. 'Forgive me, Sir Robert. My mind is so full of suspicion in these dark, heretical days. So many liars, so many enemies of the Church – one under every rock, or so it seems. It is my duty to question you rigorously to discover the truth. But if you swear you did *not* meet Jean de Malemort secretly, then I must, of course, believe you.'

Ivo began packing his sheaves of parchment away in his satchel, discreetly watching Robert as he seethed in his chains. When the documents were all stowed away, he took up his tablet again and opened it, his stylus poised and ready.

'Now, Sir Robert,' he said, smiling at the furious prisoner. 'Now all that unpleasantness is behind us. Do kindly continue with your intriguing story – be so good as to relate to me what happened to you next. And be mindful of the passing of time – four days, Sir Robert. Your trial begins in just four days! How did you pursue your exclusive treaty with the Great Khan in the face of such unexpected competition from this pestiferous priest who represented Genoa?'

Robert twisted in the saddle and glared at General Subutai. 'You have the temerity to ask me this,' he said, 'after what occurred with the Great Khan? You had promised to use your influence to aid me, yet I was humiliated there. I was rebuked like a child by the khan in front of the whole court.'

They were riding north of the smouldering city of Otrar, along the east bank of the Syr Daria. After Robert had left the khan's *ger*, Subutai had soothed his ruffled feathers and asked Robert to accompany him. He promised to show him something interesting. Then, after a mile or two of silent riding, Subutai said he wanted to ask Robert a favour – at which point the Englishman had exploded.

Subutai reined in his pony; he stared at Robert with his odd tawny eyes. 'I did help you. I presented you to the Lord of the Steppe. To the most powerful man in the world. I put you into his presence. Three times. Is it my fault that you do not understand patience? We have been teaching you our ways for months now – yet still you charge straight in like a lustful yak after a cow in heat.'

'Why did you not inform me that the priest representing Genoa was here?'

'You misunderstand our relationship, *Elchin Baghatur*. I am not your *servant*. I am not here to keep you *informed*. I am your friend and sometimes, when it suits my own purposes, your protector. But that protection could easily be withdrawn. Mark my words. You have come here to enrich yourself with trade. I do not object to that. You do not yet realise that glory is greater than riches. Perhaps you will grasp this one day. However, you also do not seem to understand that we Mongols do not *owe* you riches for the hardships you have suffered. You are owed nothing by us. And instead of acting like an honoured guest, you are behaving like a spoiled child. Learn to be patient. Help the Great Khan achieve his objectives. Help him destroy the shah and his armies. Genghis Khan *will* reward you. Has he not already demonstrated his largesse? He has given you command over a hundred of his men – the power of life and death over a *jagghun* of Mongols. He has given you a helping of his own wealth – twenty ponies, two hundred herd animals. And the honour of a title – *baghatur*! He has, in truth, rewarded you handsomely for your service – yet still you demand more.'

It occurred to Robert to say, 'I came here to save my brother!' but he bit back that remark. Since leaving Tana he had spoken to no one of Gilly's plight, and preferred the Mongols to think of him as a man who was simply seeking wealth.

In fact, part of his fury at Subutai stemmed from the priest's hissed words in the khan's *ger*. Could they be true? Had Ziani lied to him? Was Gilbert in captivity in Soldaya, not Jerusalem? He could not possibly know. But the priest had certainly sown the seeds of ugly doubt in his mind.

'Is that why you brought me here?' Robert said. 'To reprimand me for my childishness – *and* also to ask me to do something for you?'

'I came here to show you something,' said Subutai.

The general kicked his horse up onto a sandy bluff that over-looked the wide Syr Daria, and there he reined in again. Robert reluctantly followed him up.

'That,' Subutai said, pointing at the far side, 'is the Kyzyl Kum.'

Robert looked beyond the river, beyond the strip of dusty grass grazed by a tethered donkey, beyond a field filled with weeds. And saw, beyond the ass, a barren landscape that extended as far as the eye could see. Dry rock, grey scree and dark red sand all the way to the distant horizon.

'It is a desert,' he said. 'Do you think I have not seen one before?'

'Somewhere, perhaps three hundred miles south-west of here, across that merciless expanse of sand, is the city of Burkhara, where the vast wealth of Khwarazmia lies waiting for us, *Elchin Baghatur*.'

Robert stared into the shimmering red-yellow distance. He had heard of the fabled wealth of Burkhara. He also knew Subutai was now attempting to manipulate him.

'Let me tell you, Robyert, how things stand with the war at present. And what the Great Khan has in his mind. General Jochi is taking his two *tumet* – a little less than twenty thousand horsemen – and is heading north-west, up the Syr Daria – following this very river north – to capture the towns of Signak, Jand and Yanikant. He will probably achieve all that over the next two or three months.

'General Jebe will soon be riding south-east with another *tumen* to capture Banakat on the lake. He will also join up with the remaining troops in the Fergana Valley. This joint force will stay in the valley to threaten the shah – who is, we believe, still near Samarkand – from the east.

'Generals Odegei and Chagatai will remain here with a strong force to complete the capture of Otrar – the citadel still defies us, as you know. And that monkey Inalchuq is yet to be punished.

'But the main Mongol force, under Genghis Khan and me, will be riding out into that wasteland –' Subutai pointed at the endless Kyzyl Kum across the wide brown river – 'with four *tumet*. Forty thousand men. The Great Khan means to take Burkhara by surprise – and he will do it. He means to be at their gates within ten days, or even a week. For who could possibly imagine moving such a large army as ours, so swiftly, over such an inhospitable territory as the Kyzyl Kum? Then, once he has captured Burkhara, he will turn back on himself and advance on Samarkand *from the west*. Do you understand, Robyert? The Great Khan seeks to trap Muhammad Shah's army in Samarkand, his greatest city, and end his years of misrule, and his miserable life, there and then.'

'I understand,' Robert said. 'The Great Khan will attack the shah from both west and east, and perhaps Odegei and Chagatai might come down from the north, when they have dealt with Inalchuq. Then Muhammad Shah will be assailed from three sides. It is an excellent strategy.'

'I am very glad you think so,' said Subutai, smirking, 'since it is my strategy. Now we come to the favour I wish to ask of you,' he continued. 'I desire you, Robyert, *Elchin Baghatur*, to lead the Great Khan's army safely across the Red Desert, with your No.4 scouting *jagghun* as the tip of the spear. You have some experience of this, I believe. It is a great responsibility, but Genghis Khan believes you are more than equal to the task. You will need to range ahead of the army and find water, if it exists, and guide our *mingghat* to the oases you locate. It will be very arduous, but—'

'Wait, wait… How can you ask me this? After all I have already done for you. I am a high envoy, an ambassador, not some desert guide. My task here is to make a treaty with the Great Khan, not lead a Mongol army across an impassable wasteland.'

'You are a capable man – the Great Khan recognises it. It is a great honour to be given this task. It means that the khan has confidence in you. Do you think the Genoese – that long, skinny priest – would be asked to undertake this? No, *Baghatur*, only you are so favoured by the Great Khan.'

'Let us make the treaty, give me what I want, and then I will do what you ask.'

'There is no time, Robyert. We march in a few days. How long would you be wrangling over weights of silver and bales of silk? Weeks, and maybe months?'

'No. I have been badly used. I was led to understand that if I gave the Great Khan the city of Otrar, he would discuss the treaty. I did my part. Yet I was rebuffed. Do you think I am a fool?'

Subutai sighed. 'Robyert, why must you be so difficult? Do you not understand that you have no choice? The khan has *asked* that you do this for him. He honours you by asking a favour. If you refuse him, will that make him more – or less – likely to grant you the treaty? What do you think? Hmm? More or less? And, if you make him angry, might he not send you from his court for ever?'

'I want a guarantee. I want a solemn promise from the Great Khan that he will begin negotiations over the treaty when we reach Burkhara. I want him to make a public announcement. And I want the Genoese gone. I insist on *that*. If you do that, we will talk about the Kyzyl Kum.'

'When Burkhara is *captured*. If I can persuade Genghis Khan to swear that he will begin discussions with you the day after the city falls... will you agree to undertake this arduous task?'

'And have the Genoese delegation sent away?'

'What purpose could they possibly have here if *you* are to be given the treaty?'

'Not good enough. Tell me you will expel them from all Mongol lands.'

'Agreed. They shall be sent away the moment the Great Khan announces his treaty decision. Now will you please lead us safely over the Red Desert?'

'I will think about it,' said Robert.

Chapter Twenty

Robert had a great deal of thinking to do. Not just about the desert. Father Pietro had said that his brother Gilbert was a prisoner in Soldaya. That made no sense. The priest had also said that the Venetians were using Robert to gain their treaty – that Niccolò Ziani had lied to him. Robert tried to look at these statements one at a time and fathom the truth. Could Ziani have lied to him? Yes. It was conceivable. Ziani was a merchant through and through – a man who would surely lie if it meant that he gained wealth. If the Venetian merchant had lied, there would be a reckoning, but until Robert returned to Tana, there was no way of ascertaining whether Ziani had lied or not. On the other hand, Father Pietro *was* a known liar – he had masqueraded as a Pisan in Tana to deceive the Venetians.

So Father Pietro may well be lying.

There was one way to find the truth. Early next morning, Robert summoned Taghachat and a dozen of his riders from the No.4 *jagghun*, and he walked his horse slowly through the camp to seek out the tent of the Italian priest and his Rus' bodyguards.

The priest occupied a *ger* on the northern side of the encampment, a good mile from Robert's home. It had not taken Taghachat long to discover its whereabouts.

Two of the Mongols' elite Day Guard stood outside the door of Father Pietro's *ger*, which Robert noted was smaller than Noyan Khuyag's home. They were grim-looking men in full lamellar armour, with tall spears and curved swords. One of them went inside to alert the priest to Robert's presence while the other delivered a stern warning. 'The Great Khan knows that you are in rivalry with this *gadaad khun*,' he said, 'and he has instructed both the Night Guard and the Day Guard to ensure there is no violence between you. If you attack this *gadaad khun* holy man, or if any of your men do so, I and my brothers of the Day Guard will immediately kill you all.'

Taghachat growled at that remark, and the dozen riders of Robert's *jagghun* fingered their hilts. But Robert said calmly, 'I come only to speak with the priest. No more than that.'

And there he was: Father Pietro, coming out of the door of the *ger* with one big burly man behind him. The Rus' had a half-healed wound on his cheek, and Robert recognised him as the one at whom he had thrown his dagger at the ferry. He smiled at the man.

'What do you want, Templar?' said the priest, speaking in Italian. He showed no fear at all at being confronted by the Englishman and his armed followers.

'I want to know what you meant by saying my brother is a prisoner in Soldaya,' said Robert, in the same language. 'How do you know this? Have you any proof?'

The priest smiled unpleasantly. 'So you have come to your senses, then? You have realised that Niccolò Ziani is a slippery liar, who is only using you for his own purposes. You have come to understand that all Venetians are back-stabbing Judases.'

'You seem to have an inordinate hatred for Venice – for a priest from Pisa.'

Father Pietro spat on the grass. 'My mother is from Pisa. My father, God rest his soul, was a merchant of Genoa and, before the rivalry grew so hot, he had many friends in Venice, partners in several commercial ventures. Including your *master* Ziani.'

'Let me guess,' said Robert. 'Their joint venture did not prosper?'

'Ziani tricked him, cheated him, and stole all the gold he invested in the venture.'

'And what was this venture?'

'Slaves,' said Father Pietro. 'Circassian slaves, collected from north of the Caucasus and sold to the Sultan of Egypt. Ziani claimed the ship carrying them sank in the Mediterranean and all the livestock was lost. My father was broken by it. He had borrowed to invest, and he was ruined. He took his own life after that, God have mercy on him. I went to live with my mother in Pisa.'

'That is a sad tale. I can see that you blame Niccolò Ziani for your troubles.'

'I blame the whole filthy pack of them – from the Doge of Venice downwards. Liars all, sunk in the sin of avarice. And God will have his vengeance on them soon.'

'And you think that Ziani is now lying to me?'

'I know he is. Your brother Gilbert is in Soldaya. He lies in a house owned by Barisone Adorno, as an honoured guest but kept securely. Barisone is the Podestà of Genoa, the greatest man of our city. His son is Lanfranco Adorno. Now, Templar, do you understand?'

Robert did not. But the name Lanfranco was indeed vaguely familiar to him.

'Lanfranco Adorno was a Templar,' said Father Pietro, 'one of the knights captured at Damietta with your brother Gilbert and all the rest. Barisone Adorno ransomed his son – and all the rest of them – around Christmastide last year and brought them all to Genoa. He freed his son, naturally, and one of the Templars, Guillaume de Toulouse, died of a sickness he caught in gaol in Jerusalem. Your brother was held securely in Genoa for a while, then he was sent to Soldaya on the Crimea for safekeeping – far from prying eyes, far from any of his Brethren who might attempt to rescue him. I heard recently that your brother is in good health and spirits, too.'

'And your podestà – this Adorno… He will free my brother Gilbert, if I ask him?'

'Ah, well… Barisone Adorno paid out a very large sum for all the captives – and it was not all his own money. The richest merchants of Genoa contributed generously to fund the ransoms. And they would dearly like to recoup their outlay.'

'So I must pay a huge sum to the merchants of Genoa if I wish to free Gilbert?'

'This is how matters are conducted among knightly folk such as yourself, is it not?'

Robert said nothing.

'However, if you were to give up your treaty, withdraw from the Mongol camp and return to the West, I'm sure something could be arranged with the podestà that would have your brother quickly restored to you. If you went back to Tana… why, Soldaya is not so far away. A few days by boat across the Sea of Azov.'

'You want me to withdraw, so that *you* can secure a plum treaty for Genoa?'

'You may put it like that.' Father Pietro smiled nastily at him. 'I have my family's finances to restore. My poor father left us all mired in the most shameful poverty.'

'No,' said Robert. 'I will not withdraw. I have fought too hard for this treaty. And without the treaty I cannot pay the ransom for my brother to Adorno. Ziani will not help me without the treaty. Furthermore, priest, I trust you no further than I can spit. I will let the Great Khan decide who shall be awarded the prize. He favours me. I've done him excellent service since I came out east.'

'If you do not withdraw from the khan's court, Templar, I shall have no option other than to report this matter to Barisone Adorno. We are old friends – and distantly related. I am sure that the podestà will follow my urgings, when I tell him of your greed and intransigence, and he will have his prisoner in Soldaya, your poor little brother Gilbert, immediately put to a painful death.'

Robert stared at him for a moment, his intestines clamped in an icy vice.

'I have made my decision, priest.' Robert remounted his horse. 'Ziani might have lied to me. I do not know. But I *do* know that I will never see my brother again unless I gain the treaty. But know this… If you or your podestà, or any of you Genoese, harm so much as a hair on my brother's head, I shall destroy you. I shall burn Soldaya to the ground – even if it costs me my life.'

'Withdraw from this contest, Templar,' said Father Pietro. 'You cannot win. I warn you – leave the Mongol khan and his encampment immediately, or you will suffer the consequences!'

Robert did not bother to reply. He simply rode away.

–

He dismissed Taghachat and the men of the No.4 *jagghun* and went for a long ride, all the way round the still-burning, ruined city of Otrar, trying by vigorous exercise to get a purchase in his mind on the events of the past few days: Gilly in Soldaya; Father Pietro's threat to have his brother executed; thinking, too, about Subutai's request, and the power of the Great Khan's animosity.

When Robert returned to the *ger* in the encampment outside Otrar, in the late afternoon, feeling easier in his mind, he was surprised to find a pile of sacks and boxes in the place he slept.

On further investigation, he discovered that one of the heavier sacks contained a mass of coins – irregular silver discs with Arabic writing on one side and a six-pointed star on the other, with tiny animal figures inside its decorated lines.

He guessed that there were more than five hundred of these items – a type of Khwarazmian silver coin called a dirham – in the sack. He buried his hand in, pulled out a shining handful and allowed the coins to trickle through his fingers in a delightful, chinking stream. This was more money than he had ever owned before in his life. But if the Genoese had truly ransomed Gilly from the Sultan, if Father Pietro had not lied to him – and that was difficult to credit – it would be only a tiny fraction of the ransom they would require him to pay for his brother. But he knew then that he had made the correct decision at Father Pietro's *ger*. He would continue to pursue the treaty, despite the priest's threats; and with God's help he would soon secure it. The only way was through the treaty. With the gold the treaty would bring him, he would have enough to buy Gilly from Adorno.

While he was thinking, he examined the other sacks – the boxes, too, left in his sleeping place – and found they held fine-woven textiles, a long white silk robe with a bold pattern of tigers, a small bag of precious gems, a few brass jugs of various sizes for holding wine or water, a dozen Chinese porcelain cups – one of them sadly broken – painted with thin trees and mountains, an earthenware jar holding pickled cucumbers, and a wooden box containing a glossy, sticky mass of dates.

Khuyag was lolling on his couch-throne in the north part of the tent, sipping from a huge porcelain cup containing wine and indulgently watching Robert as he truffled like a hound through the various containers with growing wonder and delight.

'Your share,' he slurred, when Robert asked where this bounty had come from. 'You share of the Otrar loot – so far. The Great Khan's treasury did the first division of the spoils this morning. They counted it out and allocated it to each *tumen* and each *mingghan*. I made sure you received a *jagghun* captain's share, since Genghis Khan made you *akhmad*. My *noyan*'s share is yonder.'

Khuyag jerked his head in the direction of the woman's side of the tent, and for the first time Robert noticed an even larger pile of goods in boxes, bags and containers, all mounded up by the *ger* wall. 'We're going to need another wagon and a strong camel to pull it, when we move,' said Khuyag, smirking drunkenly at Robert.

'My thanks to you, *Noyan*,' said Robert. 'You have been a good friend to me.'

'My thanks to you, *Elchin Baghatur*. For without you, we would not have taken Otrar for many months. You might have claimed an even bigger share of the loot, my friend, but, since the Great Khan has already rewarded you, this seemed sufficient...'

'I am truly grateful,' said Robert.

'There's something else, too,' said Khuyag, wiping away an oily tear from his cheek. 'I never thanked you... for saving my life. When you pulled me from the rubble at that foul breach. I was too proud to acknowledge it then. But I do now. And I can never ever repay you. I owe my life to you. You are... my brother!'

Robert noted that Khuyag had reached the maudlin stage. He also saw that he had a raw patch on the left side of his head – a burn. All the carefully arranged plaits were gone from that side and a strip of pink skin was glistening with moisture beads.

'Where are Sarantuya and her mother?' asked Robert. 'You need to dress that burn – that wound looks ugly. Painful. You must attend to it now before it goes bad.'

'It is nothing,' said the *noyan*. 'I was in a house when part of the burning roof fell on me. There is a little pain – but I have this fine Persian wine to soothe it!'

'Khuyag, shall I call one of your men? One of the *mingghan* servants—'

'It is nothing, I tell you. Leave me be. My women are with the Great Khan, but they will be back soon. My lovely wife Sarantuya will tend to me when she returns.'

'Noyan, I really think you should—'

'Do not fuss me like a woman – or some nagging old servant. I have plenty of wine. Leave me be! But speaking of servants… I received a message from your faithful old Cuman dog. He told a Golden Eagle, who told one of my guards, to tell you to meet him at the bathing place this evening. He has something interesting to show you.'

'Altan?' said Robert. 'I had better go, then.'

'Stay with me. Have some wine! I will teach you Mongol drinking songs.'

'I must go… The bathing place, you said?'

'Go if you must, brother. That just means all the more wine for me! Ha ha!'

Robert mounted his gelding and rode slowly towards the section of the river Alys where it was his custom to bathe. On the way, he stopped at the *ger* where Karacha was staying with Minquat, the Mongol trooper whose men had protected his wagon full of treasure when they were leaving Otrar.

Minquat was not there, but he found the merchant sitting on the floor and playing chess in the tent with a boy of perhaps ten years – Minquat's son. The boy fetched a flask of *airaq* and two cups, and then left the *ger* to give the two men privacy to talk.

'How goes it, my friend?' asked Karacha. 'Has the Great Khan agreed to set his seal on our wonderful treaty yet?'

Robert told Karacha everything that had happened since they last spoke.

'They want me to lead the way across the Kyzyl Kum – if I do this, they say I will be given the treaty. But I do not know if I can trust them to keep their word.'

'A Mongol's promise *is* sacred,' Karacha replied. 'But rarely made. The Mongols I traded with would often lie, and cheat and wriggle, and use all manner of subterfuge. But if you could get one to swear on their heathen Sky God, to make a solemn promise to you, I found that their word was iron. It is a matter of honour. Mongols delight in trickery, but not when a divine vow has been made.'

'Thank you, Karacha. That is useful. Now, tell me, do you know any man who has deep knowledge of the Kyzyl Kum? Altan has never been across it.'

'I have crossed that desert. Twice, there and back both times. I went to Nurata with a camel train of silk five years ago, when I was still a stripling. And I took a dozen mules loaded with fragrant tea from Cathay over to Burkhara more than two years ago. It is a brutal journey – they say the Kyzyl Kum is waterless, but that is not true. Our old camel-master knew of several good oases, wet in all seasons, even the driest, and we stopped and watered at them on both journeys.'

'Do you think you could find these oases again?'

'It was not me who guided the train, Robert. And to miss a landmark – some hill or patch of scrub – and wander in the desert without water is to invite death.'

'But do you think you could do it?'

'Truly, my friend, I do not know.'

'And your old camel-master? Do you know where he is now?'

'Not here. If he was in Otrar when the siege began, he is surely dead.'

When Robert reached the bathing place by the sandy bank of the Arys, he was surprised to find Altan was not there. It was near dusk. Had he tarried too long with Karacha? He did not think so; the Cuman had not said that he was in a hurry – just to meet him here, at the bathing place, where he would show Robert something.

Robert dismounted, tied the gelding to a scrub-bush and wandered over to the excavated bank to look down at the green river. There was no one in sight when he looked around. The nearest *gers* were two hundred paces away, with no one visible around them. He also knew that the Mongols did not like to wash themselves in rivers – they considered it unlucky and, indeed, it was forbidden to them during the spring and summer months – so there was no one about whom he might ask if they had seen his old servant.

Then, suddenly, there *were* people on the bank.

A huge man with hair like dry straw sprang out from under the overhanging lip just two yards in front of Robert's boots. The attacker seemed to leap out of the ground itself. And more men were following him – two, three, four men, armed with swords, spears and knives. They were Rus' – that was Robert's first thought. His second, an instant later, was this was a trap and he was a dead man. These were the consequences Father Pietro had threatened that morning. The priest had acted fast.

Without thought, Robert fell back into a fighting stance: right foot forward, left foot back and braced, his knees slightly bent. His left hand grasped the lacquered sheath of his new sword. His right seized the hilt, and he drew the weapon in a smooth shining arc just as the first Rus' attacker came charging at him, shouting something in his own language, his sword raised, ready to strike.

Robert twisted his body to avoid the sweeping downward blow, a hard vertical chop. As the man came blundering forward under his own momentum, Robert stepped quickly sideways and sliced across his own body, low and hard. The blade hacked into the back of the passing Rus's left knee. The man stumbled a few paces, his tendon severed, and collapsed in an ungainly heap. The Mongol blade was keen – very sharp indeed – and light to wield, too. But Robert did not have time to finish the sprawling man. Two others were on him now, one jabbing with a spear at his belly, the second coming round on his left and slashing at him with a thick-bladed knife.

He jumped left towards the man with the knife, placing this attacker's body between him and the jabbing spearman. The man slashed at his face with his heavy blade; Robert dodged and struck – an upward sweep that took off the knifeman's extended arm below the elbow. This was an exquisite sword, Robert thought, sharper than a razor. He stepped back to avoid the inevitable blood fountain.

Two men down. The spearman rushed forward, howling his hatred, jumping over his fallen comrade, who was screaming and clutching his severed arm. Robert tracked the spearman's line of attack, waiting, perfectly balanced on both feet. When the spearman was committed to his strike, Robert flipped the spear aside from its path with a tap on the shaft with the sword. Then, reversing the direction of his blow, he sliced sideways into the man's neck, ripping through meat and tendons.

The fellow dropped his spear and went down to his knees like a dropped sack of oysters, gore pumping from his neck. Three down. Yet there were two more opponents still facing him, both armed with swords – more cautious men, apparently. The man with the severed arm was screaming distractingly. The fellow with the gashed neck was lying prone on the turf, drowning in his own blood. But these two men were properly wary, their relish for combat dampened by seeing three of their friends so efficiently maimed.

Robert danced in. He was angry now. A chilly anger. He wanted to punish these men – destroy them. There would be *consequences* for their murderous attempt. And for Father Pietro, too, if Robert survived this bout. There would definitely be consequences for the priest.

Robert attacked. A step, another step, and he engaged the first man: a clash of steel, sparks flying. The second man, a fellow with a big shaven head, ran in and chopped at him. Robert sidestepped to avoid the blade, then rapidly ducked a wild lateral blow from the first man. He jumped right and hacked his blade into the back of the bald man's head, the curved Mongol steel sticking fast in the back of the man's big skull. His victim went down, ripping the sword from Robert's grasp.

Robert now turned, empty-handed, to face the last man standing: a short, dark-haired fellow, who grinned at him nastily, showing broken teeth. Robert smiled back at him, entirely unafraid.

The Rus' lunged with the sword – a straight Western blade, similar to an arming sword. Robert backed out of reach and circled the man, nearly tripping over the abandoned spear as he stepped left. The dark swordsman advanced on him again, swishing his sword, still grinning. Robert could hear his comrades calling encouragement – enjoining him to kill the unarmed man, to slaughter him.

The dark-haired Rus' attacked, his sword sweeping towards Robert's belly. The Englishman was forced to jump back, then duck under a cut at his head that hissed half an inch above his scalp. The swordsman slashed at his back and Robert dive-rolled forward, very fast, to avoid the sword's slice. He found himself, by chance, lying on the turf very near the abandoned Rus' spear.

He gathered the long weapon up and got to his feet in one smooth movement.

The dark little man came at him snarling, then shouting and swinging his straight blade, left – a feint – then right, the real, potentially lethal blow. Robert batted the sword from its line with the wooden spear shaft, stepped in and kicked him in the balls. A solid boot between his spread legs.

The man flew backwards and landed breathlessly on his arse, his head thrown back, clutching his groin. Robert jumped forward and thrust the spear into him, the tip driving in hard under the man's chin, up and up and into his dark skull. The steel point burst out the other side in a welter of blood.

The first man – the blond one with the ruined knee – was mewling, crying and crawling away across the blood-smeared grass. Robert retrieved his Mongol sword, levering it from the enemy's head. He pulled the spear loose from the other fellow's throat, and went over to the crawling man.

He watched the man scrabble on the grass for a few moments, a cold rage still consuming him. Then he jammed the spear into the crawling man's lower back, shoving it all the way through, pinning him to the earth. He took a handful of the man's greasy blond hair, pulled his head back and sliced his throat open with the sword. Then he finished off all the other Rus' attackers who still breathed.

Even when they were all lifeless, the remnants of his anger were still strong in him. He felt he had been badly used in the Mongol lands. Tricked and betrayed by those he had trusted. Threatened. Ambushed by enemies. He had had enough – it was time to take decisive action. He took several deep, calming breaths, thinking about what he might do now. Then he cleaned the excellent sword, dried it, sheathed it, and went down to the river to bathe his face and wash his bloody hands clean.

In the gathering gloom, he turned his back on five torn bodies, leaving the Rus' casually scattered on the riverside turf in their ultimate positions of death and, without saying so much as a simple prayer for their souls, he mounted up and rode back into the encampment towards Khuyag's *ger*.

As he rode between the first two *gers*, an old Mongol man he did not know came out and saluted him, grinning, banging a fist hard against his own heart.

'Five men, *Baghatur*!' the old man crowed. 'One against five – and you killed them all without taking a scratch. It is the work of a true warrior, a true Mongol *baghatur*!'

Robert strode into the tent, saw that Khuyag was gone, and spotted Altan seated on the cushions in his usual place. He went to stand over the Cuman.

'Where were you today, old man?' he said coldly.

'I was with... With a friend,' the old steppe warrior said nervously. He was staring at a large patch of fresh blood on the sleeve of Robert's *deel*.

'The widow?'

The Cuman nodded. He got to his feet. 'What occurred? Are you hurt?'

'No. Someone used your name to lure me to the river, to the washing place, where five assassins waited.'

'What happened?' Robert turned to see Sarantuya at his side. She looked distressed, her lovely face pinched with worry. 'Have you been injured, Robyert?'

The Englishman gave them a brief description of what had occurred. He was still coldly furious. 'They were creatures of Genoa. Armed Rus' bodyguards – Father Pietro's men.'

'We must go to the Great Khan and make our formal complaint,' she said.

'I have no doubt *you* will tell Genghis Khan all about it, lady, when you make your report on me. Tell me – do you talk directly to the Great Khan when you inform on my doings? Or do you speak only to Subutai? Or do you pass on your intelligence about me to another of his servants?'

Sarantuya stared at him, saying nothing. All the colour had left her face.

'Don't tell me you deny you have been spying on me?' he said.

'I... I do not understand what you mean, Robyert.'

'Spying – *tagnuul*. It was you who taught me this word – the passing of secret information about someone to his enemies. You have been spying on me, informing on me to General Subutai and Genghis Khan ever since I set foot in this *ger*.'

'The Great Khan is not your enemy. I know that he holds you in high esteem.'

'Oh, is that so? But you do not deny spying. Worming information from me, discovering my deepest secrets, betraying me to your master? You do not deny *that*!'

Suddenly Sarantuya was very angry. 'You believe I have *betrayed* you?'

'You told the Great Khan my secrets. You gave him information about me. You are an informer – the lowest of the low! You told the khan or his creature Subutai that I had served as a scout with Aaron the merchant in the desert lands in Syria. That I found water for them. I told you and your mother and no one else the story of that time. And, armed with the knowledge that you gave them – that only you had – Genghis Khan and Subutai are able to make use of me. They can now twist me to their purposes – compel me to do their bidding against my own will.'

'I am Mongol. Genghis Khan is my kin – and my khan. My first loyalty is to him.' Saran's face was bone-white; her black eyes flashed like twin pools of rock oil. 'Yet I have never said anything to Genghis Khan or to Subutai that would harm you. Nothing. Indeed, I have urged my uncle to accede to your request for a treaty. I have begged him to help you. Subutai put you in my *ger* – with Khuyag's grudging permission and Genghis Khan's knowledge. He told me to teach you our language, to look after you, to watch over you, and to keep you safe – and to keep him informed of all your doings. Yes, I admit it. I report on you to the Great Khan. But nothing I have ever said, either to Subutai or to the khan, has harmed you!'

'Your spying denied me the treaty – the reason I am in this God-forsaken land. Instead of my treaty, they force me to cross a desert. Because of you, I'm denied the only thing my heart desires.'

They were facing each other. Staring into each other's eyes, faces just inches apart.

'Is that the *only* thing your heart desires?' said Sarantuya, and quickly looked away.

'Why did you do it?' Robert's anger had gone, replaced with sadness, an aching sense of loss. 'Because of this, I know now that I can never, ever trust you again.'

'If you had your treaty, the *only thing your heart desires*, you would be gone — riding back to your own western land in triumph, bearing your prize home. Is that not so?'

'It is why I came here.'

'Had you ever considered that there may be some who do not wish you to leave?'

Chapter Twenty-one

With a flat hand, Robert shaded his eyes from the sun that scorched him from almost directly above and looked out to where Karacha was pointing.

The parched rocks and sand of the Kyzyl Kum were brownish-grey in this part of its huge expanse. But Robert thought he could make out, a few miles distant across a landlocked sea of rippling dunes, a small, white skeletal object near a fold in the dun earth. In the far distance, a flat-topped mountain, bleak and grey, rose out of the plain; there were dots of green on its parched flanks.

It was not full-blown spring, yet the air was already oven-hot well before midday. Robert could understand now why there had been such urgency in the Mongol command to cross this feared Red Desert as quickly as possible. In a month's time, it would be almost too hot to breathe the air during the daytime. Even now, his lips and mouth were baked stiff and cracked; the skin on his face and hands, where it was exposed, was red and raw, and he had stopped sweating – which he knew was a very bad sign. There were less than a few mouthfuls of gritty, brackish water in the second leather water-bag slung from the gelding's off side. The first bag was bone-dry.

'You think this is it?' he said to Karacha.

They had been riding for four days: four endless, skin-roasting days, when even the moisture on their eyeballs seemed to dry up; four days of plodding through clinging sand and clattering over rocky plateaus before dropping down into shadowed, baking canyons; four days of scanning empty vistas, reckoning their way south and west only by the shadows of the brazen sun, searching beyond hope for an oasis Karacha said he only half-recalled – whose very existence Robert had begun to doubt.

The riders of his *jagghun* had been sent out in pairs to scour the land ahead, making great sweeps on their exhausted steppe ponies, with orders to report back any signs of greenery. Anything at all. Karacha had given them all the information he could remember – which was horribly scant. Yet, almost miraculously, one pair of No.4 *jagghun* riders claimed to have been successful, and they had led Robert and Karacha to this very place where he now scanned the shimmering horizon.

The countryside was flat in this part of the desert, seemingly lifeless but for a few tiny, frightened lizards that scuttled among the rocks, and the big carrion birds that wheeled above like winged demons, waiting for their inevitable demise. But this small white skeletal object in the far distance *was* surely a tree. Was it not? Or had been a tree. And trees grew near water.

'It was more than two years ago,' replied Karacha, testily. 'I was not in command of the camel train, and I was more concerned with care of the goods – making sure the silk did not dry out – than on recording the scenery. But, yes, maybe, I think perhaps I remember this place, and that old white thing is a tree, too. The land falls away steeply there and at the bottom is a pond, green with algae, but filled with sweet water. There was a spring there, too, which feeds the waterhole.'

'Enough to water the whole army – four *tumet*?'

Karacha shrugged.

'What say you, Altan?' Robert looked at the Cuman, who was protecting his balding head with a floppy hat of woven millet straw. 'Is that the fabled Tirik Oasis?'

'The steppe is wide,' said Altan. Robert had to suppress a jolt of rage.

'I am aware of that,' he said through his teeth. 'I believe you have shared this valuable piece of wisdom before. What I am asking you is whether you think this is the oasis the whole God-damned *jagghun* has been searching for these past four days?'

Robert was not exactly *angry* with Altan. But there was tension between them. That morning, after a surprisingly chilly night, Altan had informed Robert that this was the last day of his service.

'I said I would be your man for one year and one day. And that time has passed.'

'You are leaving me?' Robert had been appalled by the prospect.

'I have not decided what the future holds,' Altan had said. 'The steppe is wide.'

The loss of his servant was not the only thing preying on Robert's mind. He was fairly sure now that he understood the working of the trap that had been set for him at the riverbank: Father Pietro had probably asked a Mongol trooper to give one of the Golden Eagles a message, to give to the door guards at the *ger*, inviting Robert to the bathing spot where the lethal trap was sprung.

He had complained to Subutai the next morning, informing him that, despite the Great Khan's order, the Genoese party had instigated violence against him. Subutai had been impressed that he had managed to defeat five enemies – but had been even more delighted when Robert told him that he would lead the scouts over the Kyzyl Kum… if Genghis Khan agreed to his bargain.

The khan had decreed, in front of his court, swearing by Tenggri, the Eternal Blue Sky, that he would begin treaty negotiations with the ambassador of the Republic of Venice once the city of Burkhara had been captured. He also sent his Day Guard to bring the priest before him, to explain himself and answer Robert's accusations.

But Father Pietro was gone. He had fled in the night through a hole in the rear of the *ger* – with the rest of his Rus' men, but without most of his possessions.

Robert's feelings about the disappearance of the priest were mixed. He was glad Father Pietro was gone, but he was still extremely angry. He wanted, almost more than anything else, to destroy the man.

The priest had attacked him. And he was a threat to Gilly. The simplest course would be to kill Father Pietro, which would satisfy Robert's urge for revenge *and* his desire to protect his brother.

Then there was Sarantuya.

They had not spoken since the angry exchange, when he had accused her of betraying him. Of spying on him. And how he regretted those ill-tempered words! For three days he had held on to his grievance, tenaciously going over in his mind the terrible crime she had committed against him. The gross breach of his trust. But even as he recalled her 'crime', he could feel his own argument dissolving – melting away under internal scrutiny. She was not his wife – not his woman, alas. And the fact that he loved her so much, so painfully, so passionately, was not in the slightest part *her* fault.

She was not obliged to keep his secrets – he had never asked her to – and he was a stranger in her *ger*, her guest; in effect, a guest of the Mongol nation. Why would they not wish to investigate his true intentions and reasons for visiting their lands, and abiding among them? He tried to picture a Mongol coming to Hadlow, and how his father might have welcomed him. Henry would have been far from courteous. And Robert knew how alien a Mongol would have seemed to the people of Kent.

That was not how Robert had been treated in the Mongol camp. After the initial unpleasantness, the Mongols had been welcoming, even generous. He'd been praised as a warrior, even rewarded.

Yet, after the bitter argument with Sarantuya, he had not returned to the *ger*. He had bedded down with Taghachat and his No.4 *jagghun*, telling himself that he needed to get to know the men of his command. And two days after their quarrel, he had ridden out across the river, ahead of the Great Khan's army, without saying a word of farewell. Even Khuyag, who was marching with the main host, and who clapped him on the back before his *jagghun* rode away, had sensed something was off.

It was too late, Robert reflected. To his regret, he had broken their fragile friendship with his intemperate words. It seemed likely that he would never see Sarantuya – his lovely Saran – again. But then, at least, the sinful temptation that had plagued him these past few months would be gone.

'Since you press me, *ezen*, I cannot swear that is the Tirik Oasis,' said Altan, breaking into Robert's intimate thoughts. 'But I suspect there is water. See… look at that camel. She can smell it.'

There was a hard struggle going on behind them. Two of his *jagghun* troopers were trying to restrain the feisty old she-camel, which carried such food as they had, their baggage and equipment. One trooper had a taut rope attached to the camel's jaw and was nearly being dragged off his feet.

–

'It is a small oasis,' said Robert the next morning. 'Not enough for the whole army, but it might serve a single *tumen*. However, my guide Karacha tells me the town of Nurata is but a single day's ride beyond the desert watering place. They have stone water tanks there, huge reservoirs built into the rock of their fortress home. If we could capture Nurata, then we would have ample—'

Genghis Khan held up a hand to silence Robert.

The Lord of the Steppe looked over at Subutai, who was mounted on a small pony beside him. These two great Mongol warlords were side by side, out in front of the vast army, but still somehow diminished by the baking yellow-red plain that stretched all around them for hundreds of miles. Behind the Great Khan, Robert observed an apparently endless sea of soldiery: rank upon rank of Mongol faces, impassive and silent on their ugly steppe ponies under their horse-tail banners, coloured and styled according to their own *mingghat* and *tumet*; tens of thousands of men, each one ready to do the Great Khan's bidding, fulfil his lightest wish, ready to kill and die for his glory.

And Robert, too, was bound to this man – to these two men. He was responsible for finding enough water for the khan's horde – all forty thousand of them – or they would perish.

281

'General Subutai, will word of Otrar have reached the people of Nurata yet?'

'Yes, Great Khan. They will surely know about the fate of Otrar.'

'Then take only one *tumen*. Water them at the oasis the *Elchin Baghatur* has found for us, then ride on to Nurata. You know how to achieve this. I will follow with the rest of the army. All four *tumet* will be inside the walls of Nurata and drinking from their reservoirs within three days.'

Genghis Khan turned in his saddle and looked back at the ranks of his men – line after line of horse-warriors. Their impassive faces were caked with dust and dirt and dried sweat. No water could be wasted on mere washing, and they had left the verdant banks of the Syr Daria three sun-baked days ago. Above the silent ranks, the horse-tail banners hung limp in the breezeless desert air.

'We are Mongols. We live and die under the Eternal Blue Sky. We can ride a few more days without water!' He turned back to Subutai. 'Do not fail me, General!'

–

Subutai, Robert and Khuyag rode slowly towards the huge iron-bound gates, built of vast baulks of sun-bleached timber and set into the thick sandstone walls of the desert fortress of Nurata.

The town had been constructed with its back to a mountain, the mud-coloured houses seeming to bulge out of its civic bounds and clamber up the rocky lower slopes as if to escape the heat of the streets. Over there was the turquoise dome of the famous Juma Mosque, a place of pilgrimage, its lapis roof reflecting the sun like a mirror. Beside it stood its spindly green-tiled minaret. Above the town, set into the mountain rock, Robert could make out the square stone sides – and corners, too, darker than the rest – of the vast rectangular water tanks, the reservoirs Karacha had told him about.

These tanks, which collected winter and autumn rainfall from the mountain slopes, sustained this desert settlement and

282

surrounding lands all through the spring and summer heat. The tanks were smaller than Robert had imagined, but they still held more than enough water to sate a Mongol army – even one of forty thousand men. They were also inaccessible unless one controlled the town.

A high semicircular double battlement, crenelated like a Christian fortress, arced around the front of the town, anchored on both sides by the cliffs of the mountainside. Four square towers manned by archers were set into it. There were no convenient secret passages here, Robert thought, glancing over at a worried-looking Karacha. No tunnels. Or, if there were, he did not know them.

If they wanted to take this town, they would have to get over those walls under the lethal eyes of the tower archers – a prospect that made him shiver despite the heat. He could see warriors up on the walls now: the glint of polished steel; hundreds of men, maybe even thousands, defying them.

The Mongols were here, before these fortifications, with only a single *tumen*, just ten thousand light cavalry, a paltry force with which to breach those formidable high walls. And time was not on their side. They could not just sit down here in front of the walls and wait for months, as they had done before Otrar. The Mongol horsemen were already perilously thirsty – a delay of even two days in capturing this town, and thousands of riders and their horses would die. Robert scanned the walls once more: there would not even be a breach this time, when the moment came for the assault. It would be wooden ladders, guts, and the sheer bloody determination to get inside the town.

The doors of Nurata were opening, and a stream of riders was coming out – spearmen, well mounted and richly dressed, riding fast towards the Mongol party. But too few for an attack.

'Give them the Choice,' said Subutai to Robert. 'Say it in Persian, say it in Turkish, whatever these mangy goats understand. You know the words now.'

The pack of Nurata dignitaries reined in a dozen yards in front of Robert. He glanced behind and saw the whole *tumen* was spread out all over the plain about two hundred paces back from the Mongol delegation. Subutai had ordered them to form up in open order, each horseman three paces from the next. It gave the impression of a more powerful host. And all the grooms and servants, and even some of the older children, had been ordered to mount their ponies and assemble in the rear of the ranks, to add to the illusion of overwhelming Mongol strength.

'Go on,' said Subutai. 'Don't be shy, *Elchin Baghatur*. Give them the Great Khan's Choice.'

Robert began in Persian. 'This man is General Subutai *Baghatur*, Lord of the Mountain Wolves, General of the West Wing. He is the faithful servant of Genghis Khan, Khan of Khans, Lord of the Steppes, Conqueror of Cathay, Destroyer of Otrar. The general speaks with the Great Khan's voice today. I shall translate his message to you.'

Robert paused and scanned the dark, bearded faces of the Nurata warriors.

'The message is this,' he continued. 'Surrender to me now and receive my mercy, O people of Nurata, or I shall annihilate you all and leave not one stone of your town standing upon another. Throw open your gates this very day and kneel in the dust before me, and all who are innocent shall be spared. Resist me, and I shall slay all living things inside your walls. It is time now to make the Great Khan's Choice!'

The delegation from Nurata began to chatter among themselves.

Robert, speaking a little more loudly, repeated his full message in Turkish.

To his astonishment, the leaders of Nurata, almost as one man, dismounted from their horses and knelt down before Subutai, putting their foreheads in the dust.

One old white-beard, looking fearfully up at Robert, said in Turkish, 'We humbly surrender to the mighty Genghis Khan. Nurata is his to do with as he wills!'

Chapter Twenty-two

Four days later, the riders of No.4 *jagghun* of the Golden Eagles entered the outskirts of Burkhara. Taghachat, Robert's lieutenant, came galloping back to his *akhmad* to report the first sighting of the city, and even he, a veteran of a dozen campaigns, could not keep excitement from his voice.

'The city of gold,' he shouted as he whipped his pony towards Robert's gelding, which was perched on a rocky outcrop, overlooking the broken lands all around. 'We have reached the city of gold, *Akhmad*. We have found it at last!'

His excitement was pardonable, Robert thought. There had been little loot acquired at Nurata. After the surrender of the elders, Subutai and his *tumen* had swiftly taken possession of the town. The general had decreed there was to be no looting, no sacking of palaces, no rape of their women.

A certain amount of tribute had been offered and received, of course, as was the Mongols' due as the new lords of Nurata, and the levels of the reservoirs had been lowered significantly as ten thousand men watered their thirsty horses and refilled their long leather water-bags – but there had been no repetition of the wanton and catastrophic destruction Robert had witnessed back in Otrar.

Indeed, there had been hardly any violence or theft at all. One Mongol trooper, the leader of an *arban*, had got drunk, raped a local girl and stole her opal necklace. Subutai had had the soldier publicly beheaded in the main square of Nurata as a warning to the other troopers to keep their discipline. A solemn bargain had been made when Nurata surrendered, and Subutai was bound to keep it.

Two days later Genghis Khan had arrived with the other three *tumet*. And there was feasting in and around Nurata, with thousands of *gers* pitched in the surrounding desert sands. Even though a great many beasts had died in the desert, the Great Khan still slaughtered hundreds of animals from his own herds to provide meat for all. The celebrations lasted long into the star-lit desert night.

Robert found the town delightful. There were several canals that ran alongside the streets, fed by the rock reservoirs, which gave Nurata a wonderful coolness even in the midday heat. He made his lodgings in a breezy chamber in the upper part of the emir's palace, an elegant room with billowing white curtains. He bathed, ate well, drank sweet wine mixed with water, and slept for many hours, recovering from the rigours of the punishing journey and luxuriating in his fine surroundings. The next day he visited the Juma Mosque and, after removing his dusty boots and entering the cool, airy space, he marvelled at the beautiful, intricate carvings and fine lattice work on the soaring interior. God is everywhere, he told himself; his Brethren had taught him that. Even in this Saracen temple. He knelt down on one of the soft carpets, decorated with embroidered Arabic script, and in the midst of a dozen Nurata worshippers, he prayed to the one true deity.

He asked God to keep Gilly safe in his captivity – wherever that truly was – and when he was done, he felt as invigorated as if he had received Holy Communion in the Temple Church in London.

They were soon on the march again, though, and pushing their horses once more through the desert heat to reach Burkhara before word of their coming could reach that city. Robert slept under the stars that next night, wrapped in his warm cloak. He looked up at God's perfect universe and pondered the Mongol way of war. How much better it was, he thought, when the enemy recognised the power of Genghis Khan. He had not thought much about the Choice before, but now he saw the wisdom in it – alongside the horror. The example set by the total destruction of Otrar meant Nurata had chosen to surrender, and survive, which was surely better than the vile slaughterhouse of defeat.

Yet the Choice was not an infallible way to open an enemy's gates. General Tolui, Genghis Khan's youngest son, delivered the same ultimatum a few days later, outside the gates of Burkhara. The Choice was refused, with a shower of arrows loosed at the departing Tolui's party, killing one Mongol trooper. Robert only heard about this some hours later, when Altan brought the news to his new *ger*, which was pitched three miles outside the city.

Upon arrival at Burkhara, the whole Golden Eagle *mingghan*, including his No.4 *jagghun*, had been stood down with the gratitude of the Great Khan. *Mingghat* from the khan's other *tumet* would make the assault on the walls of the city. And, knowing what horror that meant, Robert was glad of it and gave thanks to God.

Altan's woman, Jargal, brought him a cup of wine, and one for her man, and they sat in the men's part of Robert's *ger* while Altan related all the day's news.

'They have thrown a ring of steel round the city,' he said, 'but the Great Khan has also been wise enough to leave a few gaps in his lines. There is a spot half a mile wide by the Water Gardens to the south that has not a single Mongol trooper. Khuyag told me that old Tuguldur offered to put his Black Lynx *mingghan* there, but Subutai slapped him down. You understand why, *ezen*?'

'The Great Khan is inviting the foe to make a run for it,' said Robert.

Robert's new *ger* was not as large nor as comfortable as Khuyag's, but it did have the merit of belonging to the Englishman. He was no longer a guest in someone else's house – and that gave him a feeling of liberation. On the other hand, he no longer shared an intimate space with Sarantuya – and her absence was a constant ache in his heart. If only he had tried to apologise to her, to beg her forgiveness, then maybe... He brutally shoved that painful thought away. Best not to dwell on it. Best to empty his mind of all traces of the woman he loved. The only woman he had ever loved.

Altan had procured this smaller *ger* for Robert after a negotiation between the two men about the new nature of their relationship. The year and a day of Altan's service were over, and he pointed out that he was now free to leave. But the idea of being parted from the Cuman dismayed Robert.

He asked Altan what would persuade him to remain. They had shared a few cups of *airaq* and a long discussion, and it had been decided that Altan would stay. He was now to be termed Robert's 'brother-sergeant', a title used in the Order for warriors of great skill who were not gently born, and who supported the aristocratic knights in battle. It was a meaningless term, of course, in the Mongol army where noble birth was of little consequence, but it allowed Robert to reward Altan for his services, both past and future, and to keep him by his side.

It seemed fitting, too, to Robert. Brother-sergeants were often older and more experienced than their knights. Often, within the Templar precincts, they acted as mentors to the younger knights. Both men were secretly very pleased by the new arrangement, although neither would admit it.

By way of compensation for his labours, Robert had given Altan half his herds and flocks and half of the string of Mongol ponies granted to him by Genghis Khan, with the understanding that Altan would care for them all – his and Robert's – or employ others to do so. Robert had also given the Cuman a small sack of silver dirhams, part of his share of loot from Otrar, and all of the utensils, the copper jugs, the Chinese cups and the bolts of cloth that he had acquired after the city had fallen.

Robert retained the bulk of the coin, but he still had only a few possessions. The Templar credo of simplicity and poverty remained strong in his heart. One purchase that he did indulge, from one of the many skilled armourers who followed the dust of the Great Khan's host, was a full suit of Mongol armour, of the kind worn by the troopers of the heavy cavalry *mingghat*. This included a small round iron shield, which was surprisingly light and strong, and a lamellar coat made of thin iron plates sewn onto a leather undergarment, which fell below his knees when he was mounted, and which came with armoured shoulder pieces that covered him fully right down to his elbows.

He bought a lamellar iron coat for his horse, too, to protect its front and flanks in the melee, and an iron faceplate with a steel spike, as well as a new saddle, with high front and back in the Mongol style, to hold him securely in place during combat. He purchased a new helm, too, with a bold scarlet yak-hair plume – which Subutai told him was his right and his duty to wear as a *baghatur.* The helm had long iron sidepieces and a broad lamellar neck covering. Half a dozen twelve-foot Mongol spears, a plaited leather lasso, and a new horse whip completed his equipage.

He was now equipped as a heavy Mongol cavalryman, with as much protection as any English knight when he rode into battle. And he *was* going into battle – he knew that in his bones. Burkhara had defied the Great Khan and, until it fell, he could not obtain his precious treaty.

Altan disapproved of such a weight of metal on a warrior. He was a light horseman of the steppes to his finger-bones, who was protected by no more than his thick *deel*, his fur-lined hat and reindeer boots, and who relied on the speed of his pony and his skill with the bow to keep him alive.

After a supper of grilled lamb skewers, cooked by Jargal – the widow of one of the Golden Eagles troopers killed in the disastrous breach assault on Otrar – Altan and Robert fell easily to discussing the conduct of the siege of Burkhara over some more captured red wine.

The city was markedly different from Otrar: bigger, for a start, but also much richer. Despite what Taghachat had once claimed, Burkhara *did* have a defensive wall, a stout barrier around the city pierced by seven gates. But the wealth of Burkhara had meant that it had expanded far beyond the confines of the wall, and the outer suburbs – known as the *rabad* – extended a good mile outside the heart of the old city. The grander houses out there were fortified and defended by the shah's men.

'They say Burkhara and Samarkand are brothers,' said Altan. 'Similar but subtly different. They say Burkhara is a city of God and Samarkand a city of Man. *Shah* Muhammad rules in Samarkand – in Burkhara, the *Prophet* Muhammad holds sway.'

'They do seem to have a surfeit of mosques,' said Robert, who had ridden round the outskirts of the city the day before. 'And I can see why Taghachat called it a "city of gold". I've never seen a place as rich!'

'They have a canal that feeds water to all the farms and fruit gardens, to the tanneries and workshops, and all the old palaces as well,' said Altan. 'It is called "The River that Brings Gold".'

'We must take the city first, Altan,' Robert said, 'before we start tallying up its treasures. And that task may be neither quick nor easy!'

–

The city of Bukhara was, however, captured both quickly and easily, and Robert, Altan and the No.4 *jagghun* – and, indeed, the whole Golden Eagle *mingghan* – played almost no part in it at all.

The khan's strategy – dreamed up by Subutai, his cleverest general – was an astonishing success. The gaps that the Mongols had left in their encircling formation proved decisive. The wealth of the city – or rather, its striking inequalities of wealth – also proved a significant factor.

Genghis Khan had sent his agents out secretly into the poorest parts of the *rabad*. These men, often locally recruited, were armed with golden bribes and honeyed promises, and their aim was to encourage the downtrodden workers in the Burkhara farms, potteries and tanneries – the very lowest of the low – to rebel against their hated masters. While the Great Khan's men were spreading sedition in the slums, the governor of Burkhara, with ten thousand of his most loyal troops, took advantage of the gaps left deliberately in the encirclement and fled the city in the dead of night.

The governor marched his small army in great haste south-west in the direction of the Amu Daria, a mighty river, the twin of the Syr Daria, which also flowed north into the Aral Sea.

While parts of the *rabad* burned, and rioting peasants and workers stormed the palaces of their lords, Genghis Khan took two of his *tumet* and set off in pursuit of the fleeing governor.

After a brief chase, the Great Khan trapped the Burkhara forces against the muddy banks of the Amu Daria and slaughtered them to the last man. They had been given the Choice – and had chosen to defy him. And when this news got back to the city, the remaining leaders of Burkhara opened their gates, came down from their high walls and knelt in the dust before their conquerors.

The siege of Burkhara, the city of gold, had lasted no more than twelve days.

–

Three days after Burkhara fell, Genghis Khan summoned Robert to an audience. The shah's captured soldiers – all those who had resisted the Lord of the Steppe – were being methodically put to death. Robert had to look away as he rode slowly past row upon dismal row of bound, kneeling men waiting to be beheaded; his horse shied away from the reeking piles of headless corpses.

He was making for the citadel in the centre of the city, which had once been the seat of the shah's government. There was more misery on show in the central market square, where thousands of the city's artisans were being assessed for their skills, and either recruited into the Mongol army as specialists or sold into slavery. Robert ignored these unfortunates, too, as he tethered his horse to a rail and walked up the broad stone steps to the doors of the governor's vast marble-and-gold palace.

The Mongol guard on the inner door, a member of the Great Khan's *turghaut*, or Day Guard, greeted Robert with suspicion – but he clearly knew who the Englishman was. After he had removed the fine Mongol sword and belt from around Robert's waist, and a dagger from his inner belt, he used Robert's title *baghatur* as he ushered him through the door into the khan's presence.

Robert was shocked by the opulence of the room – once a debating chamber of the Burkhara Grand Council. The blaze of gold shone from every side, from candle sconces to the cupboard door handles, from huge jugs and washing bowls on the creamy marble sideboards, to the finials of the curtain rods and even the studs in the exquisite hardwood furniture. The walls were gleaming white stone veined with delicate blue lines, and a vast double window opened on to a view of the city below. The Lord of the Steppe, in a simple white robe that might have been used for sleeping or bathing in, was sitting on a plain blue mat on the sumptuous silk carpet, eating a plate of green melon slices and drinking from a clay mug of water. Generals Subutai and Jebe sat beside him on similar mats, as well as another grizzled Mongol officer whose name Robert didn't know.

Genghis Khan wiped his sticky hands and mouth on a white silk cloth and flicked it over his shoulder. Robert noticed that a servant swooped in and caught the napkin before it hit the carpet.

'Have a slice of melon, *Elchin Baghatur*, if you are hungry,' said Genghis Khan. 'Burkhara is famous for its melons. This one is very sweet. Or I can have the servants bring chilled wine, if you prefer. Perhaps a simple cup of honest *airaq*?'

'There is only one thing I require from you, O Great Khan,' said Robert.

Genghis Khan smiled. 'Always so impatient. You do not change, my friend!'

Robert, at a loss for anything intelligent to say, simply bowed low before his khan.

'Very well. I keep my word – and you shall have your treaty. I suggest you gather my Chinese scribes tomorrow, here in the palace gardens, to begin working out the terms of our agreement and, if it is to our mutual satisfaction, I will set my seal on it. I am not in the mood to haggle with you over mere trifles, *Baghatur*

– you have pleased me with your loyal service. Our business shall be concluded in a very short time, I should think. One week or two – three at most – and you shall have what you desire. Is that good enough for you, my most impatient *baghatur*?'

'You are most gracious, Great One,' said Robert, bowing again.

'I am indeed. Now, to more important matters. I have information that may be of interest to you. This is Boldog, *noyan* of the Snow Leopard *mingghan*. He has just arrived in Burkhara from the east with news. Boldog and his men have been shadowing the shah's army in Samarkand.'

The Mongol officer inclined his head stiffly at Robert. He was a grey man of middle years, his face weathered but curiously expressionless. Robert nodded back.

'Tell him, Boldog. Tell this Englishman what your spy saw in Samarkand.'

'Great Khan, I do not think it wise for us to share our secrets with—'

'Tell him, *Noyan*. You may trust the *Elchin Baghatur*. As I do.'

'As you command, my Khan. I have a man, a trooper of the Leopards. I shall not give you his name, but he is a brave man who is currently employed as an under-gardener in the palace grounds in Samarkand. My man says he saw a foreigner, a tall *gadaad khun*, received by the court of the shah only a week ago today. He was admitted to the presence, with all due courtesy, in the Blue Pavilion in the Lavender Garden, and spent nearly an hour conversing with Muhammad Shah. My man said this *gadaad khun* was treated as if he were an honoured guest by the shah, given fine food and iced sherbet to drink. I am told he is already a great favourite of the old queen, Terken Khatun, the noble mother of the shah and joint ruler of the empire.'

'What did he look like, this foreigner?' said Robert.

'A dark man, dark clothes, hair cut in a ring on his head, shaven here…'

'Father Pietro,' said Robert.

'Yes,' said Genghis Khan. 'The priest who serves Genoa. The one who sent his men to kill you. As if only five *gadaad khun* could slay a mighty warrior such as you!'

Robert was so distracted by this news, he missed the Great Khan's compliment.

He had located his enemy; at least, he knew where his foe had been a week ago. With the Shah of Khwarazmia. Which also put him completely out of Robert's reach.

'Now tell him about the letter, *Noyan*,' said Genghis Khan.

Boldog cleared his throat. 'We — that is, two of my riders — intercepted a courier who was travelling west from Samarkand. He was one of the priest's foreign guards, a big man with a badly scarred face. He had a letter on his person written in a strange manner, in a foreign tongue — a code, perhaps, that we cannot decipher—'

'Just show him the letter, Boldog,' said Genghis Khan.

Noyan Boldog reached into his *deel* and withdrew a creased letter written on thick paper. It had a few rusty stains on the outside, which Robert assumed were the courier's blood. Reluctantly Boldog passed it to Robert, who opened its folds and looked at the words inside. They were in Latin: a language that, as far as he knew, no one but the priest and he could understand this side of the Caspian Sea.

The letter was addressed to Barisone Adorno, Podestà of Genoa, and began with the usual obsequious greetings. It informed Adorno that the priest had been most unlucky in securing a treaty with the Mongol khan, but that he had hopes instead of forging a more lucrative agreement on behalf of Genoa with the Emperor of Khwarazmia...

'You can read it?' asked Boldog. Robert nodded. He was intent on the Latin words, mouthing them to himself as he read.

When Robert looked up, Genghis Khan said, 'Tell us, *Baghatur*, what is the meaning of the priest's secret message?'

'A treaty. He writes that he failed to make a treaty with you, Great Khan, so he has gone to the shah to make one with him.

He believes the Khwarazmians will win this war, and he is telling his master how valuable that outcome will be for Genoa.'

'He is wrong.' Genghis Khan's words had a chilling effect on the whole room. 'And if that dog is ever again in the Mongol lands, his life is forfeit. He received my hospitality, he took my gifts – then joined my enemies. You may *not* kill him, *Elchin Baghatur*, if you catch him – I know you dearly wish to. You will bring him to me and it shall be done properly. I shall do to him what I did to the Governor of Otrar. I shall fill his mouth with molten gold, I shall block his ears with boiling silver. This treacherous *gadaad khun* priest shall know what it means to betray *me*!'

'You have my thanks, Great Khan, for this information,' said Robert. 'Tell me... How soon before you march on Samarkand to defeat the shah and punish this priest?'

He tried to keep all traces of eagerness from his voice as he asked this question.

Genghis Khan said, 'There is nothing about the shah's intentions in this letter? No suggestions as to his future plans?'

'No,' said Robert. 'He writes to his masters in Genoa about some trifling affairs at home. He makes no further mention of the shah beyond his wish to make a treaty.'

'You will be so good as to render a translation of the letter for my clerks, will you not, *Baghatur*?' said Boldog. 'So that they may ponder the text thoroughly.'

'Gladly,' said Robert. 'But when will you be marching on Samarkand? I should very much like to be with you when you defeat the shah and capture the priest.'

There followed a slightly odd silence. Robert wondered if he had said the wrong thing. He saw Boldog glance at the Great Khan, and raise an eyebrow.

Genghis Khan nodded at the *noyan*, as if to give him permission to speak.

'Muhammad Shah is no longer at Samarkand,' said Boldog. 'He has divided his army. The bulk of his forces under a senior general have seemingly gone east, while the shah himself has taken a powerful force south. We think he is heading for Balkh, perhaps, where he means to cross the Amu Daria and continue westward—'

'He grasps the situation,' said Genghis Khan, shutting down his spymaster and taking back the letter from Robert's hand. 'They have divided their army. But I fear we have tired the *Elchin Baghatur* with our talk for long enough. I look forward to speaking with you again when our treaty is drawn up. You have our permission to leave us.'

Robert bowed. He was thinking about the contents of the letter. About the part that he had not mentioned to his hosts. The latter part that read:

> I see no further purpose, my lord, in keeping the prisoner Gilbert of Hadlow alive in your prison in Soldaya. His brother has not responded to our threats and inducements. He is an intransigent dog and stubborn. It would be best if you made an end of Gilbert of Hadlow, and fed his body to the fishes of the Black Sea. Indeed, I urge you to do so immediately, Podestà, and expunge all record of his imprisonment in Soldaya. The Templars will not ransom him and neither, I think, will his older brother. Therefore he is of no further value to us.

'Perhaps I may be allowed to accompany you back to your *ger*,' said Subutai, rising to his feet and smiling at Robert. 'There is a small matter I should very much like to discuss with you.'

Chapter Twenty-three

'You have travelled in the desert lands beyond those mighty water-ways the Tigris and the Euphrates,' Subutai began. 'I believe you might have mentioned this to me before.'

This was a polite fiction. Robert had discussed his many weeks of travel in those parts with Aaron and the Habbani only with Sarantuya, but she had evidently passed this information on to Subutai. Yet Robert had other things on his mind, so he did not take issue with this blatant untruth.

'I have been there,' he said. 'I travelled with a camel train east from the Syrian desert to the Sea of Ravens, then north across the high Caucasus Mountains and beyond into the Kipchak lands, all the way north to the shores of the Sea of Azov.'

'Would you be good enough to tell me what you know of those distant lands – in as much fine detail as you can remember?' said the general.

So Robert obliged him.

But, as he related his experiences in the West with the Arab merchant tribe, the rest of his mind was occupied thinking about his imprisoned brother and the contents of the priest's letter. It demonstrated that Father Pietro's threat had been real. Gilbert was – or had recently been – a prisoner in Soldaya. It also meant that Niccolò Ziani had probably lied to him – unless the Venetian had not known about Podestà Adorno ransoming his brother and the others. Robert would confront Ziani about it when he returned to Tana. Either way, his brother was still a prisoner. And he still had to bring the treaty to Ziani to effect his rescue. Much more importantly, the interception of this letter had probably saved his brother's life. But only for the moment. Yet the priest could easily write another one. Therefore, Father Pietro must be prevented from doing so. Permanently.

Thus engaged with his own thoughts, Robert was unprepared for Subutai's next question – which was, he soon realised, the true reason for this conversation. They were riding with an escort of Mongols through the ruined streets of the *rabad*, with burnt-out buildings on either side, the headless corpses lying like abandoned dolls in the gutters. The stench of death hung in the air.

'You want me to scout for you on the trail of the shah?' Robert asked.

'In a walnut shell, yes,' said Subutai.

'What is your plan?' said Robert.

'The Great Khan is turning back east, to deal with the bulk of the Khwarazmian army, as he always planned to do. But he has given General Jebe and me the honour of finding the shah himself. And he is running west. Perhaps he plans to flee all the way into the territory of his fellow-follower of the Prophet, the Abbasid Caliphate – I do not know. Perhaps the shah will take refuge in Baghdad or some other city in the West. However, I should like you, *Baghatur*, to accompany my *tumet*. You have been in those parts. And there will be spoils for you and your *jagghun* on the way.'

'What about my treaty? That is all I truly care about.'

'Guide us west, and I will release you to return and collect your treaty when the document is agreed. And when we have found the shah and defeated him, I will give you my permission to depart the army with your precious treaty and return home.'

'You would go to Baghdad?' said Robert. 'You think the shah will run so far?'

'He may – to escape our wrath. Or he may grow some hair on his balls, turn and face us in battle. Who can say? I only know now that he is heading west.'

Robert had already made up his mind, but he was enjoying toying with Subutai.

298

'I should like to see Baghdad in Mongol hands, General,' he said. 'I would like that of all things. But I have had my fill of war and death.' He gestured at the corpse of an old woman hanging from a cherry tree. A crow was feasting on her eyes.

'What a steaming pile of horse shit, Robyert! You are a warrior. Life *is* struggle. In war or peace, it makes no difference – there is always struggle. We are born fighting and, if we are fortunate, we die fighting. The greatest pleasure for a warrior is to see his enemy destroyed, to take his life and herds, and savour the lamentations of his women.'

'Christ has taught us to turn the other cheek to our enemies,' said Robert.

'I will remind you of that Christ nonsense, *Baghatur*, when we have that priest in chains, on his knees in front of you. Father Pietro is with the shah. You heard that spymaster Boldog. Where Muhammad Shah goes, the priest surely goes, too. So when we catch up with the shah, we catch up with the priest. Now, answer me this, Christian, and answer me true… When we do catch Father Pietro – when he is in our hands – will you meekly turn the other cheek? Or will you destroy him?'

–

The Englishman felt oddly hesitant as he approached the *ger*, despite the friendly nods of the two Golden Eagle guards outside the familiar red door. Once inside, Khuyag himself rose up from his couch-throne to embrace him as a comrade, and Robert felt even more uncomfortable in his skin.

'Come, sit, brother, drink some *airaq* with me,' said Khuyag, ushering him to his old place on the left of the tent, calling out to Sarantuya to bring them a drink.

Robert's welcome here was understandable – Khuyag had been a recipient of another portion of loot since the fall of Burkhara. He knew this because Altan had already claimed Robert's share on his behalf – a hundred fat-tailed sheep to add to his flock, and five beautiful Persian horses.

'I have come to say farewell – and to thank you for your kind-
nesses,' said Robert, looking at Khuyag, then Sarantuya, and even
throwing a glance at Temulun, who was sitting on the women's
side with a drop spindle, spinning a lump of raw wool into yarn.
The old woman grinned and nodded at him without ceasing her
work.

'You will stay and eat with us a last time,' said Sarantuya. 'We
will roast a lamb!'

'No, no,' Robert said. 'I must leave at dawn with Subutai and
his *tumet*. I have all my affairs to arrange before then. I will be
busy till long after midnight.'

'You are hunting the shah?' said Khuyag. 'Oh, how I wish I
was coming with you. Think of the jewels in his treasury... O,
brother, you have all the luck!'

'I heard that the rest of your Golden Eagles are going east
with the Great Khan to follow the main part of the Khwarazmian
army and destroy it. I'm sure there will be plenty of loot for you,
brother. And remember, when I have the treaty from the khan
in my hand, I will buy anything valuable you wish to dispose of,
anything at all – and I will always give you the friendship price.'

'You do not have your treaty yet?' said Sarantuya. 'Did not
the Great Khan grant it to you? I understood he made a public
declaration of his decision in Otrar.'

'He did – and he will surely give it to me. But it is taking longer
than I had anticipated. His clerks – those clever old Chinese crows
who infest his treasury – want everything to be set down in exact
terms. They are irritatingly precise. Today they are concerned
about not being free to trade with some Muslim merchants in
Kashgar and Urumchi, and about future dealings with their silk
producers in Cathay. I am leaving Karacha, with my full authority,
to work out the fine details. He will stay with the khan's court
and wrangle with the clerks. Subutai wants us to depart swiftly.'

They conversed a little awkwardly for a while – with Robert
ever-conscious of his ill behaviour last time he had spoken to
Sarantuya. And of how startlingly beautiful she looked that day.
Then he took Noyan Khuyag outside and showed him his gift.

It was a cart stacked with wooden casks of wine – more loot from Burkhara – and he had to insist vehemently that he had no time to drink with the *noyan* that day. While Khuyag was carrying a cask into the *ger*, Robert stole a moment with Sarantuya.

'Meeting you has changed my life,' he said, grasping her hand. 'I cannot explain how leaving will tear my heart in two. But know that it will. I want you to have this token from me, so that a part of me is with you always. You remember I told you all about the saints? They are God's holy agents who protect us here on Earth. Well, I want you to have this, Saran. Take this token, and always keep it safe.'

Robert took the silver St Christopher medal on its leather thong from around his neck, slipping it over his head, and he pressed the small metal disc into Sarantuya's hand.

'This medal has lain next to my heart for many difficult and dangerous months, over thousands of miles of hard country. It has always protected me well. The saint stood guard over me in the wilderness. If you wear it next to your heart, Saran, I know it will protect you, too.'

His voice was choked with emotion as he said this; his face close to Sarantuya's, their eyes locked. 'If you ever need me, if you are ever in danger or difficulty, send a messenger to me, with this medal as the token of truth, and I will come to you. Wherever I may be, whatever I am doing, I will come. Send a message, and by St Christopher's beneficence, I will come to you, even from the depths of Hell itself.'

'Robyert,' she said, her eyes filling with tears. 'To me, you are the—'

'It's good strong stuff,' said Khuyag, coming out of the *ger* door with a huge smile on his battered face. 'Sweet with the taste of cherries. You always had a nose for good wine, brother, and these Burkhara people, while they might all be cowardly weaklings, know how to harvest a vineyard. Come and have a little cup – just one cup before you ride off beyond the Amu Daria!'

'I cannot, brother. I have stayed too long. I must go. Farewell to you both!'

'Ha! Look at her, *Baghatur.* Look. She's crying. Women, so weak, so ready to weep. What are you crying for, woman? Our friend will be back soon. Won't you, brother? Go and catch the shah, loot his wonderful treasury, then return to us very rich. We will have a good long drink then, eh? I'll save some wine for you. What do you say?'

But the Englishman had nothing to say. He smiled, turned and walked away.

–

It was a summer of war. A summer in the saddle, with only rare days out of it, and precious little rest. A summer of burning towns and scorched fields. Before they departed, Subutai received news from Boldog of the Snow Leopards that the shah and his army had been spotted on the road to Balkh.

They left Burkhara within the hour, Subutai's force marching south-east down the right bank of the Amu Daria, with Robert's No.4 *jagghun* in the vanguard, and the three *tumet* that made up the bulk of Subutai and Jebe's command in the centre of the column, under their high horse-tail banners.

Robert gave instructions to his outriders – the men who rode ahead of his *jagghun*, the very tip of this Mongol spear. They were to stop and search any rider they met. Always to be on the lookout for any hidden letters written in a foreign tongue. The idea that constantly plagued Robert's mind was that Father Pietro would dispatch another letter to Adorno: another sentence of death for his brother.

The marmot-men, those clever engineers, oxen teams hauling their huge wooden vehicles stacked with timber, missiles and equipment, followed at the rear of the Mongol column, moving at their own slower pace. Behind them came the herds of sheep, goats and camels, and the spare horses, the tents and baggage.

After the first few days on the march, the column was spread over a distance of some twenty miles, but Subutai still urged Robert in the vanguard to make more haste. They paused at

Termez, a town at the mouth of a fertile valley, with the high white-peaked mountains of Afghanistan away down on their left and, when the engineers finally caught up with them three days later, they crossed the Amu Daria on a fleet of rafts constructed for them by these expert artisans.

After the laborious all-day crossing, the swift Mongol cavalry plunged straight south towards the old town of Balkh. Within a day they were picking up signs of the passage of a mighty army: abandoned bits of equipment; flattened earth; thousands of burnt-out campfires; and places where huge numbers of horse had been fed and watered.

At a campfire, three nights after the crossing, one of Jebe's captains told Robert that his master estimated the shah commanded an army of more than fifty thousand, mostly heavy cavalry, easily outnumbering the Mongols. 'But *they* are running away from *us*, *Baghatur*, which tells you something!' said the young horse warrior with a savage grin.

At the gates of Balkh, an ancient town of low mud walls and high spindly minarets, a place noted for the breeding of the local two-humped camels, Subutai had Robert once again give the Great Khan's Choice to the inhabitants, locked up tight behind their thick earth walls. After only an hour's delay, the gates were swung open and the old town surrendered without a fight.

They took tribute in Balkh in the form of food, fodder and fresh pack animals; then they washed, feasted and slept in comfort. But the pickings were lean, since the shah had already stripped the town bare when he passed through it only two weeks earlier.

Subutai left a small garrison to hold Balkh, under a Mongol officer – a *noyan* who had been injured falling off his horse – and they set off again the next day, this time heading south-west, the direction of travel based on information provided by the Afghan elders of Balkh – who, it seemed, had very little love for their fleeing shah.

Herat, they said: the shah was going to Herat – where he had claimed he would line the walls with his fifty thousand men and defy the Mongols till the heavens fell.

Subutai sent this information back to Genghis Khan using the swift Mongol messenger service: hand-picked men known as Arrow Riders, so called because they were said to travel almost as quickly as an archer's shaft. These elite messengers, much admired by the rest of the troops, managed this astonishing feat of speed by changing their ponies at manned waypoints along all the main roads in Mongol-controlled land, and so they were able to continue riding for two or even three days without rest.

It was courtesy of the Arrow Riders that Robert received a letter from Karacha, two days after leaving Balkh, which informed him in his partner's elegant Persian that his treaty was nearly ready for the Great Khan's seal.

One week later, the vanguard of the Mongol army arrived at Herat, and Robert reported back to Subutai that, once again, the shah had not lingered. Indeed, Muhammad Shah had stayed only a day in that town and had immediately scurried onwards.

Encouragingly, the nobles of Herat claimed that large numbers of the shah's soldiers were deserting his cause. The city also opened its gates to the Mongols without delay – they did not even need to be given the Choice – and Subutai treated them well, only levying quantities of food and forage from them, and in return giving Herat a Mongol governor and garrison to rule over them.

After three days' rest – sorely needed by both the men and their horses – the chase resumed. North, this time – the Shah was fleeing north with all speed, the Herat elders said. He had taken the hard road through the Kara Kum desert towards Merv.

For four roasting days, Robert and his *jagghun* doggedly followed in the trail of the shah's army through the blistering Kara Kum. It was not, in the end, as cruel a journey as they had endured through the Kyzyl Kum, at least to Robert's mind, although the air seemed hotter by day and colder at night. In the freezing darkness, wrapped in his cloak on stony, gritty ground, he longed for the temperate climes of England – or even Acre. He fretted about Gilbert a great deal. His brother had been imprisoned now, in various locations, for more than two years.

If Gilly survived, Robert realised, he would be a changed man. He would no longer be the bold Templar knight. Two years in chains would have wreaked havoc on Gilbert's body, as well as on his warlike spirit. But Robert could only do what he could. When Father Pietro was dead, the Englishman knew he would feel a lot easier in his own mind. There would be no turning the other cheek, no mercy – the quicker Robert could achieve the priest's death, the better. But only the Venetian treaty held the power to free his poor brother from Barisone Adorno, Podestà of Genoa. Only by getting the treaty to Niccolò Ziani – whether he had lied or not – could Robert save Gilly.

The next night in the chilly desert, Taghachat, his iron-hard lieutenant, joked over their usual rations of saddle-softened mutton strips and *airaq*, that they should have crossed the Amu Daria near Burkhara and come directly south-west across the sands to Merv. They would then have saved themselves many weeks of travel, and a thousand miles of worn-out saddle leather. 'We could have put our feet up in Merv and waited for the shah to come to us,' he said, chuckling at his own joke.

'You should mention that to the shah when we catch him,' said Altan. 'Tell him that he owes us suitable compensation for wasting so much of our precious time!'

And Robert laughed for the first time in days.

But the shah was not at Merv, they discovered, when they arrived, sun-blistered and thirsty, a day later. And, although the people of that ancient city immediately threw open their gates without a fuss, Subutai immediately helped himself to a good deal of their wealth, food and fodder. The army was ragged after six weeks of hard travel, and many of their herd animals had died in the desert.

Subutai ordered a three-day rest period – and the people of Merv were further obliged to give a lavish feast to an army of thirty thousand tired and hungry men.

They recovered their strength and resumed the chase: proceeding next to the city of Nishapur, travelling west over the mountains, but avoiding any of the fortified towns along the route. Subutai was concerned the shah was getting further away from him; Robert was equally worried that Father Pietro was slipping from his grasp. But Subutai's southern outriders captured a group of Persian deserters the next day, a full cavalry regiment who were riding south to their homes in Tabasayn.

'The shah is done,' their officer proclaimed, falling to his knees to beg for his life. 'He has no food and no silver to pay his loyal men. Allah has forsaken him!'

Subutai spared them – which rather surprised Robert. When he questioned the general about his mercy, he said, 'I like to encourage men to desert the shah. I wish all my enemies to know that I will never punish those who surrender.'

There was no mercy, however, for the fortress-town of Manj in the highlands, just off the main road to Nishapur. The town had been built on a high peak, with only one narrow path winding up towards its stone walls, and the denizens, believing themselves safe from attack, blew trumpets and shrill whistles, and shouted insults down at the Mongol column snaking along the road far below. They even bared their bottoms from their ramparts in an insult to the whole Mongol army.

General Subutai halted the army and, using a single *mingghan* of mountaineers – tough tribesmen from the high Altai region – he scaled the steep sides of the Manj eyrie in one afternoon, stormed the ramparts, and slaughtered every living thing inside the walls.

General Jebe and his *tumen* reached Nishapur ahead of Subutai and the main column, and when he called on the city to surrender, he was partially defied. Nishapur would accept a Mongol governor to rule over them, the defenders said from atop their walls, but they would not pay the Mongol army any tribute; nor would they feed and water such a multitude without proper payment.

Jebe immediately agreed, which made Subutai, when he arrived, incandescent.

Robert was present when the two men clashed in the large headquarters *ger*, which was pitched a mile outside the walls of Nishapur. Jebe was in joint command of the army with Subutai, but he had less experience than the *baghatur*, and commanded fewer men. Usually, the two generals were of the same mind and were able to collaborate amicably. But, on this day, they were not.

'Are you so stupid that you do not understand the Great Khan's Choice?' said Subutai, his odd yellow eyes flashing. 'It is our protection and our greatest weapon – but it must always be observed without exception. Nishapur defied us. We must annihilate the city, or we will surely lose credibility in the whole of Khwarazmia.'

'Have you seen those walls, you bloodthirsty old goat?' Jebe responded. 'Forty feet high – and there must be ten thousand desperate men protecting them.'

'So? We captured Otrar, which had a similar number of defenders. I took Otrar with fire and steel while you were off merrily picking apple blossom in the Fergana Valley.'

Jebe took two deep breaths. To Robert's surprise, he did not lose his temper.

'It took you five months to capture Otrar – and you only took it, I hear, because this fellow –' he shot a finger out at Robert – 'opened up a window and let you in.'

Subutai opened his mouth to say something, but Jebe rolled right over him.

'We do not have five months. Where will the shah be in five months? Who knows? He is not in Nishapur – we do know that. So why waste our time subduing a stubborn city? So that others will fear us? If they don't fear us by now, they never will. Give them a governor and let us ride on. We must hunt down the shah, as the Great Khan ordered us to. *That* is our mission.'

Robert could see Subutai recognised the truth of this. So the Englishman said, 'We cannot let the shah slip through our fingers just to make a point.'

Subutai glared at him then, but he did concede the argument to Jebe.

They provided Nishapur with a governor and a single *jagghun* of Mongols as his personal bodyguard, then rode on north and west through the mountains, following in the retreating shah's footsteps. More men were deserting the shah, Robert's scouts reported back to him. And no couriers from Father Pietro had yet been intercepted. Was that good news or bad? Robert did not know.

The Khwarazmian army dwindled the further it retreated: failure breeds failure, retreat saps morale, as his Templar instructors would have reminded him. Now only thirty thousand horsemen remained under the shah's command, according to the Mongol scouts' best estimate.

Then Damghan – a medium-sized town halfway between Nishapur and Ray, the regional capital – defied them, and Subutai was able to unleash his frustration on their walls. It took him three days, but Damghan eventually fell to his dismounted cavalry – who used ladders and ropes and extraordinary courage to get over the walls. The city was destroyed with fire and steel.

The Mongol horde rolled on. Four days later, they caught up with Muhammad Shah.

Chapter Twenty-four

Robert dismounted and bent to look at the swollen tendon on his gelding's off foreleg. The animal was tired and footsore, Robert knew that, and he intended to give him a good few days' rest when the wranglers brought up the ponies later that day and they made camp. He was about to mount when Atlan, who was still in the saddle, said, 'A rider is coming – coming in fast. That's Taghachat. He must have seen something.'

Taghachat had indeed seen something.

'Carriages, *Akhmad*, up ahead, very fancy, gold painted – they look wealthy. The draught horses are pure black. Such big, beautiful animals. And a guard of about forty mounted men – lancers, I think. I have told our people to stay back and keep watch.'

'Could be a trap, *ezen*,' said Altan.

Robert nodded in agreement. He looked to his right, at the range of dun-grey mountains to the north. A hundred miles beyond those was the southern shore of the Sea of Ravens. There were dozens of gulleys and valleys that came out of the broken hills here, plenty of places to hide an ambushing force. You could, indeed, hide an army in these defiles. To his left was open plain, some farmland and a few patches of dense woodland. You could hide a sizeable force in there, too. Yet his keen-eyed outriders had reported nothing. And the shah had never set an ambush for them before...

Robert said, 'Taghachat, send one rider back to Subutai, and report what you've found. I'll take a closer look. Altan will be with me on the road, and... give me two *arbat* – no, three. The rest are to spread out, north and south. I want riders on both my left and right flanks. Hold them here in readiness for if it goes bad, and get archers up in those rocks there. If they follow us, hit them hard.'

With Altan at his side and thirty troopers at his back, Robert trotted up the road, and after an uneventful half a mile, he turned a corner and saw what Taghachat had described.

A four-wheeled carriage was halted in the centre of the road about a hundred yards away, with one rear wheel taken off and its weight supported by a pile of flat stones. Beyond that was another, much more drab vehicle. A young female, wearing little outer clothing, was standing lookout on the roof.

Two men were crouched over the removed wheel from the nearer, finer carriage, hammering at the iron rim. The vehicle was egg-shaped, open-sided, and painted a bright blue, with designs of plants and flowers painted on it in delicate gold. From a hundred paces, Robert could see inside, where two gorgeously dressed figures were seated on cushions, shaded from the hot sun.

Robert held up a hand to halt his men. There were enemy cavalry all round the carriages: lancers in crimson jackets with bold pink and gold sashes, and conical steel helmets also covered with crimson and gold cloth. Robert could see about two score of these warriors. But there could be more, hidden from sight. He squinted at the enemy. Wait! Was that what he thought it was? Three men, one in black, bareheaded. Was that a tonsure? The others big, blond, burly and bearded.

'Attack and feigned retreat,' he said, loud enough for every man to hear. He could hear thirty bows being drawn from their wide scabbards on the horses' flanks.

His heart was thumping. *Could it be today? Could today be the day I end the most dangerous threat to Gilly's life?*

'Now!' he said, drawing his sword. And thirty arrows were launched into the air towards the mass of carriages and men on horseback. The three *arbat* surged forward at the gallop, following their flying shafts, with Robert in front, pointing his curved sword at the enemy cavalry.

Which immediately fled.

As the smaller Mongol force galloped towards them, the Khwarazmian lancers, to a man, turned their horses' heads and immediately galloped away down the main road, dust flying, their flamboyant crimson-and-pink jackets disappearing into the distance. *Failure breeds failure; retreat saps morale*, he thought. In the middle of the pack, Robert thought he could just make out a tall, lean dark-robed man and his two burly attendants. These three riders were among the first to flee.

'Halt!' shouted Robert. 'Disengage!' Even if that were the priest galloping down the road, the very real threat of ambush made pursuit without reconnaissance too dangerous. He would not risk the lives of his men so casually.

It would not be today, but the day of reckoning was close. Robert could feel it. He reined his horse in, yards away from the first carriage – the decorated one – and, looking in through the open side, he saw an old woman wearing an elaborate golden crown, who was staring down her long nose at him.

Beside her was a younger woman, very pretty, who had drawn a tiny gold-hilted dagger and was brandishing it and trying to look fierce and brave.

'Do put that away, Laleh,' said the older woman in Persian. 'You will only hurt yourself.' Then she addressed Robert in the same language. 'Young man, I am Terken Khatun, queen mother to the coward Muhammad Shah, shame of my loins. We are your prisoners. Now, if your men would kindly fix my broken carriage wheel, my handmaiden Laleh and I are entirely at your disposal.'

'I accept your surrender,' said Robert. 'But I must ask you a question – and if you answer me truthfully, you and your women will be treated with all due respect.'

'Ask, then,' said the queen.

'What is the name of the foreigner in the dark robe who accompanied you?'

And then Terken Khatun told him everything she knew about Father Pietro.

Much later, Robert personally accompanied the two carriages – the second one contained eight young women of the shah's harem, dressed in diaphanous wisps of silk – back to the main encampment, and delivered all the women over to Subutai's bodyguards.

Robert was a troubled man on that half-day journey. But it was not the virtue of the harem – nor that of the queen and her servant – that most troubled him. He had sworn to protect them while they were in his charge, so he duly accompanied them. What troubled him – apart from the escape of Father Pierto – was what he had found inside the queen's exquisite carriage.

Underneath the seat on which Terken Khatun had been sitting was a huge coffer filled with silver coin and jewels: what remained of the fabulous royal treasury of the Khwarazmian empire. The wealth encapsulated in that coffin-sized wooden chest would have been enough to make Robert one of the richest men on Earth. He could not help thinking of how much Khuyag would have enjoyed this moment, had he been with them. And this, of course, made him think of Sarantuya, and a shaft of pain pierced his heart.

Even Altan's head was turned by the discovery of that dazzling hoard.

'You know something, *ezen*,' he had said, when Robert showed him the full glittering contents before they set off back up the road towards Subutai. 'We could load all that up on a few ponies and ride into the hills. Just the two of us. Or we could bring the *jagghun* with us. There is more than enough wealth for ninety-two men. The Sea of Ravens is just three days' ride north. We could find ourselves a ship and...'

Robert actually thought about it. It would be enough to ransom Gilly from his prison – and still have enough to set Robert up as a lord somewhere. But this would mean stealing from his comrades.

'Would you truly do that, Altan?' asked Robert. 'They would catch us, you know.'

'Hmm. The steppe is wide, *ezen*,' said the old thief, grinning like a gargoyle.

'Get thee behind me, Satan,' said Robert, grinning, too. 'Better still – get up the road, Satan, and scout the way. I want all this loot safely in camp and under guard by nightfall.'

—

The shah's army was drawn up in the plain before the great city of Ray, across the main western road near the tiny hamlet of Tehran. It was an impressive sight: a glittering array of thousands of men and horses, their bold banners waving in the wind.

Robert and Subutai, and their various attendants, viewed the battlefield from the elevation of a long shoulder of hill about two miles away, to the south of the highway.

The road ran roughly from east to west, and the shah had placed his army on both sides of the eastern end of the thoroughfare, two miles outside the city walls. Ray had a famous watchtower, Robert had been told, atop which a huge bonfire burned to guide people in fog or in the darkness along the Silk Routes to this great trading city. He could make out the tower's elegant shape in the distance, but no fire burned there this hot morning. No guidance was required by the approaching Mongols.

At first, Robert was puzzled by the shah's decision to fight *outside* the walls, on the plain below the mountains to the north, rather than making use of the city's defences. Then he looked more closely at the lines of steel-armoured horsemen, rank upon rank, that faced them on the plain.

Subutai spoke then, seeming to read his thoughts. 'He wants to unleash his heavy cavalry against us. They are his finest troops. He wants to send them all at us in one great glorious charge that will sweep us away like leaves before a broom. He knows that we have the power to scale city walls – or to batter them down. We have proved that time and again. He does not want a long siege.

He wants to ride us down, crush us under the thundering hooves of his superior heavy cavalry.'

Robert could see Subutai was right. The polished armour of the Persian knights flashed and flickered in the bright sunshine all along their line. They were massed in ranks: proud noblemen in fish-scale coats and elaborate helms, on enormous armoured horses. The sheer size of the Persians and their destriers only became apparent when a mounted messenger rode along the face of the army – a servant on a pony, a normal-sized beast. He appeared a mere dwarf beside the tall Persian knights, his pony a delicate foal in comparison to their hulking chargers.

To the north of Robert and Subutai's position, Jebe had massed his light cavalry *tumet* on the plain, with some additional light *mingghat* taken from Subutai's commands. They, too, sat astride the main road, half a mile away from and facing the enemy. Robert could see the figure of Jebe riding slowly along the line of Mongol horsemen on his steppe pony, stopping from time to time to address stirring words to the units. From time to time, he heard the sound of their cheers.

The Englishman had dressed in his full armour that morning, and had selected the strongest horse from his string: a short-legged, thick-headed, wide-bodied beast called Bear, an animal well suited to carrying his full armoured weight. Bear himself, like the taller Persian horses, was also armoured with a coat of lamellar iron plates covering his front and flanks, and a full faceplate of steel with a spike jutting from his forehead, which made him resemble a muscular unicorn.

This was the kind of warfare for which Robert had trained his whole life: the clash of steel-clad knights in open battle. And he was more than ready for the fray after so long and hard a chase.

In part of his mind, he was thinking about Father Pietro. The old queen had told him that the priest was attached to the shah, an honoured member of his retinue, and that he was still hoping to get the Emperor of Khwarazmia to make a treaty with him on behalf of the Republic of Genoa. Would Father Pietro be on the field this day? That question buzzed in Robert's mind. It was possible. The priest was proficient with a sword, as Robert knew from the friendly bouts they had had in Tana. And where else could he be but with the shah? Robert prayed, then, to both God and St Christopher. 'Send me the priest, O Lord. Send the evil one to me, holy Christopher. Let him come face to face with me on this field of war, so we may settle this matter.'

Altan, who was sitting his mount beside Robert, had deigned to wear a steel helmet that day, but no other armour, and he refused to swap his short steppe bow for the long steel-bladed Mongol lance that Robert carried. The rest of the No.4 *jagghun* had been assigned a position at the rear, with the Golden Eagles, guarding the baggage. Robert was relieved they would be in a safer position on this day of bloodshed.

'Do you think Muhammad Shah is actually here?' Robert asked Subutai, as they surveyed the enemy ranks. 'In all this time, I have only ever seen his dust.'

'You see that big banner there, *Baghatur*?' said Subutai. 'The blue one with the gold embroidery. In the centre of their line, on the road itself. There's a horse with a golden bridle, and silver glinting from the saddle. I believe that is Muhammad Shah. It could be a decoy. But in my bones, I believe that is the Emperor of Khwarazmia himself.'

Robert squinted at the enemy line, a good two miles away. He could not, of course, make out the faces of the foe, but he could clearly see the big blue-and-gold banner. If Father Pietro was anywhere on the battlefield today, he would surely be beside the shah.

The Khwarazmian army ranged against them on the plain seemed to dwarf their own Mongol force. Jebe had only a little over ten thousand riders with him down there, stretched thin across the road – while Muhammad Shah seemed to have almost three times that number arrayed against him. Moreover, the Mongol *tumet* had been marching hard and fast for weeks – all pushing themselves daily beyond their usual endurance limits. Every single Mongol trooper in Subutai and Jebe's ragged force was dog-tired and saddle-sore. Half the ponies in their herd were now lame.

Yet there was a strange buoyancy among the ordinary troopers, a quiet confidence; Robert had sensed it in the tired grins and the campfire laughter the night before. They felt their victory was finally at hand. They had hunted the shah and his army across half the world, and here and now he had been brought to bay. The lines were drawn. It was a late summer day with a nip of autumn in the air, and God himself, or the Eternal Blue Sky, was surely observing this clash of mighty foes.

'Into thy hands, O Lord, I commend my spirit this day,' Robert prayed silently.

Jebe began the attack. A red flag waved at one end of the lines on the plain, and a corresponding one flashed out at the other. Jebe lifted his hand, his sword glinting. He gave the order, and the ranks of cavalry in the Mongol lines below Robert's position began to advance. They came forward at a walk, ten thousand horses in three thin lines moving slowly over the dusty plain.

Robert watched them, his heart stirring with pride. The Mongol cavalry was a magnificent sight: the three disciplined lines of the impassive horsemen, riding under their high horse-tail spirit banners, the black tufts of hair and coloured ribbons stirring in the breeze. These spirit spears, or *sulde*, were the souls of the *mingghat*, the essence of the warriors, guarding them as they advanced.

The Englishman had ridden with these iron-tough men; he had fought and bled with them. He knew their quality. They were his comrades, and now they were going into battle without him. A part of his soul ached to ride down the slope and join them, to hurl Bear at the shah's invincible knights. But he had his own orders. He glanced sideways at Subutai, who was tugging at his wispy beard.

At five hundred paces out, the first Mongol line came up to a trot, opening the gap between it and the second line. Even at this distance, Robert could feel the ground gently vibrating as three thousand Mongol light horse moved towards the enemy. Another command was given; a rattle of drums, a squeal of trumpets, and the first Mongol line was now at the canter, closing fast with the Khwarazmians. Behind them, the second and third lines of horse were also lengthening their gait.

The shah's men responded with a huge warlike shout that rippled along the line and echoed across the battlefield. And soon the arrows were flying out from Khwarazmian archers, a few hundred infantry who were stationed just behind the front lines of gleaming heavy horsemen.

The Mongols, now three hundred paces out, responded in kind, the riders drawing their bows at the gallop and loosing from the saddle. Shafts fell like black rain onto the enemy battle line.

Robert could already see disruption in the ranks of Persian horsemen. The Mongol arrows were clanging and clattering off the steel plates of their armour; some, too, were finding gaps. The horses were disturbed. Here and there a charger reared and pawed the air. Robert could see knights who had already fallen from their saddles.

The first line of charging Mongol cavalry swept up to the face of the enemy formation, and loosed a barrage of arrows directly into their shining ranks. At this close range – a mere dozen yards – their iron-tipped arrows penetrated the steel plates of their foes. Then the light horsemen swept away, moving along the opposing line, left to right, still loosing lethal arrows into the enemy ranks from a distance of a spear's throw, before galloping away, turning in the saddle to loose a final shot.

The Englishman could now see gaps in the enemy ranks: the shah's men stumbling this way and that, struck down by the arrows, and some warriors on foot, some even running forward to heave their javelins at the swift-passing Mongol horsemen. One Khwarazmian stallion, driven mad by the pricking arrows, was kicking out dangerously and having to be restrained by four strong men. A riderless horse with a red-and-gold saddle galloped right across the face of the line, its reins trailing. One armoured knight, dismounted, ran out of the ranks to curse and rave at the Mongols, waving a sword. He was instantly skewered by a dozen black shafts and soon fell to the ground, motionless.

Then the second wave of three thousand Mongols hit the shah's heavy cavalry: another cloud of shafts, arcing up and buzzing like deadly flies into the faces of the Khwarazmians. Their neat lines were already shaken by this brazen attack. By its relentlessness. Wave after wave of Mongols closing and loosing their shafts directly into the faces of the armoured knights, the equivalent of throwing down the gauntlet of challenge, then spinning their little ponies about and riding away.

The shah's archers were loosing, too. Here and there a Mongol warrior was fatally skewered, knocked clean from his saddle. Yet for the proud Persian heavy cavalry it was a special kind of torment. They had to stand in their places and simply take it, with no way to retaliate.

The second wave galloped all the way along the line, shooting swiftly and lethally as they went, before peeling away and withdrawing with only light casualties.

Now the third Mongol wave hit the Khwarazmian line: another shower of black shafts, the clatter of arrow heads hitting steel; another mass of thundering horsemen passing right along the line, hooting, taunting, and loosing their arrows into the faces of the enemy at a distance of only a dozen yards. And now they, too, were retreating, turning to loose once more – the parting shot – before riding insolently out of range.

The Persians had finally had enough. An enormous shout arose from the bristling ranks of knights, all along the line: the clarion cry that Allah was great and Muhammad was his prophet.

The whole Khwarazmian line charged. As one, the half-mile row of heavy horsemen erupted from their positions, surging forward in a great shining mass to follow the departing Mongols, catch them and slaughter them to a man.

Robert did not know if an order had been given, or if every knight had decided at the same time to charge. But the big Persian horsemen exploded onto the battlefield.

Such was the Persians' speed and ferocity that they soon caught up with a few of the rearmost Mongol riders – the dawdling ones, the wounded, the ones with arrow-struck horses – and fell upon them like ravening wolves on a fold. Skewering them with their lances, hacking them down with shining swords, trampling their bodies before spurring onwards, eager for more blood to shed.

The rest of Jebe's command – ten thousand unarmoured horsemen, clad only in wool *deel* and fur hats, disorganised, milling all over the field, seemingly spent after their exertions – all turned tail and fled in terror from the righteous fury of the Persian cavalry.

Chapter Twenty-five

From his position on the hill south-east of the battlefield, Robert watched, heart in mouth, as the Khwarazmian horsemen two miles away erupted from their positions on either side of the road.

Jebe's cavalry was spread all over the plain below him. His men had made three bold, stinging attacks on the shah's lines; then they had retreated. Now, as the Persians flooded towards them – more than twenty thousand knights on armoured horses – the Mongols ran for their lives.

The shah's horsemen galloped across the field – a magnificent sight, the fish-scales of their armour reflecting the sunlight. A great wave of dancing light and steel; the ground shaking beneath the pounding hooves of their heavy chargers. Their lance tips reached out to seek the lives of their fleeing foes. Any opposition they faced was crushed without mercy, ridden down beneath their hooves. No man or beast could stand in the way of this thick wave of silver and hope to live.

Yet the Mongols were lighter and faster than they – and somehow eluded them.

Jebe's men galloped out of range of the Persian spear points – their smaller, fleeter ponies bearing a lighter load. Some Mongols turned in the saddle and loosed shafts at the pursuers. And, just as the Persian cavalry seemed to be tiring of their furious gallop, the last of the Mongols on the field seemed to coalesce in a feeble, wavering defensive line. A pathetic attempt to resist the foe.

Robert could see Jebe out in front of them, giving his orders. A thin line was slowly forming; now two lines: a few thousand tired Mongols turning to face an unstoppable Persian wave.

The Khwarazmian cavalry gathered themselves for one last mighty effort. They surged forward once again, the knights shouting their victory, calling upon their god.

The fragile Mongol lines crumbled. When the foremost Persian knights were within a few spears' lengths of the Mongol line, Jebe's men turned their nimble little ponies and fled once more, racing away as fast as they could, always somehow staying just out of reach of the labouring Persians – who, by now, were scattered over two miles of battlefield.

The hardiest knights were only a dozen yards behind the fleeing Mongols. But many more of the shah's cavalry had already halted, the armoured men gasping for air on their blown horses, both man and beast panting, wheezing, heads drooping. Some of the knights had even dismounted, and were soothing their sweat-lathered mounts and drinking thirstily from their water flasks. Their horses were spent, and many of the men were used up, too. Yet the Persians believed they had been left in possession of the battlefield – and many were already cheering their triumph to the skies.

Robert looked over questioningly at Subutai, who squarely met his gaze.

'Yes, it is time,' the general said. Then louder, 'Flag men – give the signal.'

Two dismounted Mongols ran forward to the edge of the bluff on which Robert and Subutai were stationed and, brandishing huge yellow flags, they faced north and waved the bright cloths backwards and forwards. Two miles away, in the low grey-green hills to the north of the field, an answering pair of flags – equally bright – was waving its reply.

Robert turned in the saddle, and looked down at the reverse side of the bluff on which he was placed. He could see rank upon rank of fresh Mongol cavalry below him, patiently waiting, shielded from sight by the hillside – a full *tumen*, ten thousand men, all the heavy cavalry *mingghat* placed in the front ranks, their lamellar armour reflecting dully in the shadows. He knew a similar number of heavily armoured Mongols lay in hiding to the north. It was indeed, as the general had said, *time*.

'Advance,' yelled Subutai. 'Forward for the Great Khan. Forward for victory!' A trumpet sounded, squealing harshly, and a dozen kettledrums struck up their deep, rattling beat.

And ten thousand fresh Mongol cavalrymen began to move forward.

Robert could feel Bear's excitement between his thighs, the powerful animal quivering with a suppressed desire to gallop ahead like a yearling. He restrained his mount, patting his thick neck. And the cavalry walked slowly down the sides of the hill and emerged onto the plain – the *tumen* flooding out behind him. There were Persians scattered right across the field, and he could see the nearest knights staring with incredulity as an overwhelming force suddenly appeared on their flank.

The kettledrums beat out the order to trot, and a shiver ran through the whole of Subutai's *tumen*. Ahead, Robert could see some of the exhausted Khwarazmian knights already running, some whipping their horses to greater speed. Away to his right, the second Mongol ambushing force was even now emerging from the hills.

Subutai gave another order: the trumpets pealed; the drums were thundering now. Robert was moving up to the canter on Bear. He reached forward and pulled the Mongol spear from its socket by his right stirrup, the curved steel hook catching the sunlight. He spun the shaft to horizontal and tucked it tight under his right armpit. He could see the faces of the enemy now, a hundred yards in front of him: frightened faces; angry faces. Men with looks of bleak despair. Many were turning their backs on the battle, spurring their tired horses – or scrambling away across the field, as fast as they could on foot. A brave handful were turning to face the threat.

The heavy *mingghat* were in a line now, angling across the field, left to right, heading for the centre of the mass of Persians. The mad drums urged Robert to the gallop, the driving beat pulsing in his ears. He felt Bear surge forward under him, as eager as he was for the clash. The nearest Persian was no more than thirty paces away. Robert dropped the reins over the saddle horn and, guiding Bear only with his knees, he hefted the round shield in his left hand, took a better grip on the spear.

The whole enemy mass was now moving across the battlefield like a great shoal of silvery fish. Persians were scrambling back towards their original lines, swarming, thoroughly panicked, acting on dread instinct, blundering into one another. Their movement was all one way: backwards.

Then the Mongol cavalry crashed into them.

Subutai's first *mingghan*, a thousand heavily armoured men on galloping horses, smashed into the loose mass of the shah's hesitant or retreating men. Robert selected a tall horseman with a green plumed helmet – an older man, mature, perhaps a leader of some kind. He guided his horse towards the man, gave Bear a final kick, and lunged forward with the spear. The foot-long blade took the man in the centre of his back, and the needle-sharp steel was driven right through his fish-scale mail.

The blade punched deep into the rider's lungs. But the steel hook stopped any further penetration, thumping hard against his ribs and knocking the man clean out of the saddle.

He fell away, arms flailing; as he fell to his death, the spear came free of his flesh.

Robert kicked Bear forward again, shouting out 'St Christopher!' just as an enemy horseman closed in and swung overhand at his head with a sword. Robert caught the blow on his iron shield and shrugged it away, but the enemy was now too close to strike with his spear. He swiped the edge of the iron shield at him, striking at his knee and hearing the crack of bone. The man shouted the name of Allah and hammered at him again with his sword – then he was gone, swept away in the melee.

Robert saw an enemy in shining armour striking at Subutai with a spiked mace, saw Subutai fend off the clanging blow with his shield, and Robert closed in, lined up Bear, put back his spurs, and surged forward. He drove the bloody spear tip hard into the attacker's left side. The man screamed and twisted in the saddle, clearly mortally wounded, and the long spear was torn from Robert's right hand as the man fell away.

Robert turned Bear to the right and whipped the curved Mongol sword from its scabbard – just in time. A dismounted Khwarazmian knight with a long spear was lunging at him, the cruel point streaking up towards his face. He batted it out of the way with his sword with an instant to spare. Crack, clash – they exchanged blows, the man's snarling face filling Robert's vision. Bear bowed and bucked his head, catching the man on foot with the steel spike on his faceplate, ripping into his belly. Then Robert, with Bear now thundering past the staggering wounded man, slashed down and back at him, and caught him across the face, the blade thwacking across the bridge of his nose.

The Englishman found himself swept forward in the crush, cutting left or right whenever a target presented itself. There was no room to turn Bear. The battlefield was now a logjam, no space for manoeuvre, with the bodies of horses constantly barging into one another as men hacked and sliced at any foe within sword-reach. Persian and Mongol hammered at each other; wounded men slid from the saddle, screaming, and were trampled under-foot. Robert sliced at a Persian's fish-scale armoured shoulder, but the blade slid off harmlessly. Then a huge jolt rippled across the whole tightly packed mass of panicked men, as the second Mongol *tumen* crashed into the far side of the Persians.

There was suddenly a clear space directly ahead of Robert. And all around him, the shah's horsemen were now fleeing, galloping back to their lines. A full-on rout had begun. The cheering Mongols took full advantage. They all surged forward again. Robert could see jubilant faces around him. And they were all spurring in the same direction. The Mongols swept right across the battlefield, unstoppable, like a vast broom, brushing the shah's terrified horsemen before them.

And the Englishman, shouting for joy, was swept along with them.

Robert found himself on the heels of a galloping Persian, and saw the knight ride down one of his own infantry archers in his haste to make an escape. The Mongol tide was washing up against the Khwarazmian battle line now – what was left of it. For all the enemy were fleeing – infantry, too, most streaming west towards the distant city of Ray. But some archers were trying to head north – running for the hills and the Caspian Sea, throwing aside bows and scrambling for their very lives.

Robert saw a tall figure in a gold-encrusted suit of armour, just a few yards ahead of him. The lean-faced man, with trailing moustaches, wore a bejewelled helm. This great nobleman was yelling, shouting at his companions, trying to rally them. Ordering all his reluctant men to stand, bellowing at them, berating them, desperately trying to stem the onrushing tide of Mongol horse.

The shah. It was the shah himself. Muhammad of Khwarazmia was waving a curved sword in the air, the silver blade engraved with gold, and urging his bodyguards – big men with elaborate moustaches, dressed in coloured silks and polished steel – to stand with him and hold back the foe.

And beside the shah, Robert – his heart leaping like a salmon with wild joy – saw a dark-clad figure on a big horse, wearing a shining steel cuirass, a flanged mace in his hand. It was Father Pietro.

Their eyes met in hatred across a dozen yards of battle-filled space. Robert urged Bear forward with his knees, knocking other horses out of the way, pushing towards the priest, batting a screaming Persian from his path with his sword, almost without thought. And the treacherous priest saw him, accepted his unspoken challenge, turned and rode forward to meet him.

Father Pietro swung the mace and Robert took the blow – a surprisingly heavy one – full on his shield. As the priest rode past, Robert slashed at him, sweeping the blade over Bear's head and clanging it against Father Pietro's polished back armour with no visible effect.

They both turned their horses, and rode at each other once more. And this time – to Robert's utter astonishment – the priest drew back his arm and hurled the mace directly at Robert's face from a distance of three yards. He had never seen a move like it before. It was unthinkable to *throw away* your weapon. The mace came at him very fast, end over end. Robert ducked, but the mace caught him a ringing blow on the crown of his helm. A flash of light, then his eyes darkened for an instant.

He heard the priest yell out, 'To Hell with you, heretic!' and felt the impact as the two horses collided, chest to chest. But such was Bear's strength that the other animal snorted and reared away. Robert found himself slipping from the saddle; his vision blurred, fading in and out. He hauled himself back upright, swung blindly left with the curved sword and hit nothing but air.

He was aware that Altan – solid Altan – was beside him, bow in hand, loosing deadly shafts, one after the other, as quick as thought, into the packed ranks of the enemy. Robert recovered a little; he shook his head, and found his sword still in his hand – *thank a merciful God*. He looked about wildly for Father Pietro. There were Persian knights and Mongol horsemen all around, duelling, shouting, smashing at one another with sword and shield. But the priest had disappeared.

A Persian cavalryman came straight at Robert, and launched a tremendous sword cut at his head. The Englishman blocked and countered with a blow at his foe's waist. He struck hard and heard the man curse and spur away. Then he caught a glimpse of the priest – a flash of clerical black. He was behind the shah and his bodyguards now, his arming sword drawn. Robert saw a blond man, heavily bearded, almost certainly a Rus', canter forward and get between him and the priest. Robert kicked Bear onwards, trying to reach his foe. But a knot of madly battling Persians were in the way.

Altan rode across his front, forcing Robert to rein in, the old Cuman drawing his bow and loosing again and again, sending shafts impossibly fast into the heaving knot of men around the shah. In all the chaos of neighing horses, shouting men and milling bodies, Robert scanned the field wildly, desperately, peering through the blood-splashed moving tableau of battling horsemen.

But the priest was nowhere to be seen.

A Persian lord – one of the shah's companions, spurred out of the crush – shouted something and swung at Altan's unprotected back with his sword, a lightning blow that crunched into the Cuman's lower spine, immediately drawing a line of blood across his brown *deel*. Before Robert could react, a Mongol cut at the Persian from the left, and another skewered the man with his spear.

But Altan had been wounded. He yelled out and spilled from the saddle, and disappeared under the churning hooves. Robert had no time to tend to him. He urged Bear forward, the animal forcing his way into the thick scrum of men around the shah. Robert looked about, desperately seeking Father Pietro. Then he did catch a glimpse of the priest, just once. He desperately tried to turn his horse and drive in that direction, but was held firm by the vice of sweaty animal flesh.

'To the Devil with you!' Robert shouted, driving his spurs into Bear's flanks, breaking the animal's skin, and the powerful horse bullocked forward, shouldering weaker horses out of his way.

A figure loomed – another big man, blond beard. A flash of steel, and Robert took a crunching sword blow on his steel helm, and again he saw flashing lights, colours. Purely by instinct, he lashed out with the shield and caught the man across the jaw. The strap on his shield snapped; the iron disc came loose and clattered away. But the big fellow's beard was bloody, his face a ruin.

Robert pushed Bear forward once more. The knot of enemy horsemen was dissolving in front of him, some fleeing. A dense cluster of Mongol heavy cavalry swept in from the left – a mounted mob overwhelming the shah and his few remaining companions. The Mongol blades flashed; the sound of steel on steel rang out clearly. The Mongols were shouting in glee. Shouting their triumph.

The shah was unhorsed now, his richly caparisoned mount suddenly riderless, and his aristocratic followers all driven back.

All except one. One Persian brave knight surged forward into the sea of Mongol riders around the fallen shah, and was instantly hacked from the saddle. Around the fallen shah was a ring of Mongols, stabbing down, slashing, laughing at his pain. But Robert had no eyes to watch the death throes of a mighty monarch – his gaze was fixed on Father Pietro, who was now twenty yards away, furiously lashing his horse and galloping free from the melee.

Robert dug his heels hard into Bear's broad sides, urging him onwards. One last effort. The priest's poor horse, he saw, had three arrows stuck deep in its belly and off-side haunch, and as Robert bore down on him, the animal's legs folded and it began to tumble. The priest kicked both his feet free of the stirrups, and jumped at the last instant as the animal collapsed on the turf.

Robert was on him, his sword raised to strike. Father Pietro dodged under Bear's neck, moving at the speed of a weasel to the Englishman's left, and as the horse passed him, he hacked at Bear's flank. Robert felt the animal flinch under him and looked down to see blood, then white bulging entrails spilling from the opened belly, underneath the protection of his lamellar armour.

He turned the animal right around, but Bear was now whimpering with pain, and Robert reined in and stepped off the great-hearted beast, his curved sword in his hand.

He faced Father Pietro directly – standing still, his vision coming and going. Blood beating in his head like a drum from the two massive blows he had taken on his iron helmet. He saw no other foes near him, only the Genoese priest. No one but him within twenty paces. No one alive, at least.

Father Pietro began to walk slowly towards him.

Each had no more than a sword apiece, but Robert's head was full of dancing lights.

The priest attacked: he took two fast steps and lunged at Robert, high on the left. The Englishman parried, letting the enemy blade slide past his face an inch on the left, but he was slow and dizzy; he could now hear a loud ringing noise in his ears. The sound of bells. Church bells. Yet there were no Christian churches within a thousand miles.

Father Pietro half-circled him and slashed at his belly, and Robert just swayed out of reach. He saw the movement of the priest's steel blade as a long sheet of silver. Beautiful but deadly. He stumbled forward, now feeling the overwhelming urge to lie down and sleep. The priest hacked at his head, and Robert feebly blocked and made a half-hearted counter-attack: a wavering lunge that Father Pietro all but ignored, just gently knocking Robert's limp blade aside.

'You cannot even fight,' sneered Father Pietro. 'No wonder they kicked you out of the Order. Time to die, heretic. I wish I had the leisure to see you burned.'

The priest flung himself on Robert with a flurry of blows – left, right and left again, Robert saw the steel shift in the air like a line of light trailing rainbows, but some memory in his muscles – the result of years of training – kept the priest's blows from cutting into his flesh. The Mongol sword in his right hand was moving, sweeping, blocking, parrying the attacks almost of its own volition.

He heard Gilbert's voice – so clear, that it was as if his brother was standing next to him. He said, 'Kill him. Kill this priest, brother – or he will kill you – and I will die, too.'

But Robert stood there, dazed, his sword drooping, the world swimming madly around him.

'Time to die, heretic!' said Father Pietro. He stepped in and lofted the arming sword, and brought it down in a powerful arc towards Robert's unprotected neck.

The Englishman moved. He leapt like a panther – his curved sword reaching out, across his body, sweeping up to his left, their relative movements perfectly judged. The Mongol blade caught the priest's right arm below the elbow and, with their combined power – the priest's downward pressure as he struck and Robert's upward sweep – the blade sliced through Father Pietro's forearm.

The priest screamed – a terrible sound of pain and failure. His right forearm and hand, still gripping the sword, flew high in the air. Father Pietro stared in astonishment at the severed stump of his arm and, moments later, at the bright blood jetting out from it onto the torn grass.

Robert took another step in, raised his sword, and struck once again – the excellent Mongol blade finding the priest's thin neck and cleanly removing his head from his body.

–

'You admit it,' said the *enquêteur*. 'You freely admit that you murdered this priest Father Pietro.'

There was but one candle in the cell that day, and Father Ivo of Narbonne was forced to squint to even see the skeletal, half-naked Englishman crouched at the back of the cell. Ivo was in a foul mood. He had sent a dozen letters off to his bishop in Bordeaux in recent weeks, many containing queries of his own, and had so far received no reply to the most important of them. He, too, felt the urgency of the looming trial. He needed answers before this whole business was brought into the light. And time was swiftly running out. He had only three days left to uncover the truth.

'I did not murder him, Father. I met him in battle and slew him in single combat. There is a difference. Besides, I had good reason to demand his death. He had set his killers on me.'

'We shall see what the duke makes of this. As I am sure you have realised, in just three days you must face His Grace's justice. Just three days – you hear me?'

'I am aware of the passing of time, Father, even in the darkness of this stinking pit.'

'Then go on, man, go on. There is no time to waste! Continue your story.'

–

The Great Khan's horsemen had swept the entire Khwarazmian army away. They were defeated. Any enemy soldier who was not already dead or wounded was now running for his life. The heavy *mingghat* rampaged across the field and through the shattered enemy lines, killing and maiming, hunting down individuals and skewering them on their spears, until they, too, were spent. Then Jebe's light cavalry rejoined the field after their feigned retreat, and a rout became a slaughter.

The returned Mongols chased the survivors across the field with whoops and catcalls, making a game of shooting the beaten foe down with their bows, or slashing at them with their curved swords as they rode past, laughing. One group of the shah's infantry rallied and made a desperate stand, two hundred men forming a tight ring of defiant spear points. But the Mongol light horse merely galloped all around them, surrounding them on all sides, then shot them down, one after the other, with a killing rain of arrows, until not one Khwarazmian spearman was left alive.

They desecrated the shah's corpse, cutting off his battered head and mounting it on a spear to parade jeeringly around the battlefield until Subutai curtly gave them the order to cease.

Robert sat oblivious to the carnage around him, staring at Father Pietro's headless, one-armed corpse. His buzzing head seemed to swell and shrink in time with his beating heart, until Taghachat and some of his *jagghun* riders, released from their baggage-guarding duty, found him and brought him a spare horse. Poor Bear was long dead.

With Taghachat's help, Robert mounted and slowly rode back to the line where the doomed shah had made his last stand, and there he dismounted. Leading his remount by the reins, he walked over to another horse he recognised, nuzzling at a fallen rider, and Robert crouched down on the turf.

Altan was still alive, but only just. He was unable to move his legs, and he lay in a small lake of his own drying blood, looking up at the Eternal Blue Sky. He recognised Robert and, when the Englishman gently took his hand, he smiled and tried to speak.

'We did some fine things together, *khuukhed*,' he mumbled, his eyes unfocused. 'We rode the wide steppe, we slew our foes and took their herds and made their widows weep, we found your quarry in the wilderness, the Great Khan. And I put a shaft in the shah today, I think. My arrow marked a Persian king. But now... Now I have had my time... Now my long journey is done.'

Robert found that he was weeping. He squeezed Altan's cold hand, but the Cuman did not respond. His eyes were closed. Then Altan opened his eyes a crack and whispered, 'Take the widow Jargal into your *ger*. She is a good woman and can cook – adequately. But she is very poor. Give her my share of the herds and horses.'

Then he died.

They buried Altan on a hilltop south of the battlefield, with a view towards the endless grasslands to the east, and Robert said a prayer over his grave, asking God to forgive his heathen ways and grant him a place in Paradise. Then he returned to the camp to seek Subutai and orders.

Chapter Twenty-six

Summer turned to autumn, and with that came the rains. Over the next two weeks, Robert nursed his battered head in the rear of the column with the other wounded, while Subutai and Jebe chased the remnants of the shah's beaten army a hundred miles west to the town of Hamadan – a march through drenching rain over roads that soon became quagmires. Hamadan opened its gates when offered the Great Khan's Choice by Subutai, and the Mongol commander learned there that the shah's last few regiments were disbanded and the remaining soldiers had dispersed, unpaid, many taking up banditry, others fleeing to the safety of the Abbasid Caliphate and its wealthy capital Baghdad.

And at Hamadan the Mongol army was finally allowed to rest.

Robert and Subutai were sharing a cup of *airaq* in the general's *ger* outside the town gates. The rain was pattering hard on the felt roof, but they were snug inside by the hearth-fire. Robert was distracted, thinking of Altan, and how he missed his Cuman friend, and so he did not hear the general. He looked up and saw Subutai was holding out a folded piece of paper sealed with wax.

'This came today by Arrow Rider,' he said, grinning at Robert.

Robert took the letter. He opened it and read the message by the flickering light of the hearth-fire. It was short and written in elegant Persian.

> The treaty is completed. The terms have been agreed and the Great Khan has set his seal on it. All it lacks now is your seal. Return to Samarkand quickly. Let us grow rich together. Karacha.

He looked up at the general, and smiled at him in return.

–

Robert took a single *arbat* of Mongol troopers – ten men – and, leaving Taghachat in command of the *jagghun*, he set off early the next morning.

It took thirty days to reach Samarkand. They each took three spare horses and rode twelve hours a day. The weather was appalling for much of that journey; the rains made the roads boggy and difficult to navigate, and pebble-hard hail and icy sleet in the mountains froze their bones at night in their fireless, cheerless camp. Autumn was fast becoming winter and, on the thirtieth day, ragged, as lean as deer hounds and tired beyond belief, they arrived outside the gates of Samarkand. A gentle snow was falling. It was mid-November, Robert calculated, perhaps a week after St Martin's Day, and he had been gone from this part of the world for a full nine months.

Samarkand was a shock to Robert. In his imagination, it had been a glittering city of gold, the 'brother' of Burkhara and its equal in splendour. He had envisioned it as a place of artificial lakes and cool pleasure gardens, of tall, exquisite mosques, gilded mansions and stately cypress trees.

What he found was a freezing ruin, its fire-scorched walls reduced to rubble, with burnt-out buildings and stinking, rubbish-strewn streets. Legions of maimed beggars roamed the streets. The filthy canals and lakes were filled with detritus – dead bodies, broken furniture, half-burnt wagons, and all manner of goods discarded by drunken Mongols during the sack.

Leading his *arban* through the shattered streets of Samarkand, Robert was filled with an overwhelming sense of the pity of war. He glanced in through broken shutters at derelict houses. Their mounts stepped over mounds of loose rubble and black puddles full of half-melted snow, all the while fending off gangs of ragged children, who swarmed around begging for a little bread.

They stopped outside a grand, relatively unscathed house in the eastern part of Samarkand near the Chinese Gate, the main portal on that side of the city. It was a two-storey mansion with arched windows, a shady verandah and a wooden door strengthened with iron bars.

It must have possessed a hidden lookout post, too, for the moment Robert stepped off the gelding, the door flew open and a tall man came running out, loudly crying his name. Robert stared at the man: a thin face under a green silk turban with an aigrette nodding in the crown, a long lean nose, a neat oiled and perfumed black beard. 'Welcome at last to Samarkand, my brother,' said Karacha.

It was a joyful reunion. When the horses were stabled, and troopers of the *arban* settled in their quarters behind the house, Robert washed and changed his clothes and met Karacha in the main living room in the centre of the mansion. He was amazed at the opulence of the room: silk carpets; huge cushions as soft as clouds; a low table fashioned from black hardwood inlaid with gold; and an obsequious Uzbek servant, who served him cool wine in delicate green glass vessels, and a plate of salted pistachios and delicious wafer-thin biscuits flavoured with honey and rose-water to nibble on.

'To whom does this great house belong?' Robert asked, munching a second delicious biscuit and eyeing the expensive silk hangings, and the coals glowing in the huge copper brazier.

'To you,' Karacha replied. 'Or, in truth, to the House of Karacha, of which I own a one fifth share, and you own two fifths, and Niccolò Ziani possesses the other two on behalf of the Republic of Venice. That was the arrangement you wanted me to make, was it not?'

'And where did all this –' Robert waved his half-eaten biscuit at the general luxuriousness all around him – 'come from? You spent that treasure we took out of Otrar on *this*?'

'I made an investment in our mutual concern. And while you have been off chasing the shah, I have been busy here. Trade has been good these past few months. I will show you all the accounts after dinner. I think you will be pleased.'

Robert noticed that his friend Karacha was looking a little smug.

'What trade? I have not even read the agreement with the Great Khan yet.'

'Ah, yes, I shall make an appointment with the Chancery tomorrow.'

'Chancery?'

'We have *government* in Samarkand now, Robert. It is no longer run like an army camp. His Excellency Yelu Ahai and his staff of Chinese officials manage the affairs of the Great Khan in all territories east of the Amu Daria. They are holding the treaty for you, until you are ready to set your seal on it. Do you have a seal or a signet ring?'

'No. But I can write my own name on the document. Or just make my mark.'

'I will have a seal made for you, Robert. We must appear as official as we possibly can. Now, shall we go through to eat our supper? I have so much to tell you.'

Karacha had indeed been busy. Although the treaty was not yet ratified – it required Robert's seal for that final step – the Persian merchant had already begun trading on their behalf. He had been buying up booty taken in the sack of Samarkand, and the looting of Burkhara, and from Otrar, Signak, Banakat and half a dozen other towns besides. The Mongol custom was to pool all spoils and share them out to every man who had taken part in the battle and, as a result, there were many ordinary Mongol troopers with one small piece of jewellery, or a single ingot of precious metal, or a bolt of silk, or a fine carpet, or a delicate glass vase that he did not particularly value. And lo, here was the House of Karacha, where such things could be traded for things that he *did*, in fact, require or desire: weapons, for example – a good new sword, or a strong, light Persian scale-mail coat; a warm woollen blanket; a new saddle or stirrups fashioned from iron; a barrel of sweet wine from the vineyards of the Zagros mountains; fine food – honey cakes and sherbet – or just a sack of rice.

All these items were provided from the storerooms of the House of Karacha – and handsome profits had been reaped over the past six months. When their lavish meal was over, Robert and Karacha went down into the warehouse, in the basement of the house, and Robert duly examined the accounts. When he saw the final figure that showed the profit in the equivalent of pounds of silver, he felt dizzy with elation: he realised that he was, in fact – even with only his two fifths share of that sum – moderately rich. Not wealthy enough to pay the extortionate Adorno ransom, of course, and free his brother. But he was worth more money than the manor of Hadlow had yielded in ten years.

The Chancery of the Ulus of Turkestan was to be found in a building a few streets away from the House of Karacha, and it was guarded by a pair of armed Mongols, with swords at their waists and spears in their hands. But they allowed Robert to enter with no difficulty, and he found himself inside a huge marble-clad foyer, with refined servants in neat blue silk gowns, each man with a long queue of black plaited hair falling down his back, all seemingly hurrying here and there. There were several seats at the side of the vast room, and three or four nervous-looking people sitting waiting.

A Chinese man at a desk looked up from his files and said in Mongolian, 'You are welcome, sirs. Yelu Ahai, the Master of the Treasury, is expecting your visit. He will summon you shortly.'

Even though Robert was braced for a long, dull day, they were made to wait little more than a few moments. Very soon, to the visible annoyance of the other people waiting in the foyer, they were being ushered through a set of doors to an even larger chamber – also clad in creamy marble – where one man was sitting at a writing desk with a pile of papers, a quill and ink pot. He was writing something and held up an outward palm without looking at them, while he completed the line he was scratching. Then he set the pen in its stand and stood up.

Robert was surprised at how tall he was. This man was several inches taller than him – and the Englishman was no pipsqueak – and his wispy beard fell almost to his waist.

'You will have come to see me about your tax,' said Yelu Ahai in Mongolian.

Robert frowned at him. 'Tax?' he said.

'Your Excellency,' said Karacha, answering in that tongue, 'may I introduce myself and my partner—'

Yelu held up one finger for silence and said, 'I know who you are. You are Karacha, the merchant from Otrar. He is the *Elchin Baghatur*, and I can assure you that you *are* both here to speak to me about your tax, whether you recognise this or not.'

'I am Karacha, Your Excellency, and this is indeed the *Elchin Baghatur*. But we are in truth here to speak about the trade treaty recently arranged between us and the Great Khan.'

'I believe that is what you think. And I do indeed have that treaty in my possession, waiting for your seal. But before we attend to that, I must inform you of the tax that you will pay to the Ulus of Turkestan on the profits you make trading in this realm. I think one fifth part of your profits, delivered to this office every quarter, would be appropriate, don't you? You will receive a receipt.'

'With the greatest respect, Your Excellency, this is outrageous,' said Karacha. 'We were promised an exclusive treaty by the Great Khan himself, which includes the freedom to trade in all his realms on behalf of the Republic of Venice, without let or hindrance, and what you are now suggesting is an impossible imposition on our—'

'I took the liberty of perusing the treaty myself,' said Yelu, 'and there's no mention of an exemption from tax. All the Great Khan's subjects must contribute to the upkeep of his Ulus, and the burden must fall most heavily on those who profit most.'

'Perhaps we might contribute one hundredth of our profits to the Ulus, merely as a gesture of goodwill, to be paid twice yearly. But I must also warn you that, despite any wild rumours you may have heard, our profits have been miserably disappointing over these past few months...'

Robert had agreed to let Karacha speak for him. The merchant had a far better grasp of the trading of his house. He only half-listened as the discussion went back and forth between Karacha and Yelu. Both seemed to be enjoying themselves – and Robert knew that whatever figure was arrived at, he and Karacha – and Ziani, too – would still be satisfied with the wealth they were accruing.

'I must insist,' Yelu was saying. 'I insist, at the very minimum, that you pay one tenth part of your profits in tax to the Ulus. But, on a completely different subject, I wonder if I do indeed have the treaty here ready for your seal. Things sometimes get lost – that is the curse of bureaucracies. Things are mislaid, even important documents like treaties—'

'We accept,' interrupted Robert. 'When I have set my seal on the treaty, and I have the document, and three copies, in my hand, *and not before*, I shall make an agreement with your Chancery to pay a one tenth part of our profits, every quarter.'

Karacha gave him a sour look, but said nothing. Robert shrugged at his partner.

Less than an hour later, Robert was striding out of the office of the Master of the Treasury with a bulky leather satchel containing four tightly rolled parchment scrolls under one arm, with Karacha trailing despondently after him. Robert was smiling broadly, beaming at the whole world, even at the collection of poor souls still waiting in the anteroom. His smile fell upon a tall woman, made even taller by her elegant Mongol headdress, standing at the counter, speaking to the clerk.

It was Sarantuya.

Chapter Twenty-seven

The sound of his footsteps echoed as Father Ivo of Narbonne descended into the gloom. Gutto, the gaoler who bore the candle, went ahead and fumbled with the bolts on the door, then threw it wide open.

And Ivo entered the fetid cell full of righteous fury.

'Liar!' His angry voice resounded off the slimy stone walls.

Robert, at the rear of the space, blinked, and blinked again as his eyes slowly began to adjust to the blinding candle.

'Father Ivo? Is that you?'

'It is I. And I have come here – one final time – to call you a liar. And to tell you that, because of your lies, half-truths, prevarication and misleading answers, I shall have no more dealings with you. You may rot here in this pit until the duke brings you to trial and hangs your carcass from the gallows. Then God will send you to the true Hell, where you will pay for your lies for eternity.'

'What has happened, Father? Tell me.'

'I have received a letter at last from my master Bishop Géraud, and the answers to several urgent questions. My bishop has been in contact with his brother... Yes, I see you shrink at the news. Rightly so. Bishop Géraud de Malemort has been speaking to his beloved brother Jean de Malemort, Seneschal of the Poor Fellow-Soldiers of Christ and of the Temple of Solomon – and once your superior. My bishop was summoned to his poor brother's deathbed to hear his confession!'

'Jean de Malemort is dead?'

'He is with Christ and the angels now – God rest his soul!'

Robert closed his eyes and muttered a prayer. Then opened them and looked at Ivo.

'You call me liar... Father? Why say you this? Of what lies do you accuse me?'

'You know full well.'

'I do not.'

'You told me – indeed, you *swore* to me that you did *not* have any secret meetings with Jean de Malemort. And vowed that the Seneschal did *not* send you on a mission for him, for the Order – out into the wilds of the Syrian desert. Yet, when Bishop Géraud asked his poor dying brother – at my request – whether this was true, Jean de Malemort admitted he *had* dispatched you on a mission, an important and difficult task to attempt – a mission to the great Mongol khan. That was by far your blackest lie. You were *not* sent away from the Templars in disgrace over some footling game of dice – you were dispatched on a secret mission by your superior, Jean de Malemort. You lied to me.'

Robert said nothing. He dropped his chin and tightly closed his eyes.

'For that reason, Robert of Hadlow, liar and deceiver, I wash my hands of you. You can wallow here in sin until your trial – which is two days from now. I shall not speak to you, nor shall you see me, nor shall you taste my food and wine again. You will languish here until they drag you up to the hall in chains, where you shall receive a full measure of justice from the duke's court.'

With that, Ivo moved briskly to the doorway, nodded to Gutto and stepped outside. The light of the candle began to fade away. The hinges squealed, and just as the door was about to slam shut, Ivo poked his tonsured head back in.

'I will give you one last chance to tell the truth. Will you cease your lying?'

Robert said quietly, 'What is it that you wish me to say?'

'The truth – and nothing but. Are you even capable of doing that?'

Robert said nothing for a while. Then he slowly nodded his matted blond head.

The *enquêteur* came back into the cell.

'First answer me this… Were you expelled from the Order of the Temple?'

For a long time, the Englishman did not speak. Then very softly, he said, 'Since you seem to know already, I will admit it. I was not expelled. I remain a true and faithful Knight of the Order.'

'Were you dispatched on a secret mission by Jean de Malemort?'

Another painful pause. 'Yes.'

'And was this mission to seek out the Tartars – or, as you call them, Mongols?'

'It was.'

'Then you must tell me all of it. *All of it*. And do not lie again. If I even suspect that you are departing from the truth, or distorting it in any way, I shall be gone for good.'

–

Some hours later, Ivo sat at his writing desk in his small room above the dungeon and composed himself. He flexed his fingers, selected a quill, dipped it in the open ink pot and began.

> My Lord Bishop, I am delighted to inform you that my clever ruse has been successful and the English prisoner has, at long last, made a full confession to me of his sins and rendered an accurate account of his actions since his feigned departure in apparent disgrace from Acre in spring of the Year of Our Lord Twelve Hundred and Eighteen.
>
> I devoutly hope that what I have to report to you will please both you and your august royal master, Louis of France, and will give His Majesty a large amount of material to use against his serpentine, Satan-worshipping enemies – indeed, the enemies of all good and decent Christians, the heretical Poor Fellow-Soldiers of Christ and of the Temple of

Solomon. I pray this may be so, and that your master will be pleased with my endeavours in Vienna. Robert of Hadlow, as we suspected, was dispatched by the Seneschal Jean de Malemort, your brother, as an agent involved in the secret workings of their diabolical Order, and his mission, as revealed to me, was as follows…

–

Robert was alone in his chambers in the House of Karacha, with a brazier warming the room, and the snow falling outside his shuttered window. He was thinking about his true mission, the real reason he was in Samarkand: the shining dream that had caused him to travel thousands of miles and endure so many dangers and hardships – his shining dream of a victory for Christendom, a victory for the glory of Jesus Christ. He remembered it all so clearly…

He recalled the lessons in Arabic, Turkish and Persian he had received before his departure from the Holy Land, lessons given by local language masters in cloisters deep beneath the Templar fortress in Acre. He recalled the discreet meetings he had held with Jean de Malemort, his mentor and friend, in the Seneschal's private quarters.

'You can never tell a soul about your mission, Robert,' Malemort had said once, putting a hand on his shoulder. 'You must take it to your grave. Even if they put you to the question – even if they burn the flesh from your bones – you cannot breathe a word. Never. Even if we succeed, no man can ever know the part you played. Have you the strength to carry this burden?'

'I believe so,' said Robert.

'I believe it, too. I have watched your progress for some years. Your faith is as strong as iron, as immovable as a mountain. You are a true Templar Knight, Robert. That is why I chose you for this arduous task. Your only weakness is a love for gambling, a predilection for dice. But we can make use of it...'

So Robert had agreed, and sworn an oath that he would never reveal the mission. Yet even as he made his vow, he questioned it. 'If we succeed, Seneschal, the truth will surely emerge.'

'I hope and pray it will not,' said Malemort. 'There are forces in the world, Robert, even in Christendom, even among our highest born, who would use this knowledge against us. If you love our Order, if you love God, you must be silent for ever.'

He recalled, too, the indignity of his trial in Acre, after the play-acting with being 'surprised' at dice. He remembered that humiliation with a wince, even though Malemort had arranged it all.

Yet it was the last words Jean de Malemort had said to him, that same morning in Acre directly after the trial, that were branded on his soul. 'Go with God, Robert of Hadlow,' Malemort had said, embracing him like a loving father. 'Go with my full blessing, and remember that you hold the fate of our Order, the knighthood of Christendom, and the Church itself in your safekeeping.'

With those words, Robert had been dispatched into the desert with only a water bottle, a staff and his unshakeable faith, to seek out Jean de Malemort's ally, Aaron of Sana'a, and his wandering tribe of Habbani merchants somewhere in the wastes of Syria. The whole adventure lay ahead of him then: the brutal journey through the desert; trading through Anatolia and Trebizond, and on into Azerbaijan and Georgia; across the high Caucasus all the way to Tana, where he had been told a friendly reception awaited him with another of Jean de Malemort's friends – a wealthy Venetian merchant, a man who would smooth his path, equip him for the journey and propel him eastwards.

The only wrinkle in the blanket had been the news Niccolò Ziani had given Robert in Tana about Gilbert's capture at Damietta and imprisonment in Jerusalem. Robert had wanted to abandon the mission to find the Great Khan – or at least delay it – until his brother could be freed. But a message from Malemort ordered him to press on with his mission, and Ziani also urged him to proceed east.

'We shall free Gilbert together, Roberto,' Ziani had promised. 'Once we have the treaty, I will raise the ransom price myself. I swear this to you. But first we must attain this precious treaty.'

Niccolò Ziani was not a devotee of their cause. His relationship with Jean de Malemort was one of mutual assistance: a purely businesslike arrangement. Ziani did not believe, as Robert and Malemort both fervently did, in the absolute necessity of this last desperate throw of the dice.

And, so far, the mission had been a success. Robert possessed the treaty – indeed, the scroll was lying there now, beside its three copies, on the desk in front of him. And, while this treaty would – praise God – free his brother from the Genoese, it was not the true reason he had journeyed so far and suffered so much. It was not even his most urgent concern that afternoon in Samarkand. For it was time, now, at last, for Robert to enact the final part of his mission – the part that mattered.

All was in place for the final stroke. Subutai was in position in the far west with a powerful army of two full *tumet* – twenty thousand battle-hardened Mongols. The general had made his winter camp on the shores of the Sea of Ravens near Rasht – an ancient town Robert had actually recommended to Subutai as being the perfect mild spot to see out the cold months.

This piece of deft persuasion had the merit of being perfectly true – Robert had visited the place with Aaron, and had tucked it away in his mind. So Subutai was on the Caspian with his *tumet*, five hundred miles from Baghdad, a distance his troopers could cross in a mere ten days.

Ten days' hard ride from his winter camp at Rasht, and Subutai could be outside the walls of the city of Baghdad, giving a suitably cowed Abbasid Caliph the Great Khan's Choice.

Robert was certain that, in time, he could convince Subutai to make that journey. The general trusted him. They were friends. It also made excellent sense from a military perspective. How many of the shah's troops had fled to Baghdad after their defeat? Thousands. And they must be crushed.

From Baghdad it was only six hundred miles – so Aaron had assured him – to *Jerusalem*. Just twelve days' ride for the desert-hardened Mongol army. Once Subutai had conquered Baghdad – and he could easily do it – the Mongol general would be in striking distance of the Holy City itself.

And that was the true prize.

A Mongol army, appearing like magic out of the empty deserts to attack the Saracen enemy from the rear – *that* was the shining dream. Achieving that was his secret mission. That was why Robert had come east. Not for Gilly, not for the treaty, but to engineer the capture of Jerusalem.

This would be the master stroke that would save Christendom. To win back Jerusalem for the Christians in the Holy Land – and to hold it: that was the plan Malemont had conceived, and that Robert was tasked with executing. That was the coup that would finally win the war in Outremer.

Robert had seen the awful face of conflict in the Holy Land – a war that had lasted a hundred years or more, a war that had ravaged the Latin kingdoms and cost many thousands of Christian and Saracen lives – and he now possessed the means to end that endless blood-soaked struggle.

He knew how precarious the hold of the Christians was on their strip of land along the Mediterranean. For the Ayyubid Sultanate in Egypt held sway over almost the entirety of the land that had nurtured the Saviour of mankind. The Ayyubid armies of the Saracen warlord Safadin were everywhere triumphant from Al-Yemen, the homeland of Aaron's tribe, to the city of Aleppo, the great Arab fortress of northern Syria. The Pope himself had called for a new great pilgrimage, a new holy war to rescue the Christians of the Latin kingdoms and return Jerusalem to the control of its Christian king. This was why Gilbert and all the other Templar Knights had been sent off to Damietta.

Robert, too, was playing his secret part in this new great pilgrimage. What greater cause could there be than to retrieve the Holy Land for Christ? What greater glory could he win on Earth?

Jean de Malemort had revealed his plan to Robert over several private sessions. The battered armies of Christ in the Holy Land, even supported by the great military orders such as the Templars and Hospitallers, even with fresh infusions of knights from France, Hungary and Germany, were simply too weak to beat back the Ayyubids alone. If only, Jean de Malemort had said, they had a powerful ally in the East, a puissant Christian king who might come to their aid. And that is when their talk had moved to the legend of Prester John, and the idea of help from an unexpected quarter.

Robert no longer believed that Genghis Khan was Prester John; that illusion had been shattered early in his acquaintance with the Mongols. But the notion of an unexpected invasion from the east by a powerful ally of the Christians was still enticing. The Great Khan was not *against* the true faith – he claimed he tolerated all religions equally – and he had proved himself more than capable of destroying the armies of the worshippers of the Prophet. If Robert could persuade the Great Khan to unleash his *tumet* on Baghdad, then to go one small step further...

There was a knock at the door, and Robert, irritated to be roused from his deepest and most secret thoughts, snapped, 'Yes?'

An Uzbek servant, one of dozens who kept the House of Karacha, who provided Robert with his daily food and drink, poked his shaven head around the door jamb.

'Lord,' he said in Turkish, 'there is someone here to see you. A visitor.'

'Who is it?' said Robert, still deep in his thoughts. 'What do they want?'

'A teacher, who says they are here to give you a lesson in the Mongolian tongue.'

Sarantuya walked into Robert's luxurious suite of rooms in the House of Karacha surrounded by her own beauty. She wore a long coat of brocaded silk in iridescent green, touched here and there by golden thread, and a tall, slender square headdress of the traditional Mongol type, which made her appear even taller and more elegant than ever. Her face was powdered white, as pure as the snow outside, except for her tiny, cherry-red painted lips and a fine flick of kohl beneath both her large dark liquid eyes, which brought them out like a splash of spring water on the purest jet-stone.

Her hair was bound up in an elaborate glossy bundle underneath her vertiginous headdress, making her neck look impossibly long and luscious, the fine black tendrils of hair that escaped it like the delicate fronds of some rare and precious flower.

Robert stared at her with his stupid mouth hanging open as she glided effortlessly into the room. He was used to seeing Sarantuya as a hard-working Mongol wife, often bloodied to the elbow from working with raw meat, or red-faced from crouching over the *ger* hearth to cook the nightly *shulen*. Even when they had hunted together, she had been brisk and boyish, in practical leathers and a shapeless cloak, leather-booted, armed with knife and bow, and smelling strongly of horse. Now she was the vision of loveliness – a perfect line of beauty, like calligraphy in human form.

Robert could not speak. She moved to him and he took her hands in his and found they were as cold as ice. He looked into her bottomless eyes, and was lost.

He felt the pull of his love for her more powerfully than he had ever felt love before. This emotion was beyond words, beyond the physical plane. It was a merging of two souls. He led her towards the brazier in the middle of the room, his brain struggling to say something, anything.

'I came to resume where we left off,' Sarantuya said, her voice husky and deeper than usual. 'With our Mongolian lessons, I mean. I saw you in the Chancery with Yelu Ahai. I saw you, and I knew that I *must* come here to your house, to see if...' She faltered and stopped. For the first time, Robert recognised that she was unsure, vulnerable…

He pulled her to him and kissed her. And it was real – and all of it was true.

She kissed him back, hungrily, passionately. Their clothes seemed to shed themselves from their bodies, like leaves falling from an autumn tree. On the soft silk carpet they were soon joined together, naked, eager, each as voracious as the other, kissing, biting, bucking into the other's body, grasping at the other, squeezing and plunging, until they found a solid rhythm, and thrust and rocked and thrust until it was over – surprisingly quickly, but with the wild, abandoned, reckless intensity of a cavalry charge – and then lay back, panting and joyful, in the puddle of their clothes.

Robert realised he had still said not a word to her. So he kissed her again and held her hard against his sweat-cooling body. He could feel her heart thudding against his ribs. And slowing, her body relaxing, gently melting into his.

Out of the corner of his eyes, he saw something silver glinting around her neck. It was the St Christopher medal that he had given her all those months before, worn on a leather thong and now lying over her white, cherry-tipped breast. They stayed there for a long while, holding each other, listening to the sounds of their own breathing. Then Robert disentangled his limbs and took Sarantuya gently by the hand, lifting her up and leading her to his chamber, where they slid between crisp white linen sheets, together.

And there they kissed again.

Chapter Twenty-eight

Robert had never experienced anything like it. His half-remembered relations with girls in his youth, before he made his vows to the Knights, had been mirthful, often drunken and perfunctory. He had rarely had the same girl more than two or three times before moving on to the next. It had seemed a fine, frivolous pastime, a pleasant activity that happened in the margins of his real life – his serious training in arms, and even more arduous study of Latin and Greek with the *magister*.

This passion with Sarantuya was at the very centre of his life. In his heart and mind, in his belly and loins. He longed for her when they were apart; when they were together, he sought to merge himself with her, like two essences fusing into a single being.

He had never been so happy.

The lovers were fortunate in the season. Winter had gripped Samarkand, locking it in ice and snow, which made travel near impossible. Many of the residents of the ruined city remained for weeks at a time by their hearths, if they had them. Likewise, Robert and Sarantuya spent many hours – sometimes whole days – in his chamber, making love, talking together, kissing, making love again.

She visited him every third day, under the pretext of giving him a Mongolian lesson. Yet nobody in the house was unaware of what was occurring. The servants brought food and drink, from time to time, when they were closeted together. The leader of the Mongol *arban*, who had accompanied Robert to Samarkand and was looking for fresh orders, once put his head round the door when they were kissing, grinned and went away. Robert could hear him chuckling to himself as he departed.

Karacha, however, was concerned about Khuyag.

'This is not good for our house, brother,' he said, in one of their rare meetings that winter. 'The *noyan* will make a lot of trouble for you – for us. He will surely try to kill you, Robert, when he finds out what is going on. And he *will* find out. That is certain.'

Robert recalled then the painful conversation he had had with Sarantuya about her husband in the first few hours after they had first made love on the floor in his apartments.

'He is not here, Robyert,' said Sarantuya. 'He knows nothing. Khuyag is out on the Amu Daria somewhere with Genghis Khan. I heard they were besieging Gurganj, up on the shores of the Aral Sea. My husband is five hundred miles away, fighting the Great Khan's enemies.'

Too far away to travel in this weather, Robert thought with shameful relief.

'Why are you not with the khan?' he asked.

Saruntuya's aged mother, Temulun, was ill, she explained. Genghis Khan himself had ordered his sister to stay in Samarkand until the old lady had recovered. Sarantuya often had to leave Robert to go and tend to her sick mother, who was staying in their *ger*, which was set up in one of the pleasure parks of the city, where their horses could readily graze, the steppe ponies scraping away the snow to munch at the frozen grass.

Robert insisted on giving Sarantuya special foods to take to Temulun, selected from the house stores for their healing powers: pots of calf's foot jelly, to strengthen her mother's bones; hard-dried ox hearts that could be shaved into boiling water to make healthy broth; apples and pears and pomegranates stored in straw since the autumn.

Yet the shadow of Khuyag was never far away, even in the midst of their lovemaking. 'Did you ever truly love the *noyan*?' Robert asked her one day, when they were in bed together.

'Not like this,' she said. 'But a kind of love, yes. There is a strong feeling between us.'

'He beats you. Sometimes I heard him doing it at night and wanted to kill him.'

'He only beats me when he's drunk. Or when he cannot perform as a husband.'

'I would kill him for hurting you. Would you like me to? I will do it, if you ask me.'

Sarantuya slapped him then, hard across the face. 'You would kill my husband? You already steal from him. You have stolen my love. Would you steal his life, too?'

They rarely spoke of Khuyag after that – but the *noyan*'s spectre had not receded.

Robert asked her one night about the danger of making a child with her. They had been together then for two full months, and winter's grip was beginning to ease.

'I do not think I can bear a child,' said Sarantuya. 'I long for one with all my heart. But after many years of marriage, I have never felt a quickening in my womb.'

It was a strange love affair – a secret that everyone knew. And salted with so much guilt on both sides. For all Robert's talk, he knew he could not, in truth, kill Khuyag. The *noyan* was a brother in arms; they had shed blood together on the battlefield.

There was also the question of his Templar oath. He had no confessor, no one in whom he could confide his carnal sins and be absolved. And he *had* sinned. He continued to sin with Sarantuya.

Then there was Gilly. Robert had the treaty. He should be making moves to return to Tana, and to instigate the negotiations with Ziani and Adorno to free his brother. He told himself it was too cold to travel. There was no point freezing to death in the high mountains, with the treaty gripped in his dead icy hand. But he knew he was deceiving himself. The truth was that he wanted – he needed – to stay with Sarantuya as long as he could. He could not bear to tear himself from her – even for Gilly.

He prayed every night that God would forgive him his carnal transgressions. He beseeched the Virgin to intercede on his behalf – she who knew the meaning of love so well. He called on St Christopher, too, to give him greater strength; yet when Sarantuya came to his door, the gown half-slipping off her creamy bare shoulder, and entered his chamber for their Mongolian 'lessons', all that was washed away in a flood of hot joy.

He once tried to talk about his guilt with Sarantuya, but she would have no part in it.

'Do not tell me this is not good,' she said. 'I love you – and you love me. It is natural, and therefore *right*. What does an oath matter, mere words, spoken long ago, when we have real love in our hearts? And I know that you do love me. You truly love me. I knew you loved me the instant you entered me in the *ger* on that night.'

'You mean in the chamber out there,' said Robert. 'It was in the afternoon.'

Sarantuya looked at him out of the side of her eyes, and smiled coyly, and Robert remembered the night: the impossible dream of love; the moonlight on her dark hair and the warm scent of her skin. 'Oh,' he said, as understanding dawned.

They were in love, and happy, but both knew it could not last. Spring was coming and the main roads would be open, and Khuyag would soon come south to Samarkand with the Great Khan and would be eager to seek out his beautiful wife.

'Leave him,' pleaded Robert. 'Dissolve the marriage – marry me.'

Sarantuya put a soft hand on his bearded cheek. 'You must go to the west – and soon. You must take your treaty to the lords of Venice. When the roads open, you must go and save your brother.'

So with green spring unfurling in Samarkand, Robert finally recognised that he must bid farewell to his love – the only true love he had ever known – and return to his long-neglected duty.

'Come with me to Tana, where I will tell the Venetian lord that I have the treaty. Then I will swiftly extract Gilly from his prison. We have money, my darling, we can live wherever we please.'

'We cannot live *here*. Khuyag would be humiliated. His *mingghan* would whisper that his wife cuckolded him with a foreigner. His junior officers would laugh up their sleeves. He would be obliged by honour to fight you. And then one of you would die.'

'Does it matter where we live? We could live in Tana, or London – or even Hadlow.'

'This is not practical, my love. I am a woman of the steppe. My home is a *ger*. I would live my life under the Eternal Blue Sky. What place would I have in a great city, or even in your father's English manor? You know this is true.'

Their lovemaking that afternoon had a special urgency. They knew it might be the last time. Indeed, the next day word reached Robert, through one of Karacha's contacts, that Genghis Khan had captured Gurganj after a long and bloody siege, and had massacred all its inhabitants. The khan was even now leading his victorious army back south towards Samarkand.

A day after that, Robert received another summons:

Come to my side, Akhmad, I need your wisdom.
Come west. The city of Hamadan has rebelled and
murdered its Mongol governor. It must be punished.
Red war calls your name, my friend. Remember:
glory is greater than riches. Subutai.

There were tears, and a final bout of lovemaking, sweet and sad, but with few words – what had they to say to each other at this cruel but necessary parting? They had pledged their love many times. Robert knew he must go west; if Subutai was marching on Hamadan, he would already be partway towards Baghdad... And there was the treaty, too, and poor Gilly to free from his prison.

Yet he did not know if he would return to Samarkand, to the East, or if he would see Sarantuya's face again. The thought terrified him. He had found happiness – now it would be snatched away.

'We have loved each other,' said Sarantuya, kissing Robert on the cheek like a sister at the door to his grand house as she bade him farewell. 'And we have shared a little happiness, for a time, you and I. Many people, in their whole lives, will never know that joy. Let that be enough.'

–

Dressed in his best *deel*, with the gold-adorned sword swinging from his fine Mongol belt, Robert walked into the huge *ger* that housed the newly returned Khan of Khans.

The *ger* had been transported by a hundred oxen down the line of the Amu Daria and over the shoulder of a mountain, and had stopped here, a few miles outside of Samarkand, where the Great Khan planned to rest his victorious *tumet* in the spring warmth after their bloody efforts in Gurganj.

But the war was not over. Parts of the dead shah's empire still fiercely resisted the Mongol yoke. The *tumet* would soon be obliged to march again.

The *ger* was bustling – already there had been a long stream of officials and officers who wished to speak to the Great Khan. Robert had been made to wait for three hours in the antechamber before being admitted – yet he did not resent this. It gave him time to prepare and hone his arguments.

He bowed before the Great Khan, who greeted him with his usual grave courtesy.

'I have heard reports of your success in commerce, *Elchin Baghatur*,' said Genghis Khan, 'and I am also pleased to hear you are contributing to the upkeep of my Ulus with your taxes.'

Too late, Robert noticed that the lean man sitting next to the Great Khan on a plain blue cushion was the Chinese official Yelu Ahai, the Master of the Great Khan's Treasury.

The taxman smiled at Robert and bobbed his head in return.

'I am glad you are pleased, O Great Khan,' said Robert. 'And I pray, therefore, that you will look with similar pleasure on my proposal this day, which concerns the future movements of the Mongol army in the far west, the *tumet* of generals Subutai and Jebe.'

'Speak, my brave *baghatur*,' said Genghis Khan. 'What is in your mind?'

'I have heard reports that thousands of the shah's men, fleeing the wrath of your victorious *tumet* after the death of their master, have gone to Baghdad, and now take shelter in that city of the Abbasid Caliph, a staunch ally of the late Muhammad Shah. It seems to me, O Great Khan, that it may be prudent – not to mention lucrative – if your generals were to ride west and take possession of Baghdad in your name, and add that glittering city to the illustrious list of your possessions.'

'You want General Subutai to take Baghdad? Why? The Abbasids have not attacked us. They have offered us no insult. They have not molested our envoys or murdered our merchants. Why?'

'They are sheltering your enemies, lord, thousands of the shah's troops, and in doing that, their city shows you scant respect. They defy you. Yet you are wise, Great Khan, to discern that I do indeed have a deeper reason for wishing to see Baghdad and the Caliphate safely in Mongol hands.'

Robert took a deep breath. It was time to tell the Great Khan the whole truth.

'As you know, Great One, I am a Christian from the West, from England, and representing the Republic of Venice here. This is true, but I also represent my own Brethren, the renowned Templar Knights of Christendom. We have long been at war with the Ayyubid Sultanate, which holds the lands beyond Baghdad, and we seek to wrest a territory back from them that is sacred to us – the holy city of Jerusalem and all its surrounding lands. It is the place where the son of God, Jesus Christ, made his life's work and gave us his teaching. It is where he gave his life for our sins.'

'I am aware of the Christ story,' said Genghis Khan. 'My son Tolui's wife Sorkoktani is a Christian, a follower of the wise man Nestorius. I have spoken with her about this holy child of your god, and his holy sacrifice. But what have the distant wars of Christians to do with me?'

'What I propose to you, O Great Khan, is an alliance between the great Mongol nation and all the nations of Europe. For beyond the Ayyubid Sultanate lie all the wide lands of Christendom. A man would have to ride for *three thousand* miles from here to reach the city of London, for example, in my own country – a journey that even the swiftest Arrow Rider, travelling without any halt or rest, could not cover in less than forty days!'

'Is there a mighty king of Christendom? A man with whom I could make such an alliance?'

'There are many kings – but they would all likely favour an alliance with you, O Great One. At least, I think, were my Brethren and I to advocate it, they could be persuaded to agree in time.'

'So the kings of Europe are all divided among themselves? That is interesting.'

'But there is only one Pope, Great Khan, a holy man and the head of our Christian Church, who lives in splendour in the great city of Rome. Pope Honorius is a father to all in Christendom.'

'Indeed? And how many *tumet* does this Pope have?'

'The Pope can command obedience from all the kings of Europe. He has recently ordered the knights of all Christian lands to converge upon the Holy Land to fight the evil Ayyubid Sultanate. And many thousands of our finest warriors have already heeded his call to battle.'

'But not enough warriors to defeat the Ayyubids. Which is why you need my help.'

'This is so, Great Khan. But reflect on this image – the whole world divided between the Mongol realm and Christendom. East and West at peace. You, Great Khan, ruling all lands to the east of the Mediterranean Sea, the various kings of Christendom, under the Pope's authority, ruling in the lands in the West. An alliance that would usher in a time of peace and plenty. We would trade our goods with you, and you with us, and all mankind would prosper from our worldwide amity!'

'I do not dislike this image. I should see the whole world prospering in peace.'

'Then, Great One, I beg you, give General Subutai the order to capture Baghdad immediately. That is the first step towards making this magnificent image a reality.'

'I like you, *Elchin Baghatur,* and I like your idea of a world divided equally between East and West, all of us living in peace, and I will think on this. However, I will not launch another war of conquest based on one conversation, no matter how eloquently you try to persuade me. As I say, I will think on the matter, and we shall speak again. Now, *Baghatur,* I give you permission to go—'

'Great Khan, I have been summoned by Subutai. I shall be leaving at dawn to ride to his side. May I tell him that he has permission to capture the city of Baghdad, if he believes it necessary?'

'Subutai knows his business. If he deems it necessary to take that city...'

'You are most gracious, O Great Khan,' said Robert, bowing low and moving hurriedly away backwards. 'I shall deliver your message to General Subutai.'

Chapter Twenty-nine

After a month of hard roads and harder riding, Robert found himself standing one sunny afternoon in early spring beside Subutai on the walls of Hamadan, and looking inside the burning city as the Mongol *tumet* roared through the streets, hounding the inhabitants to their deaths. There were corpses strewn everywhere. Robert wondered how much of the city would be standing by dawn.

'Tell me again what the Great Khan said,' said Subutai. 'His exact words.'

Robert took a deep breath. This was one last throw of the dice. He could win it all with what he next said to Subutai. Or...

'The Great Khan said it was necessary to capture the city of Baghdad.' Robert kept his features impassive as he uttered this black lie. 'He also said that you knew your business, and that you could accomplish the task with the men you have.'

'That is strange,' said Subutai, frowning at Robert. 'Whenever the Great Khan has mentioned Baghdad to me, he has always stressed that the city lies *outside* the Khwarazmian Empire and, because of that, we have no good reason to attack it. They are not a threat. He said those very words to me. They have not injured us. He said, if I recall, we must finish one war before starting another.'

'All I can do is report what he said to me.' Robert could feel an oily coldness in his belly, and knew it was caused by shame. But he also knew the magnitude of the cause for which he lied must override these feelings of personal disgust.

'Well, if that is indeed the Great Khan's command, I had better start the planning.'

Robert said nothing. He had turned away from the horrible scenes of death and destruction inside the doomed city below him, and was now watching a rider, a filthy man on a foam-flecked horse, who was galloping madly through the scattered Mongol encampment half a mile away.

He had a premonition he was watching his doom approach as he observed the horseman, an Arrow Rider, whip his tired mount towards the open gates of Hamadan.

Later, in Subutai's *ger*, he learned the contents of the Arrow Rider's message. It came from the Great Khan in Samarkand, was addressed to Subutai, and contained no mention *at all* of Baghdad.

Robert understood in that moment that he had rolled the dice for Christendom… and lost.

'Perhaps I misunderstood the Great Khan's words,' he said, when Subutai's yellow eyes bored into his over a plate of roasted kid for their dinner. 'My command of Mongolian is not yet perfect. I recall we spoke about Baghdad, about capturing the city… Perhaps his mind has changed.'

Subutai said nothing for a long, long time, his cat's eyes very nearly scorching Robert's face.

Then the general turned to Jebe, who was sitting opposite them both, and said, 'Genghis Khan's orders, the ones we received this day, are perfectly clear, General. We are to take our two *tumet* north to the Caucasus. The Kipchak federation and their Cuman allies have rebelled once again against the Great Khan's overlordship. Several Mongol garrisons north of the Aral Sea have been attacked. Yanikant has been sacked and burned to the ground, and a whole *mingghan* of Jochi's men were slaughtered in their beds. We are ordered to go north and attack the Kipchaks – but from the west. We are to surprise them by coming from that direction and punish them for their crimes.'

Subutai and Jebe discussed their preparations for a while, with some of the other *noyan* contributing their ideas. Robert said nothing. He kept his embarrassed eyes on his plate of goat.

As the general's supper was breaking up, and all the *noyan* of the various *mingghat* were going off to sleep, Subutai grabbed the sleeve of Robert's *deel* and stopped him leaving the *ger*.

'You could be useful to me, Robyert, in the Caucasus, since you have travelled there. You could be useful again. You *do* know the mountains, do you not? You would not lie about *this*?'

Robert swore he had indeed travelled through the high peaks of the Caucasus with the Jews of Sana'a two years before, and he recalled that arduous journey well.

'Then you must come with me. With your *jagghun*. I know that you wish me to capture Baghdad – I do not understand why. But I know this is what you desire. You have mentioned it to me several times in the past, each time employing your best persuasions. So know this... I have no strong objection to my troops sacking a wealthy city. The men of my *tumet* would relish the loot of Baghdad. But you must *not* lie to me. If I am to trust you, you must never lie to me again. Yes?'

'I do not know what you are talking about, General. I have never lied to you.'

Subutai gave Robert's *deel* sleeve a little shake, for emphasis. 'I will march on Baghdad *only* when my khan orders me to do so. Do you understand? Therefore, *Elchin Baghatur*, I will make this bargain with you today. You know I am a man of my word, so pay close attention to me now. If you will come into the high mountains with me, and guide my *tumet* according to your best skills and knowledge over those peaks, then, when we return south in a few weeks or months, as we surely will, I will seek the Great Khan's permission to take an expedition to Baghdad. Do you hear me?

'If the Great Khan agrees, Robyert, you shall have your heart's desire. But before that, think on this... When we are on the far side of the Caucasus we shall be nearer your masters' home – in the town of Tana, is that not correct? So, when we are over the mountains, I will allow you to take your *jagghun* and go to Tana, and deliver your precious treaty to them. So, now, do we have a bargain?'

Robert reined in the gelding at the top of a small stony rise and looked north. Before him were the lush, verdant hills of Georgia, rumpled like a vast green blanket. The slopes were grassy in the lower parts, thickly wooded as they rose, and only cut by the single narrow road that wound through them. The afternoon sun was pleasantly warm on his face. Beside him were Taghachat and a dozen men of his *jagghun*, and behind him − a hundred miles behind him, a good two days' ride south and east − was an entire Mongol army, twenty thousand war-hardened riders under the command of the generals Subutai and Jebe. They were camped at a town called Gandza, in the valley of the Kura. The generals were awaiting Robert's scouting report before advancing any further.

Beyond the green hills, the lower slopes of the Caucasus rose in serried ranks, a darker green, marching east to west like waves on a vast sea, almost black in places, shadowed and menacing, and beyond them, further still, was the jagged wall of the peaks, iron-grey and stained here and there with old snow, even in the warmth of April. White clouds roiled over this impossible wall of nature.

There was no human habitation in sight for miles in front of him, and yet there in the distance Robert could see a line of camels − some pack horses, too − on the narrow road. They were heading his way. The animals were fully burdened, he could see now, and all roped together. About thirty people with them, he thought. They were coming closer.

'Wait here,' he said to Taghachat. 'I shall be gone an hour, or maybe two.'

'*Baghatur*, they may be dangerous. I shall accompany you. Our riders—'

'Stay here!' Robert snapped the order in Mongolian, and kicked his gelding down the gentle slope and began to canter straight towards the oncoming camel train.

As he spurred his horse through the green folds of the hills, keeping one eye on the train and its mounted outriders, his mind leapt forward to the high peaks and what lay beyond them: the land of the wild Kipchaks; beyond that, he knew, it was only two weeks' ride to Tana.

Two weeks' ride and he would be in Niccolò Ziani's hall.

In his saddlebags on the gelding's haunches, he had the treaty he had fought so hard to win, and also one fair copy. The other two copies he had prudently left with Karacha in Samarkand. He had failed, it could not be denied, to persuade either Subutai or the Great Khan to attack Baghdad. But he had planted the seed with the Great Khan – the seed of the idea of the entire world divided between Mongol and Christian – East and West, all humanity living in harmony. And the khan had shown himself receptive. There might be a delay – a few months; a year, perhaps – but the Mongol horde would eventually ride to the aid of Christendom. Robert knew this deep down in his bones.

He dearly wished that Altan could have been with him to see this view – the black Caucasus ahead both beckoning and forbidding. He wished, too, that Altan could be with him at the moment of triumph, when he informed Niccolò Ziani that he had in his possession the treaty between the Mongol khan and the Republic of Venice. He knew exactly what he would say: that the treaty would be in Ziani's hands the very moment that Gilly was free of his chains and reunited with Robert.

But, more than anything, in that moment, the Englishman longed for Sarantuya. He knew their love was not to be – it could never be: Sarantuya was married, and she would not abandon either her husband or the steppe life that she loved so dearly; and he had his tattered oath of chastity to cling to, and his duty to Gilly, and a fine treaty to deliver that was worth a world in gold and treasure.

Yet his heart was broken.

A rider came out of the camel train, galloping hard to intercept him. Robert could not make out the features of the man's face; he could only note that it was darkened by a thousand suns, and now, he saw, the man was grinning, his white teeth gleaming in a thick black beard.

The rider reined in just yards from him. The man leapt from his saddle and Robert, too, halted and stepped to the ground. The two men ran to each other, their arms open wide. They embraced.

'Well met, my friend,' said Aaron of Sana'a, finally releasing Robert. 'I see you have remembered precisely what I taught you about our habitual routes south and the timing of our travels.'

'Of course,' said Robert, still holding on to Aaron's forearms. 'How could I forget? But I was also fortunate – God smiled upon me. I have so much to tell you, my friend. So much. And I confess that I shall need your advice and help again before this day is out.'

'You shall have it.' Then, still smiling, Aaron said, 'But tell me first, Brother Robert, what fresh tidings do you bring me to pass on to our friend in Acre? For Jean de Malemort. I trust you have good news for our cause? Tidings that will spell the ruin of our Ayyubid enemies?'

'Good tidings, I believe. Although, firstly, you must know that the legends of Prester John are false. He does not exist. But I have found another, far greater monarch, and one who may yet come to our aid. Genghis Khan – the Great Khan of the Mongols. I believe he will form an alliance with us. You may give Jean de Malemort this message... The Mongols are here in the West – and in force. Also, the Khwarazmian Empire is no more. The Mongol *tumet* have destroyed that realm and its shah in less than two years. And the Great Khan will come further west, I'm sure of it. But not yet.'

Aaron nodded at him. 'I have already heard reports of the fall of the Shah of Khwarazmia. Do you think this Genghis Khan will advance and conquer the Abbasids in Baghdad?'

'In time, yes,' said Robert. 'A Mongol army follows me – I am its guide. That is where I need your help, brother. This great Mongol army must first deal with the rebellious Kipchaks beyond the Caucasus before they can turn south and attack our enemies. And I have personal business in Soldaya. Urgent business, that I must not delay any further. My brother Gilbert is... But never mind all that. I must go to Tana first, to arrange matters. Niccolò Ziani will be expecting me. Then I must go to Soldaya...'

The absolute blackness of the cell in Vienna was illuminated with a faint glowing blue light. Robert, lying on the cold stone in his chains, looked towards the doorway. He saw a figure – a tall man – blossoming into being by the entrance. He sat up.

'Father Ivo?' he said. But it was not the middle-aged Provençal *enquêteur*.

The figure came into focus: a young man, strong, dressed in the white surcoat of a Templar, with a blood-red cross emblazoned on his chest. He seemed to be lit from within by a ghostly fire, the light radiating out and enveloping him, extending beyond the physical edges of his body.

'Gilly?' said Robert. 'You are here? You came to save me in my hour of peril?'

'I no longer walk this Earth, brother – as well you know. I died a long time ago. Therefore, sadly, I cannot free your tormented body from this prison. But I do offer succour for your soul. I come to you, Rob, with a message from Heaven. A message of love, of hope and redemption. St Christopher sent me to you, with this message. He says that despite your many sins, despite your carnal lusts, and your many deceits, despite the blood of so many innocents on your hands... The saint bids me tell you that Redemption is nigh. The time draws near, brother. The time when you must leave behind this fleshly garb. But have no fear. Be strong. For our Lord has prepared a place for you in Paradise, at the right hand of the Saviour. Be at peace, my brother.'

The vision was fading, becoming dimmer, the outlines of Gilbert's glowing body becoming faint. 'No,' said Robert. 'Do not go, Gilly. Stay a while with me.'

But all was darkness once again.

Then a noise. A creaking and scraping of iron on stone, and the sound of voices.

A yellow light, like that from a beeswax candle, spilled into the hard darkness, pushing it back. Robert could make out the figure of an older man holding the candle.

'My son,' said Father Ivo, 'I am sorry to tell you that the dreadful hour has arrived.'

Robert blinked, cuffed his eyes, and stared at the priest in the cell doorway.

'The duke's court will assemble this morning, my son, and try you as a traitor to Christendom, and you must plead your case before them. I have heard your confession, Sir Robert, and I have absolved you of all your sins – and may almighty God have mercy on your soul. But while I have shriven you, the judgment of Man is now upon you.'

'The trial is today?' asked Robert.

'Yes, my son, within the hour. My advice to you is simple – tell the truth. Tell the assembled lords who stand in judgment that you were dispatched to the Mongol lands by the Poor Fellow-Soldiers of Christ and of the Temple of Solomon. Tell them that you only acted on behalf of your Order. Tell them you merely obeyed the commands of your superior, Jean de Malemort. Perhaps then they will show mercy.'

Robert now stood before the *enquêteur*, naked but for the filthy loincloth he had worn for the past two months, his pale body emaciated, covered in scabs, scars and sores. But his spine was straight, his chin lifted, his heart high. And his mind as keen and bright as the finest Damascus steel.

'Are you ready, my son, to face the Duke of Austria's justice?' said Ivo. Behind him stood two of the gaolers, and their leader Gutto, all armed with heavy clubs.

'I care nothing for earthly justice,' replied Robert in a strong, resolute voice. 'God chose me as his servant. I know in my heart that He will not abandon me. Now, let us go up into the light!'

Historical Note

A few years ago, the journalist Matthew Parris made a passing reference in one of his excellent *Times* columns to the story of an Englishman who was captured in 1241 outside the gates of Vienna, fighting for the invading Mongol army. For me, this was a light-bulb moment. I did not quite shout 'Eureka', jump out of my bath and run naked through the streets of Tonbridge because, well, I'm a middle-aged British chap, but I definitely understood then how that excitable old Greek must have felt. 'That,' I muttered, 'is a stonkingly good subject for a historical novel. Must find out more.'

So I began to research the story. Parris mentioned in his piece that his near-namesake Matthew Paris of St Albans, a thirteenth-century monk, wrote about the Englishman, so my first port of call was his *Chronica Majora*. Information about the Englishman there was scant – however, I did discover that Matthew Paris had learned all he knew about this mysterious renegade from a southern French cleric called Ivo of Narbonne.

Some months later, I discovered a fascinating non-fiction book published in 1978 by the Hungarian academic Gabriel Ronay – *The Tartar Khan's Englishman* – which identifies the Englishman as a Templar and an accomplished linguist, and which contains an appendix called 'The Englishman's Confession' that reproduces a thirteenth-century letter written by one Ivo of Narbonne to his lord the Bishop of Bordeaux, Géraud de Malemort.

Ivo's letter to his boss is an exhortation to rouse all Christendom against the looming threat of the Tartars (Mongols). He says that 'I have with certainty proved' all that he reports about

Robert's confession to his captors in Vienna Castle. It is not mere opinion, Ivo claims, and he has no doubts at all about its veracity. He then goes on to describe the Tartars, whose army numbers a 'thousand thousand', as subhuman dog-headed cannibals who rape virgins to death and cut off their breasts to be eaten by their chiefs as 'dainties'.

But the Mongols did not eat their enemies nor, rather obviously, did they have the heads of dogs, nor were there anywhere near a million of them in Europe at the time. So Ivo, despite his earnest protestations of veracity, is an unreliable witness. He is actually, quite understandably, trying to make the flesh of the princes of Europe creep, to unite them all to combat this dire new threat from the East.

Ivo of Narbonne is an interesting character, with a shady past even before he came to Vienna to report on the Englishman. In his letter, Ivo mentions that he has been accused of heresy in the past – of being a Paterinian, a member of a heretical sect similar to the Cathars – and that he had to flee his homeland in the south of France to avoid being tried and punished – probably burned at the stake.

He describes to his bishop how, on his travels, he inveigled his way into the company of other communities of heretics in northern Italy, and was welcomed by them when he pretended to share their faith. Reading between the lines, it seems Ivo was an undercover agent of the Church, an informer who routinely betrayed the people who were kind enough to shelter him, possibly for money, or to curry favour with his masters. He inhabited the medieval demi-monde of spies, paid informants, heretics, criminals and other outcasts, and therefore we should take everything he writes about the Englishman with a pinch of salt.

However, it does seem that the Englishman truly existed, and rode with the Mongols for more than twenty years, steadily rising through their ranks. Ivo writes that Robert lost everything playing dice in Acre before he was thirty years old, and then wandered, penniless and sick, through the wilderness before, eventually, being recruited by the Mongols, who needed his linguistic skills. Ivo also says the Duke of Austria recognised Robert, after the Englishman was captured, as one of the ambassadors from the Tartar horde to the King of Hungary at Pest (before the Mongols destroyed the Hungarians at the Battle of Mohi in the spring of 1241).

And this is where I have constructed my fictional story of Robert's life: in the blank spaces between the sightings reported by Ivo of Narbonne – at Acre, probably in about 1218, and at Pest, and then outside Vienna in 1241. There is a vast acreage of time when we have no idea where Robert was or what he was doing, so I invented a Venetian scheme to win a great trade treaty with the Mongols (which they did later achieve) and used the rivalry with Genoa, which was also a prominent feature of their commercial dealings with Asia, to conjure up a baddie. However, the biggest question in my mind when I was researching and writing *Templar Traitor* was – why? Why did Robert join the heathen enemy? He must have had, I recognised, powerful motives to forsake his own Christian side. And what could be more powerful, I reasoned, than love, money and faith?

–

The search for Prester John was a recurring theme in the Middle Ages. For generations, rumours had circulated in Western Europe of a mighty Christian king living in splendour somewhere in remote and distant Asia. Some believed him a descendant of one of the Three Magi who visited the infant Christ in Bethlehem; others were convinced that St Thomas, preaching in India, had converted a powerful local king to the true faith. There was even a letter sent to the Byzantine Emperor Manuel I in 1165 that purported to have come west from 'John, Christian Sovereign and Lord of Lords'. However, this was later disregarded by most as a forgery.

Still, the rumours persisted. Catholics in the West were aware of Nestorians: heretics – but still a type of Christian – who resided in the East. When they heard of a mighty Tartar warlord who was conquering all in his path, there were many in Christendom who thought this potentate must be the real Prester John. There were also plenty of military-minded Christians who hoped this mighty king might one day ride to the assistance of the beleaguered Latin kingdoms of the Holy Land.

Genghis Khan was obviously not King John the Presbyter, but he did have several Christians in his family. His daughter-in-law Sorkoktani was a Nestorian, a member of the Church in the East, and four of her children went on to become khans after Genghis's death. So, it is easy to see why a connection between the Great Khan of the Mongols and Prester John could be made in the minds of Christians in Western Europe. Genghis Khan, although he himself worshipped the Eternal Blue Sky, was tolerant of all religions, including Christianity, Islam and Buddhism. The Khan of Khans did not care what his subjects believed – as long as they submitted to him.

Muhammad Shah, the Emperor of Khwarazmia, strikes me as a rather stupid man. The story of Otrar – the theft of the five hundred Mongol merchants' goods and gold, and their brutal murders, followed by the humiliation of the Great Khan's three envoys – is well attested by historians, and these events directly caused the war between the Great Khan and the shah. (Incidentally, the Great Khan's Choice, as it appears in this novel, is based on genuine Mongol ultimatums.) But would the Great Khan have invaded Khwarazmia – which was a huge, wealthy domain comprising all of modern Iran, as well as Afghanistan, Turkmenistan, Uzbekistan, Tajikistan and parts of Kazakhstan – if the shah had not allowed his governor Inalchuq to abuse the Mongol merchants, or had punished him for doing so? I don't think so. Genghis was focused on what is now China at the time and, indeed, broke off warring there to come west and punish Muhammad Shah and Otrar. And, once he was involved, in typical hard-core Mongol fashion, he did not stop fighting until Muhammad Shah was dead.

And here I must make a small confession: I have the shah dying under the Mongol swords at the battle of Ray (near modern-day Tehran), when Subutai's *tumet* finally caught up with his fleeing army. Actually – while the battle was indeed a Mongol victory, and happened much as I have described – the shah escaped and fled north with only a handful of his followers to the shores of the Caspian Sea (called the Sea of Ravens in this novel). He died of his battle wounds, or possibly of sickness, on a small island in the Caspian a few weeks later, abandoned by his servants and soldiers. Since no Mongols were present at his death, and it occurred, as you may say, 'offstage', it seemed neater – and much better for the flow of my narrative – to end the shah's life story at the climactic battle outside the walls of Ray.

I might have given the impression in *Templar Traitor* that, after the battle, the Khwarazmian Empire was conquered. This is also not quite true. The embers of rebellion in the shah's former domain were not dead, and in the next book in the series we see Robert of Hadlow back in action in Central Asia, as well as in the Crimea and even in fabled Cathay. I hope you join the Englishman on his journey.

Acknowledgements

I'd like to thank my brilliant brother Jamie, who read an early version of this novel and offered praise and constructive criticism in exactly the correct amounts. My literary agent, Ian Drury, of Sheil Land Associates, has also been marvellously supportive and enthusiastic about this project from the beginning, and my excellent editor at Canelo, Craig Lye, has been tireless in making this the best version of the novel that it could possibly be. My heartfelt thanks to them all.

I also owe a debt to several fine historians, whose works I used to navigate the structure and tactics of the Mongol army, the personality of Genghis Khan and his generals, and the events of the Khwarazmian war. For further reading, I recommend: Jack Weatherford's *Genghis Khan and the Making of the Modern World*; *Genghis Khan: His Conquests, His Empire, His Legacy* by Frank McLynn; and James Chambers' *The Devil's Horsemen: The Mongol Invasion of Europe*.

Angus Donald
Tonbridge, 18 March 2025